CHRISTY CARLYLE

LADY MEETS EARL

A Love on Holiday Novel

AVONBOOKS

An Imprint of HarperCollins*Publishers*

LADY MEETS EARL. Copyright © 2022 by Christy Carlyle. All rights reserved. Printed in the United States of America. No part of this book may be used or reproduced in any manner whatsoever without written permission except in the case of brief quotations embodied in critical articles and reviews. For information, address HarperCollins Publishers, 195 Broadway, New York, NY 10007.

First Avon Books mass market printing: November 2022

Print Edition ISBN: 978-0-06-305450-9
Digital Edition ISBN: 978-0-06-305441-7

Cover design by Amy Halperin
Cover illustration by Judith York
Cover photograph by Shirley Green
Cover images © iStock/Getty Images; © Shutterstock (background)

Avon, Avon & logo, and Avon Books & logo are registered trademarks of HarperCollins Publishers in the United States of America and other countries.

HarperCollins is a registered trademark of HarperCollins Publishers in the United States of America and other countries.

FIRST EDITION

22 23 24 25 26 BVGM 10 9 8 7 6 5 4 3 2 1

I'm dedicating this one to my readers. Thank you for sticking with me if you've read my books before, and thank you for giving this one a try if it's my first title you've read.

Acknowledgments

Thanks to everyone who contributed along the way to getting this book to print.

LADY MEETS EARL

Chapter One

October 1897
London

Today was going to be James Pembroke's lucky day.

Or at least, it might be.

This morning felt different. He sensed something stirring in the early morning air.

Thick fog had rolled in off the Thames and curled around the streetlamps like smoke, but as his hired hansom rolled west toward the city—delivering him to a mysterious meeting at the unusually early hour of eight in the morning—he spied a few streaks of pink and gold on the horizon. After days of drizzle, perhaps the sun would finally break free of the clouds, and that made him feel something very much like hopefulness.

The last six months had taught him the sort of lessons that chip away at one's optimism. There'd been moments when he'd considered giving up. But he'd played innumerable games of chance and followed his instincts in business often enough to know that luck was changeable. A string of misfortunes might be followed by an enormous victory, or a run of good luck could end with the flip of a card.

His own success had burned bright for so long he'd believed nothing could dim it.

Then one decision, one dreadful moment of placing his trust in the wrong person, and it had all been snuffed out. He'd lost his capital, been forced to sell his fleet, still owed money to a dodgy moneylender, and the shipping business that had made him wealthy beyond his wildest hopes was now little more than an office in Wapping with his name above the door. Even that would go soon. The lease he'd paid would run out at year's end.

Yet hope flickered like a tiny, banked ember in his chest this morning. Perhaps he could revive Pembroke Shipping. It was long past time for good fortune to smile on him again.

Lady Luck? Come on, love. I've learned my bloody lesson.

If luck was coming, he needed to be ready. An anxious tension gripped his middle—the need to do something, to move, take action. When he sat still too long, his mind tended to run through his failures again, and rumination had never done him any good.

"Let me off here," he called up to the cabbie.

James handed up payment, and the hansom rolled away into the fog.

After one look around to get his bearings, he started off toward a genteel London square with whitewashed town houses and a manicured gated green at its center. It seemed an odd place for a solicitor to do business, but everything about the letter he'd received was unusual.

A solicitor he'd never heard of requesting a meeting at an ungodly hour, revealing nothing about what was to be discussed or who he worked for, was so strange that James had initially suspected some kind of flimflam. In many quarters, he was considered an easy mark after the debacle he'd made of his last investment scheme. But curiosity had always been part of his nature. The mystery of the letter intrigued him, and after a day of pondering, he'd decided there was little risk in discovering what the solicitor had to say.

That little ember inside him even dared to hope it might be good news.

Movements ahead drew his notice. Footsteps approached through the misty air, and a moment later two elderly ladies emerged. The tall one in front wore a gown with enormous sleeves that made it impossible for her companion to do anything but trail behind.

"Good morning, ladies." He doffed his hat and offered them the hint of a smile. The taller of the two possessed a cool, untouchable elegance, and the way her chin jutted toward the sky told him she was likely titled or wealthy or both. "Can you tell me if I'm heading in the direction for Selfridge Place?"

"You are, sir," the diminutive one told him.

"You've saved a lost man. Thank you." He winked at the one who'd been helpful.

"So charming," she whispered to her companion as they passed.

Thank God he still had his charm. Affability and a wink hadn't saved him from financial ruin, but they might yet open a few more doors. Instincts had only been half his success. Reading others, gaining the trust of business associates—he'd been skilled in those ways too.

Five minutes later, he'd passed the neighborhood of whitewashed houses and entered an area of redbrick buildings. He stopped in front of an unassuming one on Selfridge Place and checked the address on the letter again. A lamp lit in a ground floor window gave the air outside a sickly yellow cast.

He might call it a bad omen if James believed in such balderdash.

The front door was unlocked, so James stepped warily inside. A man called out soon after.

"In here, Mr. Pembroke."

The sound of a chair scratching wood and then rapid footsteps came before a stout, balding man appeared in the doorway.

"Mr. Cathcart?"

"Indeed. And you're right on time, Mr. Pembroke. I do admire punctuality."

"Then we're off to a good start." James tried for that easy, jovial manner he'd used in the past when meeting new business prospects. Smiling generally encouraged others to do the same.

Not so with Mr. Mortimer Cathcart, Esquire.

The man dipped his nose, examined James above the frame of his spectacles, and then ducked back into his office like a mole retreating into his burrow.

"Do sit, sir. I deduce from your manner that what I have to tell you may come as a shock."

Well damn. Apparently, it was to be bad news. James didn't need intuition to interpret the grim set of the man's mouth and the way his eyes darted to and fro.

Unbidden, a rusty chuckle bubbled up, a sound of exhaustion. So much for his string of bad luck taking a turn today. But he was prepared. He could take it. What could be worse than losing the shipping fleet you'd spent years assembling?

Cathcart gestured toward a spindly chair in front of his desk. A spark of rebellion flared up in James. He was tempted to insist on standing while the man delivered the blow. But it wasn't the solicitor's fault he'd been tasked with bearing ill news. Indeed, he looked rather morose about whatever he was about to impart.

"Don't mind if I do," James said congenially, trying to fold his tall, broad limbs into the too-small chair. "Thank you."

Five minutes later, he was bloody glad he was seated on his arse, because nothing could have prepared him for the words that had come out of the solicitor's mouth.

"Repeat yourself, Cathcart," he barked. "Slowly."

The older man's spectacles bounced along with his overgrown brows. He cleared his throat, glanced down at the documents on his desk, and then turned nervous eyes on James.

"You, sir, are Lord Rossbury's heir. Your uncle sired no sons, and his brother, your father, died years ago. As, of course, you know." The man cleared his throat.

Yes, thank you, Cathcart. He did know when his father died, and his mother, and he kept that day and those memories firmly shut away. But he'd never forget how his uncle had offered him no home, no aid, not even an ounce of consolation.

"My condolences are yours, as is the earldom of Rossbury, as of three days ago, when your uncle—"

James didn't hear the rest of what the solicitor said—or rather, the sharply accented words faded as an emotion took hold of every atom of his being. A feeling almost as powerful as the throes of pleasurable release, warming like the first searing sip of good whiskey.

Relief. Pure, sweet solace. An elixir for all the worries he'd been wrestling for months. It flowed through his veins like summer wine, and he felt drunk with the thrill of it. He burst up from his chair, and Cathcart laid a hand over his own throat, as if James meant to accost him.

"I could kiss you, Cathcart."

"I'd prefer you didn't, Mr. Pembroke."

"Then perhaps I'll just dance a jig right here in your office." James hadn't danced in months, but he moved his feet in a pattern he recalled. Decidedly less enjoyable without music, but he had to do something with his exaltation.

"Sir. My lord. Please, may I ask you to resume your seat." Cathcart gestured toward the dainty chair in front of his desk. "I have a great deal more to tell you, and I beg you to refrain from any . . . displays until I've fulfilled my duties as set out in your uncle's will."

But he couldn't contain it. The energetic thrill of finally, once more, finding that luck had favored him. He'd been so close to despair. Holding on to hope got harder the more often doors were closed in your face, friends turned their backs on you, and you found that paying for mere necessities brought worry.

Yet he'd persevered. Reminded himself that the tragedy of his youth hadn't been a curse but a lesson—fueling his ambition and success. One devastating failure in judgment couldn't destroy him, only set him back awhile.

And it had all been leading to this. This fated moment. This strange man delivering relief in the one way James had *never* ever imagined it might come.

"How much?" He turned to the aged solicitor, standing behind the chair because he couldn't bear sitting and gripping the wooden frame until his knuckles ached. "The earldom's assets, man. Tell me their value."

He expected Cathcart's sneer of judgment in response to the blunt question. Even after years of success in the shipping industry, James knew that gentlemen who put on airs liked to behave as if speaking openly of money was a sin. Well, to hell with false propriety.

"That will take some explaining, my lord."

My lord. That was *his* title now. Bloody hell, what a turn of events for a Tuesday.

James rolled his hand in the air, urging the man to continue.

"There is an estate—"

Yes, of course. Summer-something or other. That pile in Shropshire that his father spoke of a few times in tones alternately wistful and full of loathing.

"The fire took most of the structure. A great tragedy. Much of it was quite aged and of an old oak construction."

"Fire?"

"Two years ago, my lord. Most of the valuables in the house were damaged or destroyed. All the paintings, tapestries, furnishings. Your uncle was already in significant debt at the time and never, according to the estate agent's notes, saw to any repairs."

The adrenaline in James's veins chilled, and his brain grappled with the news that he had inherited a title but no real earldom.

"And the land?" One could build on land. Not that he had the funds to do so. Yet.

"The land itself remains in the inheritance, of course. You may rebuild as you see fit." Cathcart adjusted his spectacles. "Apparently, some stones from the old Summervale estate remain and may prove useful if a new structure is ever rebuilt on the site."

"Stones? You're telling me I've inherited a title and a pile of rocks?"

Cathcart cast his wrinkled face toward James and exhibited the first evidence of emotion. "Tragically, your uncle was reduced to living in the gatehouse for the final years of his life."

James tried to rally a similar sense of compassion for the man who'd refused to take him in as a freshly orphaned boy over two decades past. None came.

"So, there is no country estate, per se. No tenants?"

"None listed. The agent mentions that many left years earlier to seek work in the city."

"Any valuables remaining at all?"

"Not as such, my lord. At least none that are listed."

"Any accounts with monies remaining?"

"I'm afraid not, my lord. At least no funds that won't be needed to cover the late earl's debts."

James scrubbed a hand over his face and let out a raspy breath. His chest had gone hollow, and that feeling, at least, was familiar. And yet a resilient little flicker of hope still burned there too. Tiny, barely a glow. But unvanquished.

"Any other property?" Had the man left him nothing but a worthless honorific?

"Ah, yes!" Cathcart rifled through documents and lifted a smaller rectangle of paper. "One unentailed property, though there has been no valuation entered into the estate's records. In fact, the agent who kept all of this in order barely mentions the manor house in Scotland at all."

"So it might be a shambles too." *That* was his usual brand of luck of late. The rotten sort.

"The deed describes a two-story manor house on sixteen acres of land north of Edinburgh and not a great deal else." Cathcart raised a brow at him. "Invermere?" He asked as if the name might jog some memory for James.

"I know nothing of my uncle, his life, or his properties. And I'm only now learning that he was apparently as dreadful at handling money as I have been."

The solicitor let out a harrumph under his breath.

"Any other good news, Cathcart? Any at all?"

"I'm sorry, my lord. You have inherited a peerage and the Scottish manor I mentioned." He paused only a moment to offer James a look of forced sympathy. "I will require your signature on a few of these documents. Then I can give you a key for the manor house and a list of accounts to be addressed."

"You mean outstanding debts."

"I do."

They will have to wait until I pay my own bloody debts.

James settled hard into the chair in front of Cathcart's desk and signed the documents with a grim sort of resignation. As he scratched away, repeating his signature over and over, Cathcart continued his irritating shuffling of documents.

Almost to himself, he mumbled, "There is one other detail."

James looked at the man and waited until the solicitor met his gaze. "Tell me."

"There's mention of a woman. A Lady Cassandra Munro, who is described as *in residence* two years ago at the address in Scotland, though with no record of rents paid by her to the earldom. She's also mentioned in the late earl's will as the recipient of a piece of jewelry." Cathcart looked at James expectantly.

"A mistress?"

"I suspect as much, my lord."

"Seems a long way to go to visit one's lover."

The old man's face flushed pink under his whiskers, and James almost chuckled at his prudishness.

"No indication whether she is still in residence."

"Well, if she is, I'm afraid it won't be for long." If that house was his single means of recouping some financial relief from this turn of events, the lady would need to find other accommodations. That's all there was to it.

James capped the solicitor's pen, laid it on the

man's desk, and stood again. "You'll send everything?" He had no real desire for the pile of papers on the desk, but he understood the weight of responsibility. And now, this one was his.

"I shall send a letter to Lady Cassandra Munro informing her of the jewelry and that you intend to take possession of the manor. Is there anything you wish me to add about how you plan to settle Invermere?"

A flare of sympathy made him sigh. The poor lady probably believed his uncle would bequeath her the house if he gave her leave to reside there. James had been the recipient of so much bad news of late, he recoiled at the notion of visiting ill tidings on someone else. But he had no other choice, and he'd do it himself.

"I'll go to Scotland. I need to see about selling as soon as possible."

"Of course, my lord."

The use of the honorific made him shiver now. His father had expected to inherit and eventually pass the title on to James. It was why, when the old earl, James's grandfather, was ill, they'd all trundled off via train to Shropshire.

That thought brought his darkest memories. The ones that haunted him, reshaping themselves night after night in his dreams for years. Even now, the smell of smoke, the sound of twisting, grinding metal as the train derailed, and the screams of train passengers echoed in his mind. And then the voice of his mother. *Stay calm, love. It will be all right.*

But it hadn't been. And he'd lost them both.

All in pursuit of this worthless title.

Hearing himself referred to as Lord Rossbury would always feel like a curse.

"HOW DARE YOU!"

James heard his housekeeper's offended bellow from a block away. Mrs. Wilton's Welsh lilt was unmistakable, and the outrage in her tone was underscored by fear. Once he'd made it past a nanny pushing a pram along the sidewalk of his semifashionable square, James broke into a run toward his town house.

The front door stood ajar, and two strangers faced down his housekeeper. His blood chilled when he spotted the men, and the simmering anger after the morning's disappointment turned to rage.

Archibald Beck's thugs? The man had always issued vague threats of "consequences" if James failed to repay his debt. There was no doubt Archie Beck was a man of violence—though he tended to dole it out through intermediaries like these men, never dirtying his own hands. It was true James had put off repaying the man for months, but this was too far. The folly had been his own. He wouldn't see his staff endangered for it.

He assessed the intruders as he pushed the open door wider and stepped across the threshold. Two beefy men in gaudy suits nearly bursting at the seams to contain their brawn.

"Step away from her." He stripped off his coat and tossed it on the hall table. As he worked the buttons at his cuffs free, he offered his housekeeper a questioning glance. "Are you unharmed?"

Her cheeks had taken on a flushed glow and her eyes still bulged in fear, but she offered him a curt nod. "I am, sir."

"These men pushed their way in and demanded to speak to you, sir." Jeffries, James's aged butler whose rheumatic knees kept him belowstairs much of the time, approached whilst leaning heavily on a cane.

"What do you want?" James positioned himself in front of Mrs. Wilton and the housemaid and footman who stood behind her. Methodically rolling up his sleeves, he guessed which man was the leader among the two. He'd be the one to feel James's fist first if things went pear-shaped.

Mrs. Wilton spoke before either of Beck's men could utter a word in reply.

"They say they've cause to remove the paintings and demanded the silver. Asked me to go into your safe and bring them everything inside, they did." She turned toward him and took a step closer, whispering, "They say there are debts, sir. Is it true?"

In truth, it was only one debt, and one grandly disastrous mistake of trusting Archibald Beck.

"Yer payment to Boss is due." The brute repeated the words in a sort of bored Cockney grumble, as if he'd said them a hundred times before.

His partner, shorter but bulkier, spoke up more loudly. "Past due. Pay up, Pembroke, or we'll take what we can for what you owe."

"Go to hell."

The short man lunged at him, and James hit him with a quick jab to the nose.

"Bleedin' hell," the man squealed, holding his nose.

James remained ready to strike again, but the small man merely glared at him.

"Get out." James spoke through clenched teeth, and the larger brute leaned in as if to hear him better. "Get. Out."

"Not until we've taken what you owe." When the larger man started for the drawing room, the butler, Jeffries, struck out his cane and braced it across the doorway, blocking the way. Then Jeffries handed James a pistol he'd drawn out of his pocket. A small thing, snub-nosed with a fat revolver barrel.

James took the weapon and pointed it at the leader, cocking the weapon, not even sure it was loaded.

"Take your partner and go while you can."

The big man looked wary and made a move to slip his hand inside his coat.

"Don't." James sprang toward him, pointing the

gun at his chest. "Tell Beck he'll get his money soon, but there will be no more bullying tactics. No more threatening my staff or invading my home. Understand?"

The smaller man began to retreat, still holding his sore nose, but the larger of the two kept still, glancing once at the revolver aimed at his chest.

"When does he get what you owe?"

"As I said, soon."

"Boss won't wait much longer. Did you stumble into a windfall, Pembroke?" Dubious though his tone was, the glower on the man's face seemed set in stone. Even as he spoke, the hateful expression was immovable.

"What I stumbled into is a title. As of three days ago, I am Earl of Rossbury."

The brute's brows arched high, and Mrs. Wilton let out a gasp, then mumbled an oath James couldn't quite make out. Jeffries released a raspy chuckle, and Jenny, the housemaid, squeaked as if she'd just spotted a mouse in the scullery.

"Tell your boss that," James said, lifting the weapon from the man's chest and then using it to wave them toward the front door.

James and his staff all let out a sigh of relief when the men relented, and Mrs. Wilton locked the door behind them.

"An earldom?" Jeffries asked in his low voice.

"Apparently."

"*My lord*, blimey." Mrs. Wilton tested the honorific with a proud little smile. "Shall we prepare to move the household?"

"I'm afraid not." James didn't have time to tell them everything. Only one thing mattered now. "I will need help preparing for a journey to Scotland."

The assembled staff members exchanged raised brow glances.

"When do you depart, my lord?" Jeffries asked.

"Immediately."

Chapter Two

*W*hen Lady Lucy Westmont made up her mind to do something, dissuading her was well-nigh impossible.

Her mother knew it, and her siblings had learned it the hard way. Most importantly, Lucy knew it about herself. She understood herself very well, truth be told. And she'd learned to like herself even though others considered her odd, and eligible gentlemen steered clear of her due to her reputation as—what had the lordling at that summer ball called her?—a meddlesome termagant.

Despite how definitively she'd informed that gentleman what a small-minded, uninteresting clodpate he was, she couldn't deny the accusations thrown her way. She could be sharp-tongued when the situation called for it, and she was extremely adept at meddling. Though she'd always viewed it more as helping.

What was wrong with being the person others turned to when they needed assistance? She was quite proud of her reputation as a young lady ready to spring to the aid of others when needed.

Fixing things was an admired skill in the world

of mechanisms. Just last week, Mama had panicked for fear they wouldn't find a piano repairman in time for this evening's dinner party. Of course, Lucy had stepped in and helped. She knew nothing about fixing pianos, but when the repairman said he was booked through next week, she'd made a visit to his shop personally. After explaining that her father, the Earl of Hallston, was a diplomat for the queen, and the ambassador who was coming to dinner was an *enormous* fan of pianos, who might need a repairman himself one day, the man arrived later that same day.

So, yes, perhaps she did meddle at times. And, yes, she could be stubborn when she'd set her mind on achieving a goal. But she always found a way to get things done.

This evening, she'd made up her mind to do two things. One, ensure that Mama's dinner party came off without a hitch, and two, keep a promise to her father that she'd do her best to be sociable. To notice who might be noticing her and to smile if any gentlemen looked her way. So far, none had yet.

But she *was* trying. She hadn't even pulled out a novel or her sketchbook once. Though she'd brought both, of course. Leaving her room without something to read or a journal to draw in would be akin to leaving home without donning any clothes. Mama claimed she treated them like a shield, a barrier between her and reality. But the opposite was true. Both connected her to the world, making her watchful and interested in those around her.

She had a modicum of artistic talent and was getting quite good with her box camera, but she knew her parents would never allow her to make a profession of either. Marriage was still the fate they envisioned for her, but Lucy was no longer so sure.

Deep in her heart, she longed to be good enough to be acknowledged for her art, as her aunt Cassandra was. After the Scottish lord her aunt had eloped with during her first Season died, she'd remained in Scotland and had made a name for herself as a famous portrait artist in Edinburgh.

Lucy admired her aunt's skill, but equally her independence. If only a woman could have such a life without first having to become a widow.

"You've abandoned me." The voice of Lucy's friend, Lady Miranda Farnsworth, pulled her out of her musings.

"I haven't. I never would." She had in fact been with Miranda most of the day. She'd been at Farnsworth House all morning before returning home for her family's dinner party. Miranda was to be married in a little over a fortnight, and Lucy was helping her decide on, well, everything.

"I have a bit of a problem," Miranda said in a near whisper.

"Please don't let it be the organza." Lucy groaned inwardly at the memory of being buried in dozens of bolts of fabric in every shade and texture the modiste had in stock. "You did already decide this morning. And that was after thorough consideration."

"No, no, it's nothing to do with the wedding. I promised you to put that out of my head for one evening." She leaned in conspiratorially. "It's to do with the place settings. I know your mama must have put a great deal of thought into them, but I had hoped I would be somewhere near Heath."

"Want me to switch them for you?"

"Oh, would you? My dear Lucy, I don't know what I'd do without you."

"Don't fret another moment. I'll slip away to do it soon."

Miranda relaxed visibly and took a sip of punch from the glass she held. "It won't go terribly against Mrs. Winterbottom's dictates, will it?" she teased.

Among her friends, Lucy was known as a devotee of Mrs. Winterbottom, who'd written *the* guide on how a lady might be self-reliant, *The Orderly Lady*. Though her book gave tips on more than social etiquette. She provided guidance on arranging one's life so that everything worked like clockwork and offered advice on never getting flustered in the face of dilemmas.

"Mrs. Winterbottom is an advocate of self-sufficiency and finding solutions to all of life's little predicaments." Lucy grinned at her friend. "She'd approve."

"Heath!" Miranda's high-pitched squeal of her betrothed's given name caused Lucy's belly to flop.

She drew in a deep breath before turning to face the tall, blond gentleman who'd crossed her parents' drawing room to greet her and his fiancée.

"Ladies." He sketched a little bow toward his bride-to-be and finally glanced up at Lucy.

Thank goodness her breath didn't catch in her throat anymore. In truth, she wondered now why he'd caught her interest at all. Perhaps it was the jolliness that lit his eyes at times. A sort of open friendliness came naturally to him, and she envied that.

Lucy had always been better at helping others than charming them. Her little brother was a charmer, and her mother could melt the hardest heart with a soft look and gentle words. Somehow, Lucy hadn't inherited those talents. But she knew how to listen closely, to put people's minds at ease, and to determine fixes when things went awry.

"You did promise me a dance," he said to Miranda with a besotted smile.

Miranda's aunt, her chaperone and companion for the evening, noted Mr. Ogilvy's approach and joined them. Lucy took it as her cue. After a polite nod at Miranda's aunt and one in Mr. Heath Ogilvy's direction, she gave Miranda's arm a reassuring squeeze, excused herself, and headed for the dining room.

At the threshold, she was shocked to hear voices, but then recognized one of them and rolled her eyes. The scent of cheroot smoke left no doubt.

Her brother and his friend Nigel stood in a far corner smoking and giggling in a manner that told her whatever they were discussing was not for tender ears.

They had their backs to her, so she tiptoed inside and slid the pocket doors closed behind her.

"Charlie, what are you doing in here?"

He nearly jumped out of his boots. "Dammit, Lucy, you'll have me in my grave before I ever set foot on the Continent." He clapped one hand to his chest dramatically and waved his friend off with the other. "Make your escape now, Nigel. I'll face the dragon on my own."

Nigel stubbed out his cheroot in a potted palm and slunk by her.

"A dragon, am I? I actually quite like that." Lucy held out a tea saucer for her brother's cheroot. "Those are dreadful. Papa would be apoplectic if he saw you."

"Well, he didn't, and as my favorite sister, you'd never tell."

"Marion is your favorite sister." Marion, the eldest, was everyone's favorite. She was that perfect combination of beautiful, kind, and intelligent. And she'd landed a duke during her first Season. *That* had set expectations sky-high for Lucy, but thankfully after her third failed Season, Mama and Papa had spared her the mortification of going through another.

"Marion who?"

"Very funny." Lucy moved down the table scanning the cards. "Now tell me if you've seen Mr. Ogilvy or Lady Miranda's cards."

"Miranda is over there." Rather than point, he flung his hand out in the general direction of the left side of the table.

"Perfect. I think we'll leave her there, near me, and move him."

"Ogilvy? Isn't he that sop you fancied?"

"I did *not* fancy him."

He settled back in a chair and crossed his arms. "You did. Your face always got blotchy and scrunched whenever he came to dinner."

"You're a terrible detective."

"You're an awful liar."

"Aha, here he is." Lucy retrieved Heath's card and positioned him across from Miranda. Sitting next to her would be a bit much, but she kept him on his originally intended side of the table and just moved him down a few seats. "That will do, I think."

"Mama would be *apoplectic* if she saw you do that." He smirked as he threw her words back at her.

"Then we're even." Lucy heard the strains of piano music. "And we should both get back."

"Good grief, yes, you're right." Her brother surprised her by springing out of his chair as if he was eager to return to the gathering he'd been happy to be absent from just a few minutes earlier.

"I am, but I didn't expect you to agree so readily."

"Papa wanted me to speak to Balfour. He's something to do with the French embassy. A good chap to speak to before our trip."

Lucy stalled him on his way to the door with a hand on his arm. "What trip?"

"Next spring. I'm visiting the Continent." He hooked his hands over his lapels and smiled proudly. "My grand adventure."

Lucy made it a point not to be jealous of her siblings. Or, more accurately, she tried very hard not to be. Marion was beautiful and well wed, and Charlie was handsome and a bit of a lovable rogue.

And Lucy? She was mostly content with being helpful, somewhat talented at drawing, and a "meddlesome termagant." But lately, as the days went by, she found herself wanting more. Perhaps, in some deep corner of her heart, she'd always craved an adventure of her own.

Charlie pressed a hand to her shoulder. "I'm sorry, Lu. I thought you knew about the trip. If you feel left out, perhaps Papa would allow you to come along."

Lucy chuckled and eyed him with one brow raised. "You wish to bring your sister along on your *grand adventure*?" He was one and twenty and already known for his roguish ways. She anticipated his answer.

He drew in an enormous breath that made his chest puff out and then deflate on a dramatic sigh. "No, not as such."

"Didn't think so. Just send me lots of postcards

and letters if you can tear yourself away from whatever trouble you'll get yourself into."

He pecked a kiss on her cheek and smiled, then preceded her out of the dining room.

Lucy stood alone for a moment thinking about where she might wish to travel if she had the freedom to do so. Then the piano music reached a crescendo and pulled her out of her woolgathering.

She stopped in the hallway to check with a passing maid that there were no problems in the kitchen, then beelined for the large drawing room where guests were gathered.

Miranda spied her the moment she entered, and Lucy offered her a smile.

"All is well," she mouthed to her friend, and Miranda pressed a hand to her heart in reply.

There, one good deed done for the evening. Normally, that gave Lucy great satisfaction, but the conversation with her brother had sparked a longing she'd repressed for too long. He was three years her junior, and yet was allowed far more liberty than she was. Of course, she understood the difference in how young men were treated versus young women, but she didn't have to like it. In her opinion, her parents didn't have to carry on such outdated notions.

She had half a mind to tell Papa as much and lifted onto her toes to look past the shoulders of one of her father's cronies, hoping to catch him for a moment. He held court at gatherings like this.

Just when she'd decided to try for a conversation

later and go find Miranda, Mama sailed into her line of vision.

"Lucy, thank goodness." Her mother was trying for a calm, serene manner but her voice had taken on a high-pitched tone that meant something was amiss. "Lady Braithwaite," she whispered. "The poor thing fell asleep in an armchair in the corner, and I've had Jenkins escort her to my sitting room. Would you check on her and make certain all is well? I suspect she's merely fatigued, but if we need to call for Dr. Whitaker, we shall."

"Don't worry, Mama. I'll look in on her now."

"Thank you, my girl. Betina Braithwaite is not prideful, but I can't imagine she'd like the whisperers to make sport of her because she's fatigued or had a bit too much cordial."

Lucy had little trouble slipping from the drawing room unnoticed. Her father had begun making a toast to the ambassador, drawing the attention of most guests.

When she reached her mother's sitting room, she found Lady Braithwaite on the settee, struggling to keep her eyes open. Her niece who'd accompanied her, Alice, stood in front of her worriedly, and offered a nervous smile when Lucy entered the room.

Once Lucy had reached her side, Alice confided, "I don't know if I can get her to the dining room on my own. She's rather stubborn."

Lucy had known Lady Braithwaite since childhood and rather liked her headstrong, outspoken manner. Termagants needed to stick together after all.

"I'm happy to sit with her and can arrange for a tray if she doesn't wish for the noise of the dining room. Let me see to her, Alice, and please go and enjoy the party."

The girl nibbled at her lip a moment, and then relented. "Thank you, my lady. I did have a request for a dance after dinner."

"Well, then you must go." Lucy offered her a genuine smile. If she'd been asked to dance, she wouldn't want to miss it either—depending on the partner, of course. The lecherous, elderly viscount who'd extended the only proposal of marriage she'd received during three Seasons was definitely on the To Be Avoided list of prospective dance partners.

Once the girl had gone, Lucy lowered herself to the far edge of the settee gingerly, careful not to disturb the Countess of Braithwaite.

Lucy let herself sink into the cushions. This room had always felt calming and peaceful. It was small enough to be cozy. Her mother had decorated it in soft pastels and the air held both the scent of fresh flowers and her mother's jonquil perfume.

All in all, she was happy to escape the crowded drawing room, but her thoughts still rushed with notions of traveling to some faraway land.

A moment later, the countess roused and noticed her.

"Lady Lucy, have you been conscripted to be my nursemaid, poor girl?"

"Not at all, my lady," Lucy said quietly, "I volunteered to escape with you, and now we can both have a quiet moment."

"I find myself appreciating those more and more. I have been sleeping ill of late and find that these late nights don't agree with me. Age, you see. It catches all of us." She let out a rich, deep-throated chuckle. "But you're young and must return to the party."

She reached for Lucy's arm and gave it a gentle pat.

"I'm quite distracted tonight myself, so I would appreciate some quiet too." Lucy retrieved a soft cashmere throw from her mother's chair by the fire and draped it over the countess's lap.

"Are you indeed? Tell me what's on that busy mind of yours, my dear."

"The constraints of being an unmarried lady," she said bluntly, almost absentmindedly, as she perused her mother's bookshelf for something she could read to the countess to pass the time.

"Remind me of your age."

"Four and twenty." Lucy glanced back and found the countess observing her with a hint of a smile on her lips. "You were no doubt wed by my age."

"Wed and with two children." Lady Braithwaite narrowed her gaze.

Lucy expected a lecture on the joys of marriage or dire warnings about the fate of ladies who ended up on the shelf. She inhaled deeply, steeling herself for the effort of biting her tongue when all she wished to do was speak her mind.

"Our experiences differed, but I knew my mind

at four and twenty and imagine you do too. Are you opposed to marriage entirely?"

"Not at all." Lucy's parents proved that matrimony could be a happy state, even if it did require patience—which she often lacked—and an ability to compromise—though she wasn't terribly good at that either.

"I take it Lord and Lady Hallston have left the choice up to you."

An inkling told her where this was leading. She knew she was luckier than many of the young ladies she'd come out with years ago. They were often matched with horrible men or pushed by their families into matches that Lucy doubted could ever bring them anything like love.

"Yes, though in all honesty, the choice came down to one man who was too old and not at all kind." Lucy couldn't fib about something so well-known by those in her family's circle.

"Do not give up hope, dear girl. I encouraged my daughters to wait until they were certain." The countess smoothed the blanket across her legs and leaned her head against the pink damask. A moment later, her eyelids fluttered closed.

Lucy was too unsettled to read. She replaced the book on the shelf and poked at the dying fire. Then she spied a pile of post on her mother's desk, slipped into the chair behind it, and lit the oil lamp on her desktop.

Lucy's long-standing habit was to help with organizing and responding to her mother's post, and it seemed a good way to occupy her mind while she sat with the dozing countess.

She separated what looked to be invitations from what seemed more personal correspondence and smiled when she came upon a letter from her aunt Cassandra. As was her habit, she'd decorated the outside of her letter with scribbles and flowers colored with splashes of watercolor.

After admiring her aunt's art, Lucy unfolded the missive and began reading.

The letter was warm, expressive, and demanding. Lucy smiled to see herself mentioned.

Send Lucy to me.

A little rush of pleasure shot through her, and she quickly scanned further to see what project her aunt might need her help with.

Do not allow Lucy to become a joyless spinster. She has more spirit than that. I've seen it in her since she was a little girl. As a middle sister myself, I know how easy it is to become consumed with being useful rather than experiencing any passion for oneself. She deserves more than being useful.

She read the words many times, until they were burned in her mind's eye. *Joyless spinster* cut the deepest, causing a searing kind of hopelessness that made her heart ache.

No. That wasn't her. She pushed the letter aside

as she moved on to focus on the other post in the pile, but tears blurred her vision. She swiped at her cheek and took up her aunt's letter once more.

Send Lucy to me.

Reading that line again, she let out a little gasp as she finally began to understand what her beloved aunt was trying to do.

Aunt Cassandra hadn't sent the letter as a condemnation or even a critique. It was a beacon. A lifeline cast out all the way from Scotland.

It was an opportunity for Lucy to decide for herself.

The dinner gong sounded, but the countess didn't stir. A moment later, a quiet knock sounded at the door and her mother stepped inside, closing the door softly behind her.

"I came to see how our guest is faring," she whispered as she tiptoed past the countess and came to stand next to Lucy. "What do you think it is that's ailing her?"

"Just fatigue, Mama. But I think it might be best to see to a tray for her or at least tea. I don't think she'll enjoy sitting at table tonight."

"And you?" Her mother reached out and swept a stray strand of hair the same honey-blonde as her own behind Lucy's ear. "I hate for you to miss out. I could have Jenkins come and sit with her."

Lucy stood and reached for her mother's hand. An urge had taken hold that she couldn't keep inside.

"Mama, I want to go to Scotland."

"Scotland—"

"To visit Aunt Cassandra." Lucy held out the letter. "She's invited me."

Her mother lifted a finger to her lips. "We don't want to wake Lady Braithwaite." Then she clasped Lucy's hands in hers. "Of course you should go and visit, my dear. Let's discuss it later and see if we can find a time in the spring to go together."

"No, Mama. I want to go on my own, and I want to leave now. As soon as possible."

A frown broke across her mother's face, pinching her forehead and tightening the edges of her mouth. "Lucy, what has gotten into you?"

Of course, this wasn't like her at all. For too long, she'd been willing to let everything happen for others and content with never claiming experiences for herself. But the spiritedness her aunt spoke of in her letter was there too, and it was long past time she reclaimed it.

"I'm going, Mama," Lucy told her mother with a quiet determination she'd never felt before. "I want an adventure of my own."

Chapter Three

Three days later

"This is unexpected, Papa."

Lucy's father said nothing to that declaration and merely settled more firmly against the squabs of his elegant carriage.

After breaking her fast and dressing, she'd bounded down the stairs, practically vibrating with eagerness to start her journey to Scotland. She'd expected to find a hansom cab to take her to the train station. Instead, she'd stepped out the front door to find her father's fashionable brougham at the curb. He'd appeared behind her a moment later, helped her into the polished black carriage, settled himself beside her, and had yet to say a single word. She had a terrible inkling about why he'd decided to escort her to the station, but there was a lightness and flutter of anticipation inside her today that nothing could dull.

She'd obtained her ticket the day after her parents' dinner party and exchanged telegrams with her aunt, who planned to pick her up at Waverley

Station in Edinburgh this evening. The express would get her there in a little over eight hours. She'd packed what she'd need for a fortnight stay as efficiently as possible. Only herself, one small trunk, and an overstuffed valise were to be transported to King's Cross Station.

"What merited a personal escort by the Earl of Hallston?" she prodded.

He side-eyed her with one salt-and-pepper brow arched high. "Are you implying that I don't normally attend to my daughter's safety and well-being?"

"Not at all." Lucy was used to their teasing banter, but she couldn't tell if he was in the mood for it today. "But you're usually at your club or busy with meetings at this hour of the morning."

"I canceled my meetings." When he glanced over at her, his eyes were narrowed and assessing. "If you must know, I'm still debating whether to permit you to go."

Lucy gripped the fabric of her skirt and willed herself not to retort. Her father did not respond well to rash replies. He was a man of diplomacy, a reasonable man. In fact, they'd already debated this topic and he had relented, however reticently.

Besides, they'd already pulled onto a main thoroughfare and into the crush of morning traffic. With any luck, they'd arrive at the station within half an hour.

"Bannister should be accompanying you on this excursion," he groused.

"Mama needs her more than I." The loyal lady's maid always accompanied her mother on journeys, and Lucy was more than capable of dressing herself. "Besides, I'll have Aunt Cassandra and her staff."

The harrumph her father let out was loud and brimming with all the doubts he'd earlier expressed about how much of a bad influence he expected her aunt to be. But Lucy had never considered herself missish or impressionable.

"Don't you trust me, Papa?"

He side-eyed her again, turning his face only the slightest bit, but still allowing her to feel the full force of his irritation.

"I trust you implicitly, dear girl. You're clever and competent and never get ruffled when trouble arises. I'd trust you to run the earldom, truth be told."

"But?" If the cause of his grumpiness involved more critique of her aunt, Lucy didn't wish to hear it, but she would put his mind at ease if she could.

"A young lady traveling alone—"

"But you've taught me and Charlie how to defend ourselves." Her younger brother had received more formal instruction than she had, of course, but their father had taught both of them the basics of how to handle a gun, a sword, and the kinds of punches he employed at the gentleman's boxing saloon he attended when they were in residence in London.

"You recall how to break a hold if some devil accosts you?"

"I do, Papa."

"You needn't do this as some sort of rebellion, Lulu." He rarely used her childhood nickname, and his voice softened the minute it was out. "We were never going to marry you off to Atterberry."

There had been talk at the end of her final Season about a match with a son of one of her father's dearest friends, but the young man hadn't liked the notion of marrying "a failed debutante."

"Your mother and I agree that you must choose as your heart desires."

As Lucy understood it, that's exactly what Aunt Cassandra had done, running off to marry a Scottish laird when her family had a long-standing plan for a union with the heir of the neighboring estate. But Lucy knew pointing that out wouldn't amuse her father.

"This isn't an act of rebellion, Papa, but it is a bit of freedom I crave."

He remained silent so long, Lucy's heart began to sink. Would he truly demand the coachman turn their carriage about?

But he never did. As the brougham drew closer to King's Cross Station, he patted her gloved hand once, and she knew that was his answer. Whatever his worries, whatever his doubts, he would only see her off, not thwart her plans.

Once the carriage had stopped along a line of others disembarking passengers, he finally turned toward her, his expression still grim, though his gaze had softened.

"Travel safely, darling girl, and come back to us soon. Be sensible, no matter what mad scheme your aunt concocts."

"I promise. On all counts, and I'll be back with you within a week. A fortnight at the most, or else I'll miss Miranda's wedding."

He nodded then, and rather than allowing her to climb out on her own, he exited the carriage and came around to escort her. After they'd settled her trunk onto a porter's cart, Lucy stopped him from taking her further into the station.

"I hope you and Mama enjoy your time in Wales." Lucy lifted onto her tiptoes to buss his whiskered cheek. "All will be well, Papa."

"Remember," he called to her as she strode away, "pivot, elbow if necessary, and aim for the soft spots."

Lucy chuckled, glanced back, and waved, though the crowd soon thickened and she lost sight of her father.

A moment later, she stepped onto the platform and gasped at the beauty of the station. Swathed in early morning light, the glass suspended between the steel beam arches of the roof glowed with an ethereal glow that made her feel a bit like she'd entered some grand cathedral.

As the platform filled with passengers waiting to board the Special Scotch Express, Lucy sensed the same anticipation she'd felt all morning among those in the crowd. For her, though, it was more than anxiousness for an exciting journey. She'd been seized by another feeling she found too fanciful to confess to her father.

She sensed that, somehow, this holiday would change her. That whoever she was now, she wouldn't be quite the same when she returned.

JAMES CLENCHED HIS fist within the tight confines of his glove and winced. He hadn't struck another man in years and had rather forgotten how hard a human face could be. Even three days later, bruises lingered and the cut on his knuckle was slow to heal.

"Not long now, m'lord," the driver shouted down.

James gritted his teeth. Despite his eagerness to get to the station in time for the express, the notion of boarding a train made his pulse race and panic shoot like adrenaline through his veins. The same feeling he'd had on *that* day so many years ago.

He rarely returned to memories of the train crash that had taken his parents' lives.

The cabbie seemed to know how to navigate the sea of carriages heading toward King's Cross Station. Yet, they moved with the speed of pouring molasses.

Was *everyone* traveling today?

As much as he loathed the notion of train travel, the express to Scotland departed once each day, and James wanted this matter settled with all due haste. Even now, the thought of Archibald Beck or his men revisiting his home and menacing his staff made his stomach roil.

He commanded himself to take deep breaths and felt his heartbeat begin to settle. He let his head fall back against the wall of the carriage, and it knocked harder than he'd intended against the wood.

Maybe he deserved it.

After James had invested heavily in an industrial scheme to develop cargo ships that ran on electricity, the enterprise fell apart. Injured contractors. Faulty materials. An inventor who disappeared with much of the initial investment.

Three months in, James sought a loan to keep his shipping business afloat and only later came to realize that Beck was the worst sort of predatory lender. Once the loan monies evaporated, Beck came after him for what he'd borrowed, plus an exorbitant amount of interest.

Perhaps Beck had assumed that because of the blue blood in his veins, James could liquidate assets readily, but he'd never lived that way. Never known true inherited wealth. Even his father had eked out a living on the pittance the old earl had spared him.

James had built wealth through his own ingenuity and instincts. He'd formed his own shipping company, earned the respect of others in commerce, and with one ill-fated investment scheme, his efforts had all gone to hell.

Bloody, bloody fool. How had he been such a

gullible mark for a fraudulent enterprise? Or a man like Beck? His entire adult life, he'd relied on the principle of accepting help from no one. When his uncle turned his back after his parents' deaths, James decided he could only rely on himself. Whatever he earned, whatever success he achieved, he wished to do so on his own merit, through his own hard work. Most of all, he'd steered clear of nobility, despite his father's bloodline, after the expectation of inheriting a title had gotten his parents killed. Aristocrats liked to dabble in business, yet they judged those who made their living via commerce.

Damned snobs, just like his late uncle. If he had anything to thank Rufus Pembroke for, it was the opportunity to learn that he could survive on his own.

But then he'd grown desperate for funds, and Beck had been so bloody reassuring. The actors of Drury Lane had nothing on the man's performance.

Nevertheless, James should have known better, and now he did. Never again would he trust anyone so damned easily.

"Arriving now, guv," the cabbie called down again.

James collected the suitcase that would serve as his only luggage for the trip. With any luck, this venture would be a short one. If the manor house wasn't a dilapidated pile, finding a buyer shouldn't take long.

Leaning forward, he let out an oath of frustration. The clog of traffic may have let up midway, but it seemed as if they'd all ended up in front of the station. A drove of passengers moved in a wave toward the entrance, and James prepared himself to be crushed between strangers for the duration of the trip.

He paid the cabbie, patted his chest to ensure the documents that he needed to prove his ownership of Invermere Manor were secure, and joined the sea of bodies moving toward the platforms.

A squabbling family took up the whole of the space ahead of him, and no matter how he tried to sidestep them, one or two would spread out enough to block his way. When one of the little boys stopped to collect a stuffed bear he'd dropped, stalling the entire procession of passengers, James decided he'd had enough.

"Pardon me." He turned to make himself as narrow as his bulk would allow and squeezed past the father. The man grumbled in irritation, but James got clear and was able to pick up his stride. The Scotch Express came into view and wariness overtook him. If he could just get on the train, he could stop worrying about getting on the train.

He knew he was being rude, but he couldn't stop himself from squeezing past a bickering couple who'd slowed in front of him. This time, the lady seemed most irritated, and James's sense of chivalry made him turn back and offer a belated *pardon me* as he passed.

But as he glanced at the couple, his body collided with something soft and warm ahead of him. A moment later, a block of concrete slammed onto his foot.

"Bloody hell." The shout of pain emerged at the same moment his gaze clashed with the woman he'd bumped into. Her lips were parted in shock and seeming outrage, but she'd grabbed his arm to keep herself steady and held on as if she was still in danger of taking a tumble.

He didn't mind. He liked the heat of it, the firmness of her small hand wrapped around his forearm. Under the brim of a sizable hat, James caught sight of the prettiest lips he'd ever seen. Plump and peaked and pink, tipped up at the edges as if they were used to forming a smile.

But she wasn't smiling now, and when she tipped her hat back, eyes framed by thick lashes flared with undisguised irritation.

Disappointment echoed through him when she let go of his arm and immediately started to bend to retrieve the books that had slid out of the thousand-pound valise he'd caused her to drop.

With the movement, they collided again, and her head bumped his chin. Actually, it was her hat—a gargantuan purple concoction with an enormous satin ribbon and silk flowers.

"You've ruined my hat," she said, seemingly more appalled at the offense to her accessory than to her person.

They were too close, though with the swarm of

other passengers passing by, it was impossible not to be. Still, her sweet floral and warm spice scent was so delicious, it made him draw in a deeper breath.

She watched him warily as she lifted both arms to fuss with her hat.

Green. Her eyes were green. But not a simple dark emerald or even anything as familiar as grass. They were a cool green like jade, shot through with gold strands.

"It's just a little askew." He reached up to help and she let out a gasp. He avoided touching her and focused on making the brim as even as he could. The thing was no doubt pinned on, and he sensed the moment it tugged at her hair and stopped.

Blond hair, satiny and honey colored—he couldn't help but notice.

"There. Now, stand still, don't bump me again, and I'll retrieve your books."

Another breathy gasp of outage. "*You* bumped into *me* if we wish to be accurate about the whole thing."

Her voice made him smile. Deeper than some ladies and yet with an uplifting lilt, a natural sort of joviality, even though she was annoyed with him.

"Here." He handed up a hairpin that had come loose and landed near a book.

"I say, clear off," an old whiskered man snapped at them.

"A true gentleman might offer to help a lady

rather than being rude," she said in an icy tone. Then she swept her gaze around at the other gentlemen nearby, as if daring them to bark at her like the old man had.

"Here." James offered her the final book that had fallen, and she shoved it into her valise with a nod of dismissal.

When she turned her back, he sensed others moving past him and realized he'd stalled. Watching her. Fascinated.

As she joined the line of passengers, she gazed upward, admiring the canopy of steel arches that formed the interior of the station. She even tried turning herself around, as if to take in the whole of the station in one last panoramic sweeping glance.

Why couldn't he stop looking at her?

From her voice, her accent, her clothes, she had to be a noblewoman. Likely with too much money, a great deal of education—judging by her trove of books with gilt-engraved covers—and possessed of the same haughtiness she'd used when speaking to the old man.

But she was traveling alone. That seemed utter folly for a lady so young and pretty.

By the time propriety caught up with him and he realized he should cease watching her and step forward, she'd hitched the strap of her valise higher on her shoulder and moved back into the line of embarking passengers.

"You getting on the train or admiring the scenery, chap?" A hulking tower of a man nudged

James's shoulder, and he joined the procession toward the train again too.

Almost against his will, he found himself looking for the lady in purple. Was she a pampered wife who'd been separated from her husband? No, James decided. A man would be a fool to abandon such a lady. Most likely, she was a bluestocking, independent minded enough to insist on traveling on her own.

Whoever she was, and despite her beauty, she was also undoubtedly a blue blood. And he'd sworn off amorous entanglements with noble ladies, just as he vowed to never do business with aristocrats again.

But she intrigued him, and after months of self-imposed celibacy due to his crushing financial defeat, his body responded hungrily.

Get a hold of yourself, man.

After boarding the express train, he found his car easily enough. As he seated himself, he couldn't resist a sigh of pleasure at finding it sparsely occupied. Just one old curmudgeon grumbling as he read the *Times*.

James had been too distracted by the young woman to buy a newspaper for himself. He tended to peruse one each day. An old habit of keeping abreast of news that might impact his shipping enterprise. Though now he always hoped to read some piece about Archibald Beck being exposed as the miscreant he was.

Pressing his fingers to his temple, he attempted to

stem the thrumming that had begun the moment he'd set out for the station. Without the distraction of the lady on the platform, his anxiety regarding train travel was back with a vengeance.

He'd been able to avoid travel by train for most of his adult life. But this was the fastest way, and getting the Scottish manor house liquidated quickly mattered most.

He drew in a breath that filled his lungs, letting it out slowly. He counted as he breathed, letting his eyes slide shut and opening them a few moments later.

And then, she was there, passing by his train car. The bluestocking with her gorgeous mouth. He still felt guilty for knocking all her expensive books onto the ground.

He told himself there were much more pressing matters at hand. He clenched his fists, reminding himself just how important those matters were. The last thing he needed was the complication of a train trip dalliance with a bluestocking.

No matter how distractingly fetching she was.

Chapter Four

Lucy found her train car easily enough and was pleased to discover that two ladies would be her companions for the journey. She gave each a quick smile, stowed her valise on the shelf above her head, and took her seat.

There, now it was settled. Papa couldn't stop her. Though the train remained still, puffing steam, and hadn't yet rolled from the station, her journey had well and truly begun.

Though the bubbling energy she'd felt this morning had turned to something else.

Irritation caused her to fumble with the buttons of her gloves, so she stripped them off and pressed the cool back of her hand to her flaming cheek.

Whatever she was feeling, it was *his* fault. That man. That tall, rude—

"Are you all right?" One of the ladies had taken the seat next to Lucy, and her companion sat across from them.

"Quite," Lucy told her with forced cheerfulness. "Thank you. It's a bit warm. That's all."

"Is it?" The older woman cast her gaze down,

then tipped her head as if giving Lucy's claim deep consideration. "I'm afraid my sister and I could not agree. We were just remarking on the bite in the air. Winter is on its way, and we only pray it's not yet utterly frigid in Edinburgh."

Lucy could help with this worry. She flipped open her sketchbook, the empty pages of which she was using to organize her travel documents and anything she might need to reference quickly for her trip.

"I can assure you that it won't be frigid." Under the train timetable and the stub from her ticket, Lucy found the page where she'd recorded the relevant information. "Though we may have a cold winter, the weather in Scotland is expected to be cool but not cold enough to freeze."

"How on earth do you know that?" The lady across from Lucy stared down at the journal in her hands as if it was a tome of arcane knowledge.

"*Simpkin's Prognostications of the Weather.* Not always reliable, of course, but I've found it to be quite accurate."

"You're a very prepared young lady. Well done."

"I do hope so."

"Goodness, I suppose we've yet to introduce ourselves. I am Jane Wilson, and this is my sister, Maribel."

"Lucy Westmont." They exchanged a round of genuine smiles and nods, then fell silent again.

"You do look warm, Miss Westmont. I brought a folding fan." Miss Maribel Wilson offered up a pretty dark wood fan with floral muslin stretched across its ribs.

"I'll cool down soon enough, I'm sure."

The air did have a pleasant autumn bite to it. Unfortunately, the heat in her cheeks had nothing to do with the weather and everything to do with a man whose smile had turned her knees to melted butter.

And those eyes. No one had sapphire eyes. Novelists and poets may rhapsodize about ladies with gemstones gazes, but that particular shade of deep, rich blue was extraordinary. She'd certainly never had a man with eyes in that shade look her way, his gaze full of mirth and warmth.

He'd seemed as caught up in staring at her as she had been in studying him, and *that* had certainly never happened before. Men's attention didn't linger on her.

But his had. Brazenly. Downright impudently.

The man was definitely a scoundrel of some ilk. And then he'd turned imperious and accused her of being the one to barrel into him. As if *he* owned the train car platform, and the rules of propriety and the demands of politeness simply didn't apply to him.

Imagine having such a man bossing one around every day? Insufferable.

She lifted her gloves from her lap and aligned them neatly to store them in her pocket, but a scent stopped her. Rich and clean. Pine perhaps and a hint of spice. His scent.

Gracious, she'd touched him—gripped him, actually. What had possessed her? She recalled the moment she'd noticed they were still connected after the collision, and it was because *she* held on to him. There'd been such an odd comfort in feeling the firm muscles shifting beneath her palm, knowing, somehow, that he wouldn't let her fall.

But she wasn't certain of that at all, of course. The man was a stranger, and a far too handsome one.

Forget him. Lucy needed to put the whole thing out of her mind. Good grief, Papa would roll his eyes to the heavens if he knew she'd overheated like a boiling teapot the minute she'd clapped eyes on a fine-looking man.

The door of the train carriage slid open, and Lucy snapped her head up.

A wiry, bespectacled man stepped inside. "Number Five, is it?"

"It is indeed, sir," the younger Miss Wilson told him.

Lucy realized she'd been holding her breath, hoping like a fool that it might be *him* who'd entered their train car.

"Nichols," the thin gentleman said as he settled on the bench across from Lucy. "Traveling to Edinburgh, as I'd guess you three are."

"You are correct, Mr. Nichols. At least, that's true of my sister and myself." Miss Jane Wilson turned her gaze on Lucy. "And you, young lady?"

"Oh yes, I'm going to Scotland too," Lucy told the trio of passengers. "My first visit."

The two ladies nodded and offered a kind smile, while Mr. Nichols subjected all three of them to an oddly brazen perusal. Lucy watched him assess the sisters from the toes of their boots to the tops of their heads. When his gaze reached Lucy's face, she expected the man to blush or turn away, to acknowledge that she'd caught him staring rudely.

Instead, he offered her the tiniest of smirks. A flash and then it was gone.

The two sisters were still debating the weather and took no notice of the man, but something about him set Lucy's nerves on edge. Or perhaps it had been that odd encounter on the platform with a tall, handsome stranger that still had her rattled.

Two hours into the journey, Lucy found herself grateful to her past self for remembering to pack books. And thankfully none seemed damaged from the debacle on the platform. She'd chosen Wilkie Collins to start, and getting lost in *The Law and the Lady* was almost enough for her to ignore the way Mr. Nichols made her skin crawl.

After reading a newspaper for nearly an hour, he'd settled his head against the upholstered bench and feigned sleeping. Every so often, an odd sense came over her, and Lucy would glance up to find his squint-eyed gaze on her.

"Oh, look at the time, Maribel. The dining car

should be serving lunch now." The older Miss Wilson, a tall, regal lady, was clearly the decision maker of the two.

"That sounds like just the thing we need," Maribel agreed instantly and turned to Lucy. "Won't you join us, Miss Westmont?"

"I'd love to." It was likely a futile hope, but she dearly wished Mr. Nichols would choose another train car while they were gone. Since he appeared to be dozing, they left him to his rest.

As they made their way down the corridor, Lucy told herself not to stare into the other train cars in search of a man with sapphire eyes. *Such nonsense.* The whole incident had been odd. Certainly, that was why she couldn't get it out of her mind.

"Hold on!" Jane Wilson shouted as the train took a rather sudden curve in the tracks.

"Heavens, it's worse than a ship in stormy waters."

Lucy had never been on a ship, though her father had traveled a great deal, and the stories he'd told made her long for a sea voyage.

"Only a little further," the elder Wilson sister assured them as she led the procession down the narrow passageway.

Delicious scents emanated from the dining car—fresh bread and smoky coffee—and they were lucky. Despite it already being busy, they managed to find one table with three chairs.

Yet, before they could all get into their seats, the younger Miss Wilson seemed to have a spell.

"Oh, Jane, it's coming on." Maribel stumbled a bit and gripped the back of the chair.

"She has dizzy spells," Jane told Lucy as she embraced her sister.

Lucy rushed to pull out the chair, and Miss Wilson helped her sister into it.

"I'll get you some tea and perhaps some water biscuits." Lucy gestured at a passing waiter, and the young man nodded as if he'd overheard her.

Maribel's skin had gone a pasty white. She seemed to be in a state of shock.

"Is there anything else I can do?" Lucy asked, wishing to help ease the lady's discomfort.

"There's a tonic she takes for these. It's back in our train car, the embroidered bag on the rack above our bench."

As soon as Lucy saw the waiter approaching with tea and biscuits on a tray, she stood. "I'll go now."

"It's a small blue bottle," Maribel whispered. "And thank you, my dear."

"Of course."

Lucy rushed back to their train car. Once she reached number Five, she hesitated, noting that Mr. Nichols still *seemed* to be dozing. Sliding the door open gently, she moved quickly but attempted to be as quiet as possible. Unfortunately, the embroidered bag was on the metal rail above him.

Lucy reached up, trying not to bump him or the bench, and was able to retrieve the bag. Turning, she set it on her bench and leaned over to sift through the contents. A cluster of neatly folded handkerchiefs sat on top, but when she pushed them aside, she found a number of bottles in a small compartment, each secured by a leather strap. Several of them were blue, and Lucy found herself freeing and resecuring bottle after bottle hoping to find the correct one. Finally, she noticed one labeled Dizzy Tonic, and slipped it into the pocket of her skirt.

"I see you've come back, and I get you all to myself."

Lucy stiffened, and the unease Mr. Nichols inspired turned to an icy shiver up her spine.

Before she could turn, he was off his bench and behind her, wrapping an arm around her waist.

Lucy bent her elbow, shifted slightly to the left, and jabbed back as hard as she could into his abdomen. Just as her father taught her to do.

Nichols groaned and released her.

She took the opportunity to turn and balled her hand into a fist.

He'd bent slightly, holding his stomach, and then looked up at her with that smirk she'd seen earlier. Not concealed now, it was broad and as ugly as the man's intentions.

"I like a spitfire." He straightened and wiped a hand across his mouth, assessing her as he had earlier, starting at the edge of her skirt and letting his gaze travel upward.

Lucy held her breath and shifted her feet, ready to run for the door as soon as he moved far enough away from it. She stepped back toward the corner of the carriage, drawing him closer.

But then he startled her by launching himself forward, arms out in an attempt to embrace her.

Lucy jabbed hard at the man's jaw. Pain shot up her arm, radiating out across her shoulder, but Nichols stumbled back, and that gave her time to escape from the train car.

Pushing the door aside, she glanced back to ensure Nichols wasn't on her heels. Then she slammed into a hard, immovable bulk in front of her. Arms came around her and she struggled against the man's hold until she looked up into those unforgettable dark blue eyes.

"Looks like it's your turn to bump into me." He grinned, and then his expression fell. "You're trembling."

"He—" Lucy gestured toward Nichols at the same moment the man lunged toward them through the open train car door.

"That bloody bitch assaulted me!"

The stranger from the platform immediately stepped in, pulling Lucy along so that she was behind the width of his body, sheltered from Nichols's view.

"Step back. Now." The man shouted so loudly, Lucy felt the echo of it reverberating in her own chest.

"I'll have her thrown off this train," Nichols blustered, though his voice wavered into a whiny pitch.

The stranger turned his head slightly to glance back at Lucy, a question in his gaze.

"He put his hands on me," Lucy whispered, trying to control the tremor in her voice. "I punched him."

One dark brow arched high before he directed his gaze back at Nichols. An arm shot out, and Nichols grunted. The man from the platform had Nichols by the throat.

"What's the trouble here?" A porter approached from the far end of the corridor.

"All's well." Platform Man offered the porter a reassuring smile, then released Nichols, who coughed and bent at the waist as he caught his breath. The porter hesitated, glanced at each of them in turn and then went back the way he'd come.

"Get back inside and keep your bloody hands to yourself." Without waiting for Nichols to offer any kind of resistance or reply, Lucy's stranger pushed him back and shut the door in his face.

Then he turned to her. "Come with me."

"I can't."

"If you're worried about propriety, we can say—"

"No, not propriety. I need to get this to Miss Wilson." Lucy pulled the bottle from the pocket of her skirt and grimaced as she felt a sting of pain when the fabric grazed her knuckles.

The man glanced down at the bottle, then immediately reached for her wrist.

He touched her quite freely, and for some reason she allowed it.

"You've injured your hand."

"Miss Westmont?" Miss Jane Wilson approached from the direction of the dining car.

The man, who she seemed to keep colliding with and touching, immediately let go of her wrist. Apparently, *he* had some sense of propriety.

"I worried when you didn't return." She quickened her pace and studied the gentleman pressed against Lucy in the corridor. "And who might you be, sir?"

"An acquaintance," Lucy said with an awkward lump in her throat. Two hours to get herself into a scandalous muddle. Papa would never stop telling her he'd been right all along.

"James Pembroke." He wielded that smile. Not quite the full arsenal he'd unleashed on her earlier, but a bewitching version that Lucy could see was working its charm on Jane Wilson. "A recent acquaintance, but a fond one, I hope."

This caused Miss Wilson to go absolutely pink from the lace collar of her high-necked blouse up to the sharp edge of her cheek. "Jane Wilson," she said a little breathily. Then she seemed to recall Lucy again.

"Are you unwell too, Miss Westmont?"

Lucy shifted the bottle into her uninjured hand and held it out. "Not at all. I'm well. But I—"

After the older woman had taken the bottle, Mr. Pembroke moved past Lucy and toward Miss Wilson. He lowered his deep voice and said, "The man in that train car is a menace, and I won't countenance Miss Westmont spending another moment in his company."

Miss Wilson shot a quizzical look at Lucy.

"I don't wish to remain in Mr. Nichols's company, and you and Miss Maribel shouldn't either."

Jane's finely plucked silver brows winged high, and her mouth flattened into a grim line. "I did not like the look of him from the start. But where will you go?"

"There's room in my train car," Mr. Pembroke said smoothly. "Join us, if you wish. Number One. All the way at the end."

With that, he came back Lucy's way, wearing a conspiratorial smile. He'd charmed the older woman in less time than it had taken for her to lay a punch on Mr. Nichols's face.

"I'm not sure this is entirely—" Jane Wilson called.

"It's all right, Miss Wilson. I trust Mr. Pembroke."

That almost made him stumble in his approach, and the cocky smile faded into something softer, uncertain, and vulnerable.

He gestured behind her. "This way, Miss Westmont."

Lucy turned in the direction he'd pointed and started toward the first train car, far enough to get past the one containing the odious Mr. Nichols, but after a few steps, some wicked impulse made her wait to step forward until he was closer.

James Pembroke. Soon he was just at her back. His suit coat brushed the bell of her gown.

"Are you stuck?" His words were softly spoken and laced with amusement that could almost make her forget the pain in her hand. "Or are you having second thoughts because you trust me much less than you claimed?"

Lucy looked back into that mischievous blue gaze. She couldn't say whether it was him she didn't trust, or herself and the wayward thoughts in her head since the moment she'd crashed into him.

Chapter Five

I should go and find the Wilson sisters."

"Who?" James tried to keep her talking as he focused on tending to the abrasion on her hand. He sensed she needed the distraction. It was less than half an hour since her encounter with the vile man in her train carriage, and there was still a quaver in her voice.

"The sisters who shared the train car with me and Nichols." At the mention of the man, a shiver rushed through her body. James felt it as he held her, swabbing gently at the skin across her knuckles.

"Why did they leave you alone with him?"

"They didn't. We all went to the dining car, but Miss Maribel Wilson needed her medicine, so I went back to retrieve it. That's when he—"

"After I'm finished, I'll find them. As I told Miss Wilson, there's plenty of room in this car. My only companion has been an older gentleman who's gone to the dining car too." He looked up at her, but she kept her focus on the window and pulled her bottom lip between her teeth.

"The greater question," he continued, "is what to do about Nichols."

"I stopped him. There's nothing more to be done."

"He accosted you." James spoke with more force than he'd intended. Anger simmered just below the surface, but he'd held it in check to comfort her.

"It was a . . . misunderstanding. Please leave Mr. Nichols to his own fate."

"As you wish." James nodded, but the thought of the man getting off with no consequences made him ill at ease.

She narrowed her jade green eyes as if she didn't quite believe his easy acquiescence. It was odd to meet a woman who seemed to read him so well and so quickly.

For the first time, she turned her attention toward her injured hand and his attempts to clean away the blood. After a moment, the wary beauty sat up straighter on her bench and firmed her chin.

"This isn't necessary, Mr. Pembroke. I assure you I'm quite capable of caring for myself."

Interestingly, despite the bite in her tone, she made no move to pull her hand from his grasp.

He loosened his hold, giving her the option to move away.

She didn't, and James pressed his lips together to keep from smiling. A small victory, but one of the few he'd had of late. He intended to savor it.

"Your skill at fisticuffs isn't in doubt. I'm sure the man's nose will hurt for a while." James resisted looking at her again as he spoke, keeping his attention on the task at hand.

He couldn't deny the lady's claim. This wasn't necessary. She *was* capable of using the cloth, water, and soap he'd requested.

Still, something in him wanted to do it, needed to. He told himself it had simply been too long since he'd touched a woman. Plus, the distraction of having a task to accomplish kept him from thinking about the tragic train accident that cost him his family.

Yet, she was more than a distraction. The need to help her, touch her, had to do with *this* woman.

Maybe it was guilt for being a cad to her on the platform. The rest he couldn't quite suss out. He only knew there was something about her—perhaps it was her very self-possessed capableness—that made him wish to be the one to offer her aid and protection.

"His chin, if you wish to be specific," she murmured a moment later.

James quirked a brow.

"I aimed for his nose and missed," she said ruefully. "My father always advised me to aim for the soft spots, and his jaw was not at all soft. As the backs of my fingers can attest."

He grinned then, unable to hold it back, but she didn't respond in kind. Just turned her head to study the passing landscape, much as she'd done since taking a seat on the bench opposite him and resting her hand against the bowl of water the porter had delivered.

But she hadn't kept silent or still. Beyond the

trembling he occasionally felt reverberating down her arm, there was a palpable impatient energy about her. As if she longed to be up and moving.

He understood that most of all.

"I do hope Jane and Maribel don't return to that car. Though I suppose they'll have to in order to retrieve their bags."

"Almost finished," he said quietly, an attempt to reassure her but also remind himself that he shouldn't drag this out. "I'll go and find them and bring their belongings back here."

Yet he held on for a moment longer, taking his time, reluctant to stop touching her. But, of course, he must. They were strangers, and she was a lady of propriety. As he suspected, she was a lady by birth according to the corner of an envelope sticking out of her valise. *The Lady Lucy Westmont.*

James stilled. What the hell was he doing? He avoided nobles. That was his rule. Never mind that he now was one.

Good god. There'd been so little time to let that fact sink in or consider what it meant for his future. His only goal was to liquidate the Scottish manor house he'd inherited.

But now he could foresee a future where matchmaking mamas pushed young women like Lady Lucy his way. They'd be sorely disappointed. Despite the title, and even if he could leverage the income from the sale of one property, he had nothing more to offer in terms of security than he had a week ago.

He released her hand and set the cloth aside. "Those scratches should heal soon."

"You missed a bit just there." She retrieved the damp cloth and swiped at her finger.

It seemed the lady didn't appreciate help. She wanted to be the one to care for herself.

A moment later, she stunned him by tracing her fingers across the knuckles of his right hand.

"You're injured too." She looked at him expectantly. "Who did you punch?"

There it was. A flicker of wariness finally appeared in her guileless gaze.

"Nothing worth discussing."

"That's not quite fair, Mr. Pembroke. You know about my incident."

"I do. But my secrets are my own, Lady Lucy."

"How did you . . . ?" Her pale brows crimped in question and perhaps a hint of concern.

James pointed at the overstuffed valise at her side. "I spied the edge of your letter."

She immediately gripped the envelope and shoved it deeper into the bag.

"Please call me Miss Westmont. I try not to rest on ceremony."

Was the lady completely free of pretense, or just terribly naive?

"The whole of the aristocracy rests on ceremony, does it not?"

She blinked and her very lovely mouth pinched. James realized he'd offended her. Once again, he'd been a cad. Whatever his own misgivings about noblemen like his uncle, she didn't deserve his bitterness.

"My family tries not to be so formal in private."

"Then I suspect I'd like them a great deal."

A wistful smile tipped the edge of her mouth. "Everyone likes my father, though he's perhaps the most formal of all of us." She seemed to ponder that a moment. "Diplomacy is very formal, isn't it?"

"May I ask your father's name?"

"Must you?" The question seemed to distress her much more than he'd intended.

"You wish to keep your secrets too?"

"I don't truly have any secrets," she said immediately and with an unpretentious honesty he'd begun to doubt anyone was capable of anymore.

"Still, I would prefer he did not know I needed to strike a man in the face not an hour after he dropped me at the station." She drew in a sharp breath and let it out slowly. "He'd expressed concerns about the dangers of taking this trip alone, and I reassured him. But perhaps he was right. Traveling on my own may have been folly."

"You'll be safe for the rest of the journey, Miss Westmont. I promise you that," he told her, holding her gaze and wanting her to believe him. Wanting her trust.

They had a handful of hours to go before they reached Edinburgh, and he'd ensure Lucy Westmont's safety for the remainder of the trip.

"You shouldn't make promises you can't keep,

Mr. Pembroke. So far, nothing about this trip has gone as I intended."

He appreciated her wariness. She might look like some summery goddess with her spun-gold hair, tip-turned nose, and rosebud lips, but the lady was no fool.

"Still, I will do my best not to let any harm come to you."

"I see." She cradled her sore hand, then stretched out her fingers as if testing for pain. "Are you my self-appointed protector now?" There was a bit of sharpness in her tone. And he realized that they weren't so different in their determination not to trust easily.

"Think of it as recompense for the moment we met. I was rather—"

"Rude?"

"Impatient."

"More like dictatorial."

"You seemed overwrought."

"I wasn't until you spilled my books onto the ground."

"See," he teased. "You're overwrought now."

She seamed her lips into a tense line and shot him a challenging look. "I have a sixteen-year-old brother who teases me as often as he can, Mr. Pembroke—"

"James."

"—I assure you. I'm not easily provoked."

"I do love a challenge."

"Your attempts will be utterly futile."

"Isn't that for me to decide?" In his mind, he'd already decided. Any time spent with this far too pretty and prickly lady would not be a waste. In fact, this train trip, which he'd dreaded since his decision to travel to Scotland, might have left him with nothing but time to replay his own failures, or recall the last time he'd traveled north on a train.

Meeting her had changed all that. He'd enjoyed every moment in her company and was especially glad he'd gotten her away from Nichols.

When he began to roll down his sleeves, he felt her gaze tracking his movements and looked up to find the loveliest pink blush cresting her cheeks.

She leaned forward to tidy the items he'd used to clean her wounds, arranging the bowl on the tray, folding the cloth, and setting the block of soap on top.

"I should return these."

"Allow me." He leaned forward to take them from her hands.

She swung them away, out of his reach. "I don't need to be coddled, Mr. Pembroke."

"Forgive me, Miss Westmont." James raised his hands in surrender. She seemed more defensive the longer they were in each other's company. Almost as if she felt she had something to prove. Perhaps her father's doubts about her independence rankled. "Please don't think I underestimate you."

She looked at him then, taking him in, allowing her gaze to rove boldly. If the places where her perusal lingered were any indication, she was fond of his eyes, his shoulders, and his mouth.

He smiled. Not to fluster her—though it was clear he did—or even to seduce her. He smiled to show her that he knew the turn of her thoughts and welcomed them.

"You're a scoundrel." She breathed the words so softly he wouldn't have heard them if she'd been any further away. But she was close. Achingly so. Her scent enveloped him, and her breath warmed his face.

"You know, I've never thought of myself as one, but I rather like that word on your gorgeous lips."

HE *WAS* A scoundrel. A man so handsome and so at ease in his masculine beauty couldn't be anything but.

"If you'll excuse me." Lucy swallowed hard, clutched the bowl and cleaning items to her chest, and made her way out of the Number One train car.

She moved down the corridor quickly, sloshing a bit of water, and stopped at the connection between his carriage and the next.

Closing her eyes, she drew in deep breaths until her heartbeat settled into something closer to a normal pace.

Good grief, that man. *James Pembroke.* No one had ever been able to fluster her as easily as Mr. James Pembroke. He was mercurial. At once cocky and then suddenly kind. She was able to read most people, understand them. She listened, paid attention, and discerned how best to approach them. It was a set of skills she'd learned from her diplomat father. But Mr. Pembroke confounded her.

She found a train attendant just inside the dining car who took the cleaning items from her with a nod. "Shall I find you a table, miss?"

"No, thank you." She had no desire to eat. The business with Nichols had rattled her nerves and soured her stomach, and Mr. Pembroke had made it flip-flop more times than she cared to admit.

"There she is!" Maribel pointed at Lucy, causing Jane to turn her head and then rise from her chair.

Jane waved her over, and Lucy approached the sisters, praying her cheeks weren't flushed and that her expression gave nothing away.

"We were just considering whether to return and find you. I was a bit worried about the gentleman who took charge of you."

Took charge of made Lucy bristle, but she knew Miss Wilson meant nothing by it.

"Is he a safe sort?" the younger Miss Wilson asked warily. "Jane says he's quite handsome."

"Handsome does not a good man make," Jane proclaimed authoritatively. "I would hope most ladies know that." She shot Lucy a piercing look.

"I do know that." Lucy wasn't sure she'd ever heard that precise maxim, but her distrust of handsome men was learned from three Seasons of watching the most appealing lordlings toy with ladies' affections as if they were master puppeteers.

She couldn't explain why she trusted Mr. Pembroke, even now when it was clear he took pleasure in teasing her.

"Will you join us?"

Lucy nodded. "I will, but I also want to invite you to move to Mr. Pembroke's carriage when you've finished your lunch."

"All our things are still in Number Five with Mr. Nichols."

"Then I'll retrieve them."

The deep voice drew their attention toward Mr. Pembroke, who'd entered the dining car and was approaching their table. Lucy observed that they weren't the only ladies who took note of his entrance. She'd wager he was a man who attracted feminine attention wherever he went.

"Oh, he *is* handsome," Miss Maribel whispered.

Indeed, he was. Far too attractive for his own good and apparently for Lucy's peace of mind.

"Shall I escort you back?"

"Miss Westmont hasn't even had time for a cup of tea."

"Then we can have some brought round to the train car."

"Goodness," Miss Maribel said in an awestruck tone. "Is there anything you haven't thought of, sir?"

That comment poked at something inside Lucy. It was the sort of remark she often heard from her best friend, Miranda. She wasn't used to anyone being quite as thoughtful or helpful as she was.

And they were odd qualities for a charming scoundrel to possess.

"You three deserve a bit of peace after the ugliness with Nichols."

Lucy woke with a start and sat up straight on the train car bench. Her neck, shoulder, and hand immediately protested. It took a moment to process the fact that night had fallen.

Across from her, the sisters sat side by side. Maribel leaned her head against her sister's shoulder, and both slept soundly.

She reached up to massage the ache in her shoulder and then reached further, trying to get to the knot in her upper back.

"I'd offer to help but if we woke the sisters, it would be a proper scandal." His words were low and warm, roughened by sleep.

"I don't need help. Thank you very much." Lucy glanced over to find James Pembroke looking amused.

He'd removed his suit coat and loosened his tie so that the dark lengths of fabric lay in stark contrast against the white of his shirt. His neck was exposed in a vee that revealed the base of his throat and a dusting of dark hair disappearing along his collarbone.

Her fingers itched to touch him. She should be

shocked at how freely they'd touched each other since meeting just hours before. But there'd been no awkwardness in it, no shame. It felt natural and strangely right to be at ease with him.

Yet when their gazes met across the train car, she sensed *he* wasn't at ease.

"Have I been asleep long?" She kept her voice low so as not to wake the sisters.

"A couple of hours." He ran a hand through his hair, and Lucy noticed the sheen of perspiration on his forehead.

The train carriage was cool, so his heated state made no sense.

"Is something troubling you?"

He let out a breath of shaky laughter. "Perhaps it's all the sitting still. I'm not terribly good at it."

"I understand that. I like to keep busy too."

He nodded and flashed her a sympathetic smile.

"But we'll be there soon." Lucy swept her gaze over the napping sisters. "Then we can all stretch our legs."

At her words, Lucy couldn't help but notice that his gaze flickered toward her legs. A scoundrel, indeed.

"You've never told me what's taking you to Scotland. I'm going to visit my aunt."

"Business takes me to Scotland," he said evenly. His tone seemed meant to dissuade further inquiry.

But Lucy was nothing if not curious. Especially about him.

"So, you're a businessman?"

He nodded but didn't look her way. Suddenly, the passing landscape—too dark for him to see at night—fascinated him. While he watched, he pulled at the tie that lay loose around his neck and wrapped the fabric into a ball in his hand, as if anxiety plagued him.

"What sort of business?" Lucy ignored every sign James Pembroke gave to indicate that he didn't wish to be prodded for personal details.

Such a curious man.

In her experience, gentlemen were quite pleased to speak about their accomplishments, sometimes to a yawn-inducing degree.

Whenever she was anxious, talking tended to ease her mind. Even if the topic was inane. The mere diversion of conversation could work wonders.

She nibbled at her lip, wondering what she might say that could put James Pembroke at ease.

"Will it be a long stay in Scotland for you?" She flicked her gaze above his head. He carried no overstuffed valise as she did, though he might have given the porter two trunks to stow for all she knew.

"Not if I can help it." He loosed one of his charming grins, like an arrow that shot straight and swift, disarming her completely.

Lucy swallowed hard and told her brain to generate a witty reply. None came.

He turned back to the window, a hint of a smile still curving his lips. As if he was satisfied that his devastating grin had the desired effect of making her tongue-tied.

"Keep your secrets if you like, Mr. Pembroke," Lucy said in a tone meant to indicate she did not care a whit, though it emerged with all the irritation she felt.

Lucy paused and studied him as she would some perplexing gentleman across the length of a ballroom. There was tension in his jaw and lines of worry creased his forehead. She could see it. He wasn't at ease in the way he'd been when they were alone.

Perhaps it was the sisters' presence that had cooled the rapport between them. Or perhaps he'd never been as intrigued with her as he'd seemed. If three Seasons had taught her anything, it was that affections were changeable.

After a few minutes of silence, he said quietly, "I'm afraid I'm not fond of train travel."

"Why is that?"

He drew in a deep breath. "An . . . incident from when I was a child. Nothing I wish to discuss."

"I see." She wanted him to tell her more, but would he?

They were strangers after all. Strangers who would part soon.

Much as she expected, he fell silent but continued to twist the fabric of his tie between his hands.

"My father is the Earl of Hallston." She wasn't certain why she blurted the confession. Perhaps the hope that if she answered the question she'd avoided a while back, he might say more too.

It worked, at least to get his attention. He tipped his head. "I've heard of your father. He's known as a philanthropist."

"Oh yes, Papa is always looking for ways to help others."

He shifted on his bench, finally letting the balled fabric of his necktie lie loose on his thigh. "I know you're afraid of him learning what happened with Nichols—"

"It's more that I don't wish for him to know I encountered the very sort of danger he feared the moment I stepped onto the train. I don't wish to disappoint him more than I already have."

"I can't imagine you being a disappointment."

Lucy blinked as the heat of a blush warmed her cheeks. "That's very kind to say." So kind it made her suddenly embarrassed, not sure where to look or what to do with her hands. "I failed for three Seasons, you see."

"Failed?" He squared his gaze on her, more intensely than before. Brows drawn into deep furrows, he stared, almost as if he was seeing her for the first time. "How did you fail?"

Lucy quirked a brow. Was he truly determined to make her spell it out? "To find a husband, Mr. Pembroke."

"None were up to snuff, hmm?" His expression softened.

"None suited me." Lucy decided it was fair to leave out that woefully few had offered.

"Nothing wrong with considering an important

decision carefully. We all should." The vehemence in his tone made Lucy suspect he wasn't referring to her failure on the marriage mart.

She agreed with the principle. "Oddly, Papa might say I am impulsive, but I suppose I know myself and try to make good choices."

Despite the ugliness with Nichols, she still felt this trip to Scotland was one of those good choices.

The sisters shifted, and they both glanced at the two, expecting them to wake. Though they didn't, Mr. Pembroke fell silent. Lucy wanted to continue quizzing him. But he'd drawn in on himself, crossing his arms and shifting his gaze out the train car window once more.

"I'm the sort who talks more when I'm anxious. It seems you prefer to talk less." Lucy leaned toward him. "I'm sorry if I made it worse."

"You couldn't make anything worse," he said with unexpected warmth. Then he turned toward her and lowered his voice to a whisper, "And you've done nothing wrong. I've enjoyed talking to you, Lucy Westmont."

"And I you." The whisper caught in her throat, as if she was confessing something significant.

"I hope you enjoy Scotland. See a great deal and read a great deal." He glanced at her book-filled valise.

"I wish the same for your visit, Mr. Pembroke. Except perhaps the reading part."

Lucy smiled but it immediately faltered. This

was it. Their goodbyes. Soon they'd part ways and likely never see each other again.

Something about that felt wrong, almost impossible to fathom. But she did her best to push such wistfulness aside.

This was the first solo journey of her life, and there would be all sorts of new experiences ahead.

Chapter Six

James found a hired carriage and the driver agreed to take him to Invermere easily enough, though he did remind James that the thirty-mile journey would cause them to arrive late—too late for visitors was the implication. But, in truth, he wasn't a visitor. He owned the damned place. Waking the servants was an inconvenience he'd normally attempt to avoid, but everything about this trip was urgent.

Beck's loathsome smirk flashed in his mind and then the fear he'd seen in Mrs. Wilton's eyes. He would not allow anyone else to suffer for his failures.

But before the journey to Invermere, James had an appointment. At least he hoped the Scottish solicitor he'd contacted would come despite the short notice, and they could conclude their initial business quickly.

"Meet back here in half an hour?"

The driver tipped his cap, and James gave him a wave.

As he started away from the station and headed for Princes Street, James couldn't resist scanning the crowd for a lady in an elaborate plum-colored hat. She wasn't hard to spot. Lady Lucy Westmont stood with the Wilson sisters as the three collected their luggage from a porter.

A pointless yearning washed over him, and though he could push it away with logic—she was better off not knowing a man like him, wasn't she?—some part of him couldn't quite accept that they'd never cross paths again. Their acquaintance was entirely unexpected, and she was quite the most provoking woman he'd ever met, but also the most appealing, and he knew that, despite the brief time they'd known each other, he would re-member her.

In fact, he feared he might never forget her.

He lingered there on the pavement, putting on his gloves, though he hated wearing them, and straightening his tie, though he knew his clothing was impossibly rumpled after the nearly nine-hour journey.

What was he hoping for? That she'd look his way and approach him, just to draw out a connection that seemed to fluster her more than anything?

He had nothing to offer a lady like Lucy Westmont. At least not yet.

Goodness, there was such allure in *yet*. How tantalizing the future seemed if he could somehow connive to have her in it.

Her father, when she'd begrudgingly admitted his name, was one of the most well-known noble-men in London. A leader in charitable endeavors, powerful in the House of Lords, and known to invest in public works programs. James had almost invested in a scheme that involved a bevy of civic-minded noblemen. He'd been prepared to make an exception to his usual no-nobles rule because it had been a sanitation project that, while it would have earned him little profit, would have done a great deal for Londoners. Though the project eventually fell through, James recalled that Lord Hallston's involvement was a beneficial draw.

But what was his plan regarding Lucy? To show up in London months from now and burst back into her life, when she'd likely have forgotten their strange little interlude on a train to Scotland? Or found herself a suitor ready to give her more than he could now? She deserved that.

When his woolgathering cleared, he realized the ladies were, in fact, moving toward him.

His mouth went dry, his palms warmed, and his mind scrambled for how to explain himself as he'd stood watching her—them—for far too long.

"Did you already miss me, ladies?"

"Mr. Pembroke, we meet again," Miss Maribel Wilson said in a teasing tone. "I'm surprised, as you seemed in such a hurry to see to your business affairs."

"Indeed I am."

"Where do they take you?" Lady Lucy asked, coming forward to tip her head, sending the purple flowers fluttering in the breeze as she looked up at him. "Or is that one of your many secrets too?"

Her eyes were twinkling. Even after all day on a train, a vile encounter with a bounder, and her worry about not meeting her father's expectations, she was full of life and mischief.

"I have a meeting." James lifted his pocket watch. "Good grief, I'm late."

He'd lost track of how long he'd stood watching her with the Wilson sisters.

"How far do you need to go?" She pointed toward the far edge of the station. "Should you hire a cab?"

"It's not far. The Guildford Arms. Just up Princes Street on Register Place."

"What a marvelous coincidence!" Miss Jane Wilson's voice raised to a girlish pitch and all of them looked her way. "Why, according to this map, that's quite close to where we're heading for dinner at the Café Royal." She came forward and scooped her sister's arm into hers. "Shall we make the journey together?"

Without waiting for any reply, Miss Wilson strode off at a brisk clip, her more diminutive sister nearly hopping to keep up.

Lady Lucy lingered at his side.

"Are you coming too?" James offered his arm in a gentlemanly gesture he hadn't practiced in months.

"I'm not. My aunt's carriage is due to collect me any moment."

"So this is goodbye."

"Again," she said with a smile.

Hell and brimstone, he was acting like a besotted fool.

"I wish you well, Lady Lucy Westmont. Again."

"The well-wishes are returned, Mr. Pembroke, for whatever mysterious business you've come to Scotland to conduct."

It was James's turn to chuckle. He appreciated her curiosity and almost wished he was as mysterious a man as she teased him about being.

She began to turn away and something pinched in the vicinity of his top waistcoat button—a sense of disappointment that felt ridiculously sharp for the brevity of their acquaintance.

"You'll return to London afterward, I take it?" In that moment, he wanted to promise things. To call on her when he returned. But he wasn't even certain when he would return, and he wouldn't dare make promises that he couldn't keep. Even after a day of knowing her, he knew Lady Lucy Westmont deserved better than that.

"That is the hope."

Somewhere in the distance, a clock's bell tower rang the top of the hour.

"I must be off."

"Of course. Don't let me keep you."

"You'll be all right?"

"I have sharp elbows, Mr. Pembroke. I'll be fine."

James nodded and held her gaze longer than he should have. Foolishly, he didn't wish to be the one to break the connection between them. But Lady Lucy, clever woman that she was, did so first. After returning his nod, she lowered her gaze and then turned away to watch the line of carriages and cabs approaching the station to collect or drop off travelers.

He turned too, exiting the station and starting off in the direction the Wilson sisters had headed. In only a few minutes' time, he'd reached the intersection of West Register Street and spotted the Guildford Arms. As the sisters mentioned, Café Royal was not far away.

Though he looked, James didn't spot them among those at tables in the well-appointed restaurant, but he did spy a man at a window-facing table in the Guildford Arms, looking out expectantly. Could he be the Scottish solicitor?

Inside the crowded pub, James made his way to the man. "Mr. Abercrombie?"

"Aye, found me, you have." The thin man in spectacles shot out of his chair and offered James a relieved look. "And I presume you are Lord Rossbury."

James was sufficiently taken aback by the use of his honorific that he could only nod and settle into the other seat at the man's table. The solicitor raised a hand to the barmaid. Not long after, a pint of ale he didn't particularly want arrived at the table.

"Thank you for meeting me on such short notice."

"Aye, nae trouble, my lord. I received communication from Mr. Cathcart, your solicitor in

London." He indicated documents laid out neatly in front of him. "He refers to a property north of Edinburgh. I understand you've inherited all of it, the land, the house, and presumably the property therein."

"I have." James sipped at the ale and found it tastier than he'd expected. "Has there been any time to look into the property itself? Particularly its current state of repair?" He'd only reached out to the man days before and didn't expect miracles, though what Cathcart had said about one of his uncle's past mistresses being in residence gnawed at his conscience. Was she still there? Did she consider the pile hers, and, most importantly, had she allowed the whole thing to fall into disrepair?

"There's been nae opportunity for anyone to make the trek as of yet, my lord." He grinned a toothy, crooked smile and shot a bony finger in the air. "But I have secured a surveyor, you'll be best pleased to hear. A man I've worked with before. Trustworthy. Efficient. He's to get out as early as Monday if that suits."

"As soon as possible." James swallowed down another gulp of ale, and though it warmed his insides, he was beyond pleased when the barmaid deposited bread and cheese on their table too.

"If you dinnae mind a bit of impertinence, my lord, is there reason for the rush?"

The man *was* impertinent, definitely more so

than Cathcart would have been. But after the last few months, James had come to value straightforward, honest people more than he ever had in his life.

"I'll let you be impertinent if you'll allow me to be blunt. I need the funds, Abercrombie. Desperately."

The solicitor nodded solemnly, seeming to understand James's situation more deeply than James had yet to explain. Abercrombie shuffled his papers for a bit, and James watched the man's bushy brows rise and fall while he made notations on a small pad of paper at the edge of the documents.

"The previous valuation is from nearly a decade ago, but just based on that sum, I could inquire into a loan for you with the manor house itself as collateral."

"No more loans." James was painfully linked to the worst reprobate in London because he'd been fool enough to take the man's loan. Until that debt was cleared and James was solvent again, he wouldn't borrow another penny.

"Understood. Then I will wait to hear from Dickson on Monday, and we will proceed from there."

"Any notion of how long it will take to sell the place?"

"Hard to say. Much depends on the state of it." He flicked a finger down the letter he said he'd received from Cathcart. "Lady Cassandra Munro?"

"My uncle's mistress."

"Knew her husband, I did." The older man's expression turned rueful. "An utter rapscallion. A charming one, but a rotter, nonetheless. If you'll pardon me saying so, my lord."

"Speak freely, Abercrombie. I prefer it." James wasn't sure precisely how much he wanted to know about the lady, especially if he was going to be forced to put her out once he reached Invermere. A flare of pity was already beginning to spark for a woman who'd traded a charming bounder for his cruel, humorless uncle.

"The husband still alive?"

"Nae, gone years back. Lost at sea. The man was a privateer."

After his years in shipping, James knew of such men. Generally, they were intelligent, strategic, and fearless to a dangerous degree. "I truly hope she's no longer in residence. Perhaps after the death of my uncle, the lady has moved on."

Clearly, finding paramours was not a challenge for her.

"Could be, my lord. But if she remains there, I suspect she willnae be moved easily. She was a pirate's wife and a curmudgeon's lover. I've no' met the lady, but she seems one to have a strong constitution."

James tried and failed to stifle a groan. "Sounds as if you believe I have my work cut out for me."

Abercrombie assessed James under his brows. "Oh aye, I most definitely do."

THREE QUARTERS OF an hour after James and the Wilson sisters had left her at the station, Lucy sat huddled on a bench as the sky darkened and the air grew chillier by the minute. She'd been smart enough to tuck a scarf into her valise and wrapped the soft knitted length around her neck, burrowing into its comforting lavender scent.

She thought back to the telegram she'd sent her aunt and was certain she'd listed the correct time. Besides, the express arrived once a day, so the train's arrival wasn't any great secret if Aunt Cassandra or her driver had misplaced her telegram.

Lucy cast her gaze one way down the lane of carriages arriving and departing in front of Waverley Station and then looked the other direction, just as she'd done dozens of times in the last thirty minutes. She had no notion of what Aunt Cassandra's conveyance might look like, but no one could ever mistake her aunt.

Her beauty and the rich auburn shade of her hair made her stand out in a crowd.

Where are you, Aunt Cassandra?

Lucy stood and groaned at the stiffness in her legs and back. She *had* been sitting too long, and waiting in the cold was pointless. She'd never been one to wait on someone else fixing her dilemmas.

Lucy strode toward the line of carriages, and as she did, a weathered growler pulled to the curb and the driver immediately climbed down. He scanned each gentleman and lady outside the station as if searching for someone.

"Are you seeking a passenger, sir?" Lucy called as she strode toward him.

"Lady Lucy Westmont?"

"Yes!" Lucy rushed toward the driver, some of her worry and weariness ebbing away. "You were sent by my aunt?"

"Aye, my lady, hired by Lady Cassandra Munro." The man removed his hat and clutched it to his chest, offering her a nod. "Forgive my late arrival."

"What matters is that you're here now." Lucy indicated her trunk. "I'm ready to depart immediately if that suits you."

The old man looked off into the night sky. "You'll arrive long past dark, my lady." He nudged his chin toward Princes Street in the direction the Wilson sisters and Mr. Pembroke had headed. "Could take you straight to a hotel and collect you for the journey at first light if you prefer."

"Please, sir. I'd like to go now. This evening." She was eager to see her aunt and desperate to properly start her Scottish holiday.

The man stared down at her a moment, and Lucy held his gaze. Both their breaths puffed out in front of them. Everyone she'd met on her travels so far—starting with Papa—had underestimated her. Except perhaps Mr. Pembroke. She willed the driver not to do the same.

"Very well." Within a few minutes, the burly

older man had the trunk strapped to the back of the carriage and offered a gloved hand to help her inside.

"You've no other luggage?"

"This valise." Lucy lifted it high with a bit of a groan. She really had packed too many books.

"Name's Tavish, my lady. We'll make the journey in a couple of hours if the weather holds."

"Thank you."

"Use the blanket there to keep yourself warm."

The moment Lucy settled into the carriage, the exhaustion of the day's events settled over her in a wave of fatigue. She felt an ache in her shoulder from when Nichols had grabbed her arm, and there was a taut soreness in her knuckles.

But then a warmer memory came—the gentleness of James Pembroke's touch as he'd tended to her and held her hand. They'd been so close, spoken to each other softly, and she'd been near enough to memorize the shape of his mouth and note the lighter silver flecks in his dark blue eyes.

All those memories and she'd only known the man a day.

It was foolish to think on him. *Give one's energies to what one can reasonably achieve rather than fueling whimsies*, as Mrs. Winterbottom would say.

James Pembroke was a man who liked his privacy and seemed determined to share nothing of himself. True, she'd been reticent to mention her father, but if he'd truly wished to know her, he would have made an effort to do so.

Her holiday had only just begun. In the days to come, she'd find a great deal to do and see, and the events of her train ride to Scotland would be overtaken, surely.

She closed her eyes and tried to push aside the memory of James Pembroke's smile, his pine and spice scent, and the fact that he'd touched her more intimately than any man ever had in her entire life.

Chapter Seven

*J*ames blinked at the velvet sky above his head and then realized, as he sat up quickly, that it was the upholstered ceiling of the carriage he'd ridden in from Edinburgh. And it was no longer moving.

They'd arrived at Invermere.

He opened the carriage door and found the driver settling his single case of clothing on the gravel under their feet.

"Looks like someone's still awake," the driver said, pointing toward a far window in the front of what James could only make out as a looming and broad manor house, its uppermost edges outlined in moonlight.

"Very good," James mumbled in return, then dug in his pocket for a coin to tip the man before he departed.

His gut twisted in wariness even as a desperate kind of eagerness propelled him forward. This wouldn't be as simple as he wished it to be. He knew that with certainty. His instincts, as much as he doubted them after the investment debacle and business with Beck, were not entirely faulty.

Movement caught his eye at a lit window. Someone peeking out to see what strange carriage had arrived unexpectedly, no doubt.

With his fist, he rapped twice on the front door before he noticed a knocker lower down.

Lights spread to more windows on the ground floor, and he could hear a woman's voice.

Lady Cassandra, I presume.

The gentleman who answered the door examined him in the bright glow of the entry hall lamps.

"Good evening," James started congenially. "May I speak with Lady Cassandra Munro?"

"Her ladyship does nae receive visitors at this hour." The diminutive gray-haired man's burr was thick, and his tone was a perfect mix of wariness and irritation.

"Forgive the hour." James kept his tone light, striving to let none of the anxiety he felt seep in. "I'm afraid it's a matter of some urgency."

That gave the man pause, but only a second's worth. "It's impossible, sir. I can convey a message to her ladyship if you like."

"May I ask your name?" James had shocked the older man with the question.

His bushy brows winged high on his wrinkled forehead. "Drummond. Butler to Lady Cassandra."

"Well, you see, Mr. Drummond"—James leaned in as if he wished to convey a secret to the man—"it's also a matter of some delicacy."

The man wasn't movable. James could see it in his eyes. He wondered at the fact that he'd even bothered to open the door at all. A moment later, he began to close it, offering James a nod of dismissal.

James shoved his boot into the gap at the same moment a tall, imperious-looking woman in a dark, high-necked gown approached.

"Her ladyship is not at home. Leave a message or simply leave and come again some other day. Preferably during receiving hours." The lady's accent was as polished as the lens of her brass-rimmed spectacles and as sharp as any elocution tutor in England.

James would guess she was the lady herself if not for her drab gown and starched white collar.

As if she heard the questions whirling in James's mind, she stepped up beside Drummond, creating a bulwark to keep him out.

"I am Mrs. Fox, her ladyship's housekeeper, and if you tell me your name, sir, I will let her know that you called."

Charm wasn't going to work. He shoved a hand into his inner coat pocket, pulled out a copy Cathcart had provided of the letter he'd sent to Lady Cassandra regarding ownership of the manor house. Apparently, the lady hadn't been at home to receive her copy.

Rather than explaining, James lifted the document and held it out for the woman to read for herself.

Mrs. Fox snatched the paper from his hand and stared up at him in shock, then she handed it to the butler at her side.

"I've inherited my uncle's title and this manor. When will Lady Cassandra return?"

"We're not certain. She was called away unexpectedly."

"May I?" James gestured to the long hallway behind her.

The housekeeper and butler cast each other a glance and parted, allowing James to step inside. The moment he did, a beast the size of a small pony galloped toward him on enormous furry feet. James stopped midstride, holding still, waiting to see if the creature intended to attack or merely sniff.

The dog decided sniffing was sufficient, and somehow James passed muster. The giant hound sat directly in front of him, tipping his head up as if waiting for James to make the next move.

"Good dog," he told the beast warily, patting its dark gray head.

"Hercules, ye're a disappointment as a guard," the old man grumbled.

The peacock-blue walls in the hallway were crowded with colorful paintings, and a few full-size statues dotted the foyer. In a doorway midway down the hall, James spotted a couple of other servants lingering.

He sidestepped Hercules and made his way down the hall. Every room he passed was cluttered with bric-a-brac, overstuffed furnishings, and art. Not a single wall stood bare.

James couldn't imagine the furnishing style had

anything to do with his uncle. Most of this had to be hers. Lady Cassandra Munro's belongings. Her house in all but deed.

Behind him the servants had clustered together and spoke in panicked, hushed tones.

"Do ye intend to lodge here?" a young man, likely a footman, asked rather cheekily.

"I am the owner of Invermere, so it seemed a waste of funds to secure a hotel room. I'd like to begin inspecting the manor at first morning light."

"Without her ladyship at home?" a young red-headed girl in a mob cap said in a voice of utter disdain.

"I'm afraid I cannot wait on her return. But she will be back soon?" James preferred to do this as civilly and respectfully as he could.

"We expect her tomorrow unless she's delayed another day."

"Very good. I look forward to meeting her."

The footman let out a disgruntled scoff. "Aye, say that now, ye do."

Mrs. Fox and Drummond convened near the doorway. The housekeeper still clutched the letter in her hand and pointed to it throughout their whispered discussion. Finally, they both lifted their gazes to face him.

"I can prepare a guest room if ye'll wait in there." Drummond strode forward, moving quickly for a man of his years, and led James toward a lavish drawing room decorated in pink and gold. A fire crackled low in the grate, and that in itself was too tempting to resist.

"Thank you kindly."

The old man merely nodded, stepped out of the room, and closed the door. Metal snicking metal, then the click of the lock tumbler falling sounded behind him, and James swung to face the closed door.

Had they locked him in?

He twisted the latch and found that the door was indeed locked.

Bloody wonderful.

"Mrs. Fox? Drummond?" He banged at the thick wood, then paced in front of the fire, relishing its warmth. When no reply came, he slumped onto an overstuffed settee with a sigh.

At this point, he wasn't sure if he cared if they'd locked him in for the night. Better than locking him out in the cold.

Now that rest was near, exhaustion was having its way with him. All of it could wait on a few hours of sleep, couldn't it? Lady Cassandra, getting out of this damned room, figuring out what property was whose, informing the lady that she'd need to find a new home—first thing in the morning, he'd tackle all of that.

He settled onto a gold damask settee in front of the fire with a sigh of relief, then leaned his head back, letting the overstuffed upholstery cradle the back of his neck.

The moment he closed his eyes, a memory came.

Pale green eyes fringed with sable lashes—Miss Lucy Westmont scowling at him, shocked and shaken, and then soft, curious, and as fascinated with him as he was with her.

Shame he'd never see those pretty lips and heart-stopping eyes again.

GOTHIC WITH POINTED arches, inset windows, and a turret. That's the sort of house Lucy thought Aunt Cassandra would love. She expected Invermere to be a dramatic, sprawling pile with overgrown vines, a garden gone wild, and maybe some broken statuary littering the grounds.

As the carriage slowed and they made their way up the gravel-covered drive, Lucy braced a hand on the edge of the carriage window and stared out on the moonlit landscape, trying to get a glimpse of the house her aunt loved so well.

When it came into view, Invermere took her breath away.

It wasn't tall with castle-like crenellations. There were vines. They hugged half of the front of the house, climbing all the way up its two stories. But the house itself was classical, its face spread out with a rectangular sturdiness. A manor designed with symmetry in mind, and the style was exactly what Lucy would have wished if she could design a home of her own.

Yet its simple outline wasn't what first caught her eye. Lucy's gaze was drawn initially to the windows.

So much glinting glass. Three in a row on either side of the front door and seven in a row on the upper story. As the carriage took the final curve, she noticed that the side of the house had the exact same number of windows, most of them shuttered at this hour.

"And here we be, miss," the driver called as he pulled the horses to a stop directly in front of the entry door. A warm glow lit a few ground floor windows, and Lucy was thankful for that.

How she dearly hoped her aunt was inside and might still be awake to greet her.

"Shall I wait, miss?"

"I'll be all right," Lucy called up as she lifted a few shillings out to him. "Thank you for getting me here safely."

The man touched the edge of his cap and turned the horses to start the journey back up the drive.

Lucy couldn't stop staring up at the windows. She couldn't wait to be inside when early morning light spilled through. Perfect light for painting, and she suspected that aspect must factor into her aunt's love of the place.

"Hello, miss."

Lucy nearly shot straight out of her boots. She hadn't noticed that someone had opened the front door. The lady stood dressed in what seemed to be her nightdress and held a single candle, her hand braced around the flame to keep the breeze from snuffing it out.

"I'm Lady Lucy Westmont, and I'm here to see

my aunt, Lady Cassandra. She invited me. I know she may be abed at this hour—"

"We were told to expect you, my lady. Come in." The woman lifted an arm half covered by her shawl and urged Lucy inside, then she glanced nervously behind her. "Let's get you warm and tell you of the situation."

Lucy stepped inside, and the lady helped her out of her cloak, then waited for Lucy to remove her gloves.

"Did you not receive her ladyship's message, my lady?"

"I didn't. What message?"

"A friend of her ladyship fell ill, and Lady Cassandra left yesterday to tend to her. A message was sent to the station, but we weren't certain if it would arrive too late to be delivered to you."

Disappointment gathered with the exhaustion she felt, and Lucy wanted nothing more than to sleep.

"That is unfortunate, but I hope her friend is better soon. I'll get along as well as I can until she returns. I'm sure all will be well." The housekeeper didn't seem reassured and still wore an expression of distress. Lucy noticed that she'd retrieved a folded document from the pocket of her skirt.

"That's not the situation I was referring to, my lady." The woman's voice wobbled a bit, and as Lucy drew closer, she could sense her nervous tension.

Once she moved a few steps into the foyer, Lucy noticed that several maids and a footman had gathered a little further down the hall. They whispered to each other and cast furtive glances her way.

"First, tell me your name and then tell me what's wrong." Lucy spoke to the woman in the calmest tone she could manage, though she was still shivering from the carriage ride.

"Elmira Fox, miss. I'm her ladyship's housekeeper. And this is McKay, Senga, and Mary." She gestured toward the other servants huddled nearby. Then the lady stunned her by calling out, "Drummond!"

A moment later, an older man appeared, somewhat bleary-eyed but neatly dressed. The butler, Lucy guessed.

"I've got him contained," the older man said with a relieved sigh. "Checked on him a few minutes later, and he'd nodded off like a man who's had nae sleep in days. If we keep our voices down"—he pinned Mrs. Fox with a knowing look—"he'll be out until dawn, I wager."

"How can it be true?" Senga stepped forward, twisting her apron in her hands. The girl had been crying if her red-rimmed eyes were any indication.

"Someone, please tell me what's happened. Who is contained?" Lucy offered a reassuring glance at each of them in turn. "Whatever it is, I'm sure we can find a solution."

"There's nae solution, my lady," the young footman, McKay, said matter-of-factly, "and Lady

Cassandra will be in a right fine fettle when she returns."

Lucy could well imagine her aunt being angry at anyone who'd unsettled her staff to this degree. She was a passionate woman and fiercely loyal. But what Lucy couldn't fathom was what might have caused the worry and anger she saw on every face turned her way.

The house was quiet. Nothing seemed out of place—except for her bursting in on all of them in the dark of night.

She turned to Mrs. Fox.

"Until my aunt returns, I'll help in any way I'm able."

"It's a gentleman, my lady." Senga spoke softly and cast a wary gaze at the closed door behind her. "In there," she whispered, jerking her thumb toward the paneled wood.

"An intruder?" That same shiver of foreboding that Mr. Nichols had caused crept over Lucy's skin.

"Of a sort." Drummond's voice was so grave and serious that Lucy began to wonder if someone had come to harm.

"You have him locked in that room? Has anyone sent for the authorities?"

"Aye, he is, and nae, we havnae," Mr. Drummond said stridently, as if expecting to be chastised for those decisions.

"Is he dangerous?" Lucy realized that might be a question they couldn't answer. Nichols had taught her that determining the danger a man posed wasn't an easy thing to ascertain on sight alone. Mr. Pembroke was tall, imposing, dangerous in his appeal if nothing else, and yet Nichols had initially struck her as unassuming.

"A danger to our very livelihoods." A young red-haired girl who'd yet to speak stepped forward.

"And who are you?"

"Name's Mary, m'lady." The girl offered a wobbly curtsy. "One of her ladyship's housemaids."

"I'm not sure I understand. The man's not dangerous and yet you fear for your livelihoods?"

"We're nae sure he is who he says he is at all," Drummond grumbled solemnly.

Lucy frowned. The staff all seemed unsettled, and their actions didn't seem to add up, which only served to heighten her curiosity about the man they'd confined in the drawing room.

"I'd like to speak to him," Lucy told Mrs. Fox. "Has anyone tried speaking to the man?"

"We did converse with him briefly," Mrs. Fox said defensively. "Drummond may have overreacted."

"The key, please." Lucy held out her hand, palm up.

The housekeeper shot a look at the butler, who turned a nod toward the young housemaid.

The girl stepped forward and offered Lucy the key. "See fer yerself, m'lady."

Lucy took the key, and slipped it in the lock before allowing herself to pause and ponder what sort of man might be on the other side. Drummond approached, and Mrs. Fox stepped closer, as if she intended to accompany her inside.

Lucy pushed the door open, and warmth immediately spilled out. In a blink, she made out firelight, a great hound who lifted its head and turned to look her way, and a man sprawled on a settee far too small to contain him.

He looked more exhausted than dangerous.

"What exactly did he do?" Lucy whispered to Mrs. Fox, who'd moved in to stand behind her.

"Showed up like the king himself and claimed he owns the lot of it."

"The lot of what?"

"The entire house and anything in it that belonged to the old earl. Says he's the Earl of Rossbury's heir. His nephew."

Her aunt *had* taken up with an earl. Lucy had heard those rumors. He'd been an Englishman, but Lucy hadn't heard that he'd died, and she hadn't realized Invermere was his house rather than one her aunt had purchased outright.

"So the manor is his?" Lucy whispered.

"Aye, *if* he's the new earl," Drummond said in a tone of thorough distrust.

Lucy crept closer. She was beginning to worry her aunt's staff had done the man some sort of harm.

Firelight painted the edge of his face in a warm glow and Lucy covered her mouth to stifle a gasp.

James Pembroke was even more beautiful in repose. The warm fire's glow highlighted the sharp edge of his jaw, the lush curves of his lips. His dark hair was a tumble of ebony waves, with a few strands hanging over his brow and one errant curl stroking his cheek.

Even in sleep, he exuded a magnetism that drew her closer. She itched to put her hands on him because that's what they seemed to do every time they were near each other.

For a moment she almost forgot a half dozen staff members watched from the doorway. A rogue impulse made her reach out to touch his arm. She needed the reassurance that he was real, not just some mirage she'd willed into being because she'd so wished she might see this man again.

And then it struck her, realization slamming home with a nauseating truth that made her pulse race and her stomach churn.

This man who'd touched her, helped her, made her smile, he wasn't just *James Pembroke*. He was a man who meant to take ownership of her aunt's beloved manor house while she was away and could do nothing to contest his claim.

Just as she started to turn and step quietly toward the door, he roused, and Lucy, heaven help her, looked back at him eagerly. In sleep, she missed those eyes of his, and that seductive smile.

And there it was. Just a hint of a smile, bending the corners of his lips. "Am I dreaming?"

Then realization seemed to strike him too. He shot up from the settee and got to his feet, then drew closer. Without a moment of hesitation, he reached for her, laying a hand, heavy and warm, on her arm.

"Are you all right? How did you find me? Is it Nichols?" The questions tumbled out, one on top of the other.

His voice emerged husky and deep, and Lucy wished she could sit and speak with him as they had on the train.

"This lady is our mistress's niece. I'll ask you to remove your hands from her, *my lord*." McKay was a big man and couldn't manage to say anything without bluster.

James's expression went from worried to angry to a shock that made his blue eyes widen in the span of a second.

"Lady Cassandra's niece," he said slowly, as if arranging the pieces in his mind. "She's the aunt you were coming to visit?" He held her gaze, ignoring McKay and the fact that Mrs. Fox had stepped into the room.

He did release his hold on her arm, and Lucy inwardly chastised herself for noticing that most of all.

And then anger came. Anger at her own wistfulness and the ease with which she'd been dazzled by his masculine magnetism and too-familiar manner when she knew next to nothing about him. Anger that *he* of all men had to be the one who'd come to take her aunt's home.

"If only you'd shared anything of your true intentions for this trip on the train, *Lord Rossbury*, we could have had this discussion there." How might things have proceeded differently if she'd known he was a nobleman journeying to Scotland to overturn her aunt's life?

James drew back as if she'd struck him.

She was being too emotional. Flustered. Everything Mrs. Winterbottom advised against.

Lucy closed her eyes and tried counting to ten, but halfway there he spoke her name.

"Lady Lucy" emerged as a soft, gentle plea.

She sensed that he wanted to explain as much as she wanted to ask him a dozen questions. But time was what she needed. Time to speak to her aunt. And to sort out her feelings about the most appealing gentleman she'd ever laid eyes on, a man who she barely knew and yet whose scent made her mouth water.

"Can we see to a room for Lord Rossbury?" Clearly, the man's long legs and broad shoulders couldn't be contained by her aunt's settee.

"Lucy." In the repetition, there was a thread of need in his voice that made her long to turn back and give him anything he asked. In some respects, she did owe him a debt of gratitude, if nothing else.

But explaining that to the staff here and now was too much. She didn't turn back to him and kept her gaze focused on the housekeeper.

"I'll need a room too," she told Mrs. Fox and then glanced over her shoulder. "We can discuss everything in the morning, Lord Rossbury. I suspect you're as exhausted as I am."

Lucy left him standing in his rumpled clothes with gorgeously disheveled hair and a massive dog at his feet that had to belong to Aunt Cassandra and yet remained at his side like his loyal pet.

All Lucy knew for certain was that she wasn't going to let this man, no matter how charming and handsome he might be, cast her aunt out of her home.

There had to be a solution, and she had to find it.

But as Lucy followed Mrs. Fox upstairs to a guest room, her mind wasn't churning about ways to resolve the problem of James's inheritance and her aunt's potential eviction as it should have been. His little lopsided smile filled her thoughts, the way his lips had tipped immediately when he'd woken and blinked up to find her next to him. He'd been as pleased to see her again as she was to see him.

Good grief, how had one man on a train turned her head so completely? Mrs. Winterbottom would be appalled.

No more romanticizing Lord Rossbury's lips or tip-tilted smiles or anything else about his person. She had come to Scotland to see her aunt, and now she'd help resolve this matter of Invermere and keeping Aunt Cassandra in her beloved home.

That's what mattered most.

Chapter Eight

James woke with a start, yet it seemed only moments had passed since he'd closed his eyes and sighed at the quality of the mattress in the room the butler had led him to. Judging by the light slanting through the half-pulled drapery, hours had gone by, but he was still exhausted.

Rising from bed, he slipped on his shirt and strode to the window.

So, this was Scotland.

Fog crept over the ground and the horizon glowed with the promise of sun, despite the still-dim sky. Beyond the fields near the manor, he could make out rolling hills and a misty forest. Nearer the house, a breeze set gold and crimson leaves fluttering from branches.

The beauty of the countryside soothed him for a moment, then sparked a memory he'd left far behind. Childhood visits to Shropshire and the endlessly green grounds of Summervale estate with a forest at its edge. Each time he'd run too far toward the copse of trees, he'd turn back to see his mother, fear and concern etched on her face. It was how he recalled her from that day on the train too.

Shaking his head, he pushed that pain down. Those days were best left behind.

The gorgeous landscape of Scotland would make Invermere easier to sell. That's what mattered.

Fatigue hit again when he stepped away from the window, but his mind raced. An urgency to be done with this business, to be done with Beck, and to get his life back.

He should speak to the staff first thing and determine whether there were any valuations in their possession. Abercrombie would send a surveyor as promised, and James suspected any records about the manor might help speed his assessment.

As soon as the sun was up, he'd take a look at the house for himself. What he'd seen so far appeared in good repair, but that had been through tired eyes at night. And he'd been too damned preoccupied with a pretty noblewoman.

Oh hell, he still was.

Chivalrous impulse, he tried telling himself. A young woman on her own would spark protectiveness in most men. But that didn't explain why he wanted to touch her every time she was near. Why he wanted to know the taste of her, how her hair would feel sliding across his chest. He'd quieted such yearnings after he'd lost everything, but they were back with a vengeance.

Never had a woman caught his interest so quickly and thoroughly.

There hadn't been a moment since meeting Lucy Westmont that she wasn't on his mind, and the sight of her when he'd cracked an eye open on that backbreaking settee had soothed the odd stitch that wedged itself in his chest the moment they'd parted in Edinburgh.

Longing for the niece of the woman he was about to evict. *Wonderful.*

Foolishly, impossibly, he wanted to see her again. Now. There was much to say. Much to explain. But the sun had yet to come up, and despite all the ways he and Lucy had pushed the limits of propriety on the train, the staff were already wary of him, and he had no right to risk her reputation.

Though he steered clear of entanglements with noblewomen, he had some notion of how fragile a lady's good name could be in the upper circles of society.

Odd how that rule he'd set for himself for decades hadn't stopped him from this all-consuming fascination with one petite daughter of an earl.

How bloody strange to think that the death of a man he hadn't seen in nearly thirty years had now made him an earl too. Perhaps Lucy's father would give him lessons.

That thought amused him for the twelve seconds it took to remember the title he'd inherited made him even more penniless than he'd been before. Now there were his uncle's debts to settle as well as his own.

No, he had no right to visit Lucy's bedchamber. No right to his preoccupation with her at all. He had nothing to offer such a lady, however tempting

she might be. And judging by her headstrong independence, he doubted she'd wish him to.

Even if they were beyond propriety. Even if he
knew how her skin felt against his fingertips. Even
if he'd been blessed with the ability to draw a pink
wash of color to her cheeks whenever they were
close to each other.

Good god, he was in trouble.

He opened his bedroom door because he needed
to move. Perhaps a walk across Invermere's misty
fields would do him good.

He found Hercules outside his door. The deerhound got to his feet, ears perked, tail wagging, as
if he was ready for a predawn wander too.

"I admire your loyalty, good sir." James bent to
pet the dog's wiry fur. "And I shall savor it now
because you'll no doubt hate me when your mistress arrives."

James made his way downstairs as quietly as
he could, aware that beyond one of the doors he
passed, Lucy slumbered. Near one door, Hercules
paused and let out a little whine.

"Is she there, boy?" James stared at the door and
immediately realized what a fool he was.

He couldn't resist imagining her in a sprawling
bed, clothes discarded, hair spilling across the
pillow—

A light flickered at the end of the hall as Mrs.
Fox climbed the stairs.

"I heard footsteps in the hall and wondered if
anything was amiss at such an early hour." She

glanced pointedly at the door that Hercules had indicated before turning an expectant gaze back on James.

"I couldn't sleep," he told her quietly. "Thought I might go for an early morning walk."

"By all means, my lord." She gestured toward the staircase, and James took the cue.

The housekeeper followed behind, her footfalls virtually silent. Only when they reached the bottom of the stairs did she address him again.

"Shall I have tea brought up to the dining room? We lay breakfast out on the sideboard there, but not for several hours."

"Tea would be appreciated. Coffee, more so."

That *almost* brought a smile to the lady's lips. "Coffee it will be, Lord Rossbury." Something else was on her mind and on the tip of her tongue, judging by the way she started to speak and then stopped herself but remained with him in the foyer.

"Speak your mind, Mrs. Fox. I prefer it."

A tongue-lashing from a starchy housekeeper was far preferable to being locked in a drawing room again or having his coffee poisoned.

"I don't wish to be impertinent, my lord."

"I'm giving you leave to be as brutal as you like."

"In truth, I only have two questions." She swallowed once more and squared her shoulders. "Why must you sell Invermere so urgently?"

"I need funds. My uncle's title came with debts and no real assets. Except this manor house." James looked around at the elegant marble of the floor, the classical styling of the cornices, and the vibrant display of art on the walls. He couldn't imagine his uncle at home in a place such as Invermere.

"It's clear that your mistress loves the house." Even a fool could see it was more Lady Cassandra Munro's than his uncle's. "I'm sure we can come to an arrangement that suits her."

At least he hoped that was true. He didn't relish being a villain, but he would have little choice if it came to that.

"I hope so, my lord."

James offered her a nod and a sympathetic smile. Only the jerk of her shoulders, as if he'd shocked her, indicated she'd noticed his expression at all.

He could intuit her fears. He understood them and sympathized with them. As a young man making his way in London, he'd lost jobs that meant the difference between paying for lodgings and sleeping rough. As a failed businessman, he'd had to deliver the worst news imaginable to men and women under his employ.

"Whatever happens, I'll see to it that you and the rest of the staff are employed."

"I prefer to stay with Lady Cassandra." Her voice hardened to match her posture.

"Understood. And I admire your loyalty." Hercules nudged James's leg, as if the dog wanted recognition for his loyalty too, regardless of how easily given it had been. James patted the hound's head. "It says a great deal about her ladyship even before I've met her. Now ask me the second question."

"The inquiry may offend you."

"Go on." James felt a bit like he and the house-keeper were playing a game of chess, and she was about to reveal a trick move that he should have anticipated.

"What are your intentions toward Lady Lucy Westmont?"

His body reacted before he could get a single word out. Heat streaked up his neck, and his throat went dry. And Mrs. Fox, who he suspected never missed much, seemed to perceive an answer he wasn't yet prepared to put into words.

Rather than waiting for his reply, she spoke again. "Lady Lucy is very dear to her aunt, and though Invermere's staff understands discretion, I intend to ensure that no aspersions could ever be cast on her character. Especially while our mistress is away."

"I would never cause her harm or allow any to come to her."

Mrs. Fox twisted her mouth in an expression James couldn't quite interpret.

"There is a great deal of vehemence in your tone, my lord, for a lady you met last evening."

"Yesterday morning, to be accurate." Good grief, they'd only met yesterday morning. How had she burrowed in so deep?

James wrapped a hand around his neck, bow-ing his head, seeking an answer both to Mrs. Fox's query and the inexplicable draw he felt to Lucy. He could find no logic in it. Only that what he felt for her was undeniable, and that they'd formed a bond he wasn't eager to lose.

"A woman like Lady Lucy Westmont makes a powerful first impression."

A simple explanation that revealed nothing of what the lady did to him.

"I can see that, my lord." Mrs. Fox cast her gaze toward a drawing room with its drapes pulled open. A view toward the opposite side of the house from his guest room, but much the same vista. Fog-covered fields and trees in the distance. "She reminds me a great deal of Lady Cassandra. It didn't surprise me when she rose early and went straight out to the archery field as her aunt is wont to do."

"She's already up?" James snapped his gaze toward the window and spotted her. In a far leaf-strewn field, she stood with her back to the house and an enormous bow in her hands. Her hair hung in loose waves down her back and bounced above her waist as she reached for an arrow. "She looks like Artemis."

When he turned back to Mrs. Fox, her brows had arched, but she ignored his comment.

"Seems that none of us are very good at sleeping in." Mrs. Fox glanced at Lucy. "I did tell her it would be chilly at this hour, but she's rather—"

"Stubborn."

"Headstrong." Mrs. Fox cast him a look that was

sympathetic if not outright friendly. "She's been at it awhile. I'll go downstairs and have some coffee brewed. Perhaps you could determine whether Lady Lucy would like some too."

"I'll go now." He gave the housekeeper a nod of leave-taking and strode toward the front door.

"Your coat, Lord Rossbury?"

He didn't need his bloody coat. He needed to see Lucy.

In her dreams, she caught her books before they fell. There was no collision with Mr. James Pembroke, no vile Mr. Nichols, just hours of pleasant conversation with the Wilson sisters.

Only later, when the train pulled into the station, did she spot James.

He moved quickly along the platform as if searching for someone. Then their eyes locked as she stepped off the train, he lifted his hand, and asked her to dance.

It made no sense, of course. Dancing on a train platform. But when she woke before dawn, the memory of it was so sharp that her hand felt warm from the clasp of his fingers.

Her father would be horrified to know she *had* allowed him to touch her, to hold her hand, that she'd spent time alone with a man at all. Behaviors that none of her family would expect of her. Certainly nothing anyone would expect of a joyless spinster.

Even now, as she stood in a field east of the house and watched the rising sun paint plumes of orange and gold across the morning sky, the thought of him still in bed made her pulse jump in her throat. Would his hair be tousled as when she'd found him drowsing on the settee? If she woke him, would he smile at her the same way?

Mercy, how she wanted him to.

How she wished he wasn't the man who'd come to toss her aunt out of her home.

But, of course, he was, and she'd decided something when she'd woken early and searched for the bow and quiver her aunt mentioned so often in her letters. Striding through the overgrown garden to find the practice field, Lucy had repeated one phrase in her head.

I will not let him ruin my trip to Scotland.

Lifting the bow, she pulled the string taut. The heat in her muscles and the quieting of her breath as she aimed soothed the worry she'd felt since waking. She loosed the arrow and felt a rush of anticipation as it hit the target, but not nearly as close to the center as she would have liked.

Determined to do better, she turned to pull another arrow from the quiver and felt the ribbon she'd used to tie her hair back had given way. But she didn't care. Alone in a Scottish field at the edge of morning, who would see? Besides, this trip was for being freed from everything expected of her in London society.

Lucy held her draw, savoring the tension in the

string and wood, sensing that same tension in her body. In an exhale that she could see in the cool morning air, she let go.

A squeal of victory emerged when the arrow thwacked near the center of the target.

"You're quite good."

The shock of his presence made her gasp. And his voice, sleep roughened and low, sent a shiver down her spine.

"I'm not." Lucy nocked the next arrow and turned to face him, steeling herself not to turn into a melting ninny at the sight of his handsome face. "Not as good as I used to be."

"Did your aunt teach you?"

"I learned at finishing school, but Aunt Cassandra *is* a renowned toxophilite."

For a long moment, he merely looked at her. There was a new wariness in his gaze, or perhaps he'd noticed the new resolve in hers. But neither of them seemed willing to look away.

The sun had risen, lightening the blue in his eyes and highlighting a swath of dark stubble across his jaw. He wore no gloves, no waistcoat or tie. In fact, he looked as if he'd tumbled out of bed and dressed hurriedly.

"How did you know where to find me?"

"Mrs. Fox told me. And then I saw you out the window." He pointed toward the house and the drawing room that looked out on the field.

"You watched me." Heat swept up Lucy's neck and warmed her cheeks.

He merely grinned in reply.

"I woke early and decided a walk might help me think."

"And the all-hearing Mrs. Fox caught you as she did me, it seems."

"She's a watchful woman, and her distrust of me is reasonable. We are protective when we care. How can I fault that?"

"You'll understand once you meet Aunt Cassandra. She inspires that in everyone."

He finally pulled his gaze from her face and swept a look across the field and the forest beyond. "It is beautiful land."

"Yes, I've wanted to visit for so long." Lucy realized suddenly that her first visit to Invermere might also be her last. Because of James. Because of his need to sell the manor soon. Then she blurted, "Perhaps she'll wish to buy Invermere."

"I would sell to her." James stepped forward, uncertainty in his gaze. "If that's possible."

"I have no real notion of how lucrative her portraiture work might be." Was it enough to purchase an estate on acres of beautiful Scottish countryside?

"Your aunt is the artist." A statement. Not a question. Lucy could see the realization dawning like the rising morning sun on his face. "So many of the pieces in the house are in the same vibrant style."

"She loves color much more than I realized. I plan to learn from studying how she uses it."

"There's a mural on the ceiling in my guest room. Is that her work too?"

"Yes," Lucy stepped closer, dropping the bow to her side. "She told me in a letter a while back that she intended to paint a mural of some sort in every room. The one in my bedroom is a garden." Insatiably curious, Lucy asked, "What's yours?"

"Some fanciful tableau." He let out a soft chuckle and a bit of the tension between them eased. "There's a unicorn and a forest."

Lucy smiled. "I recall the letter referring to that one specifically."

For a moment, he glanced back at the manor, his expression contemplative. "She's made her mark on this house."

Lucy didn't know what to say. Her aunt's colorful spirit filling Invermere made perfect sense. Foolishly, she'd expected some wild, Gothic shambles. But Cassandra's wildness had less to do with decor and more to do with her determination to avoid being hemmed in by society's rules.

"I hope I can do the same one day."

He tilted his head as if she'd confused him.

Lucy tried not to stare at the open vee of his shirt and the muscles of his neck that moved and shifted as he looked out across the field and then back at her.

"I mean to be so colorful that I make my mark on the world."

"I have no doubt you will."

"That's a lot of confidence from a man who's known me for all of a day." Lucy expected him to tease her in return, offering some amusing quip that would bring a smile to her face and warmth rushing through her.

Instead, he took a step closer. Sunlight really did do the most marvelous things to his extraordinary eyes. For the first time, she noticed a hint of green. Not the pale olive shade of her own, but a mossy green, lush and dark.

"I used to be a man of excellent instincts. When considering an investment, I'd get a tickle somewhere around here." He pointed toward the center of his chest, lower than his heart, higher than the waist of his trousers.

Lucy stared at his hand, mesmerized as he moved it in a slow circle that pulled the fabric of his shirt taut against his stomach.

"Something would ignite in me. Like an engine, full of fire and energy, and I'd know." He shocked her by reaching out, hooking a finger under her chin, and nudging it up until their gazes clashed. "I hadn't felt it in a while until . . ."

"Until?" Lucy murmured, somehow speaking even as she held her breath.

"I met you."

"Me?"

He dropped his gaze to her lips, which she was certain were flushed, trembling, and suddenly as warm as if she'd taken a too-hot sip of tea. She knew what came next.

Finally. For the first time in her life. Here, in this chilly field under a Scottish dawn, a man who made her tremble was going to kiss her.

His fingers strayed beyond her chin, sweeping gently down her neck, then up to tuck back a strand of hair that fluttered in the breeze.

He leaned in.

She drew in a breath so deep it nearly left her dizzy.

"I thought," he whispered, his lips already curved in a dazzling smile, "that you might give me a lesson."

The comment was so unexpected that Lucy froze in place, watching mutely as he strode forward and retrieved her loosed arrows from the bale of hay a cloth target was pinned to.

"Have you ever—"

"No, but I'm a quick learner." He winked. Winked! The man was as mercurial as a summer storm.

One moment, he put her at ease in a way that she rarely felt with gentlemen, and then the next, he'd set every part of her body aflame. She didn't understand it at all.

She didn't like the mystery. Sussing out how things worked was ingrained in her nature, and knowing herself had always been one of her strengths.

But he made her respond in ways she had no precedent for, while he himself remained mostly a puzzle.

"May I?" He approached, holding the arrows

he'd collected over the quiver hooked to her belt. He waited for her to nod before slipping them inside. All but one.

At his expectant look, Lucy lifted the bow out to him. Her aunt's prized possession was a lovely thing—dark burnished wood decorated with a few leaves and vines carved above and below the grip.

Despite James's claim of having no knowledge of archery, he tested the tension of the bowstring and placed his hand on the grip like a seasoned archer. Settling the arrow, he glanced back at her for guidance.

"There's a notch." Lucy strode forward and ran her finger along the groove. "And you want to hold the grip . . ." She hesitated before placing her palm over his hand. He watched her face as she did so, as if gauging her reaction.

"A little lower," she urged, her voice breathier than she intended.

Touching him felt familiar. The man might be an enigma, but she already knew how warm his skin would be. His hand was broad and strong, and there was a dusting of dark hair starting at his wrist. They'd formed a connection on their journey to Scotland, no matter whatever else might come between them.

"Like this?" he asked in a tone as quiet as hers.

"Exactly." Lucy stopped touching him and clasped her fingers tight. Just as when they were on the train, the brief contact settled her nerves. Gave her an odd sense of comfort and yet somehow sent a strange zinging energy through her at the same time.

He overextended as he pulled back.

"Not that far." When he adjusted, she nodded. "That's it. Now aim, center your breath as you focus on the target, and let your arrow fly."

Rather than merely releasing the string, he moved his hand forward, stealing some momentum from the arrow. It flew low and landed in the bracken to the right of the target.

"May I?" Lucy lifted her hands, requesting the bow back from him.

He turned it sideways, laying it in her palms like an offering.

"Show me how it's done," he told her encouragingly.

Lucy bit back a chuckle and offered him a half smile. "I thought you'd been watching from the window."

"That was from too far away. Go on," he urged. "I want to learn."

"Your form is good. The placement of your hands, the tension you achieve in the string. But once you've nocked the arrow, the only thing that should move is your fingers as you release. Let the power in the string do the rest.

"Like this." Lucy took up the bow, nocked an arrow, and made sure he was watching.

But he'd moved behind her, so close his warmth sheltered her from the cold.

"May I?" He reached an arm around, his sleeve

brushing hers, his chest at her back. Then he wrapped his hand around hers.

Lucy held her breath and felt his whispering across her skin.

"I'm not sure—"

"Just show me, Lucy," he said, his lips near her ear. "I'll follow your lead."

His touch was light, but what she couldn't ignore was his heat. It seeped into her skin, soothing and enticing all at once. And his scent. Forest and something earthy and rich.

Lucy pulled back. James's hand came with hers.

She breathed against the string, focusing on the target. His fingers could hinder this shot, but she did as he suggested. Precisely as she would if he wasn't there.

On an exhale, she lifted her fingers and set the arrow free. It flew fast and true, straight into the target's center.

"Now your turn." Lucy turned to hand him the bow, but just as he reached for it, footsteps approached, crunching over frost-covered leaves.

"Lady Lucy, I received your note to have a basket prepared, but there was no mention of when you will require it. Did you have a time in mind?"

"A basket?" James arched a single ebony brow.

Turning to answer Mrs. Fox, an idea struck. Lucy intended to go down to the loch, take photographs with her box camera, and sketch the landscape. A perfect start to her Scottish holiday. But there was something she wanted even more—answers from Lord Rossbury.

"How about eleven?" she asked the housekeeper, intensely aware of James watching her.

"Very good, my lady." The older woman cast a long gaze at each of them. "If either of you cares for warm refreshment, tea, coffee, and a light repast have been laid in the dining room."

"I've failed her," he said quietly as he watched the housekeeper's retreat. "She sent me to encourage you to come back inside and get warm, and I got distracted."

"I had no idea I was so very distracting."

He let out an utterly masculine burst of laughter that made her feel as if she'd won a prize. But when she didn't laugh too, his brows drew together in a frown.

"You really have no idea, do you?"

"I have lots of ideas, my lord." She didn't like the implication that she was naive. Particularly from him.

"That was never in doubt." He took a step closer. "You are distracting, Lady Lucy. Never doubt it."

Lucy's defensiveness ebbed when she realized he meant it in the best of ways. As a compliment.

He lifted a hand as if he'd touch her again, but he didn't. After a glance toward the house, he retreated, opening a distance between them.

"Mrs. Fox will be watchful and worries for your reputation. She doesn't trust me."

Lucy glanced surreptitiously toward the manor

and saw the dark-clad outline of Mrs. Fox observing them from the window.

Of course, he was right. Mrs. Fox, all the servants, had a right to wonder at the events of the previous evening. Heavens, she'd taken hours to fall asleep despite the fatigue of the journey because she'd been troubled by questions.

And yet this morning, he'd appeared as the sun chased the mist from the field and wrapped himself around her so she could teach him how to shoot an arrow. Making sense of his presence had evaporated like their breaths in the chilly air.

Good grief, she'd never been this impractical in her life. In truth, *he* was the distraction.

"I said we'd talk this morning, my lord, but all I have are questions."

The transformation those words sparked shocked her. Gone was the softness in his gaze, the teasing tilt of his lips. The sunlit glow in his blue gaze dimmed. He had as effectively shuttered himself as if he'd entered a room and slammed the door behind him.

It was much like he'd behaved on the train, reluctant to reveal much of himself. As if he was a man with secrets to keep.

"May we talk later? I came to Scotland to examine Invermere in preparation for selling, and I'd like to do that this morning before your aunt arrives."

Lucy tightened her grip on the bow in her hands. His coldness was as provoking as his compliments, but in a far different way.

"Of course, Lord Rossbury. Find me when you're ready to answer my questions."

Never in her life had she been one to storm away dramatically, or even feel the urge to. That was for beauties like her sister Marion or imps like her brother Charlie. But James Pembroke's gaze on her was too much, and his scent, his nearness, did something to her peace of mind. She wasn't used to losing her wits because a gentleman looked her way, and this trip was a terrible time to start.

So she double-checked to make sure she'd retrieved all her aunt's arrows, spun on her boot heel, and commenced a march back toward the manor. At that moment, she understood the power of having the last word and then sailing on one's way. She tried to savor it.

But, of course, her busy thoughts came crashing in. She had a great deal more to say to Lord Rossbury. Pert, insouciant, sharp-tongued things. Things a termagant would say. Boiling them all down, she stopped and pivoted toward him.

He stood precisely where she'd left him, his gaze fixed on her.

"You have your reasons for being here that seem very pressing," she called across the field. "I came here for a holiday and to visit my most beloved aunt, and I'd like to get on with that too. But it seems we are to be the unwanted snag in each other's plans."

Those seemed like better last words. Weren't they?

Chapter Nine

James was beginning to think the lady was trouble.

Not the dire sort of trouble, of course. Not the kind waiting for him back in London. She was a sweeter kind, an entirely too pleasing enticement when he didn't have a moment to lose.

Nothing about this trip was to be leisurely. He wasn't on holiday, and he didn't have time for dallying with a bluestocking *with plans*.

And yet now, over an hour after he'd gone out to that archery field and ended up with his body wrapped around hers, he stood watching her yet again.

He found himself not doing what he'd come here to do. He wasn't examining the house for any needed repairs or issues, but watching her, fascinated, as she filled a small canvas with paint.

He'd planned to start examining upstairs rooms when he noticed a space at the rear of the manor. A soaring, bloom-filled conservatory with all the accoutrements of an art studio arranged near the center.

Lucy stood in profile with a patch of sunlight

shining through the high glass overhead onto her colorful canvas. Every few minutes, she'd glance up at a cluster of hanging flowers that she was apparently attempting to capture with paint and the deft swipes of her brush.

So far, she hadn't noticed him at the edge of the conservatory, and he couldn't bring himself to interrupt her work. There were days he'd loved running Pembroke Shipping. Days when a profitable shipment entered port, or a new client entrusted their products to him. But he wasn't sure he'd ever taken such utter pleasure in signing contracts and reviewing shipping documentation as she was taking in capturing the beauty of a flower in her aunt's conservatory.

Her smile wasn't fixed. It flickered on her lips when she stepped back to examine her work or laid down a bold sweeping stroke. Sometimes, she pulled her lower lip between her teeth, or her tongue would sweep across her plump lower lip.

When the enjoyment he took in watching her shot a rush of desire to his groin, he knew it was time to walk away. But of course, as soon as he moved, he caught her notice.

"Oh," she said, her tone wary and her eyes widening in surprise. "You found me." She dipped her brush into a jar of water and wiped it on a cloth before removing a smock she'd donned.

"I did, but you looked quite content, and I'm sorry to interrupt." He gestured at the canvas. "Shall I let you finish?"

She tipped her head and stared at her creation. "I think it's done. Or perhaps I'll add a bit more later."

"May I?"

Lucy stepped back, allowing him to move in closer. He had no idea what the flower she'd painted was, some frilly red hanging variety that gave off a slightly sweet perfume not nearly as appealing as Lucy's floral scent.

"Beautiful," he murmured.

She'd taken an already pretty flower and given it more color and vibrancy, while also capturing the shifting patterns of sunlight as it brightened the flower's red shade. Her brushstrokes had a lively looseness, but not haphazard. "You're very talented."

"I dabble. Nothing like Aunt Cassandra."

"Your art truly glows."

She smiled and relief washed over him.

"It's just the sunlight, I suspect, but thank you for the kind words. I love painting but don't practice enough to truly develop any skill."

"You should paint more." He waited until she met his gaze. "You're too good."

She ducked her head. It was one of the few times he'd seen her boldness falter. When she faced him again, her cheeks were flushed the most fetching pink, and she gifted him a breath-stealing smile.

"I thought we could talk in the front drawing room."

"Of course. Wherever you wish."

"If we're lucky, there should be something there that might help you." She seemed to be relishing his surprise and flashed a little smile of triumph before striding from the conservatory, leaving him to follow.

When he caught up with her and stepped into the drawing room, she waited in front of a desk with a ledger clasped in her crossed arms.

James examined the cover of the volume but could make out nothing of what it might contain.

"This is a ledger of repairs to Invermere." She held the book out to him and released it when James clasped the front edge. "I suspect that rolled-up document on top of the desk will be the manor's blueprints."

James was rarely speechless, and he'd never been this continually confounded by any woman.

"Where did you find these?"

"I didn't. Mrs. Fox did when I asked her to look for them."

He thought he'd negated whatever fragile bit of goodwill he'd built with the housekeeper when he'd taken liberties with Lucy in the field this morning. But perhaps not.

"Why are you helping me?" Despite what she sparked in him, Lucy had every right to resent him.

She crossed her arms, rested her backside against the desk, and let out a long, contemplative sigh.

"Well, as Mrs. Winterbottom would say—"

"Mrs. who?"

"Mrs. Winterbottom," she said defensively. "She

wrote a book about how best to handle life's challenges."

"An etiquette book?" He couldn't imagine such an unconventional young woman adhering to such a thing.

"Good heavens, no. I loathe etiquette books. Mrs. Winterbottom's works are different. She encourages independence, believes ladies should learn to look after themselves, and advises what to do when troubles come along."

"Sounds a bit like you."

She brightened and then narrowed one eye. "I'm not sure if you meant it as such, but I will take that as a compliment," she said with a pleased nod of her head.

James grinned and felt for a moment as if something inside him, something latched very tightly, was beginning to shake loose.

"So what does this Winterbottom woman have to do with helping me?"

Lucy straightened and faced him squarely. "She would say that a problem should be faced rather than avoided, and that the sooner one starts a difficult task, the sooner one can be done."

James couldn't argue with any of it. In fact, one of the older boys he'd befriended in his youth had a similar philosophy, though a bit less elegantly put. *When you're going through hell, keep going.*

Apparently, this Winterbottom lady wasn't all bad. But something in what Lucy had said unsettled him.

"I'm sorry to be the problem that landed on your aunt's doorstep at the same moment you did."

His apology seemed to irk her more than anything he'd yet said since walking into the room. Perhaps because it struck at the heart of the matter between them.

"Why did you land on her doorstep?" She folded her arms across her chest again, as if bracing herself for his answer.

He was ahead of her. He'd been preparing himself for this discussion since last night. And dreading it.

"I understand you inherited the earldom of my aunt's . . ." Bright green eyes widened, she notched her chin up so subtly that he wouldn't have noticed if he wasn't aware of her every move. "Her lover."

James scoffed, and Lucy's brows winged up.

"Is that inaccurate?"

"No, just hard to believe."

"That you inherited or that they were lovers?"

"The latter."

"I assure you, Aunt Cassandra is the most beautiful—"

"Of that, I have no doubt. It's only the notion that my uncle could catch the eye of such a lady."

"You didn't like him?"

"I barely knew him." He turned away because the anger tightening his throat and making his heartbeat thrash had nothing to do with her. It was an old pain, and she needn't know the details. "We were estranged."

Bracing a hand on the frame of one of Invermere's long windows, he stared out at the leaf-strewn drive. "I was told of his death the same moment I learned that he had no other heir. None of it was expected or sought."

She approached, her boot heels a soft patter on the carpet. "May I ask when he died?"

When she drew up next to him, he could feel her studying his face. Perhaps she expected to see pain or grief there. Would she think him a coldhearted bastard for feeling none of it?

"Recently, but I can't say I know the day. I learned of his passing four days ago when I met with his solicitor."

She let out a little gasp, drawing his attention. "I wonder if my aunt knows. I can't bear to think of her losing someone she cares for and her home at the same time." Lucy laid a hand lightly on his sleeve. "Why must you sell it?"

They'd taken longer to come to the crux than Mrs. Fox had, but he loathed explaining this part to Lucy most of all.

"The funds from this sale. I need them desperately."

Shockingly, she nodded as if she understood. "The Rossbury estate must be in disrepair. I suspect there's a great deal to maintain. Papa is always speaking of the expense—"

"There is no estate, Lucy. Only debts and this manor." His voice had edged up again, and he drew in a breath. "Also, a piece of jewelry for your aunt."

It was her turn to scoff. "I suppose it's kind that he thought of her a little."

"No." On this score, he wanted to be utterly clear. "He wasn't kind."

JAMES'S VOICE REVERBERATED off Invermere's window glass. Lucy understood that he deeply disliked his uncle, yet she also heard a deep vein of pain he held inside him. Whatever unpleasantness had passed in his family, it seemed he'd inherited a burden along with a title.

"You need the funds from selling Invermere to pay the estate's debts. That part I understand, but why the urgency?"

"Because there's more. Reasons that have nothing to do with my uncle's bloody title."

Such bleakness came into his voice that Lucy's own throat burned. She held still, determined to give him the time to gather his thoughts, hopeful that he would trust her enough to divulge whatever troubled him so.

He paced from one side of the room to the other and then back again, but just when he turned to her as if to explain, a sound in the hall drew their attention.

A whispered *shh* followed by other murmured voices and a distinctly canine whine gave the eavesdropping staff away.

"We could talk elsewhere," Lucy whispered to him. "A walk to the loch?"

A few clouds hid the sun, but it was still a temperate day, and going down to the loch was high on her list of things to do during her visit. Of course, her plan had been to sketch or take photographs, but that could wait for another day.

He stared at the door and nodded, then started across the room.

Lucy stopped him by planting herself in his path and pressing a hand against his waistcoat. The warmth of his body against her palm was oddly reassuring.

"We could climb out the window," she whispered. "That way they won't even know we've gone, and no one will think to follow."

"Until we get so quiet, Mrs. Fox bursts in to salvage your propriety," he teased in a low voice.

Lucy imagined Mrs. Fox as the protector of her chastity and rolled her eyes. Without waiting for his agreement, she crossed to the window and was pleased to find it lifted with very little effort and barely any sound.

She waved James over. "You should go first and assist me."

"I'm starting to think you've done this before." He smirked at her, but then obeyed and put a leg out the window. The man was so tall and the window so low that it was merely a matter of stepping over the sill and down to the ground. Lucy imagined attempting the same with her much shorter limbs and failing entirely.

James leaned in once he was out the window.

"It's easier if you put both legs over, balance on the sill, and I'll lift you down."

"Well, now I'm beginning to suspect *you've* done this before, my lord." While she spoke the words, she did as he suggested, planting her bottom on the windowsill and pivoting to swing her legs out. Through every movement, his hand was on her to keep her from falling.

Then she faced him, looking down into his handsome face, and he placed his hands on her waist.

She realized her breathing had gone shallow.

Even during a waltz, a man would only have one hand on her waist, the other clasping her hand.

Something about this moment, the way he touched her, felt unbearably intimate. And he felt it too if his tight grip and the flash of heat in his gaze were any indication.

"Brace your hands on my shoulders, Lucy." The command in a raspy tone sent shivers up her legs, all the way to her center.

But, of course, he was being practical. She liked practical. She could be practical.

Reaching out, she placed one hand on each of his broad shoulders. He was not a man who would ever need to pad suits. Under her fingertips, his muscles bunched and flexed as he lifted her from the sill and lowered her down.

It took all of a moment, but Lucy held his gaze after her feet touched the ground.

"There may be a flaw in this plan," he said, still whispering as if the staff might overhear.

He stood so close, his breath feathered warmth against her skin.

"What's that?"

"Do either of us know the way to the loch?"

"I do, of course."

"I should never have doubted you." He sketched a little bow and lifted his arm in the wrong direction. "Lead the way, Lady Lucy."

Lucy took a few steps in the correct direction and then stopped. James grunted and stopped short behind her.

"We should skirt those hedges and then wrap around. If we take the direct path, they'll see us from the house."

A masculine chuckle rumbled at her back. "You really are determined on subterfuge. Go too far with this and they'll think I've absconded with you."

"Perhaps you're right." Lucy didn't mind that they'd frown at the two of them spending time alone, but they needn't give the staff more reason to distrust him. "Let's just take the main path. It's not far."

"You've come this way often?"

"No, not often." Lucy glanced back in surprise and nearly tripped on a stone in the path. "But I did have a wander this morning before heading to the archery field."

"I'm sorry you may not have much more time to explore Invermere." A bleakness came into his eyes.

"One man is to blame, as far as I can tell." The

late Earl of Rossbury. "If your uncle had paid his debts or gifted the manor to Lady Cassandra, you wouldn't be here, and Invermere could be hers as long as she liked."

He said nothing to that, and Lucy started walking again.

"She wrote about walks down to the loch in many of her letters, even sending sketches of the view of the water in various seasons." As soon as the words were out, she saw that view for herself and bounced on her heels. "There it is."

The loch was more beautiful than she imagined. Clouds hung in the sky, dark shapes reflected in the deep blue water. Heather dotted the ground and colored the distant hills. She had to come back with her camera or paper to sketch.

"My uncle is to blame for a great deal."

The darkness in his tone drew her attention from the view.

"But he's not the only reason I'm here now, or why the sale of Invermere must take place soon."

Lucy had sensed that from the start, but now, seeing the misery in his gaze, she was afraid of the rest of the story.

"I have debts too. I made . . . an error in judgment and lost a great deal as a result."

"What did you lose?" Tragedy lay behind his words and she wanted to know the whole of it, not just out of concern for her aunt but out of a desire to know him.

"Everything." He swept a hand through his hair, then let out a shaky laugh. "My shipping business, the trust of colleagues, my peace of mind."

"I'm so sorry." Lucy had heard of men of business and even noblemen who dabbled in commerce losing their fortunes at gambling tables or because of a bad investment. Such falls from grace and wealth could happen, it seemed, overnight. And in her parents' social circle, more than one gentleman had been snubbed as dishonorable for being unable to pay his debts.

"I've been working for months to rebuild." He shook his head.

"And funds from the sale of Invermere would help?"

"In essence, yes."

"There's something more." Lucy felt it in every word he spoke, a tautness and resistance, as if he was parsing out what he wished to share and what he was determined to conceal.

The wind kicked up, tugging at her hair and the skirt of her gown. James stared at her a moment and then turned and stalked away. He paced as he had in the drawing room.

"I'm being impertinent. My mother often tells me my curiosity will be my undoing."

At first, Lucy wasn't sure if he'd heard her, but soon after, he came back and reached for her. He placed a hand gently on each arm.

But he still wasn't going to tell her the truth. Lucy read the reticence in his gaze and something else. Fear?

"I admire your curiosity. I even like your impertinence. But it's best if you don't know the rest."

Lucy shivered, both because of his implication of some dark secret he refused to reveal and the sudden nip in the wind. James chafed her arms under the warmth of his palms.

"What will become of my aunt?" Lucy would let him keep his secrets if he wished to, but Aunt Cassandra's future mattered most.

"I swear to you that I will deal with her fairly."

"I hope so." In her heart, she knew so. Whatever he'd decided to hide from her, Lucy knew that James Pembroke was not a bad man. If anything, his arrival at Invermere was entirely prompted by circumstances he would change if he could, most of which were beyond his control.

Of course, she feared that wouldn't soften the blow of her aunt learning that her beloved home must be sold, but Lucy didn't doubt James would keep his promise.

A cool drop of rain fell on her forehead, and James reached up to swipe the dampness away at the same moment a drop landed on his nose.

"We should get inside."

He was right, but Lucy lingered a moment. Once they entered the house again, there would be no more speaking openly or using each other's given names. None of the closeness that seemed to come naturally when they were on their own.

"If Aunt Cassandra arrives this afternoon, this may be our last chance to speak privately."

"I don't know about that." He stared back toward the house. "You seem quite adept at climbing out of windows."

"And the first whiff my father hears of that, he'll be on the fast train to Edinburgh."

"They don't know you're an escape artist then?"

"I'm not sure they know me all that well at all." Lucy didn't mean to cause the sadness in his eyes. She didn't want pity, especially from him. "But maybe that's my fault. For the most part, I've always done what was expected of me."

"And now you're ready to rebel?" The words in his warm, low voice sounded like a challenge.

"I am."

His mouth twisted in a teasing smile. "I'd like to see that, Lady Lucy Westmont."

"Then keep watching, Lord Rossbury."

Chapter Ten

The next day, Lucy managed to avoid him almost entirely.

He saw her walking the fields near the house and heard the staff mention that she'd gone down to the loch to sketch, but she didn't seek him out, and they never spoke.

By the end of the day, as ridiculous as it was, he missed her. Missed speaking to her, being near her. Being the object of her attention.

Yet he wasn't sure how to approach and found himself full of unspent energy as night fell.

Stepping into the sitting room he'd been locked in the night he arrived, he was glad to find a fire in the grate. None had yet been laid in his guest room, and he was loath to trouble the staff. In addition to the palpable resentment, he now sensed the unease that had set in when their mistress hadn't appeared as expected the previous day.

Lucy was anxious too. One of the times he'd seen her fleetingly, she'd come down to speak to Mrs. Fox and inquire about any post or message from her aunt. Outside Invermere's windows, the patter of rain had turned into a fearsome storm, which would likely delay the lady's travels even further.

Hercules watched him from a spot in front of the fire, as if waiting for James to decide whether to stay in the sitting room or go. He didn't know himself. In truth, he'd only come down because it felt wrong to be in a house with Lucy and not see her, speak to her.

The dog lifted his head, and James dropped into a chair near him, running a hand over the beast's thick gray fur.

"I wonder what she's doing up there."

It was too early for sleep, but the one thing he knew with certainty was that she seemed a lady eminently capable of keeping herself busy. Bloody hell, the weight of the books she'd brought alone would keep the most avid reader occupied for a month.

As distracted as he'd been when they'd met, he hadn't bothered to note titles. But now he wondered what sort of books Lucy liked to read. Tomes by that Coldbottom woman, apparently.

"Pardon the intrusion, my lord."

James inhaled a deep bolstering breath before turning to face Mrs. Fox. He felt unprepared for battle, but she was the kind of woman he expected would strike when his defenses were low.

"Her ladyship asked for biscuits and a warm drink, and I wondered if you might wish for something from the kitchen."

Whiskey was what he truly wanted, but he hadn't seen a single drinks cart in the house.

"Is her ladyship coming down?" That's what he wanted too. He'd only just kept himself from knocking on her bedroom door and breaching that last shred of propriety between them.

Rather than answer his question, Mrs. Fox, who stood on the sitting room threshold, glanced up the staircase.

An odd energy raised the hairs at his nape, and he didn't need to see her to know that Lucy approached. Good grief, he was attuned to her mere presence now?

She swept into the room as if they'd planned a rendezvous, offering him a warm smile.

"I'll have my drink down here if I'm not disturbing you."

"Stay." At the arch of one tawny brow, he realized the word had come out as something of a command. "I mean to say, you're not disturbing me in the least."

Every word of that was patently false, considering that the sight of her had turned that fizz of recognition to something much hungrier.

"I brought something to read." She lifted a book almost proudly, a hefty tome with a gilded cover.

"Of course you did." James grinned but reserved the chuckle that wanted to burst free since Mrs. Fox still stood watch in the doorway.

"Biscuits for you too, Lord Rossbury?"

"Thank you, Mrs. Fox." The housekeeper held his gaze in silent warning before glancing at Lucy and then back at him.

When she was gone, he bent closer and whispered, "Is that the one that nearly broke my foot?"

"If you mean the one that you unceremoniously dumped onto the train platform, no. That was a Dickens novel. This one fell too." She tipped the book and examined its edges. "Though it seems no worse for the rough handling."

She took a chair opposite the one he'd vacated, close to the fire. For a moment, he got lost in watching the firelight illumine all the strands of polished gold in her hair. Lucy either didn't notice his perusal or was allowing it, and he hoped it was the latter.

"You don't have a book," she finally said quietly as she flipped a page.

"Oh, I do. I've simply gone cross-eyed from staring at the notations." James lifted the ledger he'd been poring over for the last couple of hours.

"Any conclusions?" She kept her eyes fixed on her book, but he sensed she was as enthralled with its contents as he'd been with reading Invermere's repairs ledger.

"Your aunt has been an excellent steward of this manor house."

"She loves it a great deal." Finally, she lifted her head and looked his way, but a frown knitted her brow. "I wonder why she didn't arrive today."

"The weather—"

"But it was clear this morning."

"Perhaps the storm swept down from the north."

"Mmm." She put her book aside, and James

straightened in his chair, thinking she meant to approach. Instead, she headed for the threshold where the door stood open.

Mary appeared a moment later bearing a tray laden with cups and biscuits and a pot of what he assumed was tea.

"I'll take it, Mary."

James started out of his seat to assist Lucy, but she strode toward the low table between the room's settees and practically had his cup full before he could make a move. She was capable enough to make everything she did look effortless.

"It's chamomile. Do you loathe chamomile?" She hesitated before offering him a brimming cup.

"I don't recall drinking much of it, but I can already assure you I'd like it more laced with whiskey."

She waited until he took the cup, then stepped toward the mantel, running her fingers along its length, snaking her hand back behind picture frames and figurines. After finding what she sought, she pulled out a small key and strode to a polished bureau in the corner.

"Aunt Cassandra keeps the spirits here," she said quietly. Then turned to him and lowered her voice even more. "She wrote to me about it in one of her letters. Apparently, Drummond was drinking her dry every time she refilled the decanters."

James imagined the surly Mr. Drummond on a few drams of Scotch and couldn't decide it if would make the old man kinder or more ill-tempered.

"I think this one's whiskey." She held up a decanter

and the contents glowed like molten amber in the firelight.

"You've never tasted whiskey?"

"Not yet." She eyed the bottle as she approached, then took a seat and bit into a biscuit.

James followed suit, shocked to find the buttery, iced confection tasted liked cinnamon. Sugar. Spice. A bit like the lady whose nearness he'd come to crave. He busied himself taking up his teacup, if only to keep her from noticing the rebellious turn of his thoughts.

"Oh my goodness." She giggled, then broke into outright laughter.

When he looked at her questioningly, she sat her teacup and plate down and rose from her chair. She reached a hand toward him, and he found himself leaning in for her touch.

"Just there. You have a bit of icing."

He sensed it instantly but hesitated. Then he swiped at the wrong side of his mouth.

Lucy moved closer. "Other side."

"Here?" He pointed in the general direction where he could feel something at the edge of his mouth. From the moment she'd walked into the room, he'd wanted to touch her. But even better if she touched him.

Clever woman that she was, she narrowed her gaze, hesitated, and then leaned in with a knowing smile. She ran her finger across the edge of his mouth, collecting the icing on the tip.

"Here. You see?" Drawing her finger back, Lucy seemed to be on the verge of licking at the sweetness herself. Then she noticed his rapt attention and lifted her icing-tipped finger out to him.

"Would you like it?"

He would have taken anything she offered in that moment. But he could see the flash of doubt in her eyes. As if she yearned to be comfortable with flirtation but wasn't. At least not yet.

James leaned forward and took the tip of her finger between his lips. Her own lips parted. Lush and full. They'd flushed a rosy shade that made him long to run his tongue along the seam.

He pulled her finger in a little further with his tongue, sucking on it gently.

Lucy licked her lips and withdrew her finger slowly. She pressed her hand into her lap and lowered her eyes.

"Delicious," he told her quietly.

She looked up at him wide-eyed, breathless, as overcome by the power of what was between them as he was.

"Shall we read?" she whispered shakily. "That is, shall I read to you? Aloud. To both of us. Or I could just tell you a bit about the book I'm reading."

"I'd like that." It was either settle for listening to her talk about her book, or haul her over his shoulder and take her upstairs. Though he doubted he'd make it two steps before alerting the ever-watchful Mrs. Fox.

She turned back to the hefty tome she'd discarded.

"Would you like some whiskey?" he asked once she'd gotten settled in the chair by the fire again. "You mentioned that you've never had any."

His hand shook slightly as he lifted the decanter and filled his tumbler. Resisting what she sparked in him was challenging his self-control.

"I don't think I should." She eyed his glass, flicked her gaze to his lips and then down at her book again.

James smiled and settled back in his chair. "You never told me the title."

Lifting the book, she showed him the cover, a rich, dark blue with gold lettering. *Scottish Myth and Folk Legends*.

"Very apropos."

"Yes, exactly." She flipped pages. "This one's about a kelpie."

"Oh?" James had read no folktales of Scotland, but some of the men who worked on his ships had stories they told about ocean monsters and sea sprites.

"A water horse," Lucy told him, her voice pitched low. "A shape-shifter that could take the form of a horse or a man. They say they lured women." She quirked a brow at that and then frowned. "And children. Depending on what you read, they're either very seductive or a bit grisly."

Her eyes took on a kind of eager glint as she flipped pages, deciding which tale to read to him.

"There's a tale here of a lady who enslaved a kelpie to work as a horse on her father's farm."

"That does sound grisly."

Lucy laughed. "The worst one may be this one. A group of children were down by the riverside and found a horse near the water. A beautiful horse. And they couldn't resist climbing atop to get a ride. One boy decided he didn't wish for a ride, but he wanted to touch the horse, but once he put his finger on its coat, he couldn't remove it."

She looked up at him, and James held her gaze as he sipped his whiskey.

Her cheeks darkened.

"What did the boy do?" he asked. "Get dragged away by the kelpie?"

"According to the tale, he whipped out a knife and cut his own finger off," she said excitedly.

"You like the grisly bits a little."

"Maybe a little. My older sister used to tell me scary stories before bed to torment me." The tormenting was teasing in nature, judging by Lucy's amused tone. "So I made up scary stories too. It became a bit of a competition."

"Are you competitive as a rule?" He was, but since he'd spent so much of his life alone, his competitiveness tended to be with himself. Pushing himself to do better, disappointed when he didn't live up to his own expectations.

"No. I just like to do things well." And she did do things well, perhaps better than most. Despite occasional flashes of uncertainty, she had a confidence about her, though he suspected she'd think it wrong to brag. Women were taught that, and James thought it quite ridiculous.

"Tell me what you're good at. Besides telling scary stories."

She shrugged.

"No false modesty. I'd like to know."

"I'm good at most things I put real effort into doing well. But mostly I'm good at helping people. My family, but friends too. My friend, Miranda, is marrying in about a fortnight, and it fell to me to make most of the arrangements."

"That seems a great deal for you to take on."

"I didn't mind." She rushed her reply so emphatically, he suspected it wasn't entirely true.

After a moment of flipping pages in her book, she added, "Most of the time."

"So sometimes you do mind?"

"That probably makes me sound dreadful."

"Not at all. I spent most of my life looking after myself. Helping others is admirable." It seemed she came from a family with a philanthropic spirit, and he had to concede that aristocrats who helped others deserved his respect.

"Of late, I've wanted something of my own." The words emerged quietly, almost hesitantly, as if she was uncertain whether to confess her yearnings.

"So you left London as the very helpful Lady Lucy and you've come to Scotland as Lady Lucy the rebellious, who will make her mark on the world."

"Are you making fun of me?" She rose from her chair and clutched her book of Scottish myths like a shield in front of her.

James stood too. "I'm not. I wouldn't dream of it. I think you're going to do exactly what you've set out to do, and I only wish I could be here to see it."

"You're leaving very soon?"

"That's my plan." He never imagined he'd have a moment of regret for wanting to resolve the matter of the Scottish manor quickly.

Observant lady that she was, she seemed to notice. "You don't sound entirely convinced, Mr. Pembroke."

"Perhaps I've realized it won't be as simple a matter as I anticipated."

She watched him, waiting, her gaze searching as if trying to see beyond his words and expression to all the vulnerable parts of himself he rarely revealed to anyone.

"Well, I hope you'll be here long enough to see a bit of my rebellion."

Chapter Eleven

James lay awake so long, his heartbeat synchronized with the tick of the clock on the mantel, slower and steadier than the patter of rain against the windowpanes. He'd given a name to every figure, including the damned unicorn, in the mural on the ceiling.

Cecil had seemed right, somehow, for that flamboyant, fanciful creature.

The fire in the grate still flickered with warmth, but he didn't need heat. His thoughts had wandered past propriety hours ago and rushed headlong into wanton.

He was a certifiable scoundrel, a wretch. Lying a few rooms down from a woman who made his body ache, not to mention making him smile so damn much that the muscles of his face ached.

That moment when he'd braced his hands on her waist as she climbed out of the drawing room window was emblazoned in his mind's eye, and he'd wager all the fortune he no longer possessed that her thoughts strayed to the same place his had.

But mercy, he wanted to find out. Was Lucy awake too?

He'd talked himself out of going to her twice already. The second time, he'd made it all the way out into the hall before turning back.

Devil and rot to propriety. He'd never needed it, except what had been required of him in commerce. Business etiquette had only ever truly been about basic civil niceties and protecting the egos of male colleagues.

Then, of course, there was his rule about avoiding flings with aristocratic ladies. Yes, he avoided affairs with noblewomen because he couldn't stand the hypocrites of high society, but he'd also wanted to save himself the trouble of ever being in danger of damaging a lady's reputation. He'd never fancied being a ruiner of virgins. Hell, even if a noble widow had been willing, he'd never wished to be the bounder who caused a woman to lose face in "good" society.

So this—this fascination—was all bloody new.

God, how he wanted her. There was no longer any use pretending otherwise. But neither would it do him any good to fool himself into believing he could be good for her beyond a night of pleasure. Her pleasure. Every fantasy he had involved giving her release rather than seeking his own. He wanted to see her lose herself that way again and again.

But beyond that, she deserved far better than he could offer.

Even if her family considered her a spinster, as she claimed, they would not welcome a penniless earl and ruined shipping magnate into their family.

Holy hell. James stood from his chair by the fire and stalked to the window, yanking back the drapes to press his forehead against the cool glass. Somehow, he'd gone from thoughts of tasting every inch of Lucy's body to calculating exactly how inappropriate he'd be as a husband.

Marriage was not a desire or even a consideration in his life. He'd been too busy, too eager to maintain his independence, too afraid of disappointing anyone other than himself. And he didn't have other men's longing for a family or heirs.

He'd lost all that and decided it wasn't meant for him. Wealth was enough.

Or so he'd thought.

Before he did something reckless, he stalked back to the bed and sank down into the cushioned mattress. The stray thought came that Lady Cassandra Munro must have furnished the room. His uncle had never given a damn for the comfort of others.

He scrubbed a hand over his face. Her expected arrival tomorrow should be a relief. The sooner she arrived, the sooner this could all be resolved. Yet now she wasn't a name mentioned by a solicitor. She was a lady adored by the woman who consumed his thoughts. A lady who'd devoted a great deal of time and care to Invermere.

Closing his eyes, he tried to think of nothing and merely imagine how it would feel to finally see the back of Archibald Beck forever.

Sleep had almost claimed him when his body tensed at a sound. Or had he imagined it? The creak of wood and a shuffling movement outside his bedroom door. Perhaps Hercules had taken up watch. The beast had greeted him yesterday morning too.

But a moment later, there came a whispered *shh* that was definitely feminine and not his imagination.

He donned his trousers and slid on his shirt as he crossed the room, working the lower buttons until he reached the door and swung it open.

Lucy stood with her hand raised as if midknock and immediately lowered her arm to her side.

Shock was instantly overtaken by pleasure. A kind of furnace lit in his chest, a warmth that made him smile even while she stood staring at him, stunned and wide-eyed.

"Oh," she said, as if surprised that *he* should answer the door of his room.

"Mmm," he replied.

"You're awake," she whispered. Then darted a worried look down the hall.

"As are you." James bent closer to check the hall for anyone else. "Is anything amiss?"

"May we . . ." She pressed her lips together, closed her eyes, shook her head, and then tried again. "May I come in?"

The lowered timbre of her voice and glint of determination in her gaze sent a shiver down his spine.

He stepped back to allow her in, closed the door behind her, and forced himself to wait and let her tell him why she'd come rather than reach for her as he longed to.

"This must seem strange." She still whispered and took his room in as she spoke.

"Unexpected, for certain." Though that wasn't entirely true, was it? Should he admit that he'd almost been at her door an hour ago?

If this was a seduction, she looked undecided about it. Or at least a bundle of nerves. That worried him, and he mentally kicked himself for assuming this had anything to do with him and not to do with the business on the train.

Perhaps nightmares plagued her. God knew they'd tormented him for a decade after losing his parents. Still did at times.

"Is something troubling you, Lucy?"

Even if she'd only come to him for comfort, he'd happily offer that.

"Um . . ." She took a seat at one of the chairs near the fire, perching on the edge and then setting the candle she'd brought with her down. "It's a cozy room. And I do love the unicorn." She gestured vaguely at the painting above his bed, which she darted glances at now and then.

Whatever it was, she was hesitant. James had always been devilishly bad at patience, but for her, he would try his best.

James lit the candle by his bedside and brought it with him to join her, taking the chair opposite hers. He sat gingerly, leaning forward, his hands clasped between his knees.

"Whatever it is, I'll listen."

She'd been staring at the flickering embers in the

grate, but at his words, she turned and gave him a beaming smile that made his breath stagger in his chest.

"You're making this easier than I imagined it would be."

"Good." James returned her smile, but he was still confused. "Making what easier?"

After a long gaze, so long it felt as if she could see his very thoughts, Lucy stood. She untied the ribbon on the robe she'd worn over her nightdress and let the garment tumble and pool in the chair behind her as she took two steps to stand before him.

They'd traded places. Usually, she tipped her head to look up at him, but now he was the one arching back.

"I've come to ask if you'd consider . . . Or perhaps I should say, I would very much appreciate it if you would kiss me."

James blinked, considered pinching himself, felt a flash of dizziness as all the blood in his body rushed to his groin.

"Kiss you?" The words felt thick and odd in his mouth, as if he'd never spoken the words, wasn't even sure what it was. Some scoundrel seducer he was.

Lucy held out her hands as if to ask for patience. "I know. It's unexpected. Maybe even unwanted—"

"Lucy—"

"But you see, I have never been. Kissed, that is. And I've never met a man who I wanted to be the one to give me my first." She drew in a sharp breath and then shot him a bold gaze. Fiercer than her usual boldness. "I want my first kiss—perhaps my only kiss—to be from you, James Pembroke, Lord—"

James stood and pressed a finger to her lips. "James is enough. I quite like it when you call me James."

"James." She let the word linger on her tongue, drawing out the sibilant end. "You'll consider my request?"

The answer was never in doubt. Perhaps even Lucy knew that because she leaned into him then, rested her palms on his chest, stared hungrily at his neck and chest exposed by his half-open shirt.

The luminous green of her eyes turned molten, hungry.

"I have news for you, Lady Lucy Westmont." He wrapped one arm around her waist. Then reached up to stroke the backs of his fingers against her cheek. "I've wanted to kiss you since the day we met."

"For two days, then?"

"It feels like longer." He slid back a strand of her honey-blonde hair, then cupped her nape with his palm.

"But in a good way?" Lucy arched back into his touch to gaze up at him.

"Mmm. A *very* good way." He bent his head but resisted going too fast and taking what he wanted. Instead, he would make it good for her. She'd gifted him with this moment, and he wanted it to be a kiss she'd remember.

He stroked the tender flesh of her neck, letting his fingers dance at the lacy edge of her night rail until he heard her breathing hitch. Then he bent to nuzzle the same spots, brushing his lips against where her pulse beat wildly.

"James," she breathed as she gripped his shirt front. "Please."

He kissed the edge of her mouth, and she lifted onto her toes, leaning into him. Nothing had ever felt so right. Holding her. Touching her. Somehow, it felt as if it was meant to be from the start. Yet he didn't understand it and wouldn't have bet on ever being gifted with anything as precious as Lucy's trust.

Finally, he touched his lips to hers, and Lucy instantly let out a breath of relief. As if she'd been waiting for this moment, waiting for him for as long as he'd been waiting to feel this way about anyone.

When her hand went to his shoulder, he swept his other arm around her, pulling her soft, warm curves against him.

Then, just as he deepened the kiss, she stilled. Stiffened in his arms.

"Do you hear that?" she whispered, pulling back to break their kiss.

He did, though the blood rushing in his ears made it difficult.

Music. And singing. Neither terribly good but both offered with gusto. They grew louder.

"What is it?" James was loath to let Lucy go but

released her when she lowered her hand from his shoulder.

Then she shocked him by reaching down to clasp his hand and draw him toward the window, which she very accurately had identified as the direction of the sounds.

As she stepped to the glass, the singing ceased, and some man's voice called out.

"Cassandra, come to the window, love."

Lucy turned back, her eyes wide and glittering in the candlelight. "He thinks this is Aunt Cassandra's window."

"Or he's a thief trying to cause a distraction."

Lucy pressed her face to the glass and then lifted the sash before James could stop her.

"Hello there," she called out almost congenially, "you have the wrong window."

Good grief, the woman was being helpful to a potential housebreaker.

"Let me." James drew up beside her. "You have no idea who this man is."

"He has a lute and is too deep in his cups to remember which window is my aunt's. How can he be a housebreaker?"

James frowned at the woman whose lips were pink from his kisses. God, he wanted to go back to just two minutes before.

"Begging yer pardon, lass," the man shouted up in a slurred bellow. "But who the hell are ye, and what have ye done with my woman?"

James stuck his head out the window. In the

moonlight, a tall, stout, bearded man stood wearing an odd hat, an overlong coat, and holding what did in fact appear to be a lute.

"Who are *you*, man? It's one in the bloody morning."

"He seems soused," Lucy said as she braced her hands on the windowsill next to his. "Can we have your name please, sir?"

"I already asked him that."

"You weren't very polite." She pushed her arm against his teasingly, and James wanted nothing more than to shut the window, pull the drapes, and go back to kissing her.

"Cassandra!" The man crooned her name as if it was part of his song. "My bonny lass. Bonniest of all lasses."

Lucy chuckled. "He's smitten."

"He's drunk and a terrible singer."

"Sir, I'm Lady Lucy Westmont. Cassandra is my aunt, but she's not at home."

"I'm coming up."

Whether the man misheard her or was too lost in his own drunken reverie, James couldn't be sure.

"Coming up what?" Lucy whispered as she leaned further out the window.

James laid a hand across her back, gripping a handful of her nightgown to keep her secured inside.

"Can I have a look?" The window was tall but too narrow for both of them to lean their upper bodies out of at once.

Lucy retreated and James leaned out. It took him only a moment to realize the man below was not in his right mind.

James ducked back in. "I think he means to scale the side of the house."

Lucy gripped his arm. "Good grief, he'll injure himself."

"I don't think he'll get far and will realize his folly." James reached for her, to offer reassurance, but Lucy bolted away from him and ran for the door.

"We have to stop him." The moment the breathless words were out, she took off down the hall, her footsteps thudding loudly and Hercules following in her wake.

By the time Lucy had donned a cloak and her boots and made it to the stairwell, James was waiting for her with a lantern he'd obtained from somewhere.

"You're coming too?"

"Of course. I won't let you go out there alone." He wore a strange expression. The intensity in his gaze made her wish they were back in his room, that his fingers were still stroking her skin, that the kiss they'd started had gone further.

She already missed that intimate moment.

But there was a taut squareness to his jaw now too, as if he was clenching his teeth. Lucy couldn't decide if it was the disappointment of being interrupted or a sign of regret.

"It's raining. We should go before he tries scaling the side of the house and breaks his neck," she said, and preceded him down the stairs before her true feelings spilled out.

"Prepare yourself," he said quietly, his footsteps just a pace behind hers. "I heard movement downstairs. The ruckus has woken the staff."

"Maybe they know him."

"Indeed, we do, my lady." Mrs. Fox stood watching them from the bottom of the stairs and then busied herself turning up the gas lamps in the foyer. "I've sent McKay out to deal with him, but I'm sorry that his antics disturbed your sleep." She said the words to Lucy but glanced once at James too.

He'd stopped next to her, and his nearness was both comfort and temptation now. Her cheeks were still warm, probably pink, but she didn't care what conclusions Mrs. Fox might draw. She'd thought long and hard about her decision to go to his room and didn't regret a moment of it.

"We'll send him on his way if you wish to return to your rooms." Mrs. Fox told them over her shoulder as she unlatched the front door. "Hopefully, a few more hours of sleep can be salvaged."

"But who is he, Mrs. Fox?" Lucy's curiosity wouldn't let her sleep.

"Blackwood, lass." The man himself burst through the front door, stumbled, and then righted himself by reaching for one of the statues nearby. He patted its marble arm awkwardly and murmured, "Thank you, darlin'," before continuing into the foyer and approaching Lucy.

James stepped forward and planted himself in front of her. Lucy sidestepped and laid a hand on his arm to let him know his chivalry wasn't needed here. The man seemed overly jovial, if anything.

"Angus Blackwood." He pressed a fist to his mouth to unsuccessfully stifle a burp and squinted as he examined her. "Ye are Cassandra's niece, aren't ye? Ye've the same fire in those sea-green eyes of yours."

Lucy drew in a breath when the man pointed at her. He took a step forward as if he might touch her, but James deflected him, sweeping his arm down against Mr. Blackwood's.

"Don't," he said simply, but with the deep, cold voice he'd used with Nichols on the train.

In response, Blackwood lifted his hands in surrender, then smiled. "Understood."

"McKay can drive you back in your carriage—" Mrs. Fox started.

"Is there no hospitality left at Invermere, Fox? I'll no' make that trek again this night of blighted weather."

Rain battered the windowpanes, whipped by the wind, as if emphasizing his point.

"Perhaps we could prepare a room for Mr. Blackwood." Lucy didn't know why, but she was curious about the man. He was as colorful as any character she'd ever met, and getting to know him seemed a way of knowing her aunt better. If it wasn't one in the morning, she'd ply him with coffee and questions.

"He has a room," Mrs. Fox said quietly and a little defeated. "Make your way up when you're ready, Mr. Blackwood."

He doffed his red-ribboned hat and sketched a little bow that caused him to stumble.

Lucy reached out to grab his shoulder, and James took his opposite arm.

"Are you sure this is a good idea?" he whispered over the man's head.

"He's in no state to do anything but rest."

James offered no answer, merely held her gaze.

"Let's get you upstairs, Mr. Blackwood."

The older man smiled at each of them in turn and let them lead him to the foot of the stairs. There, he shook off James's hold and reached for Lucy's hand where she held his upper arm.

"Cassandra mentioned you," he said, watching her as they ascended the stairs.

"Did she?" Lucy wanted to know how her aunt spoke of her but feared she'd hear words like *joyless spinster* again. Or worse, James would hear her described that way.

"Said you were a brilliant girl, but trapped."

"Trapped?"

"Family responsibilities, duties, social nonsense. A banked fire, she said. Waiting to burn bright."

Lucy's throat went dry, and tears stung her eyes. It was prettier than calling her a spinster but a truth she hadn't allowed herself to see for too long.

Angus Blackwood said no more but pointed at a door straight ahead the moment they reached the top of the stairs. Once he'd toddled inside, he turned to shut it.

Lucy reached for the handle to stop him from closing it all the way. "Will you be all right?"

"A bit of a sleep, some apologies in the morning, and one of Cook's breakfasts, and I shall be right as rain." He smiled sleepily, his eyes half closed, then they slid open. If not sober, he looked to have a moment of clarity. "When is she back?"

"Tomorrow, we hope. Perhaps the afternoon or evening."

That answer seemed to bring him relief. "Good. Miss her something fierce, I do."

Lucy lifted her hand, allowing him to close the door behind him.

"Are you all right?" James asked, his voice filled with concern.

"Yes." She wasn't. That kiss had set her body humming with a need, an ache, she'd never felt before. And the way her aunt had described her to Mr. Blackwood somehow made that ache worse.

James reached for her hand, led her further down the hall, out of view of the foyer downstairs, and wrapped her in his arms. He knew. Somehow he knew without her saying a word that she needed the simple comfort of his warmth, his scent, his strong arms sheltering her.

Tucking her cheek against his chest, she closed her eyes and listened to the steady, solid beat of his heart.

"I've got you," he whispered against her hair.

Lucy swiped at dampness on her cheek and realized a tear had fallen, unbidden, unexpected. Suddenly feeling foolish, she couldn't face him and just wanted to return to the privacy of her room.

James seemed to sense this too. When she lifted her head, he cupped her face, swiped at the tear with the pad of his thumb. Then he bent to kiss her forehead.

"You do burn bright. Don't doubt that." With that, he let her go and turned to head down the hall to his room.

Lucy watched until he slipped inside, wishing she could go with him. Wishing for his lips on hers again. The day before she'd vowed not to let the man affect her holiday, and now she wasn't looking forward to outings and sightseeing so much as waking up to see him again.

Chapter Twelve

The next morning, James poured himself a cup of coffee and settled into a chair in the drawing room with a view of the stairwell. He heard staff moving about, preparing the house for the day and their mistress's arrival, but he'd seen none of them and that suited him. From the minute he'd awoken, he'd hoped Lucy would be the first person he'd see.

He'd hated leaving her alone the previous night. She'd needed comfort, and he'd given what he could, but he needed to know what had brought her to tears.

And he needed to tell her that he planned to make a quick trip into the city before her aunt's arrival. The surveyor Abercrombie promised to send had yet to arrive, and nothing could move forward without a fair valuation of the house and property.

"Drummond thinks I should call you out." Angus Blackwood's deep, rumbling voice sounded from atop the stairwell. "Pistols at dawn."

James stepped into the hall to face the man.

"Unfortunately, it's past dawn, so you've missed your chance." James wanted to dislike Blackwood for derailing his moment with Lucy, but there was an affability about the man that even his drunken foolishness of the previous night couldn't conceal.

"So it is. Not the early riser I once was." Blackwood moved slowly down the stairs like a man afraid to make any sudden moves. When he reached the bottom, he arched one bushy white brow. "Swords in the afternoon?" The older man gestured at the fireplace at James's back.

A collection of blades hung above it. James guessed Cassandra's first husband, the sea captain, had collected them from various places.

"Cassandra likes swords, so we have plenty to choose from."

"Swords aren't my forte, I'm afraid. Is there a third option?"

The man's lined face creased into a smile. "Will ye settle for an unfriendly inquisition?"

"Do your worst, Blackwood. Though if you want coffee first, it's on the dining room sideboard."

"Drummond already plied me with the dark brew and my belly cannae take more." He took a spot on the settee, resting his bulk against the cushions with a sigh. When he closed his eyes, James wondered if he might nod off. But a moment later, he straightened his shoulders and focused clear eyes his way. "He tells me you've come to take my lady's home."

"Unfortunately, I have come to take possession of the property."

"Not unfortunate for yerself though. Inherited the whole lot, have ye?"

James saw no point in dissembling. There was something about Blackwood that made him suspect the man would see through such attempts anyway.

"In all honesty, the lot consists of a title and this manor house and very little else. But, yes, it has all fallen to me."

"Good god," Blackwood said with a growl of disdain. "I knew the man was a rotter, but he always seemed a tightfisted one."

James nodded. "A rotter indeed, and not at all a generous man. But he was a gambler, and apparently an extremely unlucky one."

"That I knew. The gambling is what ended them. Thought he'd stopped as a result, but apparently he didnae." Blackwood pinched the skin at the bridge of his nose. "Wish I'd met her before that bastard got to her." He side-eyed James. "No offense to ye as his kin."

"Say what you will. I've no love for the man, and I suspect the knowledge that I would inherit made him miserable."

"Fell out with him, did ye?"

James let out a bitter chuckle. "That's one way to put it."

"Tell me the tale," Blackwood urged. "If there's to be no duel and yer lass hasn't come down yet, we've time."

James studied the older man and saw something

of himself. Like he'd once done, Blackwood used his charm and easy manner to disarm. There was no reason not to tell the man the truth. The man couldn't have a terribly high opinion of his uncle, as it was.

"I was orphaned at the age of ten. He was my only living relative in England, and he disowned me. More or less." James couldn't help a rueful smile. "Primogeniture doesn't give a damn about family rows."

"He was more than a rotter, then. A right villain."

James couldn't disagree, but acknowledging it with Blackwood made him curious. "How did Lady Cassandra become connected with Rossbury?"

"Why did she take up with the devil is what you're asking." Blackwood grimaced. "Poor timing. She'd lost her Lord Munro, a wild one he was, if the stories are true. Suppose Rossbury seemed tame. Stable. But he wasn't, was he? Had that gambling problem. And that disgusted her as much as his coldness."

"And then she met you?"

"Aye." Blackwood's voice grew deeper, his eyes almost misty. "And oh, lucky day that was." He seemed far away, as if replaying a memory in his mind. Then he turned his hooded gaze on James again. "And what of your lucky day?"

"Mine?"

"The young lass coming to visit now is just a coincidence?"

"It is. We met by chance on the King's Cross Station

platform and introduced ourselves during the journey. I had no idea she was Lady Cassandra's niece. I would have never wished to ruin her holiday."

"But if you hadn't journeyed to Scotland on that train, at that hour, you might have never met her. Fate has you in its sights, my boy." Blackwood chuckled and tipped his head, assessing James with unnerving intensity. "Fond of her, are ye?"

"I am." James found little point prevaricating to this colorful character of a man whose openness invited the same, or to himself. Not that he'd willingly volunteer any other details.

Blackwood's body rumbled with a knowing chuckle. "That was unexpected, I take it."

"Completely." James took a sip of coffee and shook his head. "Nothing about this journey has gone as I'd expected."

"Life does go that way, doesn't it?" Blackwood stared at the fire and let out what seemed to James a wistful sigh. "But I must say, *we* knew this day was coming. Or at least I told Cass so, the minute she got word the old devil had taken ill."

"Did she contact him?" James surmised the two had lost touch at the onset of his uncle's illness. And it sounded as if Rossbury hadn't had the funds or the physical strength to travel, but had Lady Cassandra gone to him?

"No, she'd come to loathe him and avoided his correspondence. She's a glorious woman, my Cassandra, but speak to her of practicalities and she doesnae want to know." He leaned forward, stretching out his arms to warm his hands by the fire. "I told her that bloody English earl wouldnae leave her a thing. Half expected some solicitor to toss her from Invermere long before ye." With a wave toward James, he added, "No insult to ye."

"Seeing as Drummond wanted you to kill me in a duel, I'll settle for an insult."

They exchanged a smile, and James felt an odd camaraderie with the man.

"So he truly left her nothing?"

"A piece of jewelry, according to Rossbury's solicitor. But, no, not the manor." James had never been proud to be related to Rufus Pembroke. Hell, he'd nursed his own resentments of the man all his life, but since arriving at Invermere, since meeting Lucy and learning more about Lady Cassandra, he truly understood what a small, cruel man he'd been.

"And you mean to sell quickly?"

"My shipping business needs an influx of capital." James tapped his fingers on the chair. He spoke as if Pembroke Shipping had merely hit a wave of low cash flow but more and more, he wondered if he could ever truly piece the enterprise back together.

"Never heard of an earl who's a shipping magnate before."

"I never intended to *be* an earl, and quite honestly my business has faltered." The memory of what he'd once been, and might never be again, was hitting hard of late.

Until meeting Lucy, the business had been his first waking thought and the last consideration before he closed his eyes. She was, without a doubt, a much more pleasant preoccupation. But without his business and his wealth, he fell far short of being a worthy suitor.

"So Invermere could prove to be your salvation." Blackwood settled back, stretched his arm along the back of the settee, and sighed. "I cannae but wonder what Cass will make of that."

"I would prefer to sell to her ladyship, of course. If she wishes to buy Invermere." James had hoped to save the discussion of the sale for Lady Cassandra's arrival, but he was curious to discover what Blackwood knew of her finances.

"You've no idea what sort of lady ye're dealing with, do ye?" Blackwood shot him a searching look, eyes narrowed. Then he stood and approached a corner of the room. With his back to James, he shuffled objects around, then emerged with a canvas he propped on top of a table, letting it lean against the wall nearby.

"You'll meet her soon."

"Lady Cassandra, I presume." The woman in the painting stared out at him confidently, the same sort of boldness he'd come to love in Lucy's gaze. And she hadn't been precious with her self-portrait. Her hair hung haphazardly, as if she'd captured her waves in pins and the wind had blown half of them free. Lines bracketed her mouth and the edges of her bright green eyes.

"A formidable woman, I promise ye, but not a wealthy one." Blackwood kept his gaze fixed on the lady in the portrait and offered her a gentle smile. "Stubborn, and that's the worst of it."

James swallowed a gulp of coffee as Blackwood returned to his spot on the settee. None of this was going to be easy. He'd known that much before he arrived, but he could have never guessed how quickly it would seem impossible.

"I could buy the place from ye twice over before the day is done."

"Can you?" James sat forward in his chair. "I'll agree to that, Blackwood."

The older man let out a laugh that cracked across the room like a shot. "Aye, and she'd have my head for it, man. Or at the very least, never forgive me, and I cannae bear to lose her."

"But you'll let her lose her home instead?"

"I did mention she was stubborn, did I no'?" Blackwood's lips tugged up in a sympathetic smile. "Heed me, Rossbury, that wee niece of hers is much like Cass. I wager you'll understand the extent of a lady's stubbornness soon enough."

James focused again on his coffee, determined to avoid the topic of Lucy for fear of giving too much away. Who knew what Blackwood would report to Lady Cassandra when she arrived. Though for all he'd heard of the lady, he suspected she was as intelligent and perceptive as her niece.

"Good morning, gentlemen."

James stood and turned at the sound of Lucy's

voice, and the usual sense of pleasure he felt at seeing her came with new feelings. Hunger and a fierce impulse to protect her.

Even while she shifted her gaze between them warily as if meddling men was the last thing she welcomed. How much of their conversation had she overheard?

"Perhaps we should allow Aunt Cassandra to have some say in her own affairs."

Apparently, she'd heard enough to be piqued on her aunt's behalf, and that James understood.

"Good morning, lass." When James stood, Blackwood had followed suit, though with the snap and pop of joints and a tired groan. "Trust that I will bow to Cassandra's will in all things, lass. His lordship and I were simply having a kindly chat." He swung his arm in James's direction. "Though I have yet to ask him how ye came to be in the same bedchamber last evening."

"Blackwood—" The protectiveness James felt for Lucy turned to something raw, and Blackwood immediately seemed less endearing.

"It's all right." Lucy's calm rebuff stalled him.

YEARS OF ETIQUETTE lessons and learning the rules of ladylike propriety meant Lucy knew how she should react to Mr. Blackwood's provocative statement. And beyond what she knew, her response was usually visceral when she did something wrong. Her skin would give her away first, turning from pink to strawberry red. Then her pulse would jump in her throat or blood would rush like crashing waves in her ears.

Today, she was thrilled to find old habits and silly rules could be overcome.

Upon her first glimpse of James, she'd struggled not to drop her gaze to his lips or go to him, touch him, greet him as she truly wished to.

But she couldn't manufacture an ounce of the anger and concern she saw in his eyes. She felt no shame for what she'd done, what they'd done. And absolutely no regret. Only frustration that they'd been interrupted by the man who was apparently her aunt's lover.

That man watched her now with a kindly expression. No judgment. Just a look of amusement, as if his words had been a tease rather than a condemnation.

"Since you were attempting to climb the walls of Invermere to get into my aunt's bedchamber, Mr. Blackwood, I trust you understand and would not dare question me about anything so delicate."

"I do understand, Lady Lucy. And by putting me in my place, I ken ye are well and truly Cassandra's kinswoman." The Scotsman bowed his head but couldn't manage to look abashed. "What I also understand is that you've come to Scotland for a holiday and haven't had much of one yet."

"There's still time." Lucy glanced again at James. An outing was one of the things she wished to discuss with him this morning—the idea that they might fit in some sightseeing before Aunt Cassandra's arrival.

"Have you explored the city?"

"No, but I'd like to. It's on my list."

"Edinburgh is a grand notion for a day trip."

James started to speak, cast her an odd look, and then fell silent. But she wanted to hear from him much more than make small talk with Mr. Blackwood.

Lucy arched a brow, urging him to say something, and he stepped toward her but still seemed tongue-tied or reticent to speak in front of anyone else.

She turned her politest smile toward Angus Blackwood. "May I have a word with his lordship?"

"Of course, my lady."

Blackwood was kind enough to draw the door almost closed behind him, leaving only a respectable hairbreadth gap.

"I was planning a quick trip into the city on business," James told her when they were alone.

That caused the blush that she should have felt earlier. Because the prospect of a trip alone with him was precisely what she'd imagined from the moment she opened her eyes.

"Will you take me with you? If we're not long, we should be back in time for Aunt Cassandra's arrival, don't you think?"

"Either that, or your aunt will return before we do and think I've fled with you."

He reached for her hands, and she rested her

palms against his. All the excitement of spending a day with him still buzzed inside of her. She wanted to depart as soon as they could.

But he wasn't feeling the same. Even on short acquaintance, she was learning to read his true feelings through his usual charm.

"I need to visit my solicitor in the city."

"Would you rather go into Edinburgh alone?"

"No." He slid his thumb across the backs of her fingers. "And I'd rather you didn't go alone either, but I also don't want business matters to ruin the first outing of your holiday."

"I am capable of compromise. If anything, I've compromised too often."

"Which is why you shouldn't have to now."

"I propose we enjoy the city a bit first, then I can find myself a cup of tea while you attend your meeting."

"Lucy, I can't say how long it may take."

"I can be patient."

He laughed at that, a full beaming smile that made that fizzing start again in her middle.

Lucy rolled her eyes when he struggled to stop laughing. "All right, all right. You've seen little evidence of that, which is even more reason for me to prove it to you."

"We should leave soon."

"I can be ready in half an hour."

He arched one black brow skeptically.

Before Lucy could offer up some tart retort, Blackwood stepped into the room again.

"Cassandra may wish me to hell for this, but I think it's a grand idea." The older man thumped James congenially on the back on his way across the room. "If my lady returns before ye, I'll be here to welcome her." He cast a glance at James before turning to face Lucy. "The news of the inheritance might fall softer coming from me."

"I still hope we can be back before she arrives. With a couple hours in the city, does that seem reasonable?" Lucy didn't think anything would truly soften the news about Invermere, and learning that her niece was off on a jaunt with the man who owned her home might not go over well either.

But her aunt would want her to enjoy her time in Scotland, and whatever his reasons, the mischievous twinkle in his eye indicated Mr. Blackwood was enjoying his turn at playing matchmaker.

"If you take the train from Inverkeithing, you may."

"There's a connecting train from Edinburgh?" Lucy began to doubt her planning abilities, or at least the accuracy of *The Merry Wanderer* travel guide she'd relied on.

"Aye. Station's not five miles from the manor."

"Then we'll go. Expect us back in the afternoon." James looked almost as excited as she felt now that it was settled.

"Take my carriage to the station, if you like," Blackwood urged. "I'll go and speak to my driver now."

"Thank you, Blackwood." Once he was gone,

James drew closer. Close enough to touch, though Lucy resisted. They'd yet to speak of last night, and she wasn't yet sure if their feelings were the same.

"Do you wish for a chaperone?" He asked the question with such seriousness that she couldn't help but smile. His desire to do the gentlemanly, proper thing after they'd gone far beyond the bounds of what would be expected of her somehow endeared him to her more.

"Do you?" Lucy tried for an innocent expression.

"Not at all." He winked and leaned even closer, lowering his voice. "Though I do seem to struggle with following the rules when you're about."

"Well, I appreciate the attempt."

"Do you?" His eyes glittered, creasing at the edges as he smiled down at her.

"Of course. Having a care for my reputation is thoughtful. But I'm tired of rules and have decided to pursue what I want quite single-mindedly. I'm not willing to go back to the way I was."

He swallowed hard and dropped his gaze to her lips.

"I have no regrets about coming to your room, James. You may call me incorrigible if you like."

All the teasing fell away, and he looked contemplative for a moment, staring out the window over her shoulder. He seemed to be weighing a decision.

Lucy's breath caught in her throat. On the archery field, she'd felt certain he was going to kiss her. Now she feared he was going to set her straight about his feelings. Maybe he really did consider her nothing more than an impetuous girl.

But then he dipped his head to look at her, and it was that look that only he had ever given her. As if she was fascinating. As if he didn't want to look away.

"Meet me out front in half an hour, Lucy the Incorrigible."

Chapter Thirteen

Lucy pitched forward, and James reached out, gripping her upper arms to keep her on the bench of the carriage. She blew at strands of hair that had slipped their pins.

"Blackwood did say it was fast." James inched forward on his seat, better to serve as a buffer if Blackwood's reckless driver took another turn like he had the last. "Are you all right?"

"I am, but I shall never forget this five-mile carriage ride." She clutched the same valise she'd brought with her from London. "At least I haven't spilled my bag this trip."

"Yet." James laughed when she narrowed her eyes at that. "You don't travel light, do you? Let me carry that when we get to the city?"

"I thought I'd been quite restrained. Just my travel guide, a list of potential sights to see, and my sketchbook."

"A sketchbook? Will you allow me to have a look?"

She gripped her valise tighter. "I'm afraid I don't let anyone see my drawings."

"Fair enough." James imagined flowers, perhaps

animals, and definitely faces. Maybe even his? But most of all, he wanted her to trust that he wouldn't insist. If she wished to show him, he wanted her to do so freely.

As she'd come to his bedroom freely.

"I'll think about it," she added a moment later. "My brother and sister used to tease me because I had a passion for drawing but very little natural talent."

"That's categorically untrue from what I saw in your aunt's conservatory."

"Oh, I've gotten better. In fact, their teasing probably pushed me to do so. A need to prove myself."

James felt a resonance with that deep in his chest. "I understand."

"Do you have beastly siblings too?"

"I don't have any brothers or sisters."

She sat forward, eyes wide. "I can't imagine the freedom in that. Did it make you more independent?"

"Independence was a necessity."

The softness in her eyes made him want to retreat. Even telling Blackwood this morning felt odd, yet somehow freeing. Still, he'd never divulged such maudlin details to any lady of his acquaintance. He couldn't bear their pity or for a woman he desired to think of him as the frightened boy he'd once been. And it had always been simple because he'd never allowed himself close enough to be tempted to share his long-ago nightmare.

But Lucy wasn't just *any* lady. Somehow, after

only a few days of knowing her, his usual evasive tactics seemed wrong. He felt closer to her than he had to anyone in a very long time.

"I lost my parents when I was a boy."

"I'm so sorry." She reached across the distance between them and clasped his hand. He stilled, but she didn't let go.

He finally clasped her hand in return, but he was saved from saying more when the carriage stopped, and the driver ushered them toward the small station's platform.

"I'll carry that." James claimed her valise and found it *was* far lighter than on the journey to Edinburgh.

"Fine," she called back to him. "Promise not to peek in my sketchbook."

They obtained tickets and found they'd arrived with only minutes to spare before the morning train. There were only two carriages, and the seats were first come, first serve with no private cars.

James pointed to an open bench, allowing Lucy the window seat. When he reached up to put her valise on the rail above them, she made a little noise of protest, and he placed it on the seat next to her.

As soon as he slid onto the bench, she settled her valise near the window so that there was nothing between them. He happily closed the space until they were elbow to elbow.

"Tell me what's on your list."

"The castle, of course. Nelson's monument. Calton Hill."

James looked down as her finger traced the list she'd made.

"Camera Obscura? That sounds like something you'd like."

"Yes. It sounds fascinating. It's a mechanism that uses lenses and mirrors to give a view of the city." She turned in her seat and laid a hand on his arm, gripping the fabric of his coat lightly. "It's exactly the place I was thinking of suggesting, but I didn't know if you'd prefer something more—"

"It's your holiday, Lucy. You only need to please yourself."

She smiled in a manner that in any other young woman he'd call shy. "That makes me feel terribly spoiled." She settled back in her seat but wrapped her arm around his.

The simple gesture fired his blood and yet comforted him too. At least for this moment, she'd chosen him.

If making independent choices made her feel spoiled, he wondered at how strict and straitlaced her parents must be. This trip truly was an escape for her, and he hoped she could enjoy herself today, despite how things might change upon her aunt's arrival. This might very well be his last chance to spend time alone with her.

When he fell quiet, Lucy turned her attention toward the window. She tapped her finger at the edge of her sketchbook, and James wondered if she also sensed that this outing together might be their last.

"Blackwood is an interesting character," she said quietly. "What do you think of him?"

"He cares for your aunt a great deal. That is clear."

"You truly think so?" She turned back to him, and for the first time he noticed a dusting of cinnamon-colored freckles on her nose and cheeks.

"He offered to buy Invermere for her."

She reared back at that, and her green eyes widened.

"Will he?" She'd let go of his arm and laid a hand briefly on his thigh. "That would solve everything, wouldn't it?"

"According to Blackwood, your aunt would never allow such a thing."

She let out a long sigh. "She is a stubborn lady."

"That's what he said." James chuckled. "He thought perhaps you take after her in that respect." He side-eyed her and smiled when she let out a little gasp of outrage.

"I'm *not* stubborn," she said through gritted teeth. Stubbornly.

James let out a laugh too loud for politeness and several of the passengers nearby stared and some offered loudly whispered condemnations. As soon as he got himself under control, Lucy started, pressing a hand to her mouth to stop from making as much noise as he had.

Afterward, she smiled up at him, her shoulder nudging his slightly. He made the mistake of noticing her lips. Her gorgeous expressive lips. Then her gaze dropped to his mouth, and the desire between them became a tangible thing.

He hadn't been able to kiss her properly last night, and he wanted to make up for it now.

Reaching out, he stroked his fingers along her cheek, her skin petal soft and warmed by the sun.

Ignoring all the reasons he shouldn't, he slid his hand along her neck, cupping her nape to draw her closer.

"No!" A man's voice rose above the din of chatter in the train car. "Someone, please—"

When the passengers in front of them turned to see what caused the commotion, James turned too, still holding on to Lucy.

At the same moment, she slipped from his grasp and landed in his lap. He let out a half gasp, half groan at the feel of her sweet, round backside sliding across his groin, but then she was gone. She'd climbed over him to get out into the aisle, where dozens of documents fluttered from a suitcase on the rail across from them.

"Forgive me," she whispered to James. "I need to help him.

"Let me," she said to a bespectacled older man who was trying unsuccessfully to capture the falling papers in his arms, especially when the ladies seated around him barked at him when he tried to retrieve papers that had fallen on or near them.

The lady sitting below the railing, where the burst suitcase sat, shrieked when a tied bundle knocked her hat askew before falling into the aisle.

A few other passengers stood but weren't doing much to aid the unfortunate man.

James leaned into the aisle and scooped up what he could, then tried to assemble them into a neat pile, though whatever order they'd been in was completely lost.

"Here are these," he told Lucy, who'd knelt in the aisle to scoop stray documents from under the train benches and collect those that had drifted further up the aisle.

He helped her as much as he could, though the aisle was narrow and the minute he stepped into it, he trod on a few papers and felt like a menace.

It took a good quarter of an hour to collect every last piece they could find, and Lucy wouldn't stop attending to the man until he was settled back in his seat, busy sorting his collection, his suitcase secured as well as it could be with a broken latch.

When she approached their bench, James slid out to let her reclaim her place by the window.

"I've only seen one other person react to someone in need that quickly."

"Really? Who was that?" For the first time since they'd met, she seemed uncomfortable with his regard. As if she feared he was judging her harshly, when the opposite was true.

"She was a nurse at an East End clinic."

"I'd be an awful nurse. Blood makes me queasy, as you'll recall."

"I do, but I still admire your instinct to rush to the aid of others." Especially since he'd trained himself to look after his own survival first. And on more than one occasion, looking to his own well-being and learning how to fend for himself had kept him alive.

"Thank you." She busied herself resetting her cuffs, pushing in strands of hair that had come loose, and generally ignoring him. Then turned and asked, "Why were you in an East End clinic?"

Oh, she was good. At deflecting her unease with praise toward a new topic, but also giving him cause to reveal more of his history with her searching green eyes and endless curiosity. But he was just as skilled at deflecting unwanted attention.

"You're not a lady who particularly likes praise, are you?"

"I do." Her tone rose to a defensive pitch, then she sighed, which he took as an admission. "I like it as much as anyone, I suspect. But what you said about helping others. I'm not sure I deserve that praise. Especially since I came to Scotland to escape it."

Before he had time to make sense of her comment, the train arrived at the station and the moment it came to a stop, passengers were out of their seats, collecting luggage and moving toward the doors.

"We're here." She breathed the words and had that same dreamy look as the first moment he'd laid eyes on her. Though she'd already been to Waverley Station, so once they were off the train, she was more than happy to find their way to the street.

"The Camera Obscura is at the Outlook Tower, and it's this way according to my map." She twisted her travel guide in her hands and showed him the map.

But he trusted her navigational skills and had no interest in the map. Only in her and the joy she seemed to find in things as simple as a flower seller's cart overflowing with hothouse blooms under the chilly autumn sky.

"Would you like some?"

"No, where would I put them while we're at the tower?"

Her practicality made him chuckle, especially since he'd always considered himself the practical sort.

"When we're heading back to Invermere then."

"That would be lovely." She reached for his arm, then hesitated.

To anyone watching, they must seem a courting couple. James hated that he couldn't truly offer her anything so formal and simple. He offered his arm anyway and savored the moment she slid her hand in the crook of his elbow. Savored the fact that she trusted him and allowed him the privilege of having her body pressed against his.

Courtship or not, he wanted to touch her not because it was what was expected, but because she was becoming the only thing he thought about, day and night.

She walked quickly, and even with his long-legged stride, she tugged him along.

"Don't worry. We arrived in good time and have hours before the return train."

"I don't want you to have to rush your meeting with the solicitor."

"We have no set time, and if I must, I'll merely leave a message for the man directing him to have the surveyor sent immediately." James stopped her, guiding her off the pavement toward the awning of a shop. "Today is for you to savor."

Unspoken emotion made her eyes glitter. She didn't smile, but her mouth softened. For a moment, she looked away from him.

"Us," she said with quiet determination. "A day for us to savor. To remember."

He would remember each day, each moment he'd spent with her, but neither of them wanted to say aloud what it seemed they were both thinking. And that suited James just fine.

"Then let's go make it memorable."

LUCY KEPT LOOKING back as they climbed the tower that housed the Camera Obscura to make sure James was still behind her. There'd been a moment on the sidewalk when something seemed to catch his eye, and he'd been distracted since.

But he was there each time she looked back, smiling up at her. "Keep going. I want to see it."

She did too. They'd already been at the site for nearly half an hour, reviewing the lower floors that contained exhibits detailing history and points of interest in Scotland.

The Camera Obscura was bigger than she expected, an enormous concave bowl that reflected an actual view of Edinburgh at that moment.

James stood behind her, his hand warm and comforting at the small of her back, while they waited their turn to be among the half dozen visitors who could circle around the reflective bowl at once.

When their time finally came, James let her stand close and took a spot behind her as a lady in an enormous, plumed hat took up far more space than she should have.

The reflected image of the city was extraordinary.

"Look," Lucy said to him quietly, pointing to the movement you could see as pedestrians walked the streets in the wide panoramic view. "It's remarkable."

"Like an enormous magnifying glass." He bent closer, his body as near as they'd been that day on the archery field.

Lucy tipped her head so she could watch him, and warmth spilled through her veins. She recognized his expression. It was the same way he sometimes looked at her, as if observing something he truly thought magnificent.

When a guide ushered them along, Lucy realized she'd enjoyed watching James's reaction to the camera as much as the phenomenon of the camera itself.

"What next?" he asked when they'd made their way out of the exhibition and onto the street.

"Your meeting, yes?"

"Not yet." He glanced at his pocket watch, then shoved it back into his waistcoat pocket. "Give me another place on your list."

Lucy wasn't ready for their time together to end either. "We're close to Calton Hill."

"Then that's next." He lifted his arm again, and they fell in step together.

Lucy led them up the Royal Mile, and though they'd traveled to Edinburgh from one of the most bustling cities in the world, they both gaped at the buildings, shops, and old churches as the visitors they were.

"If only I had time to stop and sketch."

"I wish you did. Perhaps you can come back."

Come back. She understood that he meant without him. How could he make plans when his priority was to sell Invermere and return to his business, to London?

She had the fleeting impulse to ask if they might meet again when all of this was done. But he'd offered nothing beyond today, and she was determined to relish the next few hours.

"Don't worry. We'll get back in time." He mistook her lack of reply as worry about Aunt Cassandra.

"I know. Just woolgathering."

The grade changed as they climbed toward the top of the hill, and Lucy gasped at the city laid out below them in a gorgeous tableau of sandstone buildings dotted with church spires. Lucy took a few steps to get a better view, and bumped into James, who stood staring at the lovely Stewart Monument.

He wrapped an arm around her to keep her from slipping. "We seem to have a habit of bumping into each other."

Lucy pressed a hand to his chest, burrowing it under the lapels of his coat to lay her palm over the spot where his heart beat strong and steady.

Looking around, she found they were mostly alone in this spot on the hill.

"Kiss me?"

His fingers traced the seam at the back of her gown, sending shivers down her spine.

"That's an excellent question," he said with a husky teasing tone.

Lucy slid two fingers between the buttons of his shirt and a pulse of need swept down her body when she stroked his bare skin beneath.

"And your answer?"

Chapter Fourteen

*H*e couldn't answer in words, couldn't wait to taste her again.

Go slow, he told himself, but he was beyond that now.

She was too. Her hands curled around the lapels of his coat, and she pulled him closer as he bent to take her lips. It felt as if he'd held her like this a thousand times before. That's how right it was to hold this woman in his arms.

But the kiss was new. And it felt like the beginning of everything he truly wanted. What he'd been searching for too long.

She reached up to stroke his cheek and drew her fingers along his jaw. A stroke he felt like a lick of fire from his head to his toes. He traced his tongue along the sweet fullness of her bottom lip, and she let out a pleased gasp.

Under the fabric of her cloak, he traced a hand down her back, pulling her flush against him. The heat of their joined bodies warmed something deep inside him, and he let out a little growl of satisfaction when she followed his lead and drew her tongue across his lips.

"Lucy," he whispered against her lips, and she pulled her head back, breathless, her mouth flushed from their kisses.

"Don't stop." She glanced around them. "There's no one about, and I don't care about propriety. I want this moment with you."

James chuckled and bent to nuzzle her cheek, then taste the floral-scented softness of her neck.

"I hadn't planned to stop."

"Oh." Her seductive smile held so many promises.

"You're beautiful."

She blinked and her eyes turned glassy. "Just kiss me."

He did, stroking a finger along her lips and then bending to taste her. This time she opened to him, letting him taste deeply. But it was clear she wasn't content to let him take the lead. She kissed him hungrily, her hands exploring beneath his coat, pushing his waistcoat aside to get her palm against his chest.

He was hers in that moment, and she was his. And that was what he wanted. She was what he wanted, even if this kiss would be all they had.

Lucy broke their kiss first. She turned her gaze toward a couple ascending the hill a few feet away.

He'd been too lost in her to hear their muted conversation, but she was more observant.

"We should probably go," she said with all the disappointment he felt in his chest.

They still held on to each other, and she lifted her head to kiss him once more.

"You're right." He hated it, but she was being practical. He'd been practical once. Good grief, a few days had changed everything.

"You still have your meeting to get to."

"My meeting." For the first time since learning he'd inherited a Scottish manor that could mean the ability to turn his financial woes around, he considered whether there was any other way.

Not that he hadn't exhausted every other way. Not that he hadn't been trying to change his fortune for nearly a year.

Selling Invermere could finally give him back all he'd lost, but now there was also the possibility that it would cost him any connection with Lucy. Something in his gut—those old instincts he'd once believed in so fiercely—told him that once he took possession of her home, Lady Cassandra would not be happy to see him continue any kind of acquaintance with her niece.

Lucy kept her gaze focused on her travel guide as they walked, and he kept a firm hold on her arm to keep her from stumbling.

"I found it!" She stopped short, pulling him off stride. "There's a tearoom just down the lane from where you said your solicitor's offices are located."

James noted the name and then scanned the street ahead. "Just there. And Abercrombie's office should be in the building over there."

The tearoom wasn't opulent, but somehow that made it more charming. He preferred simplicity to busyness and grandeur, even when he'd had plenty of money to spend on luxuries.

"It's perfect," she said enthusiastically. "I'll be quite happy to wait for you here."

James was immediately sorry he couldn't sit with her and have a leisurely luncheon together. But even if he hadn't glanced at his watch in nearly an hour, he sensed the time slipping away. Their day together would soon come to an end.

Lucy mistook his expression and tried to reassure him. "I'll be fine. And you'll be back soon. Maybe I can recall enough of what we've seen to do some sketching."

James brushed a kiss on her cheek, and that alone bolstered him for the meeting with Abercrombie. A few minutes later, he rushed across the street, eager to have it done.

Inside a wood-paneled office with the name Abercrombie carefully painted on the outer door, James found a clerk who peered at him over the rim of his spectacles.

"May I help you, sir?"

"Lord Rossbury to see Mr. Abercrombie. I'm afraid he's not expecting me, but this won't take long."

"Unfortunately, Mr. Abercrombie isn't in until later in the day. My name is Cairns. Is there something I could help you with, my lord?"

"When I spoke to him three days ago, he promised to send a surveyor north to assess a house I've inherited."

"Let me have a look. Won't take more than a moment." The young man gestured toward a row of sturdy chairs lined up against a wall and didn't wait for any response from James before leaving his desk and entering another room.

James couldn't bring himself to sit, so he paced, but that did nothing to calm his nerves either. He could taste Lucy on his lips, still feel the warmth and softness of her body pressed against his. He wanted to get back to her. Blessedly, the young man returned only a few minutes later with a single half sheet of paper held out to James.

Mr. Dougray Dickson were the only words written on the paper.

"The surveyor, my lord. According to Mr. Abercrombie's notes, he contacted the man two days ago, and he was set to arrive today."

Bloody wonderful. "Thank you, Mr. Cairns."

James was already halfway across the threshold when he heard the young man wish him a good day.

It had been. A perfect day up to a moment ago, but now it seemed fated to go to hell.

Lady Cassandra would already be frantic to learn that her visiting niece had gone off with the man who planned to turn her world upside down, but he suspected she'd be fuming to find a surveyor there inspecting the manor as if it was a commodity rather than her home.

As he made his way back up the street toward the tearoom, he noted that blue-gray clouds blanketed the sky, hiding the sun that had warmed them during their walk around Edinburgh. It made the hour seem much later than it was, but he ducked toward a shop window and pulled out his pocket watch to double-check.

He'd lost track of everything but Lucy during that kiss on the hill.

That's when he sensed the figure in his periphery turn swiftly, a gray coat swinging as the man stared into a shop window as if something had caught his eye. There were dozens of window-shoppers up and down the busy thoroughfare, but something about the man looked familiar. He'd seen that dove-gray greatcoat earlier in the day. Though it wasn't an uncommon shade for a garment.

James continued on, walking slower now, and turned his head to note whether the man followed.

Heartbeat speeding, he forced himself to maintain his steady pace. He spied a narrow alleyway between buildings ahead, just one building down from the tearoom. Veering to the opposite side of the pavement, he ducked into the narrow space. Hardly an alley, a throughway more like, too narrow for vehicles, barely wide enough to contain the span of his shoulders.

But he turned around, his arms brushing the bricks on either side, and waited.

People passed but not the gray-coated man.

James approached the mouth of the passageway, one step away from joining the stream of foot traffic on the pavement again, and scanned the far side of the street.

He saw no one, but a shiver down his back told him he was being watched. The man's gaze was a heavy, menacing weight.

James turned and spotted the man near a storefront, on his side of the street now, just a few paces away. And worse, he recognized him—or thought he did—as one of Beck's thugs.

Would he send a watcher this far? And how did the man know he'd been in the city today of all days?

He couldn't take a chance of embroiling Lucy in anything to do with Beck.

Turning again, he made his way down the narrow passageway, hoping it would spill out into a proper alley. Then he might find a rear entrance to the tearoom where Lucy waited.

Only a few steps, and another's footsteps crunched on the gravel behind him.

James didn't want a confrontation. He required no reminder of what was owed, or of Beck's impatience for his long overdue repayment.

It troubled him every single day.

When the pace of the footsteps quickened, he spun to face the man.

"What do you want?"

The man stopped and stood watching, but said nothing.

James cursed himself for not bringing a weapon on this journey.

"What do you want?" James shouted the words this time. "You have some message to deliver?"

The man was silent so long that James had decided to ignore him and make his way back to Lucy, but the minute he started to turn, the man's voice rumbled across the distance.

"Beck wants you watched. So I watch."

James gave the man one last glance and continued down the rest of the passageway, pushing his gait as wide as he could to eat up the space between him and Lucy. Surprisingly, Beck's man made no move to follow. But the relief of that seeped away when he realized it might be because he'd seen exactly where he and Lucy had parted, and he meant to get to her first.

James broke into a sprint when he reached the crossway. Just as he'd hoped, it was a mews that ran behind the shops that lined the street.

There was no real indication that the next building was the rear of the tearoom. No signage. But James couldn't take time for much exploration. He tried the rear door and found it unlocked.

"And who might ye be?" A red-faced woman wearing an apron and white bonnet planted herself in his path after he'd barely gotten through the door. Her appearance and the wafting scent of roasted savories and baked goods made him sigh in relief.

"I confess I'm a bit lost, my good lady. Is that the way to the tearoom?" He pointed behind her.

"Ye've taken the wrong path, braw man. But aye, go on with ye."

James sketched a little bow and offered the

lady the best smile he could muster, then continued down the short hall of the busy kitchen and through a swinging door that led into the tearoom.

Lucy stood out among the other guests. She sat at the front of the tearoom and was the one lady who dined alone. Her sketchbook lay open in front of her, but her gaze was fixed on the window as she watchfully took in the activity on the street.

Had she been watching and seen him disappear from view?

The desire to go to her made his muscles ache with tension, but he preferred taking care with their next steps. The hell of it was that he couldn't be sure if his watcher had gone back to the street and followed him into the alley.

He had to choose, and exiting through the front door and joining the crowds back on the street where they could hire a carriage seemed the best course.

As soon as he started toward her, Lucy turned.

"James." The sweetness of her grin warmed him from across the room. He couldn't recall anyone in his life ever looking so pleased to see him. But somehow it also heightened his fear. Not for himself, but for her.

"I've only had tea so far. I decided to wait on food so we could dine together, but I'm famished."

"I'm afraid we have to go, Lucy."

"Just a quick bite? They have a lemon cake that

looks scrumptious." She reached for the menu at the edge of the table.

"We must go now."

The same hollowness he'd felt when informing friends that they'd lost their investment because of his foolishness opened up inside him as he watched Lucy's pleasure at seeing him turn to disappointment.

"I'm sorry. But I would not insist if it wasn't urgent."

"Has something happened?" She stood, collecting her things as she watched him, searching his face for the answers he wasn't giving her.

"Can we discuss it once we've hired a carriage and are on our way out of Edinburgh?" James helped her finish filling her bag and slung it over his shoulder before dropping a few coins on the table and leading her through the front door.

"Are we not catching the train in half an hour?"

"A carriage would serve us better." James glanced each way down the street, and though the foot traffic had thinned under the darkening sky, he didn't spot the watcher.

A hansom cab rattled by, and James moved toward the curb, scanning ahead for another.

"There's one." Lucy waved the driver down.

"Well done." James tried for a light tone, but she watched him warily out of the corner of her eye after they'd settled into the cab.

"Waverley Station," he told the driver.

"Are we catching the train, then? We could have walked in the time it will take the cab to deliver us."

James placed his hand over hers where it lay in her lap, holding tight to her bag.

"The explanation is coming, I promise. I thought the station would be the best place to hire a coach to take us to Invermere."

She had every right to be curious and wonder at his behavior. Truth be told, he wasn't relishing the explanation. But she deserved one.

At the station, Lucy seemed as intent as he to find them a coach.

"There he is!"

Before he could stop her, Lucy darted off toward a man in a weathered greatcoat. The man's coat was pitch-black, clearly not the watcher he'd encountered on Princes Street. James approached as she began a conversation with the man.

"He'll take us," she told him. "And helpfully, he knows the way. This is Mr. Tavish. He's the coachman who delivered me to Invermere."

The man touched his cap as he acknowledged James. A few minutes later, they were on their way.

Lucy settled onto the bench across from him, loosening the tie of her cloak before slipping it off. Sitting across from her reminded him of their first train ride together.

He'd expected that journey to change his life but never expected it would be because of the noblewoman he'd met on the platform.

She studied him boldly, tracing the features of

his face, even glancing down at his shoulders, his chest, his legs. As if she was memorizing him or preparing to paint his portrait.

"I'm ready now," she told him.

Her softly spoken words melted the tension of the past hour, and he smiled.

"I'm ready for your explanation."

Chapter Fifteen

Lucy had quite a bit of experience with gentlemen being appalled by her. She'd asked enough awkward questions and interrupted a sufficient number of pompous young men to see shock, offense, and even disdain on men's faces for years.

But she'd never truly cared about any of them. They were cads or fawning fortune hunters who cornered her at a dinner party one moment and were forgotten the next.

However, James Pembroke wasn't a man she would soon forget, and despite her resolve not to become smitten with the first handsome gentleman she met during this adventure of independence, she feared that she had. Become smitten, that was.

Utterly and irrevocably.

What she saw in his eyes now—fear and the desire to avoid her and this conversation—pained her in a deep part of her heart that she'd thought impervious to things like infatuation and charming scoundrels.

"I need to know—"

"I know." He didn't shout the words, but the way he cut her off made her clench her teeth.

She trusted him. So much that she'd allowed him to touch her, allowed herself to be alone with him from almost the moment they met. Good heavens, she'd gone to his bedroom in the dead of night intent on making him the first man—perhaps the only man—to kiss her.

But he couldn't trust her with whatever seemed to be eating at him from the inside out. And the worst of it was that she'd always known. He'd been reticent on the train, and she'd accepted that because they were strangers, even if there'd never truly been a moment when she hadn't felt an inexplicable connection with him.

At Invermere, he'd told her more. But still not enough. Just puzzle pieces that didn't quite fit together. Certainly not enough to get a clear picture. So why did she feel so certain that she knew him? Understood him?

She was a young lady who liked facts, and the fact was that she hardly knew James Pembroke at all.

"I'm not sure where to start," he said roughly.

Lucy held her breath, for the first time in her life not at all certain what to do. How to help.

"I want to hear it all," she told him in a near whisper. "So, whatever it is, and whenever you're ready, I'm listening."

He took a breath, and she finally released hers. This was it. He *was* willing to trust her after all.

Then minutes ticked by. She fancied she could

hear the tick of his pocket watch, or maybe it was the thump of his heartbeat.

"There was a train accident when I was nine." He rushed the words out on a single breath, then seemed to give in to the memory. A darkness in his faraway gaze told her that he could see it all clearly in his mind's eye. "One minute, we were rolling along, watching the countryside pass. My mother pointed out a kind of tree she liked. A willow tree." He shook his head and looked at her. "I was so focused on her that I hardly noticed we'd started over the bridge."

Lucy inhaled sharply.

"The structure folded like it was made of sticks. Everything next only comes in flashes. Pieces. I don't have the whole of it even now. The sounds and smells stay with me more than anything." His breathing had quickened, and he swallowed hard. "I feel it here." A fist pressed to his chest. "My heart beats erratically just as I suspect it did that day. I remember my mother's voice." His gaze fixed on hers. "She told me not to worry." The smile that curved his mouth was the saddest she'd ever seen.

Lucy reached up to grip the leather strap near the carriage door and moved from her bench to the spot next to him. He said nothing but reached out to steady her.

She laid her open hand, palm up, in her lap, leaving it there if he wished for that contact.

He did.

They held each other tightly, fingers laced.

"So now you understand my loathing for locomotives." The teasing tone she knew well did nothing to wash the misery from his gaze.

"Now you must know of my downfall. More details than I ever wished to tell you. Facts I still fear might entangle you in ways you don't deserve."

"Just tell me."

"I was very successful. Wealthier than I sometimes thought I had any right to be. And my thirst for competition and, yes, probably an ounce or two of greed kept me watchful for new ventures." He glanced over at her thoughtfully. "You'd think that after surviving on the streets of London for years, I'd understand the dangers of trusting anyone."

"That sounds very bleak."

"Safe. That's how I thought of it. Let no one in, and no one can truly harm you." He squeezed her hand, and Lucy tried not to think too much about what that single gesture might mean.

"But I'd surpassed needing to survive. I was comfortable. *Arrogant.* I needed funds after a failed business venture, and that's when he approached. A man I'd heard of in certain circles as a financier. He presented himself as an ally, a friend. He promised the world and seemed to be able to deliver."

"He befriended you?"

"He cultivated me, and he loaned me funds immediately. The quickness of it was seductive. I needed capital and he had it, and he seemed to believe in my ability to save my shipping business.

But after the failed venture, I lost the respect of colleagues and the confidence of customers. Clients went elsewhere. Opportunities dried up. I'd already lost thousands in the venture. I couldn't repay Beck in full even after selling off the ships in my fleet."

When he paused, Lucy was glad for it. The misery in his tone made her own throat ache. She'd heard of men taken in by investment schemes and ending in financial ruin. She'd heard of nefarious moneylenders who preyed on such men too. She even knew of one nobleman who'd taken his life after bringing his family to the brink of poverty when he'd lost his fortune on a failed business venture.

"Beck isn't the only one to blame. The responsibility is mine. The failure is mine." He stopped again, drawing in a long breath as if steeling himself for whatever came next. "And it's not over. Even after I sold my ships, liquidated my assets, I still owed Beck. I owe him yet."

"And selling the manor will allow you to pay him?"

"Yes. For whatever reason, he's lost patience with waiting for me to settle my accounts with him. He'd once been content with payments whenever I was able, but he's a changeable, ruthless man."

"Dangerous?"

"He employs those who are. Apparently, Beck's background isn't so different from my own. He grew up fighting in back alleys and brings those tactics to the boardroom now."

"You fought in back alleys?"

He offered her a sad smile. "I did what I had to in order to survive. Fighting in alleys wasn't common and certainly wasn't anything I sought. But competition for work, for food, for lodgings was fierce."

"I'm so sorry it was all so difficult." This time Lucy squeezed his hand and laid her other on top of their clasped fingers.

"So, you learned that Beck was unscrupulous too late?"

James stared out the carriage window and a sound rumbled in his chest, like the echo of laughter without the laugh itself.

"I was a fool. I realized everything too late."

Lucy had more pieces now, and she tried to draw the picture of this Beck man and James's entanglement with him in her mind. She understood that an unsavory lender might want their funds back and use force to get them.

"You have that look," James said to her with a little of his usual teasing tone. "Like you're scheming."

"Just trying to work it all out. Beck can only allow his brutal tactics to go so far. If he kills you, then he'll never get his money back."

"True enough, but there's a great deal of harm you can do to a man other than kill him." He turned then and looked at her, not in the heated way he sometimes did. His eyes were full of concern and a fierce protectiveness.

"You think . . . he'd harm me?"

"Before I left London, he sent men to my home. Frightened my staff. Threw around threats. They departed, but I've no idea if they came back. And"—he ducked his head, and when he faced her again, his expression had hardened—"I was followed today in Edinburgh."

Pebbles of gooseflesh rose on Lucy's skin, and she fought to hold back a shiver. "Followed by whom?"

"A man I'd seen at Beck's warehouse during a meeting."

"Did he harm you?" Lucy scanned his body as if she might be able to see through the fabric to check for bruises or scratches.

"No. The fear is what Beck likes. Intimidation. I suppose the man was meant to be a reminder."

"So somehow he heard of your departure from London."

"Which means he has probably induced some member of my staff, and I hate even contemplating how."

"You need to get back, don't you?" Lucy struggled to keep the disappointment from her voice. She'd miss him so very much. "It's why you kept emphasizing how urgent this trip was."

"At least you understand a little better." He released her hand and settled into the squabs, pushing his back against the bench. "And now you know the man I am. A fool with exceedingly poor judgment and very few pounds to his name."

He held up a finger as if he'd recalled something

more. "Plus a title, of course. I wonder what Beck will make of that."

Lucy laid a hand across his wrist. "But maybe that will help you. If he learns of your inheritance and the earldom, perhaps he'll have more patience. He'll be more convinced his money is coming soon."

"The earldom is skint, Lucy."

"But does Beck know that?"

"My god, you're clever."

Lucy beamed inwardly but she wasn't ready to allow his compliments to make her melt just yet. "And your title might work on others too. Perhaps you could secure a loan to—"

"No more loans. I can't take on more debt when I already owe one of the most unsavory devils in London."

Lucy stared at him a moment, studying his handsome face, noting the signs of worry and fatigue. Wishing with all her heart that he'd hear her without letting his fears and self-recriminations keep him from good solutions.

"I understand you lost a great deal, and you blame yourself as much as this terrible man, Beck. Once fooled, twice shy, isn't that what they say?"

"I believe it's *bitten*." He chuckled. "But close enough."

"I think you should consider any means to get out from under the man's influence." He'd assumed Invermere would allow him to do that, of course. "And I'm not just saying this as some device to keep you from selling the manor. I know you must."

At that, he only nodded. He seemed suddenly exhausted by his revelations. Though they were sitting so close their arms and thighs bumped each other's with every rut and turn in the road, he seemed to have distanced himself. Drawn inside himself. And Lucy didn't know how to get him back or follow.

HAVING IT OUT, all of the ugly truth laid unvarnished before her, brought James a sense of relief. An actual physical lightness that he could feel in his chest, as if everything he'd kept back had been ballast weighing him down.

But once the truth was out, one had to look at it, examining every ugly piece. And Lucy, in her spectacular way, wanted to find a solution. He admired her for it. No, the truth was that he loved her insatiable desire to assist others.

Nothing in him doubted that her desire to help was genuine, and she'd never once used their growing feelings for each other to persuade him not to sell her aunt's home.

And yet, he still couldn't stomach the idea of her having any connection to Beck. Perhaps she was right. The man was more bluster than a real threat, but now there was every chance he knew about Lucy, and that chilled him to the bone and twisted in his gut.

Protecting her came before everything else.

He sensed her frustration with him. When he

made no reply to her advice, she'd taken out her sketchbook and busied herself laying down light strokes with her pencil while holding the side of the sketchbook up to shield her work from his view.

"You still won't let me see?"

"These aren't very good. I'm not terribly good at drawing people." She shifted her gaze his way, then back down to her book, and let out a sigh. "All right. You may look."

Rather than merely drop her arm, she handed the sketchbook to him. The image she'd drawn was of her view from that tearoom window, and while the people were mostly blocked-in figures moving down the thoroughfare, the details of the buildings struck him as brilliant.

"You've captured so many details on the buildings' facades."

"I'm good at buildings. Landscapes, I suppose you'd say. Maybe because I mostly practiced my skills with still objects around the house. People seem ever in motion, so changeable."

"May I?" he asked before flipping pages to look at her other work.

She bit her lower lip and finally nodded. "If you must."

He found he couldn't resist, and he smiled at each new page. Each new revelation of the things that caught Lucy's eye. She'd drawn items at Invermere. A teacup. The stairwell. Her aunt's bow and arrow at rest against Lady Cassandra's intricately patterned wallpaper. Then another pattern with buttons.

"Is this my . . . ?"

"The blue waistcoat." She shrugged innocently, but he didn't miss the spike of pink along the arc of her cheek. "I liked the pattern. And the color is the same as your eyes."

"Is it indeed? You have a good eye and more skill than you let on."

She retrieved her sketchbook before he could examine more pages. "I'm still learning. I thought perhaps Aunt Cassandra would teach me a bit."

Her tone suggested that she no longer considered that a possibility.

"And now?"

"We'll arrive later than we'd planned. She may already be there now." She blinked and pressed her lips together. "I can only imagine what she'll think to find that I've gone off on the day she was to arrive."

"And with me."

"And with you. I came on this journey to take control of my fate, to make my own choices. And there is no place I would rather be than here. With you." She reached out to run her fingers along the edge of his jaw, then swept one fingertip along the seam of his lips. Tenderness, trust, affection—she continued to give him as much of her attention, show him how much she desired him, even after he'd told her what a fool he'd been, what a failure he'd become.

Lucy saw through his charm and whatever façade he projected. Perhaps she always had. And now, he could see, no, he could feel it too, that nothing had changed between them.

If anything, he wanted her more.

He took what she offered, kissing the pad of her finger, then pressing her wrist against his mouth to feel her pulse, to kiss that spot where her heart beat as fast as his. He licked at the tender flesh, savoring the sweet and spice taste of her.

Somehow, she was his. Perhaps only for this moment. Like it had been on Calton Hill, a warning in him sounded that it might be just this moment. Perhaps only for the next few hours, but right now, she was his. And he was hers. The flash of heat in her jade gaze told him she knew it too.

Impatiently, she leaned in and pressed her mouth to his jaw, nuzzling the same hard edge she'd traced with her fingers.

James waited, forcing himself to let her take her time. He expected her to kiss him, but she dipped her head, pressing her lips to the taut muscles of his neck. Then her hands worked, even as her mouth hovered, heated breath singeing his skin.

She tugged at his necktie, then slipped the button of his shirt. The first. Then the second, and immediately stroked her fingers gently along the base of his throat.

"This spot," she breathed against his skin. "I think of it often."

She flicked her tongue against the base of his

throat, at the spot where his pulse jittered wildly because of her nearness. Her heat.

His hands were on her hips, and he swept one around to cup her bottom, to pull her closer. She seemed to read his thoughts and lifted her skirts, gathering them in her hands until her stockinged legs were in view. Then she climbed into his lap. She spread her legs wide, knees resting on either side of his body.

James placed his hands on her hips, but Lucy seemed to want more.

She reached back to grasp his hand, then pulled it around until it was between them.

"Touch me," she whispered. "Please, James. I want you to."

This woman could ask anything of him, and he would give it. Anything she wished for, he'd gladly provide. A command would have worked as well as her whispered plea, but the rasp of need in her voice was what undid him.

That need was raw, demanding, and he understood it. He felt it as deeply as she did.

So whatever resistance he'd held on to, whatever cautions rang in his mind about the future and how he couldn't be enough for her, melted away.

There was just him and her, and this moment.

He wouldn't take her in a carriage. She deserved much more care and tenderness than that. But he could give her pleasure.

Sliding his hand against the warm fabric of her

drawers, he found the slit, pulled together with a satiny ribbon that gave way with the slightest tug.

Lucy shifted above him, pressing her heat against his hand, her body tense and yet so very soft.

"Breathe, beautiful."

A ragged chuckle and a flash of her smile made him smile too. When he sensed her body relax a bit against his, he slid his fingers through the damp hair at the apex of her thighs.

She hissed at that in a way that made him instantly hard and aching.

"Don't stop," she whispered.

"Never even crossed my mind," he told her as he pressed a kiss to the soft skin of her throat. At the same time, he inched his finger along her slit. So wet and hot against his skin.

She was everything he'd ever dreamed of, and somehow, she was here in his arms. Trusting him with the most intimate of explorations.

"No one has ever touched me like this. No one has ever kissed me. I wanted it to be you. I will always want it to be you." She moved against him then, arching so that he slid his finger into her. He loved feeling her explore what she liked as she bucked tentatively against him.

"That's it, sweetheart." He slid another finger inside and she let out a gasp that made him hesitate.

"More," she said almost petulantly.

"More, love." He kissed her, took her lips, danced his tongue against hers. Their hunger wasn't gentle anymore, though he stroked her only as quickly as her bucking hips urged him. Then he used his thumb to find that sweet, tender spot that made her tremble. He stroked at her slick flesh and wished he was using his tongue rather than his finger. Dreamed of being able to give her that pleasure too.

"Oh, James." Her hands were on his shoulders, then in his hair, gripping his nape. "James," she repeated, then held her breath for a beat before she broke against him, heat drenching his fingers, her body shuddering in his arms.

He held her tight, kissed her cheek, her forehead.

"That was better than I imagined," she whispered in his ear while he stroked a hand up and down her back.

"Imagined it a lot, did you?"

"More than is proper, I'd say." She still sat in his lap, her head resting against his shoulder, her lips just inches from his neck.

"There's more."

"I know, and I wish you'd show me." She let out a throaty laugh, and he felt it in his chest.

He wrapped his arms around her then, wishing the same. Hoping that the little haven they'd found in this carriage, in each other, wouldn't be torn completely apart by what came next.

"I could"—she yawned and let out a sigh that seemed to melt her further into his chest—"fall asleep like this."

"I'll let you."

"This must be uncomfortable."

"I'm quite content to have you in my lap as long as you'd like to stay, my lady." His cock protested a bit, but only because he longed to lay her out in a bed and make love to her properly.

Turning his head, he pressed one long kiss against her cheek.

But a moment later, she began to shift, lifting off his lap. He helped her stand and settle her skirts. Then she surprised him by settling in his lap again, this time with her legs stretched out on his bench and her backside balanced on his thighs.

She tucked her head against his chest, and he rested his chin against her hair. They fit together as if they were meant to be next to each other.

Having Lucy in his arms was as close to feeling content as he'd felt in so long.

That thrilled and terrified him equally. The moments in his life when he remembered feeling this way—happy, secure—everything had been ripped away from him. First his family, then his fortune.

"You'll wake me before we reach Invermere?"

"Of course."

He heard the parts of her question that were unspoken.

When they reached the manor, everything would change.

"I think she'll like you," she murmured sleepily.

James wasn't sure of that at all.

Chapter Sixteen

"We should be close now."

Lucy blinked her eyes open and straightened so quickly she bumped James's chin.

"I'm sorry," she told him as she scrambled off his lap. The side of her body that had been pressed to his felt as if she'd fallen asleep against a furnace. Her limbs felt languid, but her mind raced.

Invermere. They'd soon arrive. And she'd have to face her aunt. *They* would have to face her aunt.

Rain pelted the carriage in a steady tattoo, and the darkening sky made it easy to use the carriage window glass as a mirror.

"Good grief." Her hair was a jumble, but she decided that slipping the bits she could back into pins made more sense than taking the whole of it down and trying again. "I look terribly unkempt, don't I?"

James smiled at her, an easy, seductive smile. "You look magnificent and exactly like what you are. A lady who's been pleasured and had a nap in a cramped carriage."

"Ugh, not the picture I'd like to present to Aunt Cassandra."

"She'll simply be happy to see you."

Lucy considered that sentiment and hoped with all her heart that it was true. And more, that she could speak to her aunt sensibly about James and his reasons for selling Invermere. Of course, she had no wish to be seen to take sides, but she understood the matter from two perspectives now. The question was whether her aunt would be able to do the same.

"We're on the approach now, I think." James pointed to a stone structure that looked as if it had once formed part of a gate at the entrance of Invermere property.

"Yes." She recognized the structure from that moonlit night just a few days ago. It felt like weeks had passed since then.

While Lucy watched at the window, she sensed James watching her. Turning to face him, she felt an ache deep in her middle, as if she was already mourning the loss of their closeness.

He felt it too. A new wariness she sensed from him. All the ease of the last few hours had seeped away.

"Maybe all will be well," she said, but her tone sounded doubtful even to her ears.

James bent forward, took her hand tenderly, and then pressed a kiss to her knuckles, as if they were in a ballroom and were parting after an enjoyable turn on the dance floor.

It felt far too much like a goodbye.

But before she could say more, the carriage rolled

to a stop in front of Invermere. Mr. Tavish didn't climb down this time. There was no luggage for him to help with. Lucy dug into her reticule for a few coins, and James handed them up to the man.

"Thank you, Mr. Tavish."

"Be well, my lord and lady."

As the vehicle rattled back down the gravel drive and back onto the country lane, Lucy's heart sank. The scene she perceived through the ground floor window told her two things instantly: her aunt had returned to Invermere, and she was, as McKay would say, in a fine fettle.

In the gaslit room, she stood talking—shouting, more like—to a man Lucy didn't recognize. She was so consumed with the confrontation that she didn't notice the coach's arrival and departure.

But Mrs. Fox did. She'd opened the front door and stood at the threshold, much as she had that first night.

"Shall we?" James said tightly.

Lucy didn't take his outstretched arm, didn't move. "I'm not familiar with that man."

"Nor I, but I think I know who he is."

"Do you?" Lucy searched James's face and found nothing but anxious misery there.

"In all that's happened, I forgot to tell you." He glanced at her and then away again. "The surveyor most likely arrived today, and that man at the wrong end of your aunt's wrath may be him."

"Good grief." Lucy strode ahead of him. Not because she didn't wish to be seen being escorted by him, but because she felt an instinct to rush to the aid of the hapless man standing quietly as her aunt shouted.

"Mrs. Fox," Lucy said to the housekeeper as she entered.

The lady shocked her by laying a hand on Lucy's arm to slow her. "Her ladyship is not taking any of it well. She's in a great deal of pain, and I'll urge you to remember that. Whatever comes."

"Of course." Lucy pulled her arm from Mrs. Fox's, though the woman hadn't clasped her firmly. Something about the implication that she couldn't see her way clear to sympathizing with her aunt raised her defenses.

She loved her aunt dearly. Admired her. For so many years, she'd yearned to be more like her. Though as she approached the closed drawing room door, fear broke over her like a trickle of ice water down her back.

Never in her life had she been on the receiving end of her aunt's displeasure, but she suspected she was about to be now.

She heard James's footsteps behind her. She longed to feel his reassuring touch—his hand at her back, his lips against her cheek—but she knew he wouldn't touch her now. Not yet. Not until they knew how things would be resolved between him and Aunt Cassandra.

"All will be well," he whispered, and she adored him in that moment for trying to reassure her.

She adored him. Full stop.

Rather than step inside the drawing room un-invited, she knocked, and the raised voices on the other side quieted. Mr. Blackwood opened the door a moment later, shocking her, as she hadn't noticed him through the window.

"The lass has returned," he said with his usual joviality. "Look at ye, all cold and shivering. Let's get ye near the fire." He ushered her inside, his hand heavy on her shoulder before he shouted through the open door for Fox to have tea sent up.

Cassandra stood stock-still, staring at her, her green eyes, so much like Lucy's own, were glossy, her cheeks ruddy. Loose strands of her red-gold hair had escaped their pins. Then she lifted her arms and opened them, as if beckoning Lucy to come to her.

She went, and Cassandra embraced her as she'd done each time she'd come to visit Hallston House or the family estate in Sussex. A tight hug, an all-enveloping outpouring of affection that always made Lucy feel safe and loved.

Cassandra eased back and held on to Lucy's upper arms. "Look at you. My lovely niece." She pressed a palm to Lucy's cheek. "Are you all right?"

Lucy wasn't sure if the question was the sort of polite inquiry one makes upon seeing someone after a long separation or if her face gave something away.

"I'm well." Lucy couldn't move her head without pulling away from Cassandra's touch, but she flicked her gaze toward the man standing before the desk in the corner. He looked stoic but miserable, his mouth set in a straight line, shoulders slumped.

Aunt Cassandra must have noticed her glance because she released Lucy and took a step back. "Apparently, you've met Angus." She gestured at Mr. Blackwood. "And I know you have not met Mr. Dickson because he descended on my home unexpectedly while you were in the city."

"Mr. Dickson." Lucy nodded at the man and tried for a kindly expression.

"Dickson is a surveyor who's come to snoop about my home and measure and poke and decide how much it will sell for." Cassandra wasn't capable of a blank stare, so the one she squared on Lucy was full of emotion, but she couldn't discern precisely which emotion it was. "Did you know Mr. Dickson was coming, Lucy?"

So, it was anger. Just the thin edge of it, well restrained but breaking through.

"I did not." The truth in the barest sense, but in Lucy's experience, angry people were not interested in minutiae or complexities. Plain speaking worked best.

"But you do know why he's here." Not a question. More of an accusation.

"Yes, I do, Aunt Cassandra, and I'm sorry for it."

Her aunt looked as if she might crumple at that. She lifted a kerchief from her pocket and swept it across her forehead, then pressed the back of her hand to her cheek. She closed her eyes for a moment and the tension in her shoulders seemed to ease.

"Cass—" Mr. Blackwood stepped forward, but she stayed him with the flick of her hand.

"I'm ready," she finally said, then stood tall, chest out, chin up, drawing in a deep breath.

Lucy didn't know what she meant, and neither Mr. Dickson nor Mr. Blackwood seemed to either. The three of them exchanged confused looks while her aunt started toward the doorway at Lucy's back.

"I'm ready to meet the earl, who, without any warning or the courtesy of a letter, has come to destroy everything I've made for myself." She swallowed as if working to control her temper or hold back the bile in her throat. "And compromised my beloved niece."

"Aunt Cassandra—" Lucy found she wasn't prepared with the right words. She felt the heat of anger boiling in her chest, found herself clenching her fingers into fists. But she had no desire to add to her aunt's distress.

Then she heard footsteps and recognized the sound of James's gait.

"LADY CASSANDRA." HE said her name quietly as he approached to stand on Lucy's right. Then he sketched a bow. Never very good at the formality, he mimicked what he'd seen at formal parties and in the few ballrooms he'd spent time in. "I have been looking forward to making your acquaintance."

The ticking of the clock, the sound of servants moving about in the hall, and the labored breath of poor Mr. Dickson were all he heard as the lady took her time assessing him.

She perused him slowly, thoughtfully, examining everything from his hair to his necktie to the part of his boots that stuck out beneath the legs of his trousers. Then she lifted her gaze and stared into his eyes. Unblinking and somehow demanding.

So much like Lucy's eyes. The same shade, at least. Though there was none of the warmth and sweetness, none of the seductive boldness.

"*If* you were eager to make my acquaintance, Lord Rossbury, I suspect it was only so that you could get on with the business of sizing up my home and pocketing the proceeds of its sale. Is that about the sum of it?"

"I understand your anger—"

"I doubt that very much. Unless you have been standing where I am, how could you?"

James nodded but was undaunted. He never doubted the lady would be formidable. "I sent you a letter—or rather, I had my uncle's solicitor do so—before my arrival. I'm sorry it didn't reach you before I arrived. I should have sent a telegram, so the failure to give you fair warning is mine. Entirely."

"Well, I'm glad to know I'm blaming the right person."

"Time was of the essence, but that is my fault too."

"I'm not charmed by humility, my lord."

"You see, my lady, I made a grave error," he continued, giving pause for her barb but not letting it throw him off stride. "I failed at the business I'd built. Lost everything. Betrayed friends and colleagues. And I owe money to an unscrupulous man. None of that excuses my behavior toward you. It is merely the only explanation I can offer."

For the first time since he'd walked into the room, Lady Cassandra offered no barb in reply. Instead, she did her assessment again, sweeping her gaze up and down as if looking for something she might have missed the first time.

Mrs. Fox entered the room at that moment. Perhaps she'd been waiting for a lull in the conversation. For some reason, she'd come to deliver the tea service herself. Curious, no doubt, about how things were unfolding for her mistress.

James didn't blame her for that in the least.

"I'll pour," Lucy offered.

"Thank you, my dear." Her aunt spoke to her with genuine warmth, and James was grateful for that. Most of all, he did not want to cause a rift between them.

"Then we should all sit," Lady Cassandra announced, waving her hands as if to indicate they should all sort themselves out.

Blackwood claimed a spot on the settee. Her ladyship took the chair next to him. Mr. Dickson took the chair as far away from Lady Cassandra as possible. And James sat on the second settee opposite Blackwood.

Lucy waited until all of them had chosen a spot and took the cushion beside Blackwood. James was disappointed but not surprised by her choice. He probably would have advised it, especially since her aunt watched her closely, following Lucy's every movement as she poured tea into five cups and offered one to each of them after determining who wanted lemon or sugar or cream.

The minutes that passed while Lucy engaged in the rituals of dispensing tea seemed to give the room itself and everyone in it a chance to breathe. The tension eased.

James allowed himself a deep breath.

Lady Cassandra took a sip, closed her eyes as if savoring the brew, and then set her cup on a side table before fixing her attention on James once more.

"It seems we have bad decision-making in common, Lord Rossbury." She drew the shawl she wore more tightly around her and turned in her chair to face him directly. "I thought the worst choice I'd ever made was to involve myself with Rufus Pembroke. He had charm enough to deceive me into thinking he was a good man, but that facade fell away quickly. Quite simply, I wanted stability at any cost." She stabbed a finger in the air. "Though not marriage. Never again."

Blackwood grumbled something indiscernible at that pronouncement.

"But every time I have remonstrated with myself and hated my own choices, I've taken solace in this."

She swept her arms in an arc as if to encompass the room, the house. "I expected him to rip Invermere away from me when I no longer welcomed his interest." She lifted her shoulders, widened her eyes. "But he didn't. At one time, he'd called it a gift, of course. When he wished to woo me. But then I simply didn't hear from him."

"Or ye ignored his correspondence," Mr. Blackwood put in.

Lady Cassandra narrowed one eye at him but softened it with a half smile. "He did not evict me. No one came to put me out. So I began to feel comfortable here. As if I had a home."

"We could purchase the house—" Blackwood put in quickly.

"We've already had that conversation, Angus." For the first time since sitting, Lady Cassandra settled fully into her chair, her hands resting on the arms like a monarch on a throne. "For me to purchase, I would need time to secure the funds. A loan." She turned her gaze toward the hallway, as if she could see the paintings there. "I could offer you a down payment, and if I put up some of my artwork as collateral, I believe Lady Grimshaw, a friend and a partner in her father's bank, will lend me the rest."

James considered her offer. This was exactly what he hoped. That *she* could buy the manor herself, but the timing sounded vague. "I cannot wait long for the funds, Lady Cassandra."

"Then I will advance—" Blackwood pushed his bulk forward on the settee as if he'd stand.

"No, Angus," she snapped. "I've told you no. Respect me in this, please."

"Stubbornest woman born," Blackwood roared before getting to his feet and storming from the room.

The lady didn't even blink. "Obviously I haven't had time to speak to Lady Grimshaw, but I suspect I could have full payment for you by the end of the month."

"My lady—"

In his periphery, Lucy shot to her feet. "You can't even know if you'll find another buyer by that time. The end of the month seems very reasonable."

"*If* she can secure a loan," James said to her quietly.

Lucy sucked in a breath, dropped back onto the settee, clasped her hands, and then pressed them into her lap.

Maybe he was being a fool again. Perhaps he could persuade Beck to wait another couple of weeks. The man had waited this long, hadn't he?

"How much?" Lucy asked, her focus fixed on the surveyor. "How much is the house worth, Mr. Dickson?"

"Oh." The middle-aged man seemed shocked that he'd been given a reason to speak. "Yes, er, I haven't quite . . . I mean to say that I have not as yet had a chance to make all of my notations or produce a final report as would usually be my wont—"

"A rough estimate, man," Lady Cassandra snapped, her anger barely in check. "You've been crawling about the place for over an hour."

"Uh, yes, your ladyship, and I do appreciate you allowing me to do so."

"How much, Mr. Dickson?"

"My valuation will list the manor and its nearly sixteen acres, if the documents I've been provided are correct, as being of a market value of twelve thousand pounds."

Lady Cassandra's eyes went wide.

James felt Lucy's gaze on him and looked her way, offering her a quick nod.

That sum would be enough to pay Beck and get him out of debt.

"Thank you, Dickson," James told the man and stood.

Mr. Dickson stood too but with difficulty, struggling to collect all the documents in his arms. Lucy rose to help him when the same blueprints she'd given to James slipped from the crook of his arm.

"If I may just make a few more notes, I shall be on my way."

"You have a conveyance to take you home?" Lucy seemed to feel sympathy for the harried man. James did too. He'd only come to do as he'd been asked.

"Oh yes, miss. My carriage is in the stable yard."

"Very good. Shall I show you to the parlor across the hall?"

"He can find it on his own." Lady Cassandra had risen from her chair too. "Farewell, Dickson. I'd like to speak to his lordship and my niece alone."

"Of course, my lady."

After Mr. Dickson left the room, James sneaked a glance at Lucy. She looked as wary as he felt.

Lady Cassandra let the fraught silence continue.

Lucy spoke first. "I want to help resolve this matter, Aunt Cassandra. Tell me what I can do."

Of course, she would wish to help. But her aunt seemed in no humor to entertain assistance of any kind. James realized he'd offended her by not accepting her offer, though in his mind he hadn't yet refused or decided anything yet.

"There are two matters before us," the lady finally said, her voice low and unnervingly cool. "The matter of the sale of Invermere, of course, and the mystery of whatever is going on between the two of you." She glared at James and then softened as she faced Lucy. "Lucy and I must talk, so you must go, Lord Rossbury."

James frowned. She'd asked him nothing and might have excused him when she did Dickson if she merely wished for time alone with Lucy.

But James had no inclination to rile her. "Of course, my lady."

"I want you out of the house. I've had the staff collect your things—"

"Aunt Cassandra." Lucy took a step toward her, but the lady continued.

"There is a cottage on the property, not far

beyond the tree line. I've had a maid tidy it and prepare it for you. It should be sufficient accommodation until our two great matters are resolved."

He tried not to look at Lucy and respectfully kept his attention fixed on the lady speaking to him, but he sensed her. Felt her frustration and yearned to soothe her.

"Please, Aunt, if you'd only listen—"

"It will be all right," James told her, reaching for her instinctively.

Lady Cassandra lurched as if to plant herself between them.

"Go. Now, Lord Rossbury," Lucy's aunt commanded. "I'll send word to you tomorrow, and we can speak then."

James held back his anger and headed for the door.

"And if I find you've harmed my niece in any way, I swear I'll bury you in Invermere's garden."

Chapter Seventeen

The smaller the number, the lower the point you receive for putting your puck there. Make sense?"

"I think so." Lucy wasn't entirely sure. Her aunt's description of how to play the game had been quick, her voice still full of the tension of the meeting in the drawing room.

But now, half an hour after her aunt had thrown James out of Invermere, they stood together in the manor's ballroom.

Lucy hadn't even known the house contained a ballroom, and from the cobwebs on the high, gilded fixtures, it looked as if it hadn't gotten much use of late. At least not for dancing. The floor, on the other hand, was immaculate, constructed of a lovely dark wood and polished so thoroughly that stepping on it in stockinged feet would have certainly sent her flying.

Which was precisely the point of the little pucks that she and her aunt were meant to slide into a numbered triangle at each end of the ballroom.

The oddity of finding herself learning the rules of shuffleboard when there were quite pressing matters to discuss shouldn't have surprised her.

If anything, it gave her a bit of comfort. Her aunt was an unusual woman, one who'd always found it hard to sit still on her visits to London. And this felt exactly like her. A much more Cassandra way of spending an evening.

"Start from the beginning," she said, once she'd reset the pucks in a space for Lucy and a space for her.

"I met him on the platform at King's Cross Station."

Her aunt lifted a brow at that.

"We collided."

Aunt Cassandra rolled her eyes and waved her hand, urging Lucy to take her turn at pushing a puck toward the triangle. She shoved her stick forward, and the puck slid so fast and so far, she almost lost sight of it.

"Goodness, girl, you don't know your own strength." *That* tone sounded like the Aunt Cassandra she adored. Slightly teasing yet full of love and admiration.

"I'll do better next time."

She smiled at Lucy. "I trust you will. You've always learned quickly." Walking back and forth while staring at the triangle, she finally took up a spot and then paused for several minutes to place her cue stick just so. "You *collided* with the man. Then what?"

In the space between the question and the pressure Lucy felt to form an answer that was wholly true and yet also cast James in the best possible light, her aunt took her shot. Her blue puck slid onto the three, which was quite good, if Lucy recalled the scoring rules correctly.

"I found my seat. And later we ended up sharing a private car with two kindly sisters from Hampstead."

"There's more to that story."

Lucy wasn't quite sure how her aunt correctly surmised that, since she'd yet to look Lucy's way. She was too intently focused on the game.

"Your go, Lucy."

Lucy realized the cue needed less force. That she simply needed to focus on where she wished it to go and let momentum do more of the work. She pushed more gently this time, and the puck slid, then sputtered to a stop before even reaching the triangle.

"Damn." Lucy immediately tensed, expecting to hear her mother's voice offering some immediate chastisement. But her aunt simply let out a hearty peal of laughter.

"We have the same coloring and the same sense of competition, I see." She rolled her hand in the air. "Go on. Tell me the rest."

Lucy considered how to condense it. Push it down, in at the sides, and wrap it all up in a nice bow. It should be easy to do. She and James had only known each other for a few days.

"The carriage arrived late to deliver me to Invermere—"

"I am dreadfully sorry for that, dear girl. I hope you'll forgive me."

"Of course. And it turned out well. Mr. Tavish did eventually collect me and we made good time. Lord Rossbury was here when I arrived, and we were both shocked to see each other again. I was doubly shocked to learn why he'd come."

"But you didn't mind residing with him? Unchaperoned?"

"Invermere has a full staff. We were never alone for long without being observed." *Do not blush. Do. Not. Blush.* Lucy realized she was holding her breath and let it out slowly. *For long* was doing a great deal of work in what she'd said to her aunt, but she had not lied.

Aunt Cassandra lined up a shot and then seemed to think better of it and began pacing again. "And during this time of being *mostly* observed, you came to what? Like him? Want him? Care for him?"

"Yes," Lucy said simply. It was the easiest part of the conversation so far.

"He is handsome. That I will give you. Undeniably attractive as young men go. A fine physical specimen."

Now there was no chance of holding back her blush. In fact, she suspected her whole body had gone a splotchy pink.

Aunt Cassandra took her shot, and the movement was so fluid that there was a kind of soothing beauty in it. Lucy immediately thought it would be fun to sketch her while she engaged in the game. If she were at all talented at capturing the human figure.

"So you became enamored with this man who owns Invermere in just a matter of a few days." Her aunt turned back to her, gesturing with her cue. "That part surprises me. You had three Seasons and couldn't be swayed by any man's charms and now this . . . This man. You're besotted with him in less than a week? What's come over you, Lucy?"

Love. The simplest, purest answer welled up in her chest, like the moment before you draw in breath to break into song. But she resisted saying it aloud. James should hear it first.

Rather than answer, Lucy paced as her aunt did before a shot, lined up her puck and cue, and shoved with a confidence she hadn't felt on her earlier tries. The puck slid gracefully across the polished wood with a satisfying woosh and settled in the number two box.

"Well done!" Aunt Cassandra came close enough to give Lucy's arm a reassuring squeeze. "I suspected you'd excel at this. To be an artist, one must have a talent that joins hand and eye."

"I'm not quite an artist."

"You could be, my dear." She lined up her last puck and pulled her cue back as if she'd make her move, but then hesitated. "What would he make of that? The new earl."

"He'd encourage me."

Aunt Cassandra pushed her puck with extra force and it spun off far ahead of the target, as Lucy's first shot had.

"So, it's love." Her aunt breathed the word with such sorrow that Lucy immediately wished to comfort her. But she also felt free to admit it now.

"I think it might be. At least for my part." Lucy distracted herself with deciding where to aim her next shot, but Aunt Cassandra seemed done with the game. She walked to the side of the ballroom and set her cue on a stand designed to hold the instruments of the game.

"How far has it gone, Lucy? Must you marry the man?"

"No." She shook her head emphatically. "I won't be pressured to marry anyone."

Never needing to marry was, Lucy realized, an enormous gift her parents had given to her. Papa might encourage her to be sociable, and Mama had attended to each of her Seasons with as much enthusiasm as the first, but they'd made it clear that in such a momentous decision the choice must be hers. And the implication had always been that making no choice—choosing no groom—could be an option too.

Yet, of course, Lucy understood her aunt's meaning. By the judgment of most, the intimacies she'd shared with James in the carriage would make marriage a necessity, if one was interested in salvaging one's reputation.

But she'd honestly never considered marriage to James. Not truly. Not until this moment.

He'd promised her nothing. She'd offered no

vows of her own. There'd been something wonderful in simply relishing each moment.

The unknown quantity they had together, expecting nothing more.

Perhaps they'd both always assumed their time together would end once the business of Invermere was settled. And then there had been the question of how her aunt would react. Neither of them had spoken to the other about the future because they'd been so uncertain of what lay ahead.

Perhaps it was part of why they'd bonded so quickly, why the usual boundaries were so easily overcome. They were living entirely and completely for the time they could share.

"We find ourselves in such an enormous tangle. But life is unpredictable at the best of times. And we simply must make the best of it."

Lucy followed her aunt and placed her cue on the rack. "I'm very tired. I don't wish to be rude—"

"Get some rest, my dear. If you feel all right by dinner, we can talk again then." She cupped Lucy's cheek as she always did, then placed a soft kiss on her other cheek. "Rest well, my dear."

Lucy made her way to her room, undressed, washed, and lay on her bed, expecting sleep to take her instantly. She was exhausted. Not just in her body, but in her head and heart.

Like the stubborn fool she could be, she'd imagined that things would magically work themselves out once her aunt arrived. That James would charm her. That her aunt would understand his predicament. That the money would be found, and her aunt would keep her home while James walked away with his funds.

And yet she couldn't solve it. There was no simple, quick solution. No way to keep all the people she cared about happy.

Closing her eyes, she saw only James. She touched her mouth and traced her lips, remembering his kiss—the tenderness and the hunger.

Then she woke with a start, feeling as if only minutes had passed, though the darkness of the room told her otherwise.

But it didn't matter what time it was. She had to see James. However long she'd slept, it had been the most fortuitous slumber of her life.

She knew the answer.

Now she only had to convince the man she'd fallen in love with to agree.

"You should go." James wondered if he'd slurred the words or just imagined that he had. "She'll come looking for you if you don't."

Across the room, Angus Blackwood sat on the only comfortable chair in the little cottage James had been relegated to.

"Aye, I'll go. I'll leave the bottle. It's some of my best, don't you think?"

James eyed the golden liquid in his glass and could feel the whiskey's effects in his body and blood. The flavor was magnificent. Buttery smooth with hints of oak and a lovely searing hit as it slid down his throat.

"Blackwood Whiskey is the best in Scotland, if I do say so meself." Angus frowned and pointed at James, still clutching his glass with the rest of his fingers. "I wanted you to have a sample before I'm on my way back north for a few days. Can't leave the business unattended too long."

"Your kindness is appreciated, Blackwood."

The older man settled back in the overstuffed chair. "Not only kindness, Rossbury. I've a proposition for ye."

If the man meant to offer for Invermere again, James was determined to make the sale happen. Lady Cassandra might not get the funding she needed, and not in the time frame James needed to sell. But if Blackwood did—and apparently, he was some kind of wealthy whiskey baron—then his purchase could solve everything. Even if his lady love was angry with him for a bit. She'd eventually come to see that he'd done it out of love, and James had no doubt he'd gift ownership to her immediately.

"I'd like to hear it." James poured himself another finger of whiskey. He wasn't a man who generally indulged in drunkenness. He preferred his senses sharp, but today had been a hell of a day.

"You still have any of your ships?"

Angus's question came as such a shock that James choked on the sip of liquor he'd taken. The burn seared his throat and felt like it set his lungs aflame, and he coughed as his eyes watered.

"I have one," he said with a rasp when he could breathe normally again. "The last I ever purchased. Couldn't bring myself to part with her. Also, it's co-owned with a business partner, and he couldn't afford to buy out my share." James smiled, and it felt more like a grimace. Both had lost money in Beck's scheme.

"What kind of ship?"

"A transatlantic steamer but with an expanded engine, making it faster than most."

The old man lifted his glass, tipped back most of the contents, and let out a satisfied sigh. "That is exactly what I wished to hear. I had a feeling about ye, Rossbury." He winced. "Good god, man, may I call ye Pembroke? Or James? Repeating that man's name makes even my whiskey go down sour."

"James. Pembroke. Whichever you like. And I agree about loathing the name."

Angus raised his glass and James did the same, and they toasted from across the room.

"Ship my whiskey to America. How do ye like that idea?"

James laughed, then noted Angus's frown and realized the man was serious. "I have no shipping company, Blackwood. It's defunct. My lease is up on the offices, and long since expired on my warehouse space and docking fees."

"What if that weren't the case?"

"Maybe the whiskey has muddled my brain, but I'm not sure what you're suggesting."

"A partnership of sorts, my boy. Your ship, my whiskey."

"This is pity. You could find other companies to ship your whiskey."

"It's nae pity. Just a good opportunity, for both of us." Angus hunched forward, his intense gaze animated. "See here. Ye give me a fair price for shipping, and I get my whiskey into the American market."

"Where you don't have it now?"

"Correct. And if I'm doing ye a good turn, then I'm glad for it. But it's nae charity, Pembroke. Sometimes a business arrangement can be more than mercenary."

"And how does this help solve the problem of her ladyship's home?"

"If you can revive your business, will ye need to sell so sharpish?"

"I will. Rebuilding the company will take months and there will be costs involved." His gut tightened at the prospect of explaining his failures to someone else. "I have a debt I must repay soon. The lender is . . . impatient."

"I could advance you funds."

"No, that *is* charity."

"For the love of god, ye're as stubborn as Cass." Angus shook his head and looked, for the first time since James had met the man, a bit deflated.

"I was going to give you funds anyway—to secure Invermere for my lady. Thought we could keep it quiet. A holding fee, say, so ye willnae sell to anyone else."

"How much?" James hated that everything came down to cold hard cash for him of late, but anytime he thought of Beck's thugs at his home, his scruples melted away.

"You name the sum. As I told ye, I could buy it outright."

"Then perhaps you should." James stood and offered the bottle to Blackwood, noting that his glass was empty.

The old man nodded, and James added two fingers to his glass.

"If she learns I betrayed her—"

"Will she really not see that you do it out of love for her?"

"Independence came at a great cost for Cass, so she values it now above all else."

Angus spoke of his lady with the same fervent admiration James felt for Lucy and her determination to find her purpose and be true to her own desires, despite what it might cost her.

"I'll go and speak to her. Try again." He didn't look like he expected any more success than previous attempts, but he still smiled. "I have missed the beguiling wench."

The man was besotted, and James never expected to understand the feeling so well.

"Consider what I've said. Consider my offer.

Come and see my distillery if you doubt the seriousness of my enterprise. I leave in the morning." Ambling across the room, Angus clapped him on the shoulder. "We could help each other, my boy. I don't offer ye pity. I offer ye a means of rebuilding yer business and growing mine."

"I'll consider everything you've said, and even do so again in the morning when I've slept off the whiskey."

"Cannae ask for more than that." Angus shocked him by gripping his face in his hands. "Ye must show her no fear. My lady. She's a lioness, but one of good heart. Take my offer. Give her a chance to buy and sell to no other. Let there be peace."

"I'd like peace." More than just between himself and Lady Cassandra. For so long, he'd no peace within himself, with the choices he'd made. He longed to make choices that would bring him true and lasting peace with himself.

James turned the older man once he'd stepped outside the cottage, making sure he was pointing in the direction of the house.

Then he stepped back inside, took the comfortable chair, and closed his eyes. And there she was.

Lucy. Lovely, bold, impulsive woman. The images spun like a kaleidoscope in his whiskey-addled mind. Lucy smiling and glaring at him. Her soft hand in his. Her lush, ripe mouth against his neck. The taste of her kisses.

Oh yes, he was besotted. Smitten. Somehow, at the tail end of the worst year of his life, when he'd become a desperate, craven bastard who'd come to take a woman's home from her, he'd met the woman whom he believed—no, he damn well knew—was the love of his benighted life.

And he could do nothing about it until he got his shambles of a life back into some semblance of stability. She deserved that, at the very least.

But the bloody hell of it was that he couldn't imagine any future day of his life without her.

Chapter Eighteen

Any young woman who'd been through a London Season knew there was a lengthy list of ways a lady's reputation could be ruined. Having been through *three*, Lucy knew them all as well as she knew the correlating shades on a color wheel.

Since stepping onto the platform at King's Cross Station, she'd already ticked off several items on that ruination list: being alone with a gentleman, kissing a gentleman, letting a gentleman stroke the most intimate parts of her body until she melted into incoherent bliss.

She almost stumbled in her path at the memory of that moment. But she wouldn't be deterred. She lifted the lantern she'd brought since the clouds hid the moon tonight, hitched her skirt up an inch, and took the overgrown path a little more carefully.

Tonight, with all the knowledge she had of the means to a lady's downfall, she was taking the final step toward ruin. Yet she felt no fear. In fact, once she'd decided, she reveled in the anticipation that made her body vibrate.

She had a plan, of course, though she was honest enough with herself to know the plan might go astray. Pride was a delicate thing with men, and she respected James as much as she craved this night with him.

So she'd planned her approach, right down to practicing what she'd say and in what tone. Rallying rationales was no problem at all. This plan made perfect sense—the most sense anything had made to her in a very long time.

But she acknowledged the need for a contingency plan. That one was good too, but bittersweet.

The lights in the cottage were on. That was good. She'd hoped she wouldn't have to wake him and perhaps put him in a sour mood because of it.

"I know what I want," she practiced under her breath as she reached up to knock on the door. "I have a plan that will fix everything."

"Lucy."

That was her name, and yet she'd forgotten for a moment, because James stood in front of her only half-clothed. He was quite gloriously made. She'd imagined, of course, but even her imaginings hadn't been *this*.

A fire crackled in the hearth and provided most of the light. The golden glow of it outlined broad shoulders and thickly muscled arms, throwing into shadow an equally muscled chest with a patch of dark hair that disappeared very intriguingly into his waistline.

He turned, and his back was the most exquisite landscape of muscles. This was what chiaroscuro had been made for, those dips and shadows, mounds and hard edges.

She'd felt his strength when he caught her on the platform, held her on the train, and let her straddle him in the carriage, but she'd never seen a man's body like this. Never imagined the sharp edge of muscles could be so appealing, so much that she wanted to touch him.

Well, she always wanted to touch him. Clothed or unclothed.

Then she realized he'd turned to collect his shirt and pull it on before turning back to her. She bit back her disappointment. If all went well this evening, they'd have no cause for being hesitant about seeing each other unclothed ever again.

"I should send you back," he told her gruffly but with a yearning in his eyes that told her he wouldn't.

"I won't go, even if you try."

He reached for her then, his broad fingers stroking the edge of her cheek and jaw. "No, of course you won't. I can see you have something to say, so you'd better come in."

She smelled liquor before she noted the two glasses.

"Blackwood came by." He lifted a bottle and held it up for her to see. "Did you know he owns a whiskey distillery? Apparently, a quite successful one."

"It was good of him to visit after my aunt insisted you remove to the cottage. I'm sorry about that."

"I half expected her to put me out completely. The house may be mine by law, but it's hers in every other way."

Lucy untied her cloak and placed it over an armchair. James's reaction was exactly what she'd hoped.

"Mercy," he breathed and then stepped closer as if he couldn't hold himself back. "You look—"

"Beautiful?"

"Beautiful is a given. But the color and the—" He sketched his hand in the air. "You are stunning, Lucy." He seemed almost afraid to touch her.

The lavender satin gown had been the talk of the Hallston household when the modiste had delivered it for Lucy. The neckline was daring in front but absolutely plunging in back. Lucy had never worn it and had begun to wonder if she'd ever have occasion to.

"Good," she said quietly. "I want you to remember this evening."

He swallowed hard then, and it made her body feel warmer, wanton. There was no doubt they wanted each other with an equal ardor.

But first, her plan.

"May we sit?"

"Yes, of course." He led her to an overstuffed chair, his hand on her back where the fabric ended. Once there, he seemed loath to let her go and swept his thumb up her bare lower back before doing so.

"Would you like some whiskey?"

"Yes." She'd never had any liquor stronger than

wine at supper. But her mouth was suddenly watering, and a sip might bolster her for what she was going to ask of him next.

He poured her the slightest amount, just a line of amber at the base of a glass. "Go easy. See if you like it first."

Lucy sipped and even that felt sharp on her lips, even hotter on her tongue. A trail of flames shot down her throat. But once it reached her belly, oh, that felt nice. As if a little furnace warmed her from the inside out. "It's like liquid fire."

James laughed. "It's been called that." From the chair he'd taken near hers, he held the bottle out. "More?"

"Not yet."

She wanted to be clearheaded.

Pressing a hand to her throat, she willed her heart to stop rushing in her ears so she could do this properly.

"I think I've found a solution that will fix things." Lucy locked her gaze with James's and ignored the fact that he looked skeptical. She expected that. He was a man who'd been duped. Trusting must be hard for him. Perhaps he didn't even trust himself.

But she trusted herself and knew with certainty what she wanted. Finally.

"Go on. I'm listening."

They were too far apart. Lucy imagined how James might do it if the situation were reversed. She reached for him, and he came to her, concern bending his brows.

He knelt by her chair, took her hands in his. "What is it? You can tell me."

"Marry me."

James blinked, and then again. He looked away and then back at her. His mouth fell open, but no words came out.

The man was thunderstruck, and Lucy wasn't surprised.

This was shocking and unexpected. But it was also perfect.

"Don't you see?" She ran her fingers along his hand, up to his wrist, because touching him comforted her. "If we marry, it fixes everything. Aunt Cassandra can keep Invermere. You can pay back Mr. Beck. And we can be together as I believe we both wish to be." She gulped, because this was one of the variables she couldn't be entirely sure of. "If you feel as I do, of course."

"Lucy . . ."

"My dowry is fifteen thousand pounds. A great deal, I know. Or at least, I know it now. Honestly, I'm not supposed to know the amount at all, but you see, I handle my mother's correspondence—"

"I would never use you that way. You deserve a hell of a lot more than that." He kept one hand in hers and reached up to cup her nape, shooting delicious ribbons of warmth down her back. "Don't you understand what *you* are worth? To hell with your dowry."

She kissed him. Gripping the open edges of his shirt front, she pulled him close and seamed her lips with his, then she drew back to lick along his bottom lip as he'd taught her. He opened to her, kissing her with the same fierce longing.

Their desire was the same.

"Don't *you* see?" she said to him when they were both breathless and he'd pulled the pins from her hair. "You wouldn't be marrying me for my money but because of this." Laying a palm to his chest, she felt the wild beat of his heart. "What's between us. The way we are together."

He leaned in, and she wrapped her arms around his neck, prepared for more kisses, but he pressed his forehead to hers. "Sweet, stubborn girl. I would still be using your money to serve myself. To *fix*, as you say, my own failures. No."

"James." Lucy pulled back, one hand still on his shoulder, the other tracing the line of his shirt front. "Do you not understand that I care for you so much that I'd give you those funds freely if they were mine to give? And, in essence, they are, because my parents have given me the choice to follow my heart in marriage."

Bending his head, he took her hand and kissed it, and then her palm and knuckles. "Lucy. You would not wish to marry me if you didn't feel a need to help me. And I do adore your desire to help others." He smiled at her. "I wouldn't have you any other way. But you should be free to choose a man you don't feel the need to save. I won't let you do that."

"It's not just that. You must know that I feel—"

"I have feelings for you too, but that's precisely why I can't be the man who marries you for your money."

Lucy swallowed against how much it hurt that he was refusing her. She wanted to tell him that she loved him, that she'd want him no matter the circumstances. But she could see the determination in his eyes. The belief that he was being noble by refusing her plan. She'd anticipated this reaction, and when she fought her way through emotion, logic told her that all was not lost.

He was an honorable man, and she understood why he saw marriage to her as more advantageous to him than to her. Scratch that. He was a *foolish*, honorable man.

But she still had her contingency plan, and that was the one she was the most certain of. In truth, the one that, right now, tonight, she wanted most.

"May I have more whiskey?" She'd shocked him once more, and she hoped to again before the night was over.

He watched her warily, as if expecting her to do something else he hadn't anticipated. But he dutifully stood to retrieve the whiskey bottle and poured more into her glass.

She sipped and truly savored it this time, that instant warming comfort. But it made her feel strangely giddy too. Any tiny shreds of doubt, any lingering disappointment of him refusing her proposal, melted away in the fire of her final sip.

Casting her glass aside, she stood. James came to

her instantly, reaching for her arm as if fearing that the scant amount of liquor she'd consumed would make her unsteady.

Oddly, she felt steadier and more confident than she had in her entire life. Knowing exactly what she wanted gave her a heady kind of courage.

Looking up at him, she reached both arms behind her and unfastened the ribbon at the back of her gown. Then she started on the buttons, just a short row near her waist.

The gown made this all so much easier.

When she finished with the back, she raised her arms to the neckline of the dress. That's when the temperature in the room went from warm to scorching. She could see the moment he understood. But she didn't stop. There was no going back now.

She tugged at the straps, pulling them down her arms. She wore no corset or chemise. Nothing but this gown of satin.

James swallowed hard and took one step closer, close enough to touch.

"Lucy—"

He leaned to retrieve her cloak, and she stopped him.

"I want you to see me, and I want to be with you tonight."

She still held her gown up, braced with one arm across her breasts. Rather than answer her, he kissed the rounded edge of one bare shoulder, then the tender spot between her shoulder and neck, then her chin.

"No woman has ever tempted me more," he told her before taking her bottom lip gently between his teeth. "I've never even imagined I could want anyone the way I want you."

"I feel the same. So please, give me tonight."

A battle waged behind his lapis-blue eyes, but he never stopped looking at her. Never turned away. Their bodies fit together too well. Even now, standing chest to chest felt right.

She hoped he could see the longing in her eyes, see how sure she was of the choice she'd made.

Lucy waited, letting him fight his sense of propriety. She'd already overcome hers. But while she waited, she explored him, tracing the sharp line of his jaw with her fingertips. The stubble there was dark and shockingly soft. She nuzzled her cheek against him, whispering in his ear, "Please, James."

Maybe it was the *please* that did it. Maybe it was that she kissed his neck after whispering the word.

Maybe—and her heart wanted this to be true—he couldn't resist her any more than she could stop wanting him.

He took the final pins from her hair, running his fingers through the strands languidly, almost reverentially. "So lovely," he murmured as he swept the fall of hair off her shoulder and drew his fingers down until they snagged the strap of her gown.

Lucy dropped her arm, letting the fabric fall from her breasts. A moment later, James fell to his knees, braced an arm at her back, and licked a deliciously hot circle around her nipple. When she gasped, he simply smiled, his gaze on hers, and took the rosy puckered flesh into his mouth.

Unbidden, her hips bucked against him, somehow intimately connected with the wicked things he was doing with his tongue. When he released her nipple, he covered her breast with his palm, then turned his attention to her other nipple. A flick of his tongue made her want more, and he seemed to know. He offered decadent swirls of his tongue when he moved against her sensitive, peaked flesh.

She had her hands in his hair, ready to beg him not to stop, when she felt him gripping the bunched fabric at her waist. He tugged, sliding the satin over her hips, her thighs, letting it pool at her ankles.

James sat back on his haunches, his hands still on her hips, and gazed at her as if he'd just unearthed a treasure that was his alone. Then he scooted toward her, dropped his hands to her ankles and drew his fingertips up from her calves to the backs of her legs. He kissed her thighs, one and then the other, before pressing his lips to her curls.

"How did I get so lucky as to find you?" he asked, looking up at her with such awe and tenderness that Lucy had to fight back the burn of tears.

"We're both lucky."

He stood then, and she feared she'd said something wrong and marred the moment. But he still held her hand.

"You're certain?"

"Never more so."

He led her to a small bed at the rear of the cottage, and Lucy settled back against the soft mattress.

James watched her with a hunger that made her heart race.

"I suppose it's my turn now," he said with a seductive grin as he shed his unbuttoned shirt and began working to unfasten his trousers.

After toeing off his boots and letting his trousers fall, he climbed onto the bed, his palms planted on either side of her body.

His legs slid between hers, and he stilled, arching over her, staring into her eyes.

"I've never wanted anything more than this," he told her on a raspy whisper.

Lucy reached up and stroked her fingers through the thick fall of dark hair on his forehead.

"I've never wanted any man but you," she told him, certainty in every single word. She opened her mouth to say more. To assure him that she wouldn't stop wanting him after this single night together, or even after a lifetime at his side.

But he took her breath away. He'd knelt, scooping her backside into his hands and nuzzled his lips against her center.

One finger traced her slit, then he chased it with his tongue.

Lucy gasped at the heat of him. He'd touched her center once, but now his tongue explored and found a spot so sensitive that she bucked and gripped the counterpane in her hands as he lapped at her there.

"James." She wasn't certain what she was calling for. More, faster, deeper. But she knew what was coming.

He did too. Easing back just for a moment, he whispered against her, "Let it come, love. I want to feel you burst against my tongue."

Lucy slid a hand down to run her fingers through his hair. Then grip his shoulder, stroke along the back of his neck.

Her body drew taut as sensation built. He used his tongue masterfully, lovingly, seeming to know exactly what she needed. Then she felt the thick tip of his finger slip inside her and fireworks burst behind her eyes. She shook like she'd been shocked, the tremors somehow adding to the pleasure.

She called his name, and he was there, over her, his lips on hers.

"You're exquisite," he whispered between kisses. "We do this as you wish it. Tell me if it hurts or there's something you dislike."

"I like it all. I want all of you." Lucy felt the hot insistent press of him at her center. She was so wet, so sensitive, that she moaned as he thrust inside her and she bucked to get him closer.

There was a flash of pain, and James stilled as if he was so attuned to her feelings that he knew.

"Are you all right?"

Lucy laughed and bent up to kiss him. "I'm far better than all right."

She felt glorious. This felt glorious. Being with him, feeling their bodies connected, their breaths synchronizing as one.

He made her feel safe, desired, adored.

"I'm ready," she whispered, arching her hips up to take him deeper.

When he began to thrust, he held her gaze, his dark eyes intense, sparking with blue fire. But she thought she saw something else there too. A promise. A certainty. That this was just the beginning.

Then he shifted his hips, bent to take her nipple between his lips, and his rhythm became hungrier, faster, deeper. Exactly what she wanted.

She needed him as much as she could feel his need for her.

"Lucy," he began murmuring. "Lucy." He repeated her name like a plea.

Her name on his tongue pulled her to that precipice again. Faster this time than ever before, she dug her nails into his shoulder as she fell. And he came too. A moment after she cried out, he groaned her name.

Then he kissed her, breathlessly, and she swore she heard their hearts beating as one in that moment.

He settled beside her on the bed. There wasn't much room, but Lucy preferred it that way. They lay entwined, legs, arms, her cheek pressed to his chest.

Lucy hoped he felt as safe and content as she did. She lifted her head to ask, but he'd closed his eyes and was breathing in the slow, steady rhythm of sleep.

He looked peaceful, and there was the slightest hint of a smile on his lips.

Lucy smiled too. Stubborn, wonderful man. She didn't just want to save him. She wanted to love him for the rest of her days.

Chapter Nineteen

For the first time in his life, James woke languidly. Not gasping for air to escape a nightmare or jolting awake as if he'd heard some ominous noise. His mind and body were at peace in a way he couldn't ever remember experiencing before.

Lucy lay half splayed atop him, her leg over his, her arm draped across his chest, and her long flaxen hair tickling his chin.

This is where I'm meant to be.

He had felt this feeling before, back when he was at the pinnacle of success with Pembroke Shipping. There was a day when he realized his bank accounts were overflowing, he was turning away new customers, and friends wanted his company while colleagues respected him. Anything he wanted to buy could be his.

He recalled the moment with vivid clarity, because it was the only time he'd given more than a second's contemplation to how he might secure those things in life that one couldn't buy—happiness, contentment, love.

And he'd dismissed the thought.

Happiness came from his success, he'd reasoned. Contentment was found in financial security. And love was what he felt for his business—a kind of unwavering commitment that brought him true satisfaction. Back then, he couldn't imagine needing more.

And then Lucy came along.

A pair of bold peridot eyes and an inner strength that shone through in every choice she made, and he was never the same. Somehow, he'd known, even after that first glimpse of her gaping wide-eyed at King's Cross Station, that he wanted her in his life from that day forward.

If he'd examined the impulse, he would have rejected it out of hand. There was no strategy in it. No payoff that he could imagine. A fanciful noblewoman? A lady determined to chuck propriety aside and be blindingly hopeful that society would accept her exactly as she wished to be?

For a man who'd done his best to build himself up in the eyes of society, at least London's commercial milieu, he would have run in the opposite direction if someone told him that such a woman would beguile him completely.

And yet she had. And he was.

Not even when he'd been at the peak of his success had he felt as lucky as he did now, lying in a ramshackle cottage under a quilt made of scraps with the most determined, extraordinary woman tucked against him.

He couldn't let her go.

Selfish? Perhaps. Impossible? Considering his current financial situation, possibly.

But he had to try, even if that meant employing unusual means.

James stroked her hair, letting his fingers dance across her shoulder, stroking the soft, warm skin of her back. Lucy made a little mewling sound of contented sleepiness and nuzzled her cheek against his chest.

He waited until her breathing settled into a slow, steady rhythm and gently lifted her arm, then slid out from under her leg and out of bed. Holding his breath, he prayed he hadn't roused her, but she merely resettled under the covers, scooping the pillow into her arms where she'd previously held him.

Waking her would likely be the better choice. In fact, he suspected he'd hear about this choice later and have to explain himself.

He dressed quickly and quietly, glancing at his pocket watch.

There was no more time for delay, or even stealing another second of the truest contentment he'd ever known. He had to go.

Looking around the cottage for something to write on, he settled on a scrap of paper in a crumpled ball near the fire that looked as if it had been intended for kindling. In a bookcase with a fold-out desk, he found a nearly empty fountain pen.

Minutes ticked by as he searched his mind, but he had no eloquence to offer her. Making promises wasn't fair either. Instead, he scratched out a single line, then another, and signed with an inelegant *J*.

Little Athena, who had Artemis's love for archery, looked now like a slumbering Venus, her hair spread around her, limbs stretched across the bed, face flushed.

A kiss might wake her, but he couldn't resist. He bent without touching her, just resting his lips gently against her temple, inhaling her floral and spice scent, hoping she would understand what last night—what she—meant to him.

Then he slipped from the cottage, pulled the door shut, and headed off to try.

LUCY STARED AT the scrap of paper. Then she crumpled it again. Then smoothed it out on her thigh and let out an irritated sigh.

She'd awoken happy. Stretching like a cat, warm and sated. And completely alone.

The quilt was still warm, but James was nowhere to be found. She'd even peeked her head outside to see if he'd taken an early morning wander. Only when she'd walked back in and closed the door did the crumpled bit of paper float to the floor in front of her.

> *You're the most magnificent woman, and I'm not sure I deserve you.*
> *But I want to try.*

> *—J*

It was like a riddle, and not a particularly good one. Lucy wasn't sure she'd ever seen a collection of words that made less sense to her. The magnificent part was lovely, of course. He'd murmured as much to her last night.

The not-deserving-her part was absolute rubbish. She wasn't even certain what it meant. Caring for someone had little to do with deserving and everything to do with one's heart. James was kind, passionate, attentive—with the enormous exception of leaving her after they'd made love—and quite simply the man who made her heart leap in her chest. The only man who'd ever made her feel desired, wanted, adored.

I adore you. Those words echoed in her heart even now.

And yet he'd left her. Good grief, she wasn't even sure what time it was. She'd planned to slip back into the house last night, unseen, but sleeping next to James had been too comforting. Too precious to give up. Because she'd known, despite her hopes and her determination, it might be the only opportunity she'd have to be with him in such a way.

In all their murmurings and confessions in the throes of lovemaking, there'd been no promises. No talk of tomorrow. Of today.

She had chosen this and known the consequences might be unpleasant. So, she'd face them, knowing she had one night of passion with a man that she loved. Those memories would be hers forever.

But she still grumbled to herself when she folded

the scrap of paper and shoved it into the bodice of her gown after she'd dressed. After putting on her cloak, she shoveled ashes onto the embers still burning in the hearth and headed back toward the manor.

The morning breeze held the kind of bite that raced through you, and Lucy wasn't wearing nearly enough layers. By the time she slipped inside the front door, her teeth were chattering, and she longed for nothing so much as a warm bath.

"Lucy."

No warm bath would be imminent, apparently. Aunt Cassandra stood at the top of the stairs looking weary and worried, as if she'd been waiting there for hours for Lucy to come through the door.

Guilt joined the frustration of waking to find James gone, both chipping away at the bliss she'd felt last night as she fell asleep in his arms.

"Come up to my sitting room, please."

Lucy yearned to have a moment to herself first, to change and bathe and put on something warmer, but though her aunt had added *please* to her request, it was far more command than petition.

"Yes, Aunt Cassandra."

Those words allowed her aunt to sweep back down the hall, expecting Lucy to follow in her wake. When Lucy reached the top rung of the stairwell, her aunt was speaking quietly to Senga, who nodded and departed toward the servant's stairs.

Inside her aunt's sitting room, Lucy found the heat she craved. A lively fire crackled in the grate, and a tea service sat on a table between two rose velvet chairs, steam puffing up from the lid of the teapot.

"Sit, my dear."

Lucy chose the chair nearest the fire, and her aunt immediately moved behind her to settle a thick knitted blanket around her shoulders.

"Thank you."

Aunt Cassandra sat and pulled a similar coverlet over her lap. She watched Lucy silently for so long that Lucy guessed she was expected to confess before any more would be said. But just as she prepared herself to do so and drew in a deep breath, her aunt spoke softly.

"I know you probably wish to wash and sleep."

Despite her intention, Lucy blushed at that. Not out of shame but the clear implication that her aunt knew exactly where she'd been and what she'd done last night.

"I knew you'd go to him," she said simply. "My worst fear was that you would elope."

Lucy liked that idea and almost wished she'd suggested it. But, of course, he'd refused her proposal.

"I was pleased when I woke early and Mrs. Fox informed me that no carriages or horses had been taken from the stables, according to the stable boy. That's also when I realized you had not returned to your room."

Lucy watched the flames and wondered what she could say to make her aunt understand her choices. Or perhaps she understood them too well—she herself had eloped with Lord Munro—and just wished to offer warnings and admonitions.

"I'll let you speak now," her aunt said with nothing but compassion in her tone. "Tell me what you will. You may trust my discretion, but I would like to know your plans regarding Lord Rossbury. And, of course, his plans in regard to you."

Lucy pulled the blanket around her more tightly and settled into her chair. She did trust her aunt and knew that her reaction wasn't what Lucy had to fear. Indeed, her father's or mother's reaction, but not her aunt's. They wouldn't respond with Cassandra's compassion. At least, not at first.

"My plan is to marry him."

Aunt Cassandra nodded with a hint of surprise in her expression. "He's asked you?"

"No. I asked him, but he refused."

Something like surprise settled over her aunt's features. Or perhaps it was confusion. Her aunt's brows drew together.

"He believes he's doing the honorable thing by refusing me because I made the very practical suggestion that my dowry would help resolve the financial difficulty that he finds himself in." Lucy heard her voice rising, felt her heartbeat begin to race. "He could pay off the dreadful man he borrowed from, rebuild his business, and you could keep your home. We could gift it to you or sell it to you or whatever would satisfy your pride."

She stalled and took a breath when she felt the hot trickle of a tear on her cheek.

"I don't understand. Not you, or him, or this obsession with pride. Mr. Blackwood adores you. He would buy this house for you, or give you the funds to do so, without a second thought. My dowry isn't anything I earned. It's nothing I asked for. But it will go to whichever man I stand up in a church with and make promises to."

Senga entered the room with a basin of water, towels, and what Lucy recognized as one of her warmer, practical day dresses. She also carried a small plate of cheese and bread balanced on top. The young woman's eyes were wide as she entered, set down the items in her arms, and practically darted back out the door.

"I didn't mean to shout," Lucy said, and reached immediately for a slice of thick, crusty bread. Not until that moment did she realize she was famished.

Her aunt poured her a steaming cup of tea and set it next to her on the low, round table between them.

"We're talking about matters of the heart. Sometimes shouting is required."

"I had made peace with never marrying. But as long as I've found someone I'd like to spend the rest of my days with, of course I'd point out how my dowry will prove helpful."

"Men and money, especially a woman's money—"

"It's not just men. You won't let Mr. Blackwood help you either. It's pride. Stupid, illogical pride."

Her aunt twisted her lips, but they finally twitched into a smile. "Don't hold back, my dear. Be brutal if you must."

"I'm frustrated that there are simple solutions, ways to fix the problems that are plaguing you both, and neither of you are willing to allow those who love you to help." Lucy put her hands together, practically beseeching. "We want to help you."

Aunt Cassandra stood and went to a delicate-looking, ornate desk near one of the room's long windows. She slid open a drawer and pulled out two items, then returned to her chair.

The first item, a miniature, depicted a dashingly handsome man with a winsome smile and wild auburn hair.

"Lord Alexander Munro. He wished to help me by taking me away from an overbearing father. Perhaps your mother has told you how exacting our father could be." Cassandra shook her head as if dispelling unpleasant memories. "Alex was charming, exciting, irascible, and didn't have an honest bone in his body. And then there's this one."

The second item she handed over was a photo card depicting a stern-looking man with cold eyes, a thick beard, and a waxed mustache.

"Lord Rossbury?"

"Rufus was honest at least. He told me he could never love me, but he could provide me with things. A manor house in Scotland, for instance. A fair exchange, I thought. Until I yearned for passion in my life again."

"As you've found with Mr. Blackwood?"

"Indeed."

"Who you refuse to marry."

"That isn't out of pride," her aunt admonished with a wave. "That is pure fear."

"What do you fear?"

"Being dependent on someone and having it fail. Loving someone is always a risk."

"I'm ready for a risk."

"Is your Lord Rossbury?"

What they felt for each other was real. Of that, she had not a single doubt. Perhaps he felt the fear Aunt Cassandra spoke of. That, she could understand, but she still wasn't sure how to overcome his pride.

"Is fear also the reason you won't allow Mr. Blackwood to help you? Fear more than pride?" Lucy handed the images of the two men back to her aunt.

"I suppose it is. Angus wishes to help me because he adores me, but what if I disappoint him? What if he comes to resent me because he's given me so much? Or what if, because he's helped me so much, he comes to respect me a little less?"

"Love doesn't work that way."

Aunt Cassandra chuckled. "In my experience, love is many things, but predictable isn't one of them, dear girl. But I do adore your fierceness and determination to see every dilemma as entirely solvable."

Lucy heard what she wasn't saying too. Perhaps she thought her naive or impulsive. "If I'm not brave enough to follow my heart, what was the point of coming on this journey?"

"What will you do, since he's refused your proposal?"

Lucy's mind felt fuzzy. She hadn't taken the time to form any real plan, but as tired as she was, only one thing made sense.

The issue of what he owed to some dreadful man named Beck was at the core of his troubles. James's life was not his own until that man was out of it.

"I think I should return to London."

"Without speaking to Lord Rossbury?"

"He's not here, Aunt Cassandra. He's gone."

"But how? I spoke to the stable master. No conveyances are gone beyond Angus's, since he departed for his whiskey works this morning." Cassandra took a sip of tea and let out a contemplative *hmm*. "Perhaps Angus delivered Rossbury to the station at Inverkeithing. It wouldn't be far out of his way."

"Then I should prepare to depart too."

"You should rest, my dear. Leave tomorrow if you must."

Lucy didn't want to lose that much time. "I'll wash and rest for a bit and can still catch the morning train."

Her aunt stood and reached out a hand, helping Lucy to her feet. Then she braced a hand on each of Lucy's shoulders.

"I know that once your mind is made up, there's little chance of dissuading you. But at least I can do this much." She released Lucy and returned to that desk where she'd retrieved the images of Lord

Munro and Lord Rossbury. She replaced those and then withdrew a velvet drawstring pouch not much bigger than her palm.

"Take these," she said as she pressed the pouch into Lucy's hand. "A lady traveling alone can never be too careful or prepared."

The cool velvet slid against her fingertips but whatever was inside was heavy and blocky, with the heft of metal. When Aunt Cassandra nodded, Lucy loosened the pouch's tie, looked inside, and gasped.

The gun was so tiny it looked like a toy. An etched, pearl-handled toy.

"It's not loaded, and, no, I've never shot anyone. But I have waved it about as a threat, and it has cowed gentlemen who thought their size and bad intentions would allow them to get the better of me." She stared at the pouch in Lucy's hand. "There's more."

The other object was oblong, silver, and also etched. A sort of tube about the length of Lucy's palm.

Aunt Cassandra took it from her carefully, pointed it away from them, and pushed a lever.

"Oh my." Lucy examined the blade in excited awe.

"This is very sharp and very effective and, as you can see, easily concealed." Her aunt offered Lucy a mischievous smirk. "This one I have had to use, and I believe it may have saved my life."

The notion of causing someone physical harm made Lucy's stomach knot, but she could see the value in carrying either of the weapons as a deterrent. Especially when a lady was confronted by men like Nichols.

"Thank you. These will make me feel safer."

"Good." She took Lucy's face between her hands this time. "I'm proud of you and your loving heart, my dear. I wish I could protect you, and that desire to safeguard your well-being makes me understand your father better. I never dreamed I'd say that."

They both laughed. Then Cassandra pressed a kiss to her forehead.

"Be safe, and may you talk your very Lucy brand of sense into that gentleman you love."

"Do you still dislike him a great deal?"

Cassandra looked away as if considering her reply carefully. "Most of what I said to him was meant for his uncle. Old resentment and fear that I'd lose this house that I've come to love so dearly. If you say he's worthy of your heart, then I shall be open to being convinced he deserves it."

"I believe he does."

"Then go, my dear. Wash and rest, and McKay will take you to the station if you're determined to get back to London this evening."

Lucy settled her aunt's knitted blanket on a chair before making her way back to her room, clutching the velvet pouch full of weapons to her chest.

The gift was unexpected, but might prove useful. Because she wasn't planning to travel to London merely to find James. Lucy's main goal was to find a way to reason with Mr. Archibald Beck.

Chapter Twenty

After nearly two hours of touring Blackwood's distillery and being regaled on the difference between distillation methods, learning about blended whiskey, and getting an earful about the possibilities of distributing Blackwood Whiskey in America if he could get the stuff shipped for a fair price, James was ready to take Blackwood on as a client. But he remained unsure how to get his shipping business up and running again in the timeline the whiskey maker laid out.

Blackwood's terms were far too generous. Much of what he offered was more or less a favor because he loved the woman whose home James owned. And while Invermere was never mentioned during their negotiations, he suspected it was never far from either of their minds.

"Shall I have the documents drawn up for your signature?"

"I suppose I am the one wanting this resolved with all due haste." James fought his hesitation, fought the urge to revert to his youthful motto of trusting no one. Perhaps if he'd stuck to it, as he'd often reasoned in the past two years, there would have been no deal with Beck. No fake industrial scheme. No humiliation and loss.

But then there was Lucy. Not only was he ready to push aside his fears to become the sort of man she deserved, but her loving, kind nature, her trust, humbled him.

That's what ultimately led him to make the decision. He would risk putting his trust in Blackwood and accept the man's help. They were both businessmen, and they were both incurring risk by embarking on this venture together.

"And the house?"

Blackwood gestured at the notes he'd made during their negotiations. "This should be separate. Business and personal can never be wholly disconnected, but let's settle this formally. The house can be less formal. As I said, I'm happy to advance you a holding fee until Cass can sort out financing from her lady banker friend."

James couldn't be certain Beck would accept partial payment, but it was something to give him now rather than waiting for the process of selling the manor, either to Lady Cassandra or anyone else.

"How about thirty percent?" Blackwood offered.

"I accept those terms. The house shall be her ladyship's." Just saying it lifted a weight from his chest. He would have been miserable selling to anyone else, because causing Lady Cassandra distress would have pained Lucy.

"Bless you, man." Blackwood pressed a palm to

his chest dramatically. "We should drink to all of this good news."

"I have a better idea."

"Out with it then, business partner."

"This isn't a business idea. It's entirely personal. What do you say to us returning to Invermere to let the ladies know?"

"Ye see!" Blackwood pointed at him as he stood from his desk chair. "I knew I'd found a clever partner in ye. Of course, we should go right this minute. I'm a cad to even consider making Cass wait another second to hear the happy news."

James laid a hand on the man's arm after he'd slipped on his overcoat. "Will it be happy news? You did say she didn't want you interfering."

"She didn't want me buying the house outright, it's true. But she herself mused about a way to delay the sale. If she's keen to repay me once she has her loan, so be it."

His new business partner lifted James's coat from the rack in his spacious office and tossed it to him.

"You sure you don't wish me to sign something now, even before the formal documents are drawn up?" James had already vowed to himself that when he was in business again, he'd never again fail to read every line of every contract. He'd told himself he wouldn't accept a handshake or a man's word when making deals.

Somehow, Blackwood with his charm and open, gregarious nature had broken through his reserves.

"I trust you, lad." Angus clapped him on the

back. "Besides, I'd wager my fortune that soon we'll be family of a sort."

Whatever James's face did in response to that comment caused Blackwood to frown. "Ye do plan to marry the lass, don't ye? Any fool can see ye're mad for her."

"If I told you the truth, you'd never let me live it down."

"Oh lord no, man. What have ye done?"

"She asked me to marry her." James focused on buttoning his coat, suddenly unable to meet the man's eyes. Hell, he'd struggle to look himself in the mirror for what a fool he'd been. "I refused."

"Eejit."

"She wanted to use her dowry to help me."

"So ye refused a lass who loves ye because she's rich? Aye, ye're a right dunderheed."

"In the clear light of day, I'm beginning to agree. Do you think she'll forgive me?"

"I hope so. Otherwise, family dinners will be bloody awkward." Blackwood made a shooing motion. "Go, man. There's no time to lose. I've a lady to make happy, and ye've one to offer some quality groveling."

JAMES SLEPT THROUGH the latter half of their trip, so when he woke to Angus Blackwood nearly shoving him from the carriage, it took him a moment to register that they were back at Invermere.

The morning fog had cleared, and rays of late

morning light turned the house's limestone facade a warm caramel as it glinted off the windows.

Somehow the serenity of the weather gave him a good feeling. A sense of hope that all would be well. In terms of his business, the tide had already turned. Business with Blackwood Whiskey wouldn't remake his shipping business, but it was a fine start. And the capital Blackwood advanced him would help too.

And all he'd needed to do was battle past his pride and distrust.

But had he lost Lucy's trust already?

His gut clenched every time he recalled slipping from bed and leaving her. Was she angry with him?

Blackwood seemed to sense his unease.

"Come on, man. All will be well. Even if it takes time. You're willing to wait for her, aren't ye?"

"Forever."

Blackwood laughed at that. "Mercy, ye've truly gone and fallen hard."

On the top step, the door swung open, and James expected to see Mrs. Fox at the threshold. But it was Lady Cassandra who stood before them, her jaw slack with shock.

"I thought you'd returned to London, Lord Rossbury."

"No, I went north with Mr. Blackwood to see his distillery."

"Meet my new business partner, Cass," Blackwood put in with his usual jovial bellow and a hand slapped against James's back.

Lady Cassandra didn't even glance his way. "But Lucy has gone after you."

"She's gone to London?"

"Yes, she left early to catch the express. The girl barely took time to eat or rest."

The news landed like a blow, and James struggled to make sense of Lucy's reasoning. Then self-recriminations rang in his head. If he'd only spoken to her and explained his intentions, she'd be here, and he'd be delivering happy news.

"I've been a goddamned fool."

"Yes, it seems you have been." Lady Cassandra had no reason to empathize with him.

At the moment, he didn't know if he'd be able to forgive himself if any harm came to Lucy.

"Can one of the staff take me to the station?"

"You cannae go now, man. Come in and warm yourself. You've missed the morning express today, but you can catch it first thing tomorrow."

"Then I'll take a later train and arrive in the evening." James shook his head. "I'm going now."

A half dozen gut-twisting scenarios played out in his mind. What if Lucy encountered another man like Nichols on her train ride back to London? What if she somehow found out where he lived and visited his house in Cavendish Square? If Beck's thugs were watching his movements in Edinburgh, the man had certainly kept watchers on his home in London.

And what better way to induce him to pay up than by threatening harm to Lucy? If the man in

Edinburgh had seen them together and wired back that information, they'd know who she was.

"I have to go. Either one of your staff takes me to the station or I'm stealing Blackwood's carriage. You choose."

LUCY DIDN'T REGRET anything she'd done in Scotland, but sneaking out of the back garden and creeping down the mews behind Hallston House had her nervous about every step she took.

Her parents had been surprised but pleased by her abrupt return. Mama had been happy to see her, and Papa had embraced her the way he had when she was young, nearly swinging her off her feet. Even Charlie seemed pleased, though he'd nearly had an apoplectic fit when she told him she wished to marry a man she'd met on the train to Scotland.

He'd become convinced she was planning to elope, which made it particularly challenging to sneak away without him noticing. After one heated conversation in her chamber, she'd let him believe he'd dissuaded her. But stubbornness ran in her family. Her brother had kept a watchful eye on her for hours, so she was departing much later than she'd planned.

Thank goodness the sky was clear, and the moon was bright. She wasn't used to venturing out into the city near midnight. But there had been a passel of firsts in life of late. She couldn't lose her nerve now.

"*Are you mad? Or just determined to seek out chaos so you can fix it?*"

"Blast!" Lucy spun to see her brother marching toward her down the mews. That same moonlight that lit her way highlighted the angry frown on his face. "This isn't your concern, Charlie."

"You're my sister. Father charged me with protecting you years ago." Once he reached her, some of the anger melted into a pleading expression. "Don't do this, Lu. Eloping may seem romantic—"

"I'm not eloping."

"Then what the hell are you doing out here in the middle of the night?"

Lucy bit her lip. Nothing she said was going to put him at ease. Yet she'd never lied to him and didn't wish to start now.

"I have a meeting with someone who I must speak to."

Charlie rolled his eyes. "Hmm, let me guess. Is he tall and handsome and a penniless earl who you met on the train to Scotland?"

"No, actually." Lucy felt a momentary flare of victory, but it was short-lived because there was no chance he wasn't going to ask more questions.

"Then who?"

Lucy pressed her gloved fingers to the center of her forehead. She hadn't slept, had a headache, and just wanted this whole thing over with.

"A businessman."

Charlie's brows dipped. "What respectable businessman meets with unmarried ladies at midnight?"

"I didn't say he was respectable."

"Good god, Lu. What's got into you? You were always the most sensible of all of us, and all you ever wanted to do was help everyone."

"This is to help someone," she said emphatically.

Charlie closed his eyes, drew in a deep breath as if trying for calm and took a step closer. He laid a hand on her arm lightly. "Please, let me come with you, or at least tell me where you're going in case something goes amiss."

He was being practical because he knew it would work on her.

"His name is Beck. A con man who took advantage of James. I'm going to reason with him."

Suddenly, all the calm was gone, and Charlie clasped her arm tightly. "I can't let you go converse with a criminal in the dead of night."

His voice had risen, and Lucy shushed him, wishing she could take every word back. Charlie wasn't discreet. He was gregarious and impulsive, and he'd no doubt blurt everything she'd told him to the first person he saw. Namely, their parents.

"He's not a man my sister should have any business with."

Lucy let out a gasp. "You know him?"

"Not well, of course. I know of him."

Her brother had stunned her by potentially proving to be the most useful person in her life at the moment.

Charlie *knew* Archibald Beck.

"Tell me what you know." Now she was the one

holding on tightly to him, tugging at the lapel of his suit coat.

"I know of a club he owns." He dipped his head and then cast a sheepish gaze up at her. "I may have been once or twice." He pointed a finger at her. "Swear to me you'll never tell Mama or Papa."

"What's it called and how do I get there?"

"Lu, it's not a place for you."

"Tell me, or I'm marching in to tell Papa and Mama now."

He glared at her, and even in the moonlight she could see that his cheeks had gone a radish red as they had when they'd fought as children.

"The Helix Club," he said through clenched teeth. "Cannon Street near London Bridge."

"You're a godsend, Charlie."

The one part of her plan she'd imagined would take her the longest was tracking down Archibald Beck, but now she had a place to start.

"I'm going," she told him as she took a step away from him. "Don't follow me, and don't tell Mama or Papa."

"You can't, Lucy." He reached for her as she'd expected he would, and she took another step back.

"I'll be fine," she assured him. "I have a gun."

"Jesus, where did you get that?"

"Aunt Cassandra, of course." Lucy gave him a smile and a wink.

As soon as she turned to depart, he laid a hand on her arm. "Don't get yourself killed," he bit off

in a frantic whisper. "If I have to tell Mama and
Papa I didn't stop you, they'll never forgive me."

Lucy rolled her eyes. "I appreciate your concern. Go to bed, Charlie. I'll be back soon." She
lifted the edge of her skirt and sprinted down the
mews. She didn't hear any footsteps at her back,
and she was glad for it. Charlie would just get in
the way.

She'd dressed in black, adding a white lace collar,
hoping to be mistaken for a servant. If Beck didn't
allow ladies into his club, that might be her only
way in.

Finding a hansom wasn't hard, though the driver
gave her a long look when she told him where she
wished to be delivered.

As the carriage rattled over cobblestones, anxiety and the cool breeze of the autumn night made
her shiver. She patted one pocket of her dress and
felt the reassuring outline of the petite pistol there,
then she breathed deep and felt the slim cylinder
of the switchblade shifting beneath her corset. The
folded document in her reticule gave her a measure of peace too.

She was as prepared as she could be.

Fatigue threatened as the steady rumble of the
carriage eased away her worry, and she found a
moment of comfort in settling her tired body
against the cushioned bench.

She thought of James and clenched her fist in
frustration. A part of her was still angry at him
for leaving her alone in that cottage. But she also

couldn't deny that she missed him after only a few hours apart.

Maddening man. She understood his fear a little better after talking to Aunt Cassandra, and she certainly appreciated that trust was hard for him after the business with Beck. But she'd hoped he'd overcome it, or at least try to, for her sake.

She didn't relish facing Beck alone, but she couldn't sit idly by and do nothing. And if all went well tonight, they'd be free. James would be free, and maybe then he could consider her proposal with an open heart.

When doubts came, she pushed them aside. Stubbornly hopeful. Wasn't that what he'd once called her?

When the carriage stopped, Lucy tried to get her bearings, but this wasn't a part of the city she'd ever visited.

"You're sure 'bout this, miss?"

"This is the Helix Club?"

Shadowed by the gaslight, Lucy could only make out the driver's nod, not whatever expression he wore. "Watch yourself, miss."

He rolled off into the fog, and Lucy pulled back the hood of her cloak to look around. The man had deposited her at the mouth of an alley, but the club must have a front entrance onto the street. Didn't it?

Maybe the driver knew something she didn't, or perhaps her drab dress had worked as she'd hoped and he assumed she was a staff member at the club.

The problem with the alley was that it was weakly lit by a lantern hung on a building here and there, whereas gaslight lit up the streets in patches of reassuring light.

Unbuttoning one button on the front of her gown, Lucy pulled out the knife, tucking it into her palm. If she was going to wander down the abyss of a shadowy alley, she wanted to be prepared for anything.

One step and she heard laughter echoing off the bricks a bit further down. She could make out movement. A couple, it appeared, standing close, perhaps doing more than standing, in the shadows.

Their presence somehow reassured her.

But a few steps further into the alley and she heard movement at her back. Footsteps, heavier than hers, and coming toward her in a hurried stomp.

Lucy flipped the lever on the knife, spun, and held the blade out in front of her. "Don't come any closer."

The hulking figure skidded to a stop and raised his arms toward the sky.

"Sweetheart, please don't gut me before I've had the chance to tell you what an arse I've been."

Lucy exhaled with such relief she dropped the knife. "James?"

"I've missed you," he said roughly, then stepped forward and took her into his arms. "I'm sorry I left without explanation."

Not until she touched him, their bodies pressed

close, his breath in her hair, did she feel as if she could breathe again. She hadn't realized how anxious she'd been, how every muscle in her body felt tight, until she melted against the warmth of his body and knew he was safe and solid in her arms.

"Wait," she said, pulling away from him. "How did you find me?"

But she knew the answer even before he spoke her brother's name.

"It's a good thing he spotted me. I'm not sure your father would ever forgive me for banging down their door at midnight." He slid a strand of hair behind her ear. "I would have come earlier, but I had to take the slow train."

"I'm sorry. That longer journey must have been miserable for you."

He pulled her tighter and she glimpsed the shadow of a smile. "I had good incentive."

"You've come all this way for me, but you left me alone in a cottage with a vague note and nothing more." The anger had mostly subsided, but it still hurt.

"I was a fool. A complete and total arse to leave you. I should have explained and told you where I was going and why."

"Yes, you should have." Mention of that morning brought the previous night to mind. It was the last time she'd felt truly happy. "I miss the cottage," she said as she tucked her head against his chest.

He laughed at that and the sound rumbling in her ears made her smile.

"I had rather hoped you missed *me*."

Lucy pushed at his chest. "Of course, I did. I thought you'd gone off and put yourself in danger out of some sense of guilt or masculine pride."

He released her enough to tip his head, though she could barely see him in the darkness.

"This from a woman who *is* putting herself in danger right now?"

"I was just going to have a conversation with Mr. Beck."

"With a knife."

"I have a gun too."

"Good god, Lucy."

"Mrs. Winterbottom says—"

"I adore you, Lucy Westmont, but I'm afraid I don't give a damn what Mrs. Coldarse says."

Lucy answered by pushing up onto her toes and taking his mouth, and he responded hungrily, one hand at her nape, his fingers stroking up into her hair, the other at her back, pulling her tight against his heat.

A door opened further down the alley, and music and several raucous gentlemen stumbled into the darkened lane.

"We should go," James whispered against her lips, then reached down to clasp her hand.

He led her back toward the street and stepped to the curb to hail a hansom cab.

Lucy couldn't resist taking a few steps so she could glimpse the front facade of the Helix Club.

"Goodness, it looks quite elegant. Even respectable."

James approached until she could feel him at her back. "Beck has many respectable and successful businesses. That's the facade that makes men trust him. But this place is the epitome of Beck. A popular and lavish club on the street side, and illegal activities downstairs with an entrance in the alleyway."

"What sort of illegal activities?"

The horse attached to the hansom he'd hailed clomped its feet, as if eager to depart.

"Let's have this conversation another time and get you home?" James lowered his hand to hers, and Lucy let him lead her to the carriage.

Once he'd helped her up and Lucy settled against the cab's seat, James closed the door and smiled up at her.

"Wait, I thought you were departing with me."

"There's still something I need to do. I'll be fine, but you're sure you'll be able to get back inside?"

Lucy wanted to argue but there was a determination in his tone that made her doubt he could be swayed.

"I came out through the back garden and will get back in that way. I just have to hope my parents are still in bed. And that Charlie didn't panic and wake them."

"I don't think he would have. I assured him I had no plans to whisk you off to Gretna Green. Before I could even get to the front door, he approached down the lane on foot and accused me of lurking. He was a bit far in his cups."

Lucy closed her eyes and breathed in sharply. "I knew he was a dreadful coconspirator."

"And thank God for that. And that I could get to you in time to stop you."

Lucy tried to ignore the implication that she couldn't have helped the situation and merely would have put herself in danger. She still thought her plan had merit.

"I'll call on you tomorrow."

Lucy leaned toward him, reaching out to curl a hand around the lapel of his coat. "Please be careful."

He leaned in and offered her a too-brief kiss. "I promise."

With that, he slapped a hand on the polished wood of the cab's side, letting the driver know it was time to depart.

She glanced back as the hansom rolled away. Part of her still wanted to speak to Mr. Archibald Beck, and all of her hated the idea of leaving James to deal with the man alone.

Lucy reached up and knocked on the carriage wall. When the driver opened the small door above her head, she asked, "Would you be so kind as to turn around and take me back to where you collected me?"

$\mathcal{P}$atience wasn't a virtue James had ever learned.

In business, that had served him well. Waiting too long to take a meeting with a potential client or jump on a new venture might cost him an opportunity. Of course, it contributed to his downfall too. He'd been too eager to trust Beck's promises.

Over the past year, he'd tried to teach himself the value of waiting, reminding himself that the best things in life took tenacity and determination and, very often, time to achieve.

But when it came to Lucy, all those fresh lessons seemed to come apart at the seams.

He adored the woman. Loved her. He wanted to marry her. Logic told him they might have to wait some time to wed. Her father would wish to see that James had the sort of financial security and respectability that Lucy deserved in a husband.

And, of course, if Hallston got the slightest whiff of James's trouble with a man like Beck, he doubted he'd ever win favor with the earl at all. Never mind that he was an earl now too. Hallston was favored by their queen. James was a failed businessman in debt to a con man.

Dealing with Beck had to come first.

Which was why James found himself standing on the street in front of the Helix Club, five minutes after the hansom cab driver had departed to take Lucy back to the safety of her family and home.

It was late, but early enough for those who didn't sleep until dawn. Guests were still stepping out of carriages and into the polished brass doors of Beck's club.

James joined the throng. He made no mention of Beck, just gave the doorman his title. After a long perusal, the man allowed him inside.

It was a very long shot to think Beck would happen to be in attendance tonight, the very night James had impulsively decided to confront him. But he felt compelled to try.

He searched the guests mingling through various lavishly appointed rooms for a face he might recognize, but, of course, his vow to avoid dealings with noblemen meant he recognized no one.

Until he did.

Not a nobleman, but one of the men who'd come to his home that day before he'd departed for Scotland. The quiet, bulky one.

The man hadn't noticed him. He was too busy sweeping an assessing gaze over the club's main salon of round gaming tables.

James studied the assembly a little longer, hoping to see one short, balding man with an overmanicured mustache and a rosebud in his buttonhole. Beck had once told him that he rarely played at his own tables, but he appeared now and then just to surprise guests and hobnob with the upper crust who deigned to visit.

Tonight, it seemed, was not one of those nights.

He made his way back toward the club's entrance, then slowed when he swore he heard someone speak his name. Not his uncle's title. His name.

Turning toward the sound, he couldn't make out who'd spoken or see anyone who'd noticed him or made their approach.

"Come to pay us a visit, Pembroke, or just to pay your debt to the boss?" The man spoke from behind him and stood far too close. James froze when the stranger jabbed something into the small of his back. "Keep walking and head toward the gold door on your left."

The gold door was half-hidden by a long velvet drape. James and Beck's associate made their way toward it awkwardly, with the object at his back disappearing and then punching at his coat again. At one point, the man trod on his ankle.

"Faster. Just go."

The gold door was unlocked, and the minute he swung it a few inches, James knew where it led.

A staircase carpeted in black and lit by a dozen wall sconces led to the club's underground. The area where the desperate or debauched came for higher stakes games and to find pleasures the crowd upstairs might want but wouldn't wish to be seen partaking of in public.

James expected them to descend to the bottom

floor. He knew there was one more stairwell behind a black door that led to Beck's private quarters. An office, study, even a bedroom. But the man at his back shoved him forward, across the room, and James spotted their destination.

Upon a dais of glossy black sat an ornate marble table featuring a lady contortionist, performing a routine involving her long, shapely limbs and glasses of what looked like absinthe. Behind her, James spotted Beck and two more ladies, one seated on each side of him.

The man at his back pushed him closer to Beck. "Look what I found upstairs, boss. I wager he's come to pay up."

Beck looked happier than James had ever seen him, and he didn't know whether to chalk that up to his feminine companions or the drink. The man's cheeks were ruddy, his eyes glossy, and what James imagined was his version of a smile twitched beneath his curling mustache.

"Is that so, James? Come with money, have you? Finally?"

"I have part of what I owe. And I'll have the rest to you soon. Things have turned around for Pembroke Shipping." A generous interpretation of gaining one customer and still owning half of one ship, but James had a concrete reason to hope the tide had finally turned in his favor.

"Those weren't the terms, friend."

James dipped his head and battled his sleep-deprived brain for the right retort. The first that came to mind seemed too inflammatory, yet it somehow slipped out first.

"Financially ruining the *friends* you expect to collect a debt from isn't a stellar strategy, is it?"

Beck leaned forward. That blasted gun barrel was grinding into James's lumbar. The contortionist lady climbed off the table and glared at James for interrupting her act.

The room quieted, and a sound emerged. A wet, raspy sound, almost a squelch.

Beck's laughter. Not the menacing snicker he often paired with his threats. This sounded genuine. Sickly and entirely unappealing, but genuine.

"Not sure I wish for strategy lessons from an unlucky bastard who's lost everything."

"He hasn't lost everything."

James's heart dropped so quickly, he felt dizzy. But he couldn't waste time because he was terrified. And angry. And jaw-droppingly stupefied to hear Lucy's voice emerge from a corner of the smoke-filled room.

Maybe he was hallucinating. He was tired enough. Perhaps he'd sipped some absinthe and forgotten.

Then she stepped into view, and he was too astounded to be as furious with her as he should have been.

She wore that same awful black frock with the dainty white collar and held a tray of glasses full of absinthe in her arms, as if she'd come back after he'd put her in a hansom and obtained a serving job at the Helix Club in the last hour.

Her cool green gaze flickered his way.

"What are you doing here?" he whispered, though everyone could hear them.

"I couldn't let you do this alone," she whispered back.

"I put you in a cab not ten minutes ago." He was too frustrated to keep his volume to a whisper.

She shrugged. "We turned around." She bit her lip. "Honestly, I was willing to speak to Mr. Beck alone, if need be. But now we can do it together." She had the brass to beam at him.

"You're impossible."

"Tenacious."

"Reckless."

"Rebellious was, I believe, the word you once used as a compliment."

"Determined to put yourself in danger."

"Determined to help you get out of it."

James took a step toward her, willing the gun-toting man at his back to let him go. He glanced behind him and found the man looked nearly as shocked as he felt at the turn of events.

"Let her speak," Beck announced from his dais, then gestured for Lucy to step forward.

James calculated how quickly he could grab the woman he loved and get them both safely out of Beck's damnable club.

"He can pay you within the next few days, Mr. Beck."

"Tell us all who you are, girl."

Lucy glanced around and cleared her throat. "I'm the Earl of Hallston's daughter."

"I already knew that, love, but I do appreciate your honesty."

"That's ironic," Lucy murmured under her breath, but loudly enough for James to hear and, he suspected, others nearby.

"What was that, little lady?" Beck cast his cigar aside and leaned toward her. "You dare give me cheek in my own establishment?"

"You're a liar, Mr. Beck."

James lurched toward her and clasped Lucy's arm. "We should go. Now."

She refused to budge or to stop staring coolly at the man who'd played a role in James's ruin.

"You think you know me, girl. But I know you too." The con man's handlebar mustache twitched with his smirk. "Took some digging to find the name of the chit my friend Pembroke was walking out with in Edinburgh. To discover it was a lady with a fortune for a dowry? Clever man, James."

"Actually, he refused to marry me," Lucy told him in a strained voice.

James bit back a curse. A curse at himself for hurting her.

"Unlike you, sir, he is a man of honor."

Beck stood, and James clasped Lucy's wrist to pull her behind him.

"Clear the room," Beck said with an eerily quiet tone. So quiet that most ignored the command. "Clear the *bloody room*." This time, his shout echoed off the low ceiling, and it had the desired effect.

People began shuffling out. Most to a door that led up to the alley exit, James suspected. A few to the other half of the club upstairs. Even the ladies at Beck's side and the flame-haired contortionist departed.

Only the thug who'd ushered James into the room remained. That seemed all right with Beck.

"I take it you're paying his debt for him," he said in a conversational tone to Lucy.

"No," James cut in. "She is not."

Lucy tuned an irritated glance his way. "We plan to marry."

"Thought you said he wouldn't have you," Beck challenged.

"He changed his mind."

James wanted to quibble with her but knew it wasn't the time. There was never a moment when he hadn't wanted Lucy to be his.

"Felicitations," Beck bellowed with the wave of his ring-covered hand.

James fought the urge to roll his eyes. "We're leaving. You'll have your money." He shot Lucy a look. "I cannot vow it will be within a week, but the funds are coming. I'll wire four thousand pounds to you tomorrow."

"That's half."

"You'll get the rest," Lucy assured him.

Beck held James's gaze for an uncomfortably long stare.

James tried not to blink and attempted to decipher the man's devious thoughts at the same time.

"Four thousand pounds tomorrow, the rest within a week."

"That's not—"

"Those are my terms." He slammed his fist on the marble table the contortionist had vacated to emphasize his words.

"You'll have it," Lucy assured him, then shot James a questioning gaze. "We're going now, Mr. Beck."

James slid his hand into hers, and they turned their backs on Beck, warily making their way past his bulky guard.

"And Pembroke . . ."

James hesitated as Lucy glanced back at Beck. They were two steps from the exit, and everything in James told him they should go and not look back.

"I may have been wrong about you," Beck said in his smoke-scratchy voice.

Lucy gasped. James blinked, because he was certain he'd misheard the man. In the months he'd known Archie Beck, he'd never heard him humble himself or take responsibility for any of his misdeeds.

James half turned to look at the man.

"You're not unlucky. Not if a woman like that"—he gestured at Lucy with a far too appreciative glint in his eyes—"is willing to walk into a place like this for you."

"Then you'll leave us alone and give us a month to repay you in full?" Lucy asked him boldly.

Beck clasped each lapel of his topcoat and surveyed them, his beady gaze bouncing back and forth.

James got so bored with the man's pomposity, he was tempted to yawn. He was a dramatic devil.

"I'll agree to those terms, my lady, if"—Beck pointed a bejeweled finger at Lucy, and James wanted to break the digit in two—"I get an invite to your nuptials and an introduction to the Earl of Hallston."

"You are incorrigible." James stared out his side of the hansom carriage as it headed back toward Hallston House.

"You've said that before." Lucy knew James was angry with her, and she understood that he'd likely secure promises that she'd never be reckless again. "It turned out well," she offered with a hopeful lilt.

"Say that when your father sees Archibald Beck show up at our wedding."

"Our wedding?" Lucy snapped her head his way. "There's going to be a wedding?"

"Does that prospect still interest you?"

"So you accept my proposal?" she whispered, and her heart flip-flopped in her chest as she waited for his answer.

"I want to marry you if you'll still have me."

"Nothing has changed. You know that I will."

"One thing has changed." James reached out and offered his hand. She laced her fingers through his immediately. "Mr. Blackwood and I have agreed to a business arrangement. Apparently, I'm going to be shipping his whiskey to America. And we also agreed to terms that will allow your aunt to buy Invermere."

"That's wonderful!" Lucy kissed him—a quick, fervent press of her lips. Then kissed him again, more slowly, more thoroughly.

"Tomorrow," he said between kisses, "I'll come and speak to your father."

A trickle of panic slid down Lucy's back and made her shiver. James misunderstood and pulled away from her, slipping an arm from his overcoat to settle that half around her shoulders and pull her against the warmth of his body.

"Let me talk to him first?" she asked.

"You're worried."

"Papa is someone who makes assumptions at times. He's used to quick decision-making, but he's reasonable." Less so about the welfare of his children, Lucy had to acknowledge to herself. But she *knew* she could make her father understand how she felt about James.

"If we have to wait until Pembroke Shipping—"

"I don't want to wait. I wish I could come home with you now."

James chuckled. "Me too."

"I don't even know where you live."

He frowned. "In Cavendish Square. Not the most fashionable address, but we needn't be there for long if all goes well."

"It's perfectly fashionable as far as I'm concerned." Lucy didn't mind about where they lived. If it was up to her, she'd happily make a home with him in that little cottage at Invermere. "I needed your address because I plan to send a message tomorrow after speaking to Papa. It will be later in the day. He spends mornings at his club. Then perhaps you can come and join us for dinner."

Lucy chewed at her lip and contemplated the next challenge they'd have to face together.

Though her parents had promised her she could marry for love, she'd always known that came with the assumption that she'd marry someone of whom they would approve. Of course, they had every reason to approve of James. All the reasons that mattered to her, at least. He was kind, brave, and he loved her. Didn't he?

She turned to him within the confines of the carriage, but she had no idea how to ask such a simple yet terrifying question.

"James?"

"You're worried your father won't approve of us marrying," he said in reply as if he could read her thoughts. Well, at least some of them.

"I am a little. But not truly. My parents are reasonable people. I think they'll see in you what I do, and they'll recognize what I feel. I can't deny that . . ." Her voice caught and her throat burned. Nagging doubt in her head told her that she might be in far deeper than he was.

"You can't deny that . . . ?" he prompted.

Oh, if there was no denying it, then why hesitate? She'd told Aunt Cassandra she was ready for the risk.

"That I love you."

His eyes sparkled in the carriage's lantern and that seductive smile that made her insides quiver curved his mouth. "And I love you."

Lucy kissed him because she couldn't help herself. He gave himself to the kiss too, and then he grew sentimental, kissing her cheeks, the tip of her nose, her chin, then her forehead.

"I wish we were already married," he breathed against her skin. "I wish the work of convincing anyone that we should be was already past us."

"As do I." It was precisely what she felt, and she was half tempted to ask him to take her back to his home rather than deliver her to Hallston House. She'd feel no shame in spending the night in his arms, but allowing her parents to find that she hadn't slept in her bed overnight would only make the task ahead of them harder.

This time the hansom cab driver drove around to drop her off in the mews and waited patiently while they said their goodbyes.

"You're sure you can get inside and this time you're staying put?"

Lucy laughed and kissed him one last time. "I promise."

"Then I'll see you tomorrow."

"Remember to wait until I send word," Lucy reminded him. "It's only fair that I face him first."

As soon as Lucy reached out to open the cab door, James placed his hand on hers.

"I don't think it is fair that you face him first. Allow me to speak to him? You came for me tonight. Let me take care of you as you always do for others. Let me speak to your father."

Warmth bloomed in Lucy's chest. Her heart felt full, near to bursting, and she fought back the sting of tears.

"All right, you speak to Papa first. But then we'll face him together. I want us to always face our challenges together."

He smiled the smile that had captured her when they'd first met. "Me too."

Chapter Twenty-Two

*J*ames had been at more gentlemen's clubs in the past two days than he had in the past two years. Most of the businessmen he'd dealt with preferred talking business in offices or at formal dinners in their homes. But he knew that noblemen tended to prefer to hobnob at these lush places of leisure, and Lucy said Lord Hallston spent most mornings at his club.

He was relieved she'd agreed to let him speak to her father first. She'd done enough. He suspected her helpful nature meant she'd spent her life trying to smooth the way for others. He wanted to be the one to do the same for her.

Seeing as Lord Hallston was a diplomat, James thought it a good bet the man belonged to the famous Travellers Club in Pall Mall.

He arrived in the neighborhood at eight, knowing the earl might not arrive for hours, but it gave him time to traverse Green Park and wander St. James's Park. He circled back every so often, seeing gentlemen being delivered to the club or approaching by foot, but none of them looked like the man James had seen in newspaper coverage of the waterworks project Hallston had supported.

The doorman at the club gave him a stern perusal on one of his turns around the block. He was certain he looked like exactly what he was—a man who didn't quite belong in Pall Mall, title or not. He half expected an "Oy, what are you doing lurking there?" same as he'd gotten from Lucy's brother the previous night.

On the verge of heading back for another walk through St. James's Park, he heard a man's boisterous laughter and turned back. Two men stood conversing on the pavement just outside the club. He couldn't see either of them well. One stood with his back to him, blocking his view of the other. Yet some inner sense told him that one of them was Hallston.

He approached at a quick pace, worried they'd go inside where he wouldn't be admitted.

"Lord Hallston," he said convivially as he approached. If he was wrong, they'd just ignore him.

But the taller of the two men turned, and James knew he'd found Lucy's father. His hair was dark, but his eyes were the same shade of jade green.

"Lord Rossbury, my lord." Might as well throw his title around when it mattered most. "We haven't been introduced." James stuck out his hand the way he would when meeting a business colleague. He hoped that worked as well for aristocrats.

"I have met a Lord Rossbury. But I suspect that was your father."

"My uncle." James had no notion how close the two might have been. Not very, he suspected, but he didn't want to risk being indelicate. "I inherited quite recently."

"My condolences."

The man who Hallston had been talking to leaned in. "If you'll be a while, I'll see you inside, Hallston."

Lucy's father nodded to the man, then turned back to James.

"Shall we go in, Lord Rossbury?"

James hesitated. Presumably, if Hallston had a membership and wanted to bring a guest inside, no one would blink an eye.

"I hadn't seen your uncle at the club in years. But perhaps you'll make more use of the membership."

Did memberships pass with the inheritance of a title? James wasn't sure they did, and he couldn't imagine his uncle could have afforded club memberships if he was reduced to living in a gatehouse during his last days.

"It's warmer inside," Hallston vowed as a further inducement.

"Of course." James joined the man and headed inside the Pall Mall club.

"Hallston and Rossbury," Lucy's father told the doorman, who merely nodded genially.

Well, that worked out well. Though James wasn't ready to count anything a victory yet. Hallston still had no idea why he'd approached him.

"I like this spot." Hallston pointed to two well-worn

leather chairs near a fireplace and a table filled with sporting magazines and books.

James said nothing but claimed the seat Hallston didn't.

"Port? Brandy?"

"Coffee?" James asked. It wasn't yet nine in the morning.

In extraordinarily quick order, a steaming cup of dark coffee and a snifter of brandy were settled in front of them by a youthful waiter.

"You approached as if you wished to impart something, Lord Rossbury. Was it simply the news of your uncle's passing?"

"No, my lord." James sipped his coffee, burned his tongue, and wondered how to say all that he needed to and not bungle everything.

"Then my curiosity is piqued."

"It's about your daughter, Lady Lucy." Just straight into the fray was really the only way James knew, and, in fairness, it seemed to be Lucy's modus operandi too.

Hallston's expression went from amused surprise to distinctly alarmed in two heartbeats.

"Are you the reason she cut her trip to Scotland short?"

"In a manner of speaking, I am."

Hallston leaned forward, broad shoulders hunched near his ears, and his friendly expression turned to something much fiercer. "I'll thank you not to prevaricate, Rossbury. What is between you and my daughter?"

Before James could form a reply, Hallston settled back again and scrubbed a hand over his face. "My god, this is all down to that woman, isn't it? She's my wife's sister, I'll allow, but by the devil, we should have never let Lucy go."

James chuckled at that. He couldn't help it. The sound burst out of him.

"Is something funny?" Hallston's tone dripped with irritation and disdain.

Good god, this was going wrong. All wrong.

"Forgive me, my lord. I assure you I wasn't laughing at you." Technically untrue, but he had to save this somehow. "Just the notion."

"The notion?" Hallston's tone was beginning to rise, not to mention his volume. A few gentlemen nearby turned their heads.

James lowered his voice and tried for a light tone. "The idea of keeping Lady Lucy from doing anything she set her mind on seemed amusing." James smiled. He tried for the charming one. "But perhaps you do not find the humor in it. And for that, I'm sorry."

"Stop apologizing." Hallston narrowed one eye, his dark brow dipping down precipitously. "How long have you known Lucy? I don't recall seeing you at any events."

Oh, this was a bad idea. Dreadful.

"A week." More or less.

"This has something to do with Scotland and Cassandra. I want you to tell me quickly and quietly before I lose my temper and thus my membership in this esteemed club."

If James were one to quibble, he'd point out that the man had already lost his temper. But he knew it was his job to lower the temperature of the conversation and try, though it seemed improbable now, to earn a bit of the man's respect.

"It does have to do with Scotland. I met Lady Lucy on the journey to Edinburgh. And then we met again at Invermere."

Hallston narrowed both eyes now. "You *followed* my daughter to Invermere?"

"No, I did not." Definitely not the time to mention that Lucy had arrived after him. Neither of them had followed each other, regardless. "It was a coincidence."

"Why were you there?"

Not until that moment—very late, in other words—did James realize that there truly was no way to recount the story of how he and Lucy had met, and then remet, and then spent days alone together without it all sounding scandalous.

But he couldn't very well begin a relationship with the man by lying.

"I own Invermere. It was my uncle's, you see. And he gave leave for Lady Cassandra to reside there."

"She was his tenant?"

"More or less, yes."

"Oh good god. He was her lover."

James gulped coffee. "She was an excellent steward, and I was not keen to evict her, but I had hoped to sell the manor quickly."

"Why?"

Damnation.

"No, you needn't explain. As little as I knew Rossbury, we all knew he'd mismanaged his estate. I assume there were debts."

"Yes, my lord." Hell and bollocks, he'd nearly forgotten there were his uncle's debts to contend with too.

"I imagine she wasn't best pleased to discover you'd come to put her out."

"Not pleased at all."

Hallston sipped his brandy and stared at the fire, and James was glad for it. He needed a moment to regroup and somehow get their fresh acquaintance onto better footing.

"Lady Lucy was very kind to me, and I came to realize what an extraordinary woman she is in a very short time."

"Short indeed," Hallston snapped. "Though I can't find fault with you for realizing Lucy's excellent qualities upon brief acquaintance. They are apparent to anyone willing to see."

"And I do see. She is magnificent. Maddening at times, but magnificent even then."

"Goodness, you do know her." Hallston sighed, and somehow, it was a gesture that gave James hope. "So you wish to marry her."

"I do indeed."

"You've heard of her dowry, I take it."

"Only from her."

That shocked him, and James could tell Hallston didn't know quite what to make of that news.

"I would forgo her dowry and marry her if she were penniless."

"A pretty sentiment, Rossbury, but you know I'd never let my daughter go penniless."

"Nor would I. I intend to provide for her well. Before inheriting, I ran a successful shipping enterprise. I intend to maintain my business, even grow it."

"A nobleman in commerce?"

"Yes." James wouldn't waver on this point, even if Hallston offered them an annuity or Lucy's inheritance was sufficient to keep them afloat for years. He wished to be successful again at something he'd been good at. Even loved.

"I need to speak to my daughter. I can make no decision until then."

James already considered Hallston a man worthy of respect for the reputation he'd built for himself and the daughter he'd raised, but at that moment, his esteem for the man nearly overwhelmed him. Every day, noblemen negotiated the terms of marrying off their eligible daughters with little or no regard to the lady's preferences. He admired Hallston for making Lucy's feelings, her choices, the deciding factor.

"Come at one. I'll speak to her before then. And then we'll all have a conversation together."

James understood he was being dismissed. He stood and was pleasantly surprised when Hallston rose and shook his hand.

Stepping out onto the pavement in front of the Travellers Club, James felt buoyed by an ebullient kind of hopefulness that Hallston might, in the end, give his blessing. Reviewing the conversation between them, he knew he was far short on elegance and had left out some crucial details, but there'd been a kind of understanding between him and the earl. At the very least, an agreement that Lucy deserved the very best.

That's where the ebullience burst a bit and doubt swept in.

They'd dealt with Beck, for the most part, but the offices of Pembroke Shipping still sat dusty and inactive. He'd yet to rebuild anything.

His conscience whispered that the matter of marrying Lucy should come after all the rest was in order. After he could point to his successes once more.

But another part of him, his heart, the deepest center that didn't doubt or reproach, told him that he should not waste another moment. That being apart from the one whom he'd felt connected to from the moment he'd seen her, a woman who made him wish to be the best man he could be, was folly.

Lucy wanted him. Now. Just as he was. He'd be the most unworthy of fools to deny the gift of having her in his life.

And he would do his very best to make sure she would never regret her choice.

Now they just had to convince Lord and Lady Hallston.

"IF YOU TREAD on those hellebores, Mama will never forgive you." Charlie sat in a corner of the conservatory, lounging on one of their mother's velvet chaise lounges and intermittently reading out statistics about horses from some boring sporting magazine.

"I'm not treading on anything," Lucy bit back at him.

"You came close."

"I never did."

"How would you know? You've been pacing aimlessly and staring off in the distance for nearly an hour."

"Charlie, I entered the conservatory twenty minutes ago."

"It feels like an hour."

"You could go elsewhere."

He scoffed with dramatic offense. "I was here first."

"I'm nervous."

He harrumphed at that, then sat up and tossed his magazine aside. "All right, I can see you're dying to tell me why."

Lucy wasn't. Not really. She'd come into the conservatory to be alone. And, as proven by last night's events, Charlie wasn't a trustworthy confidant.

"Wait, why haven't you asked me about the gentleman you met out front last night?"

"What gentleman?" He screwed up his face in genuine confusion.

"You were so soused, you don't even remember, do you? Good grief, Charlie, you'd be the worst spy in British history."

He shrugged. "Probably. Good thing I've never wanted to be a spy."

"You're incorrigible." The words came out of her mouth in an irritated tone, but Lucy couldn't help but smile.

"Oh no." Charlie stared at her wide-eyed, a hand clapped over his mouth. "You're going to tell me again about the man you met on the train."

"I wasn't, actually."

"You're besotted. Utterly and ridiculously." He pointed in a zigzag pattern, up and down her body. "Don't deny it. There's proof in every stumbling step you take, every lost look at the wall, that almost mad gaze in your eyes."

"You're being dramatic."

"Says the lovestruck girl."

"I never tried to deny it."

"My lady?" Sarah, their housemaid, had stepped into the conservatory. "Lord Hallston is asking to see you in his study."

Lucy shot her brother a "see what you've done" look, to which he responded with an "it's your own fault, really" shrug.

"Thank you, Sarah. I'll be right there."

She shouldn't have come to the conservatory. She should have paced in the privacy of her bedroom or maybe even made a list of things to say to her father. Charlie was never going to be any help, and the truth was that she had gone to find him. He may be a dreadfully loose-lipped confidant, but he wasn't a terrible listener.

But now the moment was upon her. She hoped her father wished to speak to her because he and James had spoken. All morning, she'd been praying that discussion went well. But if it hadn't, it would just be the start of convincing him.

"I love him, Papa." She whispered the words that seemed the most important point she could make. Whatever Papa's misgivings, whatever arguments he might raise, he could not change the fact that James Pembroke had won her heart when no other man ever had. And more importantly, that he spoke to her, listened to her, cared for her as no other man ever had.

"Papa," she said brightly as she stepped into her father's study. "It's a lovely coincidence that you wished to see me because I was hoping to speak to you today too."

"Well, good. And we'd both like to talk with you." He gestured at her mother, who Lucy hadn't noticed sitting in a chair near the window. Her mother remained seated and the expression on her face, somewhere between reticence and worry, told her that all was not well.

She imagined all the ways a first meeting between James and her father might have gone off track. And then considered ways they might overcome any misgivings her parents had.

Something was terribly wrong if her father's stormy expression was any indication.

"Have a seat if you will, my girl."

Lucy chose a chair facing her mother's and her father finally sat on a settee angled toward both of them.

"Tell us about your trip to Scotland."

Mercy, this was *not* what she'd expected.

"Why did you return so abruptly?" her mother put in quietly.

"I . . ." Lucy had never been good at fibbing, at least not for her own benefit. She'd withheld information to aid friends. To keep secrets. But she'd never lied to her parents for any reason. Though she certainly didn't feel as free to speak openly to them as she did to her aunt.

She drew in a shaky breath and contemplated how to toe the line between honesty and true openness.

"My trip was eventful. I met a gentleman that I came to care for. I thought he'd returned to London, so I did too." Perhaps James hadn't yet had a chance to meet with her father.

"You never mentioned this," her mother said sharply.

"I returned so recently, Mama. We haven't even dined together since I've been back. You and Papa had your dinner party to attend last evening."

"How much do you care for him?" Her father's voice held no emotion, which was odd for him. Very odd.

"A great deal. More than I've ever cared for any gentleman." Lucy straightened her spine and looked at her father. "I love him, Papa, and I plan to marry him."

"Lucy . . ." Her mother pushed the word out on a gasp.

"Mama, I know my own mind. I know my own heart. Don't you trust that I know myself well?"

"First love can be rather consuming. It can blind you to a man's faults." Her mother spoke the words with a kind of quiet desperation.

When Lucy's father tipped his gaze down and worked his jaw, she realized that he was not the man her mother spoke of. Her parents were enamored with each other, and she couldn't remember her mother ever intimating that her father had faults, let alone pointing them out.

"If I were a debutante in my first Season, I would listen to words of caution more closely. But I'm four and twenty, Mama. I've waited a long time to feel this way. Even doubted I ever would. But now I know what I was waiting for. I've found it. And I don't want to wait any longer."

Her parents exchanged a lengthy look, their gazes locked as they communicated in that silent way they often did.

"May I tell you about him?" Lucy asked softly.

"Even on a short acquaintance, I feel I know all the best, essential things about him."

Her parents still held that secret communion of gazes, and after Lucy's question, they nodded at each other. Something had been agreed, but what?

Lucy opened her mouth to start reciting James's good qualities when her father lifted a hand.

"We do want to hear your opinion of the young man, of course. But maybe he'd like to hear too. Shall we have him join us?" Her father's smile was suddenly mischievous.

"I don't understand. He's here?"

Lucy dared to hope. Dared to take her father's sudden mirth as a good sign. They'd met him and they weren't scowling. Mama still looked worried, but Papa was smiling. Good grief, so much worry and now it melted into a warm, joyous flutter in her middle.

Her father stood, stepped from the room, and returned a moment later with James. Despite her father's amusement, James looked wary.

"He accosted me outside my club," her father said with false gruffness.

"Did he indeed?" Lucy smiled at James. "He wanted to catch you early."

"As patient as you are, it seems," Mama put in. "That should make for an interesting next few months."

"Few months?" James and Lucy voiced the two words at nearly the same time.

"As you've seen with Miranda, it does take months to properly plan a wedding."

Lucy felt James's gaze on her and looked up to find he liked that prospect as much as she did. Which was to say, not at all.

"Don't even think of going back to Scotland to elope," Papa said firmly. "Cassandra has enough to answer for."

"Aunt Cassandra did nothing wrong." Lucy couldn't bear her father's wrath toward her aunt any longer. "She wasn't even—"

"Terribly in favor of our courtship," James interjected.

And thank goodness he had. Lucy's parents didn't know that she'd been alone with James for days at Invermere. And really, why did they need to?

"Why is that?" Mama sounded slightly alarmed.

"James was the man who owned the home she's been living in for years," Lucy explained. "The home she loves. She didn't take to him at first."

"But you did, apparently." Papa held her gaze with a searching one of his own, but he knew her well enough to see.

"Yes, I certainly did."

"And you, Lord Rossbury?"

James turned his head to Lucy, taking her in with a look that traced all the features of her face. All the spots he'd kissed.

"The first moment I saw her, I knew. I didn't understand it. I'm not sure I fully do now. But I know that I love her beyond all reason, that I want to spend every day in her company, that I want to give her whatever she desires." He leaned in and whispered, "I adore you." Then he turned back to Lucy's parents. "I adore your daughter, and if she'll have me, I'm hers."

Lucy couldn't hold back. She leaned in, resting a hand on his arm, savoring his warmth and strength. Then pressed a kiss to his cheek.

Her mother cleared her throat. Papa let out a stifled chuckle.

"Perhaps we should forgo those months of preparation and look into a special license."

Chapter Twenty-Three

Two weeks later

*A*re you very disappointed?" Lucy asked him the question as James held her in his arms in the house they'd soon share as newlyweds. They'd finally relented and agreed to the sort of grand wedding her parents longed to give her as they had her older sister.

"I'm not an enormous fan of pomp or weddings, but I'm a quite serious devotee of you, so I'm fine with however we get our names together on a marriage license."

Lucy bounced up onto her toes and kissed him. He dropped a hand to her lower back, pulling her closer, and she deepened the kiss, sweeping her tongue in to taste him.

"Pardon, my lord." Mrs. Wilton, who James had come to suspect Lucy's mother had put on retainer, stood at the threshold of his study. The woman was suddenly as watchful as a guard dog and seemed to have an unerring ability to sense when he and Lucy were about to pull each other's clothes off in the middle of the day.

"All is prepared as you requested. The . . ." She cleared her throat. "They've cleared out now, so it's all presentable."

"Thank you, Mrs. Wilton."

She nodded, then glanced at his unbuttoned shirt before noting Lucy's half-unpinned hair.

"That will be all, Mrs. Wilton."

"Very good, my lord." She still called him *my lord* with extra emphasis, and James wasn't sure if that was for his benefit or hers.

"I'm sorry," he whispered to Lucy when the housekeeper departed.

"It's all right. She's watchful. Worried about your reputation, apparently," she teased. "Though I am glad the servants' quarters aren't near your bedroom."

"Our bedroom soon."

"Otherwise, we'd have to be quiet."

"We're *not* being quiet. I quite like the sounds you make." James pulled her in for another kiss.

Lucy pushed at his chest. "Likewise, but what was she talking about? It was very mysterious."

James wanted to slide up the fabric of her skirt and make love to his fiancée on his desktop, as they'd done once before, and as he'd been dreaming of every day since. But he forced himself to cool his wanton thoughts. He was eager to reveal the surprise he had planned for her.

"Let me show you." He took her hand and led her from the room, down the hall, and toward the back of the house.

"*You're* not disappointed, are you?" He repeated the question she'd asked him minutes before. "With this town house? This square isn't terribly popular with your parents' set, and this house isn't nearly as opulent as Hallston House."

"I love this house. It has character. And, most importantly, it has you. We'll make it our own."

They'd already talked of alterations they wanted to make. Lucy had as much affection for vibrant colors as her aunt, and he was happy to let her make whatever changes she saw fit.

Though there was one change he was insistent upon. It was the only thing that made him grateful she wasn't already living with him. Keeping it a secret from her had been difficult enough for two weeks, but it was near enough to completion that he thought it was time to show her. Especially since he wanted to determine if she preferred any amendments before it was finished. He wanted the house and everything in it to feel like her own and suited to her taste.

He stopped near the stairwell.

"Maybe you should close your eyes."

She did, but immediately peeked one open. James laughed and moved to stand behind her, lifting a hand in front of her eyes.

"May I?"

Lucy nodded. "If you must."

It allowed him to hold her close, one hand on her waist as he walked her slowly toward her surprise.

"Ready?" he asked when they'd reached the threshold.

"Yes." She drew out the word, already done with her moments of patience.

James withdrew his hand, and Lucy let out a breathy squeal. She crushed his hand in her grip and bounced on her toes.

"It's so beautiful."

"It's still a work in progress, but I wanted your opinion."

"My opinion is I adore it."

"Keep going. Take a good look."

She stepped into the conservatory as if unsure whether it would evaporate if she moved too quickly, which was so un-Lucy-like that he worried he may have misjudged. The conservatory was built in a similar style to the one at Invermere, but he'd made this one wider, as big as the back garden would permit, which allowed for a higher ceiling.

"Oh my goodness." On a table at the completed edge of the conservatory, away from the work-men's tools and materials, she found the easel and art materials he'd purchased. He was much more wary of making those choices and had sought her aunt's advice for everything.

"It's a start, I hope. Cassandra advised me not to buy too much and allow you the opportunity to choose brushes and colors you prefer."

Standing with her back to him, Lucy paused.

Minutes ticked by as she stood and took it all in. But her silence was worrying. She was never a lady without something to say.

Then she looked up, taking in the arched wrought-iron beams that supported the many panes of glass. She spun in a slow circle, just as he'd watched her do at King's Cross Station, eyes locked on the craftsmanship above her.

"What do you think, sweetheart?"

"It's so much. I'm overwhelmed."

"Good overwhelmed, right? Not 'I actually hate this' overwhelmed?"

Two things happened at once—she began to laugh, and then tears started trickling down her cheeks.

James was still confused.

"Why did you do all of this for me?" Nestling up against him, she wrapped her arms around his neck.

James laughed and wrapped his arms around her waist. "Those are the silliest words that have come out of your mouth since the day I met you."

"I want to know."

"If you don't already know, we're in trouble." He nuzzled her cheek. "I love you. You're to be my wife, if we ever manage to have this wedding. My goal is to make you happy, and based on what I saw at Invermere, and what you've told me—I do listen—painting is something that matters to you a great deal."

"It does."

"Therefore, allowing you to pursue it is something that matters to me." He'd only used funds from his business deal with Blackwood for the cost of the conservatory. That had been important to him, though he was hesitant to tell Lucy. They still didn't quite agree on the distribution of her dowry or how much of their lives her father would finance.

"Now." Lucy paused and fussed with the ribbon at the waist of her gown before meeting his gaze. "There's something I should probably tell you."

"That sounds ominous."

She glanced away. "I'm not sure what you'll make of it. Papa wanted to tell you, but I thought it should come from me."

"Go on."

"Your debt to Archibald Beck has been cleared."

James's body instantly tensed. "How so?"

Lucy pulled out of his embrace. "Please don't be angry. Papa saw to it."

"That's not what we agreed."

"There's more though. Will you listen?"

James nodded, though his jaw ached from how hard he'd clenched his teeth.

"Much of the debt was forgiven."

James barked out a cynical laugh. "Beck would never forgive anyone anything."

"Papa . . . spoke of your trouble with Beck to a friend. He did not mention your name, just that someone he knew had run afoul of Mr. Beck. And his friend exerted . . . influence, I suppose you could call it, on Mr. Beck."

"Influence."

"The man works for Scotland Yard and knows far more about Beck's nefarious dealings than I expect even you do. Obviously, Beck wishes to avoid that man's attention and ire. He spoke to him as a favor to my father."

"I did want the satisfaction of resolving it myself."

"And I think it's wonderful that we just don't have to worry about the man anymore at all." She tipped her head. "Don't you?"

James chewed on it, and still didn't like the taste of Lucy's powerful father swooping in to solve a problem that his own foolishness had gotten him into. It was his fault, his responsibility, his debt.

He spun away from her, his eyes on the town house's front door. An urge in him told him to go, walk outside, walk away before he said something to her that he'd regret. He did not like the man he was when he felt like this, like he had as a child— angry and afraid. Helpless.

But what was it he feared?

Lucy approached and placed a hand on his arm, but he didn't turn to face her.

"I know my family can be quite a lot. And, believe me, I, of all people, understand that Papa can be overbearing. He's got power, and he's not afraid to wield it for his family. And now that includes you." She drew in a sharp breath. "You've been without a family for so long—"

"No." James said the word softly. God help him,

he didn't want to shout at Lucy. She didn't deserve it. This fear was old. Decades old and compounded by the loss of his fortune in the last year. "I just . . ."

He started away from her, realizing it was the first time he'd ever pulled away from her touch. She might not understand, but he'd try to explain when these feelings had subsided.

"I just need to walk. I'm sorry."

The front door felt a thousand steps away, but he forced himself to keep going and breathed in long gulps of air when he stepped outside.

LUCY SWIPED AT her tears as she watched James depart.

She took one last look at the glorious conservatory he was building for her, the art supplies he'd chosen with care, and retraced his steps with her own.

Stopping in the hallway, she stepped into the front drawing room, checked the time, settled into the chair she'd already picked out as her favorite, and waited.

Going after him was what her heart told her to do, but her head bade her to wait. To allow him space to collect his thoughts, to cool whatever feelings were overwhelming him.

And she had an inkling what those were. She might be wrong, and she certainly preferred to hear it from him, but he'd reacted most strongly when she mentioned family. In that moment, she'd searched her mind for a way to mention his loss that wouldn't cause him pain. Now she'd begun to realize that there was no way to do so. He'd pushed those memories, that experience, out of his mind, creating a barrier against the feelings that came with those memories.

Had he ever had time to truly grieve his parents? From the little he'd told her, it seemed he'd had to turn all his attention to trying to survive almost the minute he'd lost them. Because of Rufus Pembroke and his heartlessness. Dastardly, hateful man.

What had Aunt Cassandra ever seen in him?

James mentioned that Angus believed she'd seen Pembroke as security. How ironic that he was the very opposite to his own kin, offering an orphaned boy nothing but his negligence.

James wasn't used to having a family that meddled, that tried to help and nosed in even when you didn't wish them to with advice and counsel. He wasn't used to having anyone, as far as she could tell, who cared about him enough to sacrifice anything.

But she did. Angus did. Papa did.

The fifteen minutes she'd decided to allow him were up, so Lucy stood and made her way outside. James sat on a bench, his back to her, in the square's green.

"May I join you?"

He lifted his hand to her immediately. "Please do."

Lucy settled next to him, leaned against his arm, and placed her hand in his.

"You'd think that speaking of them wouldn't bother me after all these years."

"I don't think that at all. I would never stop feeling the loss of my family under such circumstances. The derailment itself must have been so frightening."

"I still have night terrors." He swallowed and his mouth tipped up at the edge. "I still hate trains."

"Then it's lucky you own ships."

"Only one. Half of one."

"There will be more. You'll see."

He tipped his head, arched a dark brow. *This* had been a point of disagreement in the last few days. He'd sat her down one day and wished to discuss how they would utilize her dowry. She'd suggested putting a good deal of it into rebuilding his business, but he'd balked. He'd even resisted using some of the funds to refurbish his town home and only relented when she'd insisted it was something she wanted, to make the house feel more like her own.

"I'm afraid you're going to have to get used to something you may not like."

"What's that?"

"Help."

"Mmm."

"When people love each other," she said slowly and teasingly, "they wish to help each other. You know, like building them an entire conservatory and purchasing art supplies because they have a modicum of artistic talent."

"A great deal of artistic talent."

"Whatever, you see my point."

"Possibly."

"You're a hypocrite, James Wesley Pembroke, if you think it's quite all right for you to indulge me but refuse to allow me to do the same."

"But your father—"

"Or my father. To him, you're family now. If there's something he'd do for me, he'll be willing to do it for you." She clutched his sleeve, desperate to make him understand. "You know how fiercely I crave independence—"

"You're sure you want to marry, then?"

"Don't make me prove my skill at fisticuffs to you again."

He lifted his hands as if defending himself. "All right, all right. The wedding is still on. Someday."

"My point is—"

"I understand." He turned and pulled her toward him, nearly into his lap. "I must learn to live with happiness and familial love and people who wish to meddle helpfully."

"Exactly."

He nuzzled her cheek and murmured a long *hmmm*.

"Are you still considering it, or is that an acquiescence?"

"I get you in this bargain, is that right?" he whispered, his breath hot against her ear.

"Yes, you're stuck with me." Lucy pressed a palm to his cheek, traced her fingertips along his jawline. "Are you all right with that bargain? Forever?"

"I acquiesce." He gave her that smile. The one that made heat pool in her belly and travel lower, to all the places she wanted his touch. "I'm yours, Lucy. Forever."

October 1898
Scotland

$\mathcal{A}$t least we're arriving in the same carriage this time." James held his wife's hand as she leaned across to get a better of view as they approached Invermere.

"You're nervous?" Lucy glanced down at their joined hands.

She must have felt the odd tremor that rushed through him as their hired coach rolled toward her aunt's home. It was their first return to the property, and to Scotland, since they'd met the previous year.

Lucy had looked forward to the trip for months, and it had originally been planned for late summer. But two events had delayed them—the acquisition of a new ship for Pembroke Shipping, and Lucy's first exhibition of her paintings at a small art salon founded by Lucy and several artistic friends.

Both had proven to be a success.

Pembroke Shipping now had four fast, transatlantic ships in its fleet, and Blackwood's Scotch whiskey was selling well in America, even against the competition of fine stateside blends.

In her art, Lucy was most adept at capturing nature and landscapes, and had become popular in London's aristocratic circles among lady and gentleman gardeners who commissioned her to capture their prized flowers and trees in full bloom.

"There's nothing to be nervous about this visit," Lucy told him. She eased his worries with a kiss on the cheek, but James wanted more.

He cupped his wife's cheek and kissed her. She curled her fingers into the placket of his shirtfront, sweeping a fingertip across his bare chest.

"What is it?" she asked, pulling back and nuzzling his cheek. "Your heart is racing."

"How many people will be here, exactly?"

"You already know." She pushed teasingly against his chest. "Everyone will be here. Mama, Papa, Charlie, and Marion and her family."

Over the months since their wedding, James had developed a rapport with Lucy's father and mother, though he still sensed the earl and countess were watchful. As if, even now, they weren't quite certain he was worthy of their middle child.

Charlie was an ally, friendly and gregarious, and as reckless as any young man James had ever met. He considered them friends, but also felt a brotherly sense of responsibility for Charlie.

Marion and her husband had been so busy with their first child that he'd yet to meet them. James couldn't help but wonder how the duke and duchess would react to their brother-in-law in commerce.

"Angus is out front waiting for us." Lucy kissed his cheek again. "I know you're pleased to see him."

Within minutes, the carriage had rolled to a stop in front of Invermere, and the minute James helped Lucy down, Blackwood practically dragged James into a bear hug.

"Good god, it's been too long, lad."

"Pleased to see you too." James patted the man awkwardly on the back and noticed in his periphery that he was gesturing at Lucy.

"I'll just go in and find Aunt Cassandra," she called, and practically dashed through Invermere's front door.

James watched his wife go and assessed Blackwood, who'd finally released him.

"What's afoot, Angus?"

"I've nae idea to what ye're referring, good sir." Blackwood hooked an arm around his shoulders and led him inside, but before they could mount the front steps, a blur of gray fur darted straight for James.

James bent to scratch between the hound's ears. "I missed you too, Hercules."

Blackwood chuckled, a deep rumble that made James smile.

"Cass was angry as a riled bear when ye departed last October. Hercules took it hard. Moping around for weeks. She was mighty peeved that you'd wooed her hound and taken her niece from her in the space of a week."

"But she's forgiven me?" James asked warily as they crossed the threshold.

"That is a foolish question." The lady herself swept down the hallway, her trusty housekeeper following in her wake.

Lady Cassandra held out her hand and James took it into his. If she wasn't yet prepared to receive the kind of overly affectionate displays like Blackwood's from him, James was simply pleased to find her smiling at him.

"Welcome." She did bend forward to peck a kiss on his cheek. "Thank you for bringing Lucy back to me."

"We've already decided it should be an annual tradition to visit, if you'll have us." The house was hers now, and she'd been able to secure the financing as she'd hoped. Though James and Lucy had tried to gift the house to her, she'd refused to consider such an option.

Stubbornness was something James shared with Lucy and her aunt, and he understood her reasons.

Voices carried from the house's drawing room, and James felt that trembling sense of hesitation again. Not that he wasn't used to socializing with aristocrats now. Lucy had made sure that they entertained frequently, and he was gradually becoming comfortable with his role in society and the duties of his title.

But a boisterous family gathering was something

else entirely. Lucy's parents had dined at their home, and Charlie dropped in whenever he liked, but James had never had to contend with the whole lot of them all gathered in one place.

Blackwood and Cassandra headed off into the drawing room, and James suspected Lucy had been drawn into the fray already too. Laughter carried from the room, the clink of glasses, even someone plunking away at a piano.

"How does it feel to be back, my lord?"

James hadn't noticed that Mrs. Fox lingered in the hallway. The woman was as quiet as a watchful wraith, but when he turned to face her, he found kindness in her gaze. Even a sympathy he hadn't expected.

"It's a place that holds good memories, despite the brevity of my first visit. But I do recall that first night was rather unpleasant for all of us."

She nodded and offered the hint of a smile. "I've secured Drummond's promise that he won't attempt to lock you in any rooms during this visit."

"That's something, I suppose." James shot her a grin of genuine warmth. He'd always appreciated her sense of loyalty and watchfulness.

"You'll want to join the family in the drawing room before dinner. I understand there's to be a surprise."

"Is there?" That made his gut clench. He wasn't terribly fond of surprises, at least not of being the recipient of them. Or rather, the unknown still made him wary. After years of uncertainty as a

young man, he had a craving for security and stability now.

Surprises were only enjoyable when they were for
Lucy—gifts, flowers, new paint for her canvases.
One of his favorite parts of marriage was the ways
they reminded each other they were thought of and
loved.

"I've been sent to retrieve you and bring you to
the drawing room by force, if necessary." Charlie
stood at the end of the hall, a drink in one hand,
the other waving James toward him. "Come.
They're all waiting for you."

"Why?" A little muscle began to tick at the edge
of his jaw. He'd already been quizzed by the earl
and countess during dinner visits. Good grief, were
Marion and her husband going to subject him to
the same?

"Lucy has a surprise for you," Charlie whispered
to him when James approached. "An early birthday gift." Charlie pointed a finger against his lapel.
"Don't you dare tell her I told you that."

"What is it?"

"No, no. I won't go that far. She'd skewer me
with one of Aunt Cassandra's arrows."

James chuckled. She probably would.

The room was warm and smelled of woodsmoke,
mulled cider, and the faint but distinct scent of
Lucy's perfume. Scanning the room, he saw that
she was in a chair at the far side of the room, her
back to him.

James sensed everyone's gaze turned his way.

"Let me introduce you to Marion and Wakeford. Don't worry," Charlie said out of the corner of his mouth. "Marion is more of a snob than he is."

His unfamiliarity with most nobles meant that James didn't know quite what to expect from his brother-in-law, the Duke of Wakeford. What he didn't expect was the man to reach out his hand and pat James on the back as if they were old friends.

"Glad to meet you, Rossbury."

"And you, Wakeford."

A tall, dark-haired woman watched from over the duke's shoulder. Marion, James had no doubt. She took him in with one sweeping gaze, and he couldn't tell from her expression whether he'd passed muster.

"Lucy has told me a great deal about you in her letters," she said in a higher, sharper voice than Lucy's. "I shall look forward to getting to know you, Rossbury."

"And I you, Your Gra—"

"Please call me Marion. Or Sister, if you prefer." She smiled and it softened her demeanor. She seemed instantly more at ease. "We are family now, after all."

Sister. A word he'd never had cause to use in place of a name in his life. And *family* was a word he was getting used to, a reality he was coming to embrace.

Taking in the room, he realized he was a part

of this group now, even if he only truly knew one member of it well.

"Would someone please send my husband to me?" Lucy called from her corner of the room.

James needed no one's urging to seek her out. From the minute he'd entered the room, even while meeting the duke and duchess, part of his attention had been on her, the glint of gold in her hair a kind of lodestar drawing him closer.

When he reached her, he placed a hand on her shoulder, and she stood immediately to face him.

"I have a surprise for you," she said brightly.

"Do you indeed?" James risked a glance Charlie's way, and the young man arched a brow in warning. "What's the occasion?"

"I know your birthday is next month, but this gift can't wait."

That did stoke his curiosity.

Lucy was all but bouncing on her toes in excitement, and the rest of the room had gone quiet. James glanced at Lord and Lady Hallston, both of whom were watching them, amused smiles on their faces.

"Are you ready?" Lucy asked archly.

"I am." If it made her this happy, it had to be a good surprise.

"Drummond, it's time," Lucy called out in a loud voice.

Drummond? James bore no grudge against the aged butler, but he couldn't say if the Scotsman felt the same. His certainty that this would be a pleasant surprise began to wane.

A moment later, he heard Drummond in the hallway. "Come, ye wee scamp," the old man muttered. "Ah, ye sprite. I'll carry ye then."

The butler entered the drawing room with a squirming creature tucked under his arm.

Lucy rushed forward, blocking James's view, and scooped the animal into her arms.

When she turned, two glossy black eyes were turned his way.

"Darling, meet the son of Hercules."

"And Dolly," Aunt Cassandra put in as she approached. "Lady Grimshaw has a deerhound lass. She and Hercules get on well, shall we say?"

"Do you like him, James?"

He nodded and wanted to speak, but there was a knot in the back of his throat and a sting behind his eyes. "Thank you, love," was all he managed before Lucy bent closer to kiss him and shift the puppy into his arms.

The lively thing immediately licked his cheek.

"He's magnificent." As James petted the pup, he noticed that he had the same white patch on his chest as Hercules, who'd come closer to keep a watchful eye on his son.

"What shall we call him?"

"I suggest Charles," Charlie put in.

"Dickens," James and Lucy said almost in unison.

"Author of the book James knocked from my arms the day we met," Lucy said with a cheeky grin.

"The book that nearly broke my foot."

"Nearly doesn't count, darling." Lucy winked. She'd learned that from him.

"Shall we have a toast?" Lord Hallston called, lifting his glass of mulled cider. "To Dickens, the newest member of the family."

Lucy collected a cup for James, and he tried his best to hold the wriggling pup in one arm.

"And to James," Charlie added. "The second-newest member who I don't think we've ever yet toasted as a family or subjected to our favorite parlor games or too often repeated family stories." Charlie smirked at James. "You're in for quite a visit, mate."

James swigged back his cider as everyone else did, but he was grateful when everyone went back to their small clusters of conversation. He was grateful, and a little overwhelmed with it. The feeling of belonging, of being wholly embraced by a close-knit group, was strange and new, and a warmer, more comforting feeling than he'd ever imagined it could be.

He turned when he realized Lucy was no longer at his side. She strode back into the room, holding a collar and leash.

"I thought we could take Dickens for a walk."

It was as if she sensed he needed some air.

A few moments later, they made their way out of the house with Dickens in tow, and she led him on the path toward the archery field.

"Feeling better?" she asked him quietly. "My family can be overbearing and a bit too loud at times. Marion has her moods, and Charlie imbibes too much."

"They were all kind, welcoming. Perhaps I worried for nothing."

"I don't think that," she said softly. "We both knew this would take some adjusting."

"Thank you for understanding, love." James stopped her, turned, and drew Lucy into his arms.

They kissed, chuckling against each other's lips as Dickens pulled at his lead, whining to continue on.

"He sees the lights," Lucy whispered.

"The lights?"

"That's the other surprise." Even in the darkening night, he could see the flash of his wife's smile. "Mrs. Fox helped me arrange it. We're staying in the cottage tonight."

Lady Whistledown Strikes Back

by Julia Quinn, Suzanne Enoch,
Karen Hawkins, and Mia Ryan

All of London is abuzz with speculation: Who
stole Lady Neeley's bracelet? Was it the fortune
hunter, the gambler, the servant, or the rogue?
It's clear that one of the four is connected to the
crime. Society's secrets are revealed in a second
glittering anthology starring gossip columnist
Lady Whistledown, popularized in #1 *New York
Times* bestselling author Julia Quinn's Bridgerton
novels.

Worth Any Price

by Lisa Kleypas

Nick Gentry, the most seductive and dangerous
man in England, has been sent to find Charlotte
Howard, a runaway bride who has disappeared
without a trace. But when he finds her, Nick is
stunned by the intensity of his attraction to the
elusive young woman whose adventurous spirit
matches his own. And he realizes he will pay
any price to protect Charlotte from the diabolical
aristocrat who threatens her.

Give in to your Impulses!

**These unforgettable stories only take a second
to buy and give you hours of reading pleasure!**

Go to *www.AvonImpulse.com* and see what we
have to offer.

Available wherever e-books are sold.

AVONIMPULSE

"You'll Need Both Hands For This.

"When you swing the ax back, let your right one slip up the handle. But whatever you do, always hold on hard with your left, like this. Want to try it?" he asked.

When she took the ax, her fingers brushed over his.

Rye stepped back and reached around Lisa until his hands were positioned above and below hers on the long handle. Every time she breathed in, a blend of evergreen resin and warmth and man filled her senses. His skin was smooth against hers, hot, and the hair on his arms glistened beneath the sun in shades of sable and bronze.

With each motion Rye made, his chest brushed against Lisa's back, telling her that barely a breath separated their bodies.

"Lisa?"

Helplessly she looked over her shoulder at Rye. His mouth was only inches away.

"Come closer," he whispered, bending down to her. "Closer. Yes, like that."

Dear Reader:

Welcome! You hold in your hand a Silhouette Desire—your ticket to a whole new world of reading pleasure.

A Silhouette Desire is a sensuous, contemporary romance about passions, problems and the ultimate power of love. It is about today's woman—intelligent, successful, giving—but it is also the story of a romance between two people who are strong enough to follow their own individual paths, yet strong enough to compromise, as well.

These books are written by, for and about every woman that you are—wife, mother, sister, lover, daughter, career woman. A Silhouette Desire heroine must face the same challenges, achieve the same successes, in her story as you do in your own life.

The Silhouette reader is not afraid to enjoy herself. She knows when to take things seriously and when to indulge in a fantasy world. With six books a month, Silhouette Desire strives to meet her many moods, but each book is always a compelling love story.

Make a commitment to romance—go wild with Silhouette Desire!

Best,

Isabel Swift
Senior Editor & Editorial Coordinator

ELIZABETH LOWELL
Fever

Silhouette Desire

Published by Silhouette Books New York

America's Publisher of Contemporary Romance

SILHOUETTE BOOKS
300 East 42nd St., New York, N.Y. 10017

Copyright © 1988 by Two Of A Kind, Inc.

ISBN: 0-373-05415-7

First Silhouette Books printing April 1988

America's Publisher of Contemporary Romance

Printed in the U.S.A.

Books by Elizabeth Lowell

Silhouette Desire

Summer Thunder #77
The Fire of Spring #265
Too Hot to Handle #319
Love Song for a Raven #355
Fever #415

Silhouette Intimate Moments

The Danvers Touch #18
Lover in the Rough #34
Summer Games #57
Forget Me Not #72
A Woman Without Lies #81
Traveling Man #97
Valley of the Sun #109
Sequel #128
Fires of Eden #141
Sweet Wind, Wild Wind #178

ELIZABETH LOWELL

is a pseudonym for Ann Maxwell, who also writes with her husband under the name of A. E. Maxwell. Her novels range from science fiction to historical fiction, and from romance to the sometimes gritty reality of modern suspense. All of her novels share a common theme—the power and beauty of love.

To Francis Ray
salt of the earth
and sweetness, too

One

Ryan McCall climbed out of the battered ranch pickup and instantly began unbuttoning his city shirt. He had flown from Texas to a small local landing strip in Utah where he kept one of the few luxuries he had bought for himself—a plane that could get him in and out of his father's life in nothing flat. From the airstrip he had driven in the pickup over increasingly primitive roads until he reached his home in the early afternoon. He had loved every rough inch of the way, because each rock and rut meant that he was farther removed from the father he loved and could not get along with for more than a few minutes at a time.

"It was worth it, though," Rye told himself aloud as he stretched his long, powerful arms over his head. "That Angus bull of his is just what my herd needs."

Unfortunately it had taken Rye two weeks to convince Edward McCall II that his son would not, repeat *not*, marry some useless Houston belle just to get his hands on the Angus bull. Once that was understood, the negotiations for the bull had gone quickly.

Rye turned his face up to the afternoon sun and smiled with sensual pleasure at the warmth pouring over him. The Texas sun had been hot. Too hot. He preferred the golden heat of Utah's mountain country, where the lowland's fierce sun was gentled by altitude and winds smelling of piñon and distant pines. The air was dry, brilliant in its clarity, and the small river that wound through the Rocking M was a cool, glittering rush of blue.

Eyes closed, shirt undone, Rye stood and let the peace he always felt on his own land steal over him. It had been a long two weeks. His father had just turned sixty. His lack of grandsons to carry on the family name had been duly noted—about six times an hour. Even his sister, who was normally a staunch ally, had told him sweetly that she would be bringing up a very special girl for the end-of-the-summer dance Rye always held at his ranch. Rye had ignored his sister, but he hadn't been able to ignore the endless stream of moist-lipped debutantes or accomplished divorcées who were trembling with eagerness to get their perfectly mani-cured claws into the McCall pocketbook.

Rye's mouth shifted into a sardonic smile. He could af-ford to be amused by the women's transparent greed now; he was home, beyond their reach, and he thanked God for every instant of his freedom. Whistling softly, he pulled out his shirttails and leaped onto the porch without touching any of the three steps. The movement was catlike in its speed, grace and precision.

Since Rye had come into his mother's small inheritance at twenty-one, he had spent his time digging postholes, felling trees and riding thousands of miles over his own ranch. The hard labor showed in his powerful body. The lithe flex and play of muscles beneath tanned skin had attracted more than one feminine glance. Rye discounted his appearance as any part of the reason women lined up at his door, however. He had seen his father and his younger brother fall prey to too many greedy women to believe that any woman would want him for any reason other than his bank account, which meant that he had very little use for women at all.

The instant Rye walked into his house, he knew that someone else was there. The room smelled of perfume rather than the sunshine and fresh air that he preferred. He turned and saw a woman standing in the dining room. She had pulled open a sideboard drawer and was looking at its utilitarian contents with a combination of curiosity and disbelief.

"Taking inventory?" Rye asked coolly.

The woman made a startled sound and spun to face him. The movement sent black hair flying. There was no shifting of cloth, however; the clothes she was wearing were too tight to float with any movement she made. Big, dark eyes took in every detail of Rye's appearance. They widened at the breadth of his shoulders and the thick mat of hair that began at his collarbone and disappeared beneath the narrow waist of his pants. The speculation in the woman's eyes increased as she approvingly inspected the fit of his slacks.

A single fast look told Rye that his father had gone all out this time. The woman was built like a particularly lush hourglass and had paid a tailor to prove it. Not a single ripe curve went unannounced. The blouse was too well made to strain at the buttons with each breath she took, but it was a near thing. Automatically Rye put her in the "experienced divorcée" category.

"Hello," she said, holding out her hand to him and smiling. "My name's Cherry Larson."

"Goodbye, Cherry Larson. Tell Dad you tried, but I threw you out so hard you bounced. He might feel sorry enough for you to buy you a trinket." Rye's words were clipped, as cold as the gray eyes staring through Cherry, dismissing her as he turned away.

"Dad?"

"Edward McCall the Second," Rye said, heading for the staircase, pulling off his shirt. "The Texan who paid you to seduce me."

"Oh." She frowned. "He told you?"

"He didn't have to. Overblown brunettes are his style, not mine."

The bedroom door slammed, leaving Cherry Larson to examine the stainless steel flatware in peace.

A few moments later Rye emerged in boots, Levi's and work shirt. Cherry was still standing in the dining room. He passed her without a look, lifted his hat from a peg by the kitchen door and said, "I'm going for a ride. When I get back, you won't be here."

"But—but how will I get into town?"

"Wait around for a silver-haired cowboy called Lassiter. He loves taking women like you for a ride."

Rye walked to the barn with long, angry strides. The first thing he saw was Devil, his favorite mount. The big horse was tied to the corral fence, swishing flies with a long, black tail. Saddled, bridled, ready to go.

Instantly Rye knew that at least one of the cowhands had realized how he would react when he saw the woman lying in wait for him in his own home. He'd bet that the thoughtful cowhand had been Jim. He was happily married, yet he fully sympathized with his boss's desire to stay single.

"Jim, you just earned yourself a bonus," Rye muttered as he untied the reins and swung onto the big black horse.

Devil bunched his powerful haunches and tugged impatiently at the bit, demanding a run. He hadn't been ridden by anyone during the weeks that Rye had been gone, and Devil was a horse that had been born to run.

There was no one in sight as Rye cantered out past the barn. For a moment he wondered about the fact that none of his men had turned out to say hello, then he realized that the hands were probably back in the barn somewhere, laughing at his reaction to the lushly baited trap set in his lair. The men could have warned him about Cherry's presence, but that would have spoiled the joke, and there was nothing a cowboy loved better than a joke—no matter who it was on. So they had just made themselves scarce until the fun was over.

Reluctantly Rye smiled, then laughed out loud. He spun the big horse on its hocks just in time to see several men filing out of the barn. Rye waved his dark hat in a big arc before spinning Devil around again and giving the horse the freedom to run that it had been begging for.

As the trail to McCall's Meadow glided by under Devil's long stride, Rye relaxed again, relishing his freedom. The high, small meadow was his favorite part of the ranch, his ultimate retreat from the frustrations of being Edward Ryan McCall III. Usually he was one of the first people to reach the mountain meadow after the snow melted in the pass, but the melt had come very late this year. He hadn't had time to get to the meadow before he had gone to Houston to negotiate for the purchase of one of his father's prize bulls.

Before Rye had bought the ranch, the various high meadows had been used as summer pasture for cattle and sheep. Most of the meadows still pastured cattle. The small, high bowl that had come to be called McCall's Meadow hadn't been touched for ten years. Dr. Thompson had been very eloquent in his plea that Rye, as one of the few ranchers who could afford it, should be the one to lead the way in allowing a small part of his land to return to what it had been before white men had come to the West. The resulting patterns of regrowth in the plants and the return of native animals would be studied in detail, and what was learned would be used to help reclaim other lands from overgrazing.

In truth, Rye hadn't needed much persuading to participate in Dr. Thompson's study. Rye might have been born in the city but he had never loved it. He loved the rugged land, though. He loved riding through sunlight and wind and silence, and seeing mountains rise above him, their flanks a magnificent patchwork of evergreen forest, blue-gray sage and quaking aspen that turned from green to shimmering silver under a caressing breeze. The land gave him peace.

And if a man took care of the land, unlike a woman, the land would take care of him in return.

That same afternoon Lisa Johansen sat by a mountain stream and slowly trailed her fingers through the cool, clean water. The sunlight that smoothed over her was as warm and sensual as her daydream, making a languid heat uncurl deep within her as she stretched to meet her dream. *He will be like the mountains, strong and rugged and enduring. He will look at me and see not a pale outsider but the woman of his dreams. He will smile and hold out his hand and then he'll gather me in his arms and . . .*

Whether she was awake or asleep, the dream always ended there. Wryly Lisa acknowledged to herself that it was just as well; she had a thorough intellectual understanding of what came next, but her practical experience in a man's arms was one zero followed by another and another, world without end, amen. Isolation from her peers had been the biggest drawback to the kind of life she had led with her parents, who were anthropologists. There had always been men about, but none of them were for her. They had been tribal men who were cultural light-years apart from herself and her parents.

With a sigh Lisa scooped up a palmful of water and drank, letting the shimmering coolness spread through her. After two weeks, she still didn't take for granted the mountain water flowing clean and sweet and pure, day and night, a liquid miracle always within her reach. As she bent to drink again, the muted sound of hoofbeats came to her.

Lisa straightened and shaded her eyes with her hand. At the entrance to the high, small valley were two riders. She stood up, wiped her dripping hand on her worn jeans and mentally reviewed her meager supplies. When she had taken the job of watching over McCall's Meadow through the brief, high-country summer, she hadn't realized that she would need to buy so many supplies from her tiny food budget. But then, she hadn't realized that Boss Mac's cowboys would be such frequent visitors to the meadow. Since she had first met the cowboys ten days ago, they had been back almost every day, swearing that nobody made pan bread and bacon like she did.

The shorter of the two cowboys took off his hat and waved it in a wide arc. Lisa waved back, recognizing Lassiter, Boss Mac's foreman. The man with him was Jim. If they had other names, the men hadn't mentioned them and she would never ask. In many of the primitive tribes among which she had been raised, to ask someone for his full name—or for any name at all—was unspeakably rude.

"Morning, Miss Lisa," Lassiter said, dismounting from his horse. "How're them seeds doing? They slipped through that old fence and flown away yet?"

Lisa smiled and shook her head. Ever since she had told Lassiter that she was here to watch the grass seeds growing within the big meadow fence, he had teased her about runaway seeds that needed to be "hog-tied and throwed 'fore they learned their rightful place."

"I haven't lost any seeds yet," Lisa said gravely, "but I'm being real careful, just like you told me. I'm particularly watchful when the moon is up. That's when all sorts of odd things take a notion to fly."

Lassiter heard Lisa's precise echoes of his earlier dead-pan warnings and knew that she was gently pulling his leg. He laughed and slapped his hat against his jeans, releasing a small puff of trail dust that was almost as silver as his hair. "You'll do, Miss Lisa. You'll do just fine. Boss Mac won't find one seed missing when he gets back from Houston. Good thing, too. He's hell on wheels after a few weeks of having his pa parade eager fillies past him."

Lisa smiled rather sadly. She knew what it was like to disagree with parents on the subject of marriage. Her parents had wanted to her to marry a man like themselves, a scholar with a taste for adventure. So they had sent her to the United States and their old friend Professor Thompson with instructions to find her a suitable mate. Lisa had come, but not to find a husband. She had come to see if the United States would be her home, if she would finally find a place that would hold the answer to the hot restlessness that burned like a fever in her dreams, in her blood.

"Hello, Miss Lisa," the second man said, climbing down and standing almost shyly to the side. "This here mountain must agree with you. You're pretty as a daisy."

"Thank you," Lisa said, smiling quickly at the lanky cowhand. "How's the baby? Has he cut that tooth yet?"

Jim sighed. "Durn thing's stubborn as a stump. He keeps a-chewin' and a-chewin' and nothin' happens. But the missus says to thank you. She tried rubbing that oil you gave her on the gum and the baby was right soothed."

The smile on Lisa's face widened. Some things didn't change, no matter the culture nor the country. Oil of cloves was an ancient remedy for gum troubles, yet it had been all but forgotten in America. It pleased Lisa that something she had learned half a world and cultural centuries distant from Utah's mountains could help the fat-cheeked baby whose picture Jim proudly displayed at every opportunity.

"You and Lassiter are just in time for lunch," Lisa said. "Why don't you water your horses while I build up the fire?"

As one, Lassiter and Jim turned toward their mounts. Instead of leading the animals away, both men untied gunnysacks that had been secured behind the saddles.

"The missus said you must be getting right tired of bread and beans and bacon," Jim said, holding out a sack. "Thought you might like some cookies and things for a change."

Before Lisa could thank him, Lassiter held out two bulging sacks. "Cook said he had more food hanging around than he could set fire to 'fore it went bad. You'd be doing us a favor if you took it off our hands."

For a moment Lisa could say nothing. Then she blinked against the stinging in her eyes and thanked both men. It was very comforting to know that generosity, like a baby's first tooth, was a part of human experience everywhere in the world.

While the men watered their horses, Lisa added a few more sticks to the fire from her dwindling supply of wood, mixed up a batch of dough and checked the soot-blackened kettle that served as a coffeepot. To her joy, a generous supply of coffee had been included in the supplies that the men had packed up the trail for her. There was also dried and fresh fruit, more flour, dried beef, fresh beef, rice, salt, oil and other packages she didn't have time to investigate before the men came back from the stream. The sacks were a treasure trove to Lisa, who had been accustomed to seeing food measured out carefully except for the rare feast days.

Humming happily, Lisa planned meals that would have been impossible before Lassiter and Jim had come riding up the trail with their generous gifts. She had come to America with almost no cash. If there had been any money left over from the grants that supported her parents, it had always gone to help out the desperately poor among the natives. Nor did the job of being caretaker in McCall's Meadow pay anything beyond a roof over her head, a fixed amount of money for supplies and a stipend so small it could only be called an allowance.

The cabin itself was ancient. Previous students had joked that it had been built by God just after He finished the mountains surrounding it. There was a hearth, walls, floor, roof and not much else. The lack of electricity, running water and other such amenities didn't bother Lisa. She would have loved to have some of the beautiful carpets that the Bedouin tribes used to brighten and soften their austere lives, but she was more than content with the gentle sun, clean air, abundant water and near absence of flies. To her, those things were true luxuries.

And if she wanted to touch something soft and exquisitely made, she had only to open up her pack and admire her parents' parting gift to her. The yards of cloth were a linen so fine that it felt like silk. One piece was a luminous dove gray meant to be made into a swirling dress. The other piece was a glowing amethyst that was the exact color of her eyes. It, too, was destined to be made into a dress.

Despite their alluring beauty, Lisa hadn't cut into either length of cloth. She knew that they were meant to help her find a husband. She didn't want that. She wanted more from life than a man who saw her as a cross between a producer of sons and a beast of burden. Few of the native marriages Lisa had seen aroused in her anything but a mixed admiration for the women's stamina. Intellectually she knew why the nubile girls her age and younger had watched men with dark, speculative eyes and measuring smiles. Emotionally Lisa had never felt the strange fever that she had seen burning in other girls' blood, making them forget the lessons of their mothers and grandmothers, aunts and sisters.

Secretly that was what Lisa had always hoped to find somewhere in the world—the fever that burned through body and mind, the fever that burned all the way through to the soul. Yet she had never felt farther away from it than in America, where the boys her own age seemed very young, full of laughter and untested confidence, untouched by famine and death. During the few days that she had lived with Professor Thompson, waiting for the pass into McCall's Meadow to open, she had met many students; but not once had she looked at the males around her with ancient female curiosity in her eyes and fever rising in her blood.

She had begun to doubt that she ever would.

Two

"Sure smells good," Lassiter said, coming up behind Lisa as she cooked. "You know, you're the only one of Professor Thompson's kids we haven't had to teach how to make real camp coffee."

"In Morocco, coffee isn't coffee until it's so thick it barely pours," Lisa said.

"Yeah? You'll have to make that for me someday."

"Bring lots of tinned milk, then. And sugar."

"Think so?"

She nodded.

"Real horseshoe floater, huh?"

Lisa hadn't heard the phrase before. The image it conjured in her mind made her laugh. "Actually, it would probably float the horse, too."

Chuckling, Lassiter looked around the camp, approving of the order that Lisa had brought to the area. Twigs for kindling and thicker sticks for burning had been stacked

within easy reach of the campfire, along with a few larger
pieces of wood. The ground itself had been recently swept
with a broom made of twigs. The various tools that had
been broken or abandoned by other students had been
gathered by Lisa and laid out neatly on a log. The tools
ranged in size from a slender awl to a battered wedge and
sledgehammer used for splitting logs. The big, double-edged
logger's ax that came with the cabin showed recent signs of
having been sharpened, although Lassiter couldn't imagine
what Lisa had used to hone it. Nor could he imagine her
using the ax itself. The handle was four feet long, and she
was only a few inches over five feet.

The ax reminded Lassiter that he had meant to see how
Lisa was fixed for firewood. Unlike the other students, she
cooked her food over a campfire rather than on a camp
stove. Lassiter suspected that she didn't even have such a
stove. In fact, he suspected that she didn't have much at all
beyond the clothes she stood in and the bedroll that was
being aired right now over a small bush. Yet despite her obvious lack of money, she had never begrudged him or any
of the McCall cowhands a meal, regardless of how many
men there were or how often they showed up. She had always offered food no matter what the time of day, as though
she knew what it meant to be hungry and didn't want anyone to leave her camp with an empty belly.

"Jim, why don't you and me snake a few logs on down
here," Lassiter said, settling his hat on his head firmly. "We
won't have time to cut them up today, but we can get them
ready. Twigs and sticks are all well and good, but a proper
fire needs proper wood."

"You don't have to," Lisa began. "I can—"

"Durn things are blocking the trail," Jim interrupted,
mumbling. He snagged the heavy ax in one hand and turned

to his horse. "Boss Mac would have our hides if a horse tripped on 'em and came up lame."

"Miss Lisa, you'd be doing us a favor just burning them up," Lassiter said firmly as he stepped into the stirrup.

Lisa looked from one man to the other, then said simply, "Thank you. I could use some more wood." As the men rode off, Lisa suddenly remembered. "Be sure that you don't take anything from inside the fence!" That was why she was here, after all. She was to protect everything behind the fence from the interference of men, so that the meadow could slowly revert to its natural state.

"Yo," Lassiter said, raising his hand in acknowledgment.

The men didn't have to go more than a hundred feet to find the kind of wood they wanted—pine logs no bigger than ten inches in diameter, the remains of trees that had fallen and had been cured through the following seasons. As Jim and Lassiter worked, preparing the logs to be dragged to the cabin, their voices carried clearly through the mountain silence.

Lisa listened to the men while she cooked, smiling from time to time at their colorful phrases when a log was especially stubborn. When the conversation shifted to the mysterious Boss Mac, she found herself holding her breath so as not to miss a word. She knew only two things about the absent owner of McCall's Meadow: his father urgently wanted Boss Mac to marry and have a son, and his men respected Boss Mac more than anything else except God.

"Then he told that redhead if'n she wanted a free ride, she should go down to the highway and wiggle her thumb," Lassiter concluded, laughing. "She was so mad she couldn't talk for a minute. Guess she thought a few nights in town with the boss meant wedding bells." The sound of the ax rang out as branches were trimmed from the log. "And then that redhead found her tongue," Lassiter continued. "Judas Priest! I ain't never heard such language. An' her with such a sweet smile, too."

"You get a look at the one layin' in wait for him now?" Jim asked.

He grunted with effort as the heavy ax bit into wood, making a notch for the rope to rest in while the log was dragged over to the cabin. Lassiter secured the rope around the log, then mounted his big horse and took a few turns on the rope around the saddle horn. At a touch of his heels, the horse slowly began pulling the log toward the cabin.

"Well, did you get a look?" Jim asked again as he mounted his own horse, wondering what the latest candidate for McCall's bed was like.

"Sure did." Lassiter's admiring whistle lifted musically on the mountain air. "Big dark eyes to put a deer to shame. Black hair down to her bosom—and a mighty fine bosom it was, too, all full and soft. And hips? Lordy, it was enough to make you weep. I tell you, Jim. I don't know a man alive that wouldn't want to climb into that saddle."

"Hell you don't," grunted Jim. "What about Boss Mac?"

"Oh, I wasn't talking about *marrying* it," Lassiter said. "Didn't your pa tell you? A smart man don't marry a horse just cuz he enjoys a ride now and again. Look at me."

"I'm lookin'," Jim retorted, "and I'm thinkin' most women would rather have the horse."

Lisa couldn't completely hide her laughter. When the men heard, they realized that their conversation had carried very clearly to the camp. As they rode in, both of them looked embarrassed.

"Sorry, Miss Lisa," Jim mumbled. "Didn't mean to be sayin' such things in front of a girl."

"It's all right," she said hastily. "Really. We used to sit around the campfire and talk about Imbrihim's four wives and eight concubines and no one was embarrassed."

"Four?" Jim asked.

"Eight?" Lassiter demanded.

"For a total of twelve," Lisa agreed, grinning.

"Lor-dy," said Lassiter in admiring tones. "They make 'em strong over there, don't they?"

"Dumb," Jim muttered. "They make 'em dumb."

"Just rich," Lisa said cheerfully. "You herd cattle and Imbrihim herds camels, but things are pretty much the same underneath—in both places a strong, dumb rich man can have as many pretty, dumb women as he can afford."

Lassiter threw back his head and laughed. "You're one of a kind, Miss Lisa. But don't you go to thinking the boss is dumb. He ain't."

"That's God's truth," Jim said earnestly. "Boss Mac don't catch near as many girls as throw themselves at him. I'll bet he don't do nothing with the one waiting at the ranch now but kick her out on her high-rent keister. 'Scuse me, Miss Lisa," he added, flushing. "I forgot myself. But it's true just the same. Boss Mac is a good man and he'd be a happy one, too, if'n his pa would stop running secondhand fillies past him."

"I don't know about the one at the ranch," Lassiter said, smiling a very male smile. "Wouldn't surprise me a'tall if he kept her around. If nothing else, he needs a date for the dance, otherwise every gal in two hundred miles will be all over him like flies on fresh . . . er, honey."

"The dance is six weeks away," Jim protested. "He's never let a woman stay around that long."

"He's never had a woman that looked like this one," Lassiter said flatly. "She's the kind to make a man's jeans fit too tight, make no mistake about it."

Lisa made a strangled sound and nearly dropped the frying pan as a blush climbed up her fair skin at the image that came to her mind with Lassiter's words. She couldn't help wondering what it would be like to make a man burn with that kind of elemental fever. Then she remembered Lassiter's description: *Big dark eyes... black hair down to her bosom... all full and soft. And hips. Lordy!*

Glumly Lisa prodded the pan bread, knowing that the only thing a pale, slender, inexperienced blonde was likely to set fire to was lunch.

Black nostrils flared as Devil drank the wind sweeping down out of the high country. He snorted and pulled hard at the bit. There were two trails to the meadow. One followed an old rough wagon road that had been built when the meadow was first homesteaded more than a century ago. That was the trail cattle had been driven over when the meadow was used for summer pasture. Rye could tell from the hoofprints that his men had been riding that road with unusual frequency in th: past weeks. Two sets of very fresh prints told him that Lassiter's big bay and Jim's smaller cow pony had just come down out of the meadow and headed east to check on the range cattle.

The second trail hadn't been touched since the last storm. The route was precipitous, narrow, and the path all but invisible. Rye had stumbled onto it six years ago and had since used it when he was too impatient to get to the meadow's peace to take the long way around. Most horses would have balked at the path. Devil took it with the confidence of an animal born and raised in steep places.

After a long series of breathtakingly rugged switchbacks, the trail clawed up a talus slope and into a mixed grove of aspen and evergreens. The weathered cabin was just beyond the grove, at the edge of the remote meadow that was slowing reverting to its primal state. As Rye approached it, he heard the raucous cry of a whiskey jack flying through the trees and an odd series of noises that sounded rather like someone chopping wood. Rye listened for a while and then shook his head, unable to identify the sounds. The noises were too few and far between and too erratic to come from the rhythmic motions of a man chopping wood.

The horse's hooves made no sound on the bed of evergreen needles as Rye rode around the back of the cabin into the meadow. What he saw thirty feet away made him rein in the horse and shake his head in a combination of approval and disbelief. The odd sounds were indeed those of wood being chopped, but the axman who had his back turned to the woods was a flaxen-haired college kid not much taller than the ax itself. No matter how high the boy stood on his toes or how hard he swung, he lacked the size and muscle to handle the heavy ax the way it had been designed to be handled.

But the kid was getting the job done anyway. There was a ragged, gnawed-looking pile of firewood on one side of the chopping stump. On the opposite side was a much bigger, much more intimidating pile of untouched logs.

Rye reined the big black horse closer. He had cut enough wood to know that the boy was overmatched. Game, but in way over his head. He'd be all summer and well into winter before he gnawed his way through that pile of logs.

Then the kid turned around at the sound of Devil's restless snort . . . and Rye felt as though he had been kicked.

The "boy" was a young woman with the kind of willowy, long-legged, high-breasted body that made a man's blood run hot and thick. What he had thought was a boy's short hair was a mass of platinum braids piled high above a delicate face. Her eyes were a clear amethyst that took away what little breath remained to Rye. She watched him with a combination of curiosity, poise and innocence that reminded him of a Siamese kitten.

Suddenly Rye felt rage replace desire in his blood. *Innocence?* Like flaming hell! She was just one more freeloading female lying in wait for his money—and she had the raw nerve to do it in his favorite retreat.

Rye spurred Devil closer. The girl was not intimidated by the big horse. When Devil's shoulder was no more than a foot away from the girl, Rye reined in and looked her over, trying to reconcile his certainty that she was a cunning gold digger with the slender, delicately beautiful, almost solemn girl who stood watching him with fathomless amethyst eyes, her hand on Devil's shoulder as she absently soothed the restless horse.

Lisa noticed Rye's blunt appraisal for only an instant before she was shaken by a soft, slow explosion deep inside herself, an explosion that sent shock waves all the way to her soul. Emotions sleeted through her, a wild exhilaration mixed with fear, a confused feeling of having lost her footing in reality while at the same time never having felt more alive. And above all she knew a primal certainty that grew with every second she stood motionless watching the stranger who had ridden up and turned her life inside out without saying a word: she had been born to be this man's woman.

There was no hesitation, no withdrawal, no questioning within Lisa as she looked at him. She had lived on the edge of life and death in too many different cultures to flinch from the truth now simply because it was new or strange or utterly unexpected.

She could not look away from him. In electric silence she stared at his dusty boots, his powerful calves and thighs, his narrow hips, his shoulders wide enough to block out the sun, his hard jaw and shadowy beard stubble and curiously sensual mouth—and his eyes the color of rain. She was far too riveted to conceal her fascination with him, and too innocent to understand the currents of sensuality and desire that stirred her body, bringing a slow fever to her flesh.

Rye saw the subtle flush of response in her heightened color and felt a hot shaft of answering desire. Reluctantly he conceded that his father's taste in sexual bait had made a quantum improvement. This candidate was definitely not a thick-hipped, overblown rose. There was an essential elegance to the girl that made him think of the transparent, burning grace of a candle flame. There was also a shimmering, almost hidden sensuality in her that made his body harden in anticipation.

"You're something else, little girl," Rye said finally. "If you'll settle for a diamond bracelet instead of a diamond ring, we'll have a good time for a while."

The words came at Lisa as though from a distance. She blinked and took a deep breath, composing herself in the face of the overwhelming truth of the hard-looking, rough-voiced stranger.

"I beg your pardon?" she asked slowly. "I don't understand."

"The hell you don't," he retorted, ignoring the leap of his blood when he first heard the husky softness of her voice. She was young, almost a girl, but the eyes that watched him were as old—and as curious—as Eve. "I'm a man who doesn't mind paying for what he wants, and you're a girl who doesn't mind getting paid. Just so long as we understand that we'll do fine." His pupils darkened and widened as she took a sudden, sharp breath. "Hell," he added roughly, "we'll do better than fine. We'll burn down the whole damned mountain."

Lisa didn't even hear the last words. Her mind had come to a quivering halt over the description of herself as *a girl who doesn't mind getting paid*. Prostitutes were prostitutes the world over; being described as one by the man who had turned her world inside out just by riding into view made her furious. She realized that he had felt none of the soul-deep awareness that she had felt, had known none of the utter rightness of being with him that she had known. He had seen only a piece of merchandise he wanted and had set out to purchase it.

The amethyst eyes that examined him were different this time. They noted that his shirt collar and cuffs were badly frayed, a button was missing where the material stretched across his chest, his jeans were faded and worn almost to transparency, and his boots were scarred and down at the heels. This was the wealthy sultan insulting her by offering to rent her body for a while?

Caution vanished in a searing instant, taking with it Lisa's usually excellent self-control. She did something that she hadn't done since she was eight years old. She lost her temper. Completely.

"Who are you trying to fool?" Lisa asked in a voice that had lost all softness. "You couldn't afford a glass stickpin, much less a diamond bracelet."

The look of shock on the man's face made Lisa feel suddenly ashamed of herself for attacking him on the basis of something that she cared nothing about—money. Her shame deepened as she realized that, given the way she had been staring at him, it wasn't surprising that he had assumed she would be pleased rather than angered by his blunt proposition.

Lisa closed her eyes, took a deep breath and remembered something that didn't vary from culture to culture across the world: men, especially poor men, had a great deal of pride, and they were inclined to be quite abrupt when their stomachs were growling.

"If you're hungry, there's bread and bacon," Lisa said in a quiet voice, automatically offering him what food she had. "And cookies," she added, remembering.

The corner of Rye's mouth kicked up in amusement. "Oh, I'm hungry all right," he drawled, "so let's decide on a price."

"But it's free!" Lisa said, shocked that he would expect to pay for a simple meal.

"That's what they all say, and every last one of the poor little dears ends up whining for a diamond ring."

Belatedly Lisa realized that the word *hungry* could have more than one meaning. Her anger flashed again, surprising her. Usually she was the kind of person to laugh rather than swear when things went wrong, but the heat racing through her blood owed nothing to her sense of humor. The man's off-center, lazy, terrifyingly sexy smile made her furious.

"Are you this rude to everyone?" she asked, clipping each word.

"Only to little darlings who ask for it by lying in wait for me in my favorite places."

"I'm here because it's my job. What are you doing in McCall's Meadow besides wasting Boss Mac's time?"

Again, Rye couldn't keep his shock from showing. "Boss Mac?"

"Yes. Boss Mac. The man who pays you to herd cattle. Surely you recognize the name?"

Rye barely swallowed a hoot of incredulous laughter as he realized that the girl had been sent out to trap a man she didn't even know on sight. As he opened his mouth to straighten her out about Boss Mac's true identity, Rye saw the humor of the situation—and the potential for teaching what was obviously an amateur gold digger the rules of the game she had chosen to play.

"I surrender," he murmured, smiling and holding his hands in the air as though she had drawn a gun on him. "I'll be good if you don't report me to, um, Boss Mac." Rye looked down at her and asked innocently, "How well do you know him?"

The change from blunt to charming unsettled Lisa. "I've never met him," she admitted. "I'm just here for the summer, making sure nothing goes wrong with Dr. Thompson's experiment," she added, waving her hand toward the rustic split-rail fence zigzagging across the end of the meadow.

Rye strenuously doubted that she was here only to watch the grass grow, but all he said was, "Well, you watch out for Boss Mac. He's hell on women."

Lisa shrugged gracefully. "He's never bothered me. Neither have his men. All of them have been very polite. With one exception," she added coolly, looking directly at him.

"Sorry about that," Rye said sardonically, lifting his hat in a polite salute. "I'll be real polite from now on. I know Boss Mac well enough to be dead scared of his temper. Is that offer of bacon and bread still open? And cookies."

For a moment Lisa could only stand and look up at Rye's powerful, rangy frame and feel odd sensations shivering throughout her body. The thought of him being hungry, of him needing something that she could give to him, made her feel weak.

"Of course," she said softly, appalled that he would think her so mean as to turn a hungry man away from food. "I'm sorry if I've been rude. My name is Lisa Johansen."

Rye hesitated, unwilling to end the game so quickly. When he spoke it was curtly, and he gave only the shortened form of his middle name, Ryan. "Rye."

"Rye..." Lisa murmured.

The name intrigued her, as did the man. She wondered if it was his first or his last name or a name he had chosen for himself. She wondered, but she did not ask. She was accustomed to primitive peoples; for them, names were potent magic, often sacred, and always private. She repeated the name again, softly, enjoying it simply because it was his and he had given it to her.

"Rye.... The bacon and bread will be ready in a few minutes. If you want to wash up, there's a pan of water warming in the sun around at the side of the cabin."

Rye's eyes narrowed into glittering silver lines framed by sable lashes that were as thick and as long as a woman's. It was the only hint of softness about him as he studied Lisa, searching for any sign that she was pretending not to know who he really was. He saw absolutely nothing that indicated she knew that he was Edward Ryan McCall III, called Ryan by his dead mother, Rye by his friends, Little Eddy by his father—and Boss Mac by his hired hands.

Rye watched the gentle swinging of Lisa's hips as she walked to the campfire and didn't know whether to be furious or amused that she knew so little about her intended quarry that she didn't even recognize his nickname.

"Little girl, you've got a lot to learn," he muttered under his breath. "And you've come to just the man who can teach you."

Three

As Rye watched Lisa's easy, economical movements around the campfire, he decided that his father's latest candidate was different in more than her unusual, delicate beauty. Whatever else Rye might think about her, she wasn't afraid of work. Not only had she been willing to tackle a log with an ax that was old, dull and far too big for her, she had also taken the time to clear up the clutter that had slowly gathered around the cabin over the summers of student use. Used aluminum cans, plastic containers and glass bottles, as well as other flotsam and jetsam of modern life, were all stacked in neat piles at the side of the cabin.

"Next time I come, I'll bring a gunnysack and pack out that trash for you," he offered.

Lisa looked up from the frying bacon. The pan was perched on a warped, blackened grate, which was supported by the rocks that she had brought from the stream to make a fire ring. "Trash?"

"The bottles and cans," he said, gesturing toward the side of the cabin.

"Oh."

Lisa frowned slightly as she turned the bacon. Where she had come from, the pile would have been viewed as raw materials rather than junk. Broken glass would have been patiently ground into jewelry or pressure-flaked until it was a knife edge that could cut tough fibers or hides. It was a technique that she had used more than once herself, when they had lived with tribes that were too poor or too remotely located to replace steel knives when they broke or were lost. Modern steel kept its edge miraculously, but it was an expensive miracle. As for the tough, resilient plastic bottles, they would have been used to carry water, seeds, flour or salt—or even, on the shores of an African lake, as floats for fishing nets. The aluminum cans would have been worried over until they became something useful or were reluctantly discarded somewhere along the way.

"Thank you," Lisa said carefully. "If it's all right, I'd like to hang on to some of those things for now. The gunnysack would be very nice, though, if you're through with it. That way I can soak clothes in the stream and not lose them. The water runs awfully fast."

Rye stared, unable to believe that he had heard correctly about the collection of junk along the side of the cabin and washing clothes in the stream. Even if he put the question of trash aside, the other student caretakers had gone into town once a week for supplies and laundry and had carried enough equipment up the trail in the first place to make two of his best packhorses groan.

With the exception of the frying pan and bucket, it didn't look as though Lisa had carried anything new to the cabin. Her clothes were clean but showed signs of long wearing. There were patches on her jeans and shirt that had been sewn on with incredibly tiny, even stitches. He had assumed that the patches and fading were part of the new fashion trend that had clothes looking old the first time they were worn out of the shop. Now he was beginning to wonder. Maybe it was simply that she preferred to wear old, comfortable clothing as he did.

Or maybe she just didn't have a choice.

Lisa didn't notice Rye's suddenly speculative look at her clothes. She was busy cutting another piece of bacon from the slab that Lassiter had brought. She was using a broken jackknife she had discovered among the weeds in the front yard. Unfortunately she hadn't discovered a whetstone with the knife. She had ground off the rust on a convenient rock, but the blade would have had a tough time gnawing through butter.

With a muttered word in another language, Lisa set aside the hopelessly dull knife and went to the side of the cabin. She selected a piece of glass, examined its edge and returned to the fire. Casually she went back to work on the bacon, holding the glass between thumb and forefinger and cutting with light, quick strokes. When she was finished, she set the impromptu blade aside on top of a flat rock that she had found and carried to the fire for just that purpose.

"Hell of a knife," Rye said, not bothering to conceal his amazement.

"It won't hold its edge for long," Lisa said, laying the strip of bacon in the cast-iron pan, "but while it does, it's sharper than any steel."

"Lose your knife?" he asked, approaching the topic from another angle.

"No. It's just that the one I found was pretty rusty. Must have been here for a long time."

"Umm. I'll be going into town tomorrow. Want me to pick up a new knife for you?"

Lisa glanced up and smiled at Rye, silently thanking him for his thoughtfulness. "That's very nice of you, but I found enough glass around here to last for several summers."

She turned back to the bacon, missing the look that crossed Rye's face.

"Glass," he said neutrally.

She nodded. "And there are enough antlers around to keep an edge on."

"Enough antlers."

Something in Rye's tone caught Lisa's attention. She looked up, saw his face and laughed softly, realizing how she must have sounded.

"You use a point of the antler to pressure-flake the glass when the edge goes dull," she explained. "Glass has a conchoidal fracture. It breaks in tiny curves rather than a straight line. So you just put the point of the antler on the edge of the glass, press, and a tiny curved flake comes off. You do that all the way down the edge and then up the other side if you want to be fancy. The blade you get is pretty uneven, but it's hellishly sharp. For a while."

There was a silence while Rye assimilated what had been said and tried to match it with Lisa's deceptively fragile beauty.

"Are you one of those crazy physical anthropology students who run around trying to live like Stone Age men?" he demanded finally.

Lisa's soft laughter and amused amethyst eyes made tiny tongues of fire lick over Rye's nerve endings.

"Close," she admitted, still smiling. "My parents are anthropologists who study the daily life of the most primitive cultures on earth. Hunter-gatherers, nomads—you name it and we've lived it. Mom got interested in rare grasses, so she started collecting seeds and plants wherever we were and sending them on to university seed banks. The people who were working to develop high-yield, disease-resistant crops for Third World countries would use the plants in their experiments. That's why I'm here."

"You're disease resistant and high yield?" Rye offered dryly. He was rewarded by musical feminine laughter that shortened his breath.

"No, I'm an experienced seed collector who is used to camping out."

"In a word, just right for a summer stint in McCall's Meadow."

She nodded as she looked around at the clean, fertile meadow and the aspens shivering against a bottomless blue sky. "Of all the places I've been, this is the most beautiful," she said softly, closing her eyes for an instant to drink the sensual pleasures of the meadow. She inhaled softly, her lips slightly parted as she tasted the untamed wind. "Sweet, pure, perfect," she murmured. "Do you have any idea how very rare something like this is?"

Rye looked at Lisa's sensual appreciation of the sun and sky and wind for a long moment. The certainty grew in him that he had been wrong about her. She was what she had called the meadow—sweet, pure, perfect and very, very rare. She wasn't just another woman lined up for a lifetime of easy living as a rich man's wife. She couldn't be. Every one of the women who had come hunting him at the ranch had been appalled by the lack of amenities in the ranch house—the bare wood floors and stainless steel silverware, the ancient kitchen—and by his blunt promise that any work that got done around the house would be done by his wife rather than a pack of servants. And that went for the stables, as well. Any woman who wanted to ride could damn well shovel out stalls, polish saddles and bridles, and in general earn the right to put a horse through its paces.

Every single one of the women had told Rye to go to hell and had left without a backward look—which was exactly what he had had in mind. He didn't think Lisa would do that. She didn't have fancy nails to worry about. Hers were short enough not to get in the way, and they were as scrupulously clean as the wisps of platinum-blond hair that clung to her delicately flushed face. Nor did the thought of physical labor dismay her. He could still see her in his mind's eye, stretching up on tiptoe in a futile effort to bring the ax blade down with enough force to take a decent bite out of the log. She had spent a long time working on that log, long enough to leave red marks on the palms of her small hands.

He could see those marks clearly as she piled steaming, herb-scented bread and evenly cooked, crisp bacon on a plate for him.

"After dinner, I'll chop some wood for you," Rye said, his tone gruff. The thought of Lisa struggling to chop enough wood simply to cook his food disturbed Rye in ways that he didn't understand.

Lisa's hands paused as she put bacon on the battered tin plate. She didn't want Rye to feel that he had to repay her for the food he was eating. The longer she looked at his clothes, the more she doubted that he could afford even the most token amount of cash in payment. Nor did she want it. At the same time, she knew how proud a poor man could be.

"Thank you," she said softly. "I'm not very good with an ax. The places where we've lived didn't have pieces of wood big enough to need chopping before they were burned in cooking fires."

Rye bit into the camp bread and closed his eyes in pure pleasure. Tender, fragrant, steamy, exotic, the bread was like nothing he had ever eaten before. Food always tasted better in the meadow's crisp, high-mountain air, but this was extraordinary.

"Best bread I've ever eaten," he said simply. "What did you put in it?"

"There's a kind of wild onion growing near the stream," Lisa said as she settled cross-legged on the ground. "There was something that smelled remarkably like sage, too, and another plant that was very like parsley. I could see that deer had been browsing on the plants, so I knew they weren't poisonous. They tasted good when I nibbled on them. Kind of clean and crisp and lively. I put a little of each in for flavoring. Bread may be the staff of life, but variety is the spice."

Rye's grin flashed suddenly, making a hard white curve against his tanned face. Then he frowned as he thought over what she had said about tasting the various meadow greenery. "Maybe you better take it easy on the plants."

Her head snapped up. "I didn't go into the fenced part of the meadow."

"That's not what I meant. Some of those plants might make you sick."

"Then deer wouldn't eat them," Lisa said reasonably. "Don't worry. Before I came up here, I spent some time in the university library. I know exactly what the local narcotic and psychoactive plants look like."

"Psychoactive? *Narcotic?*"

"Ummm," she agreed, swallowing a bite of bacon. "Hallucinations and delirium or narcosis and full respiratory arrest, that sort of thing."

"From my meadow plants?" he asked incredulously.

Lisa smiled over Rye's proprietary "my" in reference to the meadow. She knew just how he felt. After only two weeks in the meadow, she felt as though it were her home.

"There's a plant growing not thirty feet from here that can cure the symptoms of asthma, make you crazy or kill you, depending on the dose," she said matter-of-factly. "It's called datura. Grows everywhere in the world. I recognized it right away."

Rye looked suddenly at the bread he had been wolfing down.

"Don't worry," Lisa said quickly. "I wouldn't touch datura. It's simply too powerful. The only herbs I use are for flavoring or for simple things like a headache or a stomachache or to soak my hands to help them to heal faster after hard work."

"There are things for that around here?" Rye asked, looking at the meadow and forest with new interest.

Lisa nodded because her mouth was too full to talk politely. Other cultures didn't object to a person chewing and talking at the same time, but Americans did. Her parents had been quite emphatic on that point. Burping was also prohibited. On the plus side, however, it was not considered a sign of demonic possession in this culture to eat with the left hand. That was quite a relief to Lisa, because she was naturally left-handed.

"Almost all modern drugs are the result of research into what is called 'folk medicine,'" Lisa continued. "Outside of the industrialized nations, people still depend on herbalists and home remedies to heal the sick. For ordinary discomfort such things work quite well and, compared to Western medicines, they cost almost nothing. Of course, when they get the chance, every tribe, no matter how primitive, inoculates their children against contagious diseases, and families will travel hundreds of miles at terrible hardship to take a sick or badly injured child to a hospital."

Rye savored the subtly flavored bread as he asked questions and listened to Lisa talking matter-of-factly about exotic cultures and various tribes' special expertise in medicine or animal husbandry or astronomy. Before he had finished eating, he had begun to wonder about his definition of "primitive." Lisa had been raised among tribes that could be described in no other terms than savage, primitive, Stone Age, yet there was a sophistication about her that had nothing to do with fine clothes, finishing schools or the other hallmarks of modern civilization. Lisa accepted human diversity with tolerance, humor, appreciation and intelligence. She was the most cosmopolitan and at the same time the most innocent person he had ever met.

The longer Rye sat with Lisa, the more convinced he became that the patches on her clothes weren't a fashion flourish but a necessity. Nor was the fact that she gathered trash for future use an attempt to be eccentric or ecologically trendy; she did indeed have a specific use for what she kept. She sat with lithe grace on the ground not because she had taken yoga or ballet, but because she had been raised among cultures that had no chairs.

"Amazing," he muttered to himself.

"I suppose so," Lisa said, grimacing. "I never went in for fermented mare's milk myself. The smell is indescribable. I guess that by the time we moved in with the Bedouins, I was just too old to be flexible in my tastes."

Rye realized that she had overheard him and thought that he was commenting on the Bedouin passion for fermented mare's milk rather than on his own awareness of how different Lisa was from other women he had met.

"I'll stick to bourbon," Rye said, trying and mercifully failing to imagine what fermented mare's milk would taste like.

"I'll stick to mountain air," Lisa said. "And mountain water."

The tone of her voice told Rye that she meant it. Having been raised in a dry, hot part of Texas, he could understand her passion for altitude and cold, sweet water.

"Time to earn my meal," he said, coming to his feet.

"You don't have to."

"How about if I admit that I like chopping wood?"

"How about if I admit that I don't believe you?" she retorted, looking at her own reddened palms.

He grinned. "I'm a lot tougher than you are. Besides, there's something satisfying about cutting wood. You can see exactly what you've done. Beats hell out of pushing papers and sitting on twelve corporate boards."

"I'll have to take your word for it," she said, glancing up at him curiously.

Abruptly Rye realized that a down-at-the-heels cowboy wouldn't know anything about corporate boards. He ducked his head and examined the ax blade carefully, cursing his heedless tongue. He was almost sure that Lisa didn't have the slightest idea who he was—either that, or she was a world-class actress. Somehow he doubted that she was. He did know one thing: innocent or actress, he didn't want her to realize that he was rich. He didn't want the flashes of elemental feminine appreciation that he had seen in her eyes when she looked at him turn into an equally elemental feminine calculation as she added up her own poverty and his real net worth.

"Both blades look like they've been used to quarry stone," Rye muttered.

He went to where he had tied Devil and fished around in the saddlebags he always carried. A few moments later he came back to the campfire with a whetstone in his hand and went to work sharpening the ax. Lisa watched, admiring his unusually long, strong fingers and the skill with which he worked to bring an edge up on the steel.

Once Rye glanced up and saw Lisa looking intently at his hands. He thought of what it would be like to be touching her silky body instead of cold steel, and to have her watching him. Immediately the fever that had been prowling in his blood became hotter, heavier, like his heartbeat. He bent over and went back to work on the ax, not wanting the direction of his thoughts to be revealed by his hardening body.

"Better," he grunted finally, touching his fingertip to the edge, "but it needs a lot of work before I'd want to shave with it."

Rye stepped up to one of the logs that Lassiter had dragged into camp, swung the ax and felt the blade sink into the wood. He had learned a lot about chopping wood the summer he made the split-rail fence that kept cattle from grazing in McCall's Meadow. Barbwire would have been easier to install but he had preferred to look at weathered wood zigzagging over the remote, beautiful meadow.

When Lisa finished cleaning up, she found a spot that was covered with pine needles and warmed by the fading sun. She sat and watched Rye, fascinated by his combination of power and masculine grace. The sound of the ax biting into wood was clean, sharp, rhythmic. It went on without pause or change until he bent to reposition the log. Then the rhythm resumed as muscles bunched across his shoulders, straining the fabric of the old shirt. The pile of cut wood grew with astonishing speed as the late-afternoon silence was punctuated by the whistling strike of steel against wood and the small sounds of chips falling to the ground amid dry aspen leaves.

Suddenly Rye's shirt split as the worn fabric gave up the unequal contest against the shifting power of his shoulder muscles.

Lisa leaped to her feet and ran toward him. "Your shirt!" she said, dismayed.

The back of Rye's shirt had parted in a wide, straight tear. Between the pieces of faded blue cloth, his skin gleamed over the flex and play of his muscles as he continued chopping wood without pausing to assess the damage to his clothes. Lisa's breath wedged in her throat and stayed there. The satin heat of him was tangible, as was the raw strength that had torn apart the cloth. Watching him sent the most curious sensations through her body, a shimmering feeling that made her skin flush as though with fever.

"No problem," Rye said, glancing at Lisa as he lifted the ax again.

"But you wouldn't have ruined your shirt if you hadn't been chopping wood for me," she said, biting her lip.

"Sure I would have." Rye paused to balance a chunk of log on the chopping stump. He raised the ax and brought it down on the wood with a smooth, uninterrupted motion. The wood split apart and the halves tumbled to the ground. "The shirt's nearly as old as I am. I should have tossed it out long ago. I just kind of liked it."

"Toss it? Do you mean throw it away?"

He smiled. She made it sound as though throwing away the worn shirt was unthinkable.

"Oh, no, don't," Lisa said, shaking her head in a quick negative. "Leave it with me. I'll mend it."

"You'll mend it?" he asked in disbelief, looking at the frayed cuffs. The shirt wasn't worth the thread that it would take to fix it, much less the time.

"Of course," she said. "There's no need for you to buy a new shirt to replace this one. Really."

Rye sank the ax blade into the chopping stump and turned toward Lisa. She looked as unhappy as her voice had been when she had told him that it was her fault that his shirt was ruined.

"Please," she said softly, putting her hand on his arm.

"It's all right, honey," he said, touching her cheek with gentle, callused fingertips. "I don't blame you."

Lisa couldn't control the quiver of awareness that swept through her at Rye's touch. When he saw the telltale trembling of her flesh, heat flooded violently through him. He looked from her fingers tightening on his arm to her suddenly dilated pupils and knew that she wanted him. She believed that he was too poor to replace a worn-out shirt, yet she shivered helplessly when he touched her.

The realization swept through Rye, and with it came the knowledge that he had never wanted a woman half so much as he wanted the one who stood only inches away, watching him with wide amethyst eyes as she tried to still the trembling of her lower lip by catching it between her small teeth.

"Lisa..." he whispered, but there were no words to tell her about the fever raging just beneath the surface of his control.

He fitted his hard hand beneath her chin and bent down to her. It took an agonizing amount of willpower to do no more than barely brush his lips over hers, soothing their trembling. She stiffened at the touch and then shivered wildly once again.

Rye forced himself to release Lisa when all he wanted to do was to undress her, to pour over her like a hot, heavy rain, to feel her pouring over him in turn....

Then he looked at her eyes. They were wide with surprise and curiosity and perhaps desire. He didn't know. She hadn't responded to his kiss by offering more of her mouth to him or by putting her arms around him. Perhaps she sensed the desire running through him in a savage flood and was afraid of him. She was barely more than a girl, and she was alone in a remote place with a man who was easily twice her strength—a man who wanted her with a violence that he could barely control.

The realization of his own savage need and Lisa's helplessness shocked Rye.

"It's all right, little one," he said huskily. "I won't hurt you."

Four

The memory of Lisa's trusting, almost shy smile stayed with Rye all the way down the mountain. So did the heat in his blood. He had intended to teach her how to use the ax. He hadn't dared. He hadn't trusted himself to stand that close to her. He had ached to take more from Lisa than that single, brushing kiss, yet he hadn't allowed himself even to touch the tip of his tongue to her soft lips. Smelling the sunshine scent of her hair, seeing the tiny trembling of her lips, breathing in the sweetness of her breath... It had been all he could do to keep from unwrapping her shining braids and pulling her unbound hair around him, binding them together in a world that began and ended with their joined bodies.

With a throttled groan, Rye turned his thoughts away from the shimmering temptation of Lisa Johansen. It didn't seem possible that any girl in that day and age could be so innocent, yet she had acted as though she had never been kissed. Certainly she hadn't seemed to know how to return even that chaste caress with a gliding pressure of her own lips.

The thought of such complete innocence shocked, intrigued and aroused Rye. The women he had known before had been experienced, sophisticated, sure of what they wanted from him. Sometimes he had taken what they so willingly offered. Most of the time he simply had walked away, disgusted by seeing dollar signs reflected in the women's eyes rather than real desire.

More than Lisa's delicate beauty and her unusual upbringing, it was her honest sensuality that made her so compelling to Rye. She didn't know that he was rich. She didn't look at him and see more money than a reasonable person could spend in a lifetime. She looked at him and saw a man.

And she wanted the man she saw.

Rye had sensed Lisa's passionate fascination with him as surely as he had sensed her inexperience. The fact that he himself—rather than his bank account and future inheritance—aroused Lisa was so unexpected that Rye could barely allow himself to believe it. The fact that his touch made her shiver with sensual fever rather than with greedy fantasies of money everlasting was so compelling that Rye hadn't been able to trust himself to remain with Lisa in the meadow's sun-drenched intimacy.

By the time he reached the ranch house, he had decided that he must have an objective way to judge Lisa's apparent innocence and honesty. It was as obvious as the fit of his jeans that he wanted her too much to trust his own judgment of her character. He very much wanted to believe that she was exactly what she seemed, completely unawakened yet feeling the slow heat of desire spreading through her innocence whenever she looked up at him.

Rye pulled off his torn shirt and wadded it up for the wastebasket. Just before he let go of the cloth, he hesitated. He had finally promised Lisa that he would let her try to mend the shirt. She had been so relieved that he had almost told her that he could buy all the shirts he wanted, anytime he wanted them. Then the thought of her slender hands working over the shirt, touching each fold and seam, leaving something of herself in the cloth and then giving it back to him had changed his mind. He would far, far rather have her believe that he was too poor to buy himself a shirt than to have her know that he was rich and getting richer with every day.

Ignoring the ranch account books that lay waiting within the floppy disk, Rye bypassed the computer for the telephone. He dialed a number, waited and heard Dr. Thompson answer on the fourth ring.

"Ted? This is Rye McCall. I want to talk to you about that student you sent up to watch the meadow this summer."

"You mean Lisa Johansen? She's not a student, at least not officially. She challenged our anthropology department. As soon as the tests are graded, I'm willing to bet she'll be a graduate, not a student. Of course, with her parents, it's not surprising. The Drs. Johansen are world-famous experts on—"

"Challenged?" interrupted Rye quickly, knowing that if he didn't get Dr. Thompson off the subject of anthropology, it could be a long time before they got back to the subject of Lisa Johansen. The professor was a wonderful teacher and a good friend, but he could talk a mountain flat.

"Challenged. As in took final exams in certain courses without having taken the courses themselves," Dr. Thompson said. "When you have someone with Lisa's unconventional educational background, it's the only way to test academic achievement. The poor girl's never been in a real classroom, you know."

Rye hadn't known, but beyond making appropriate encouraging noises, he said nothing. He had Dr. Thompson steered in the right direction. Now all Rye had to do was settle into a comfortable chair and let nature take its inevitable course.

"Oh, yes, it's true," Dr. Thompson continued. "She speaks several exotic languages, she can transform unspeakable things into savory stews over a campfire, and she can do clever things with her hands that make some of my physical anthropology students' eyes pop. Wait until you see her make a deadly little knife out of a piece of broken beer bottle."

Rye's gentle murmur of encouragement was lost in the professor's rushing words.

"She's a darling child, too. Such eyes. My Lord, I haven't seen eyes like that since her mother was my first and best student years and years ago. Lisa's a lot like her mother. Fine mind, healthy body, and not enough money to make a call from a pay phone—not that she would know how to, either. Lisa, that is, not her mother. Poor child barely knew how to flush a toilet when she got here. As for a modern kitchen, forget it. My electric stove frustrated her, the dishwasher made her jump and the trash compactor completely boggled her. Rather unnerved me, if you want to know the truth. Now I know how the natives feel when my eager students follow them around taking notes on odd indigenous customs. She learns fast, though. A very bright girl. Very bright indeed. Still, her parents waited too long to send her here. Now all she's suited for is the life of a vagabond herder."

"Why?"

"Time. Yesterday, today, tomorrow."

"I don't understand."

The professor sighed. "Neither does Lisa. Civilized man divided time into past, present and future. Many tribes don't. To them, there are only two kinds of time. There is a very vague 'time before' and then there is the vast, undifferentiated *now*. That's where Lisa lives. In the endless tribal present. She no more understands the Western concepts of hourly work and weekly wages than I understand Zulu. As for typewriters, filing cabinets, computers and that sort of thing... well, there's just no possibility. The only suitable job I could find for her on short notice was watching grass grow in your meadow until the school year begins in the fall. Then her scholarship money should take care of her until Geoffrey gets back from Alice after Christmas."

"Geoffrey? Alice?" asked Rye, wondering how the conversation had been sidetracked.

"Geoffrey is the brightest anthropology student I've had since Lisa's mother. Alice Springs is in Australia's outback. Geoffrey is doing research for his Ph.D. on the oral traditions of Australian aborigines, with particular emphasis on the use of—"

"Does Lisa know this Geoffrey?" Rye interrupted impatiently, feeling an irrational shaft of jealousy.

"Not yet, but she will. She's going to marry him."

"What?"

"Lisa's going to marry Geoffrey. Haven't you been listening? Lisa's parents sent her to me so that I could find a suitable husband for her. I have. Geoffrey Langdon. Her skills are admirably matched with his professional needs. She'll be able to run the camp while he works. Who knows? If she shows the same flair her mother did for fieldwork, Lisa might be able to help Geoffrey on his research."

"What does Geoffrey think of all this?"

"I haven't got an answer from him yet, but I can't imagine that he would be anything except enthusiastic. She's a pretty little thing and her parents are very, very well respected within academic circles. That sort of thing matters to young academics, you know. He might even get to work with her parents, perhaps even to collaborate with them on a paper or two. That would be a colossal boost for his academic career."

"What would Lisa get out of this love feast?" Rye asked, trying to keep the irritation from his voice.

"'Love feast?' Oh, dear, you *are* a child of Western culture, aren't you? Love has nothing to do with it. Lisa will get out of the arrangement exactly what women have always gotten out of marriage—a lifetime of food, shelter and protection. In Lisa's case, that's much more necessary than love. She simply isn't prepared to cope with the modern Western world. That's why her parents sent her to me when it came time for her to marry."

"She came here to find a husband?" Rye asked harshly.

"Of course. She could hardly marry a Bedouin herder, could she?"

There was a silence, which was immediately filled by Dr. Thompson's blithe retelling of the life of a Bedouin wife. Rye barely listened. He was still caught in the moment when his worst fears had been confirmed: Lisa was one more woman looking for a lifetime meal ticket. Innocence had nothing to do with it. The game was as old as Adam and Eve—male lust and female calculation joined in unholy matrimony.

And Rye had nearly fallen right into the musk-scented tiger trap.

Afterward Rye couldn't remember the rest of the conversation. He showered and changed clothes in a bleak rage, not knowing whether he was more angry with Lisa for being so innocently, deliciously treacherous or with himself for almost falling into her hands as though he had no more brains than a ripe apple.

Yet no matter how he swore at himself or at her, the memory of Lisa's trembling mouth haunted him, and when he fell asleep it was to dream of velvet heat enfolding him, caressing him, arousing him until he awakened with a stifled cry on his lips. His body was sweating, hard, heavy with a desire so great it was almost unbearable.

It was no better the following morning. Rye stepped into the bathroom cursing. After fifteen minutes he decided that cold showers were vastly overrated as a means of subduing lust. He stamped into his boots and ate a cold breakfast, because he knew that the smell of bread toasting would have brought back memories of camp bread and Lisa watching him, her fingers trembling almost invisibly as she handed him the fragrant, steaming food she had prepared for him.

Rye slammed the kitchen door and strode out to the barn, wishing that he could slam the door on his thoughts half so easily. In the east, rugged peaks were condensing out of the dawn sky. The cowhands were straggling out to the barn. Horses nickered and milled in the corral, waiting for men to single them out with flying lariats and gentle words.

"Morning, Boss Mac. Old Devil looks like he got some of the starch taken out of him yesterday."

Rye recognized the pale silver of Lassiter's hair even before the cowhand's drawl registered. "Morning, Lassiter. I took Devil up the back way to the meadow. You look a little tuckered around the edges yourself. Tough ride?"

The cowhand grinned, lifted his hat to smooth his prematurely silver hair and seated his hat once more with a swift stroke. "I was meaning to thank you. Cherry said you particularly told her to look me up for a ride. That filly was prime, really prime."

"Bet she came with a meat inspector's stamp on her haunch to prove it, too," Rye said sardonically.

Lassiter shook his head. "Boss, you shouldn't take it so personal. When a gal that looks like that is ready, willing and by God *able*, why the least a man can do is meet her halfway."

"That's why I have you around. Fastest zipper in the West."

The retort and the cowhand's hoot of laughter drew smiles from the men who were hauling saddles out to the corral fence. Lassiter's ability to get women into bed was legend. No one knew whether it was his silver hair, his slow smile or his quick hands. Whatever it was, the women loved it.

"How did the meadow look?" Lassiter asked innocently.

"Better than my dining room."

"Yeah, Cherry mentioned something about that. Was she really checking the silver?"

"She sure as hell was. Did she take the fillings out of your teeth?"

"It was worth every last one. Did you eat supper there?"

"In the dining room?"

Lassiter's eyes twinkled. "In the meadow."

Rye grunted, then gave in. Lassiter would keep waltzing around the subject of Lisa until he found out how Rye had reacted to having his private domain invaded by yet another woman. If there was anything on earth the cowhands loved better than a joke, Rye hadn't found out what it might be.

"At least she can cook," Rye said obliquely.

"Easy on the eyes, too. Skinny, though, 'cept up top."

Rye started to deny that Lisa was skinny anywhere, then caught the gleam in Lassiter's eyes. Rye laughed and shook his head.

"I should brand your tail for not warning me about Cherry or Lisa," Rye said.

Lassiter's teeth flashed. "You find a filly that can rope and hog-tie me, and you can put that brand anywhere you please."

"I think I already found one."

"Yeah?"

"Yeah. You've been up to the meadow so often your bay's big hooves left a trench."

Slowly Lassiter shook his head. "Not that filly. Miss Lisa's too innocent for the likes of me."

"Besides," Jim called from the corral, "she ain't given him nothing but the same sweet smile she gives every other hand. And bread and bacon that would make a stone weep. Lordy, that gal can make campfire food sit up and do tricks."

Rye was relieved to hear that Lisa hadn't responded to any of the cowhands as she had to him. However, that did nothing to cool his anger at himself for almost being taken in by her.

"Innocent? Maybe, but she's after the same thing Cherry was—a diamond ring and a free ride for life. Only difference is that Lisa doesn't know who I am."

"Didn't you introduce yourself?" Lassiter asked, surprised.

"Sure. As just plain Rye."

Instantly Lassiter saw the humorous possibilities in the situation. He smiled slowly, then laughed and laughed. Reluctantly Rye smiled.

"She thinks you're just another hand?" Jim asked, looking from Lassiter to Rye.

"Yeah," Rye said.

Jim chuckled. "An' she's looking for a husband?"

"Yeah."

"An' she don't know who you really are?"

"Yeah."

"I don't believe it. She's no hip-swinging city hussy."

"Ask Dr. Thompson the next time he comes up to the meadow," Rye said in clipped tones.

"Well, shoot," Jim complained. "She sure didn't let any of us in on the game. Don't blame her for passing up old Lassiter as hitching material, but she didn't give Blaine a second look, neither. Ain't that so, Blaine?"

"That's right," called a tall, lean young man who was squatting on his heels in front of the corral, smoking a cigarette. "An' the good Lord knows I'm a durn sight prettier than Lassiter."

There were catcalls and howls from the cowhands as they compared Blaine's prowess and physical attributes to Lassiter's. Both men took the chaffing with good nature. They had played too many jokes on the other cowhands to object when their own turn came to be the butt of rough humor. Rye waited until there was a pause in the raillery before he got down to implementing the decision that he had made in the small hours of the night when he had awakened sweating with desire.

"Well, I'm tired of being chased and cornered on my own land," Rye said flatly.

There were murmurs of agreement on the part of the hands. A man's ranch was his castle—or ought to be. Boss Mac had their sympathy in his struggle against matrimony.

"Lisa doesn't know who I am and I want it to stay that way. As long as she thinks I'm just one of the hands she'll treat me like one of you. That's what I want. Otherwise I won't be able to spend any time in the meadow at all without being pestered to death.''

There was another round of agreement from the men. Each of them knew how much Boss Mac loved to spend time in his meadow. They also knew that without the meadow to soothe him, Boss Mac had a temper that would back down a hungry bear.

"Now, I know one of you would call me Boss Mac if I went up to the meadow with you, so I won't. When I go, I'll go alone. Got that?''

There were grins all around as the men thought about the dimensions of the unfolding joke. There was Lisa up in the meadow hunting a marriageable man, and the most hunted, marriageable man in five states would be slipping in and out of the meadow without her even suspecting it.

"And I want you to stop going up there.''

The grins vanished. A joke was one thing. Leaving a small bit of a girl out in the wilderness completely on her own was another. No matter how well she cooked over a fire, and no matter how game she was in taking on a man's tasks, she was neither as big nor as strong as a man. In the West, such distinctions still brought out latent stirrings of chivalry. The cowhands would tease Lisa unmercifully, play a thousand jokes on her without a second thought, but they would never do anything that they believed would actually harm her.

As one, the men looked to Lassiter, who was their unofficial spokesman as well as the Rocking M's foreman.

"You sure that's wise, boss?'' Lassiter asked softly. "That there meadow is a long ways away from anywhere. What if she turned her ankle on a wet rock or the ax slipped when she was chopping wood or the summer flu got her and she was too weak to carry a bucket of water from the stream?''

Only the rosy flush of dawn kept Rye's face from showing a sudden pallor. The idea of Lisa being hurt, alone and
stranded up in the high meadow camp was unthinkable. She
had been so at home around the camp, so supremely suited
to her surroundings, that he had forgotten the true primi-
tiveness of the meadow.

"You're right," Rye said instantly. "I should have
thought of that. Go up, but not as often as you've been
going, or else no work will get done and I'll never have the
meadow to myself." He looked slowly from man to man,
including everyone in the cool glance. "But if any man
touches her, he'll be looking for a new arm and a new job,
in that order. Understood?"

Male smiles flashed briefly in the dawn. They understood very well, and they approved.

"Sure thing, boss," Lassiter said. "And thanks for the
visiting privileges. She makes the best bread I ever ate.
Think maybe she'd like to be a ranch cook after she's
through watching grass grow this summer?"

"Doubt it. By then she'll have given up on Edward
McCall the third and moved on to greener pastures."

Rye stood in the flooding rush of dawn and wondered
why the thought of Lisa leaving brought restlessness rather
than relief.

Five

Polaroid camera in hand, Lisa slipped through the split-rail fence into the meadow preserve. She went to the nearest numbered stake—number five—knelt and looked through the viewfinder. The silvery-green grass in front of the stake was slender and delicate, almost fragile appearing, but it had grown inches in the past week.

"Good for you, number five," she muttered. "Keep it up and you'll go to the head of Dr. Thompson's list of hardy, useful grasses. Your children will be fruitful and multiply in pastures all over the world."

She let out her breath, squeezed the button and heard the surprisingly loud clack and grind of the Polaroid's mechanism as the camera went to work. Instantly a featureless square popped out of the bottom of the camera box. She shielded the print from the sun by putting it in her shirt pocket where the exotic chemicals could develop in peace. After weeks in the meadow, the process of development was no longer so fascinating that she watched each print as it condensed out of nothing until it filled the odd paper square. These days she contented herself with sneaking quick peeks as the photo developed. She couldn't quite take the process for granted. There were too many parts of the world where the camera and its instant images would have been considered magic, and she had lived in most of them.

The tribal view of photographs as magic was one that Lisa came close to sharing. Even after Dr. Thompson had given her a book on the photochemical process, she still felt like a magician with a very special kind of magic wand every time she wielded the Polaroid and came up with precise, hand-sized images of the world around her. It was certainly easier than the painstaking process of exactly reproducing the appearance of all the plants with paper and pencil, as her mother did.

Lisa went through the meadow, photographing the plants in front of each numbered stake, changing packs of film several times. If Boss Mac's cowhands hadn't delivered fresh film, she would have been forced to go "down the hill" and into town every week. She preferred staying in the meadow, where time had nothing to do with clocks.

Seasons she understood. There was a time of fertility and a time of growth, a time of harvest and a time of barren fields. That was predictable and natural, like the rising and setting of the sun or the waxing and waning of the moon. It was just the artificial nature of weeks that took some getting used to. She suspected that for the rest of her life she would think of a week as the time it took to use up five packs of Polaroid film in McCall's Meadow.

As Lisa worked she kept pausing to stand on tiptoe and peer toward the grove of mixed aspen and evergreens at the back of the cabin. Rye would come up that way, when he came. If he came. Since the first time he had visited the meadow, he had returned twice a week and had hardly spoken to her at all. Once she had followed the tracks of his horse to the sheer trail zigzagging down the shoulder of the mountain. None of Boss Mac's other cowhands had come into the meadow by that route. Nor were there other tracks on the trail besides those of Rye's big black horse. Apparently it was a trail only Rye knew about—or dared to take.

Would he come today?

The thought brought a surge of the same restlessness that had claimed Lisa's dreams since the first time she had met Rye. She had enjoyed the visits of Boss Mac's men, but Rye's visits the past few weeks had been different. His effect on her was too vivid, too overwhelming, to be described by a word as bland as "enjoyment." He was a summer storm sweeping down from the peaks, leaving everything in his path wind-tossed and shivery and glistening with new possibilities.

She could relive in her memory the single time he had kissed her weeks before, the slow brush of his lips over her mouth, the warmth of his breath, the heat radiating from his big body into hers. When he had kissed her, she had been too shocked by the sensations bursting through her to do more than stand motionless, consumed by the instant when she had first known a man's kiss. By the time she had truly realized what was happening, he was already stepping away from her. He had gone back to chopping wood as though nothing had happened, leaving her to wonder whether he had been half so shaken by the caress as she had been.

"Of course he wasn't," Lisa muttered as she switched a used film pack for a fresh one and aimed the viewfinder at another numbered stake. "If he had been, he would have kissed me again. Besides, kissing isn't unusual here. Look at the kids who were in Dr. Thompson's eight o'clock class. Half of them were late to class because they were kissing their lovers goodbye in the corridor. The rest of them brought their lovers right into class and—oh, darn it, I ruined another one!''

Glumly Lisa stuck the botched photo in her rear pocket without waiting to see how badly out of focus the print was. She had to stop thinking about Rye and kissing and lovers. It made her whole body tremble. That was the third photo she had mangled so far today. At that rate she would need an extra shipment of film before the week was out.

Maybe Rye would bring it.

With a groan of exasperation at her own unruly mind, Lisa went to the next stake—and saw Rye walking across the meadow toward her. She knew him instantly, even though he was too far away to make out his features. No other man moved with just that blend of male grace and power, his long-legged stride eating up the distance between them. No other man had shoulders like that, a breadth and strength balanced above lean hips. And, Lisa thought as Rye drew closer, no man had ever watched her the way he did, with a combination of curiosity and hunger in his eyes. And wariness.

The wariness had been there the second time Rye had visited Lisa in the meadow, and it hadn't changed since then. She had noticed his attitude immediately and had wondered what had caused it. The wariness certainly hadn't been there the first time he had met her. She would have seen it. She had been watched by too many strangers in too many strange places not to recognize wariness when she saw it.

Seeing it now so clearly in Rye's glance made Lisa feel suddenly awkward. She wondered wildly whether she should hold out her hand to him for the brief, firm clasp of greeting that was so essentially American. And then she wondered what Rye was doing inside the meadow preserve.

None of the other cowhands had so much as set foot beyond the split-rail fence.

"Good morning, Rye," she said, and her voice caught at the hunger that flared visibly when his glance traveled over her body.

"Good morning."

Without realizing it, Lisa simply stood and memorized the features of Rye's face. She loved the forelock that had escaped from his hat to lie in sable profusion across his forehead. The very dark, shining brown color was matched in the steep arch of his eyebrows and in the long, dense eyelashes that were almost startling against the hard planes of his face. His eyes were very light, a glittering, crystal gray that was shot through with tiny shards of blue and surrounded by a thin rim of black. He hadn't shaved recently. Stubble darkened his face, gave it texture and made the contrasting paleness of his eyes even more pronounced. His mouth was wide, his upper lip cleanly shaped and his lower lip just full enough to remind her of the instant of brushing contact when he had kissed her. His caress had been unexpected, firm and soft at once, and his lips had been a teasing resilience that she wanted to experience again.

"Is my nose on straight?" Rye drawled.

Lisa felt a flush climbing up her fair cheeks. Staring was staring, no matter what the culture, and she had been caught with her eyes wide open as she drank in his appearance. No wonder he was wary of her. Around him, she wasn't quite sane.

"Actually, no," she said, rallying. "Your nose looks a bit crooked."

"The first bronc I rode bucked me into next week. Broke my nose, two ribs and my pride."

"What did you do?"

"Breathed through my mouth while I learned to ride. For a city boy, I didn't do too bad after that."

Lisa's shock was clear on her face. "You were raised in a city?"

Rye started to curse his loose tongue before he remembered that many modern cowhands started out on paved streets. A man couldn't help it if his parents had bad taste in living places. "For my first fifteen years. Then my mother died. My dad remarried and we moved to a ranch."

Lisa started to ask where Rye's father was now, then hesitated. Before she could remember if it was polite to ask about a man's relatives, Rye was saying something about the meadow. The change of subject was so swift that Lisa wondered if talking about family was a social taboo among cowhands. But if that was true, why was Jim so forthcoming on the subject of his own family?

Sunlight glancing off Rye's gray eyes distracted Lisa, making her forget what her question had been. She was accustomed to people with eyes that varied from dark brown to absolutely black. The lightness of his eyes was fascinating. Not only were there shards of blue, but in direct light there were luminous hints of green, as well.

"...think so?" he asked.

Abruptly Lisa realized that she was staring again. "I'm sorry. I didn't hear you."

"Must have been the whiskey jack making all that racket," he said dryly, knowing very well that he had been the distraction, not the raucous bird.

"What's a whiskey jack?"

"The mountain jaybird that sits on that bare pine branch near the cabin and waits for you to turn your back on a piece of bread."

"Is that what you call it—a whiskey jack?"

"Not when it steals my lunch."

There was an instant of silence before Lisa's laughter pealed. Rye felt the sweet sounds sink into him as surely as the warmth of the sunlight and the slow caress of the wind. The temptation to take her lips beneath his had never been greater. They were parted now, glistening with the recent touch of her tongue, flushed with the vitality that shimmered just beneath her skin. It would be so easy. He could almost feel how it would be, the softness of her flesh beneath his palms, the rush of her breath over his mouth, the sliding heat of her tongue rubbing against his....

Lisa realized that Rye was staring at her mouth with an intensity that made her feel both weak and curiously alive. Prickles of awareness shivered over her skin. She wondered what he was thinking of, what he wanted, and if he remembered that single, fleeting moment when his lips had touched hers.

"Rye?"

"I'm here," he said, his voice husky, deep.

"Is it rude to ask what you're thinking?"

"Not particularly, but the answer might shock you down to the soles of your little feet."

She swallowed. "Oh."

"How about if I ask you what you were thinking instead?"

"Oh!" she said, her amethyst eyes wide with dismay. "Er, that is, I wasn't really, I was just..." She tried to look away from the off-center curve of Rye's smile. She couldn't. "I wasn't thinking, not really. I was just wondering."

"What were you just wondering?"

She took a deep breath and let it out. "How your mouth could look so hard and have felt so velvety."

The pulse just beneath Rye's temple leaped visibly, reflecting the sudden hammering of his blood. It was why he had stayed away from her after that one, brief kiss.

And it was why he couldn't stay away from her.

"Did my lips feel like velvet?" he asked softly.

"Yes," she whispered.

Before the last breath left her lips, she felt the brush of his mouth against hers.

"You sure?" he murmured.

"Mmm."

"Is that a yes?" He caressed her lightly again. "Or a no?"

Lisa stood utterly still, afraid to move and thus end the moment. "Yes...." She sighed.

Rye had to clench his hands into fists to keep from pulling Lisa into his arms. All that prevented him from grabbing her was his own wariness of the heat sweeping through him, changing his body to meet the elemental femininity of hers. There was no doubt that she had wanted his kiss. There was also no doubt that she had done nothing to return it. He was hard, hot, ready, and she was standing there, watching him with curious amethyst eyes, catlike in her poise and stillness.

"Now that we've got that settled, how's the meadow doing?" Rye asked, keeping his voice normal with an effort as he stepped back from her.

The change in him dismayed Lisa. She wondered why he had stopped kissing her, if she had done something that she shouldn't have, but when she tried to ask him, the words dried up on her tongue. He was looking around the meadow as though nothing had happened between them. In fact, it was as though she weren't there at all.

"The meadow?" she asked, her confusion clear in her voice.

"Yeah. You know. Grass without trees. Meadow."

Suddenly Lisa realized that she was swaying toward Rye, her breath held, her mind quivering like an aspen leaf. And he was watching her with something very close to amusement gleaming in his uncanny eyes. For the first time she wondered if he wasn't simply teasing her to watch her blush. It would be the kind of joke that cowhands loved to play on the uninitiated, and when it came to being kissed by a man, she was definitely a novice. If it was a joke, it would explain why her heart was going crazy and her body felt like sun-warmed honey, while Rye was glancing around the meadow as though he had come to see it rather than her.

The joke was on her, Lisa admitted to herself ruefully. What was the idiom that the cowhands had used? Something to do with fishing . . . hook, line and sinker. That was it. She had fallen for Rye's skillfully presented bait and taken it in a single gulp.

Yes, the joke was definitely on her. Unfortunately her normal sense of humor seemed to be asleep, leaving her to flounder on unaided. Then she remembered Rye's question about the meadow. Gratefully she grabbed the neutral topic.

"Some of the meadow grasses," Lisa said quickly, "are growing at a rate of several inches a week. Number five has been especially productive. Yesterday I checked it against last year's records. There are more stems per plant and the stems themselves are significantly taller. I understand that the thaw was late this year. Perhaps number five does better in a cold, wet climate than the grasses it's competing with. If so, Dr. Thompson will be delighted. He's convinced that too much effort is being spent on desert grasses and not enough on the sub-Siberian or steppe varieties. Number five might be just what he's looking for."

Normally Rye would have been interested in the idea that his meadow preserve was being useful to hungry people halfway across the world, but at the moment the only hunger he could think of was the heavy beat of his own blood.

"Boss Mac must be a very generous man," Lisa continued. As she spoke, her natural enthusiasm for the meadow project replaced the cold disappointment she had felt when she realized that Rye had only been teasing her in his own way, like Lassiter with his solemn warnings about flying seeds and full moons. "This meadow would be a rich summer pasture for his herds, but he set it aside for research that will have no benefit for his ranch."

"Maybe he just likes the peace and quiet up here."

Lisa's serene smile transformed her face. "Isn't it beautiful?" she said, looking around. "I was told that Boss Mac loved to spend time here, too, but he hasn't been to the meadow the whole time I've been here."

"Disappointed that he hasn't come calling?"

The sardonic curl to Rye's mouth surprised Lisa. "No, I'm just sorry that the poor man is too busy to enjoy his favorite place."

"Oh, he's busy, all right. So busy that he told me to take over his meadow watching this summer. He just won't have time to get up here and check on things."

As Rye spoke, he watched Lisa closely, searching for signs of disappointment in her expressive face when she discovered that her carefully laid matrimonial trap wasn't going to work on Edward McCall III.

"Oh," Lisa said. "Well, what sort of thing did Boss Mac usually do up here? Will you need any help? Dr. Thompson didn't mention anything but taking notes on the growth of his grasses, taking pictures, and labeling them, and keeping the daily weather log."

The clear amethyst eyes looking at Rye revealed nothing. Lisa was watching him, but not with the breathless anticipation she had shown a few minutes before. She was as relaxed and yet as subtly wary as a doe grazing at the margin of the meadow, alert for the first hint of a predator gliding close.

"He just sort of kept a general eye on things," Rye said casually. "He spent a lot of time by the creek. Guess he liked to watch the reflections in the water."

"I can understand that. There's nothing more beautiful than cool, clean water, not even the first light of dawn."

Rye heard the note of certainty in Lisa's voice and looked at her speculatively at her. "You sound like a West Texan."

"I do?"

"Yeah. I was raised there. They love water, too. They have so damn little of it."

Lisa smiled and began to walk slowly toward the next numbered stake. "Sounds like dryland herders all over the world. There's never enough water to go around."

After an instant of hesitation, Rye followed Lisa deeper into the meadow. Her faded jeans looked soft, supple, and they fit the curve of her bottom with loving perfection.

"They must wear jeans everywhere in the world," he said.

"What?"

Rye realized that he had been thinking out loud. "Your jeans have seen a lot of use."

"They belonged to one of Dr. Thompson's students. She was going to throw them out until I showed her how to put on patches. She liked the result so much that she went out and bought new jeans, faded them in bleach and then spent hours sewing patches on perfectly good cloth." Lisa laughed and shook her head. "I still don't understand why she didn't just keep the old ones."

Rye smiled slightly. "Fashion isn't supposed to make sense. It's supposed to attract men."

Lisa thought of the dark blue tattoos, chiming anklets, nose gems and kohl eyeliner that were fashionable in various parts of the world. "It must work. There are a lot of children."

Before Rye could say anything, his breath wedged in his throat as Lisa knelt gracefully, straining the fabric across her bottom for an instant. She took the picture quickly and then rose to her feet once more with an ease that made him think how good her body would feel locked with his in a slow act of love. She had a supple, feminine strength that would mate perfectly with his male power. She would be like the meadow itself—generous, elegant, fragrant, a sun-warmed richness that would surround him, drenching his senses.

Abruptly Rye realized that he was going to have to think about something else or start wearing his hat on his belt buckle.

"What are you going to do after summer is over?" he asked.

For a moment Lisa said nothing, then she laughed.

"Let me in on the joke?" he said.

"Oh, this one is on me, too," she assured him wryly. "It's just that your question didn't make sense to me for an instant. You see, I keep slipping back into tribal time. No tomorrow, no real yesterday, just every day lived as it comes along. According to tribal time, I've always lived in the meadow and I always will. Summer will never end. It's hard to fight that way of looking at the world. Especially here," she added, watching the grass rippling in the breeze. "Here the seasons are the only hours that matter."

He smiled slightly, knowing what she meant. "And the days are just minutes marked off by the sun."

Lisa turned and looked up at Rye with an intensity that was almost tangible. "You understand."

"I feel the same way about the meadow. That's why I come here as often as I can."

Rye's quiet words confirmed Lisa's earlier guess. The meadow rather than her own presence was the lure that had drawn him up the mountain. She sighed.

"Have you worked for Boss Mac a long time?" she asked.

"Tribal time or real time?"

Lisa smiled slightly. "'Real' time. I have to adjust to this culture just as I did to the others. So…have you worked for Boss Mac a long time?"

"I've been here as long as he has. More than ten years."

"It's a long way from West Texas. Do you see your family much?"

"Too much," he muttered. Then he sighed. "No, that's not fair. I love my dad, but I have hell's own time getting along with him."

"You and your boss have a lot in common."

"Oh?" Rye said, his expression suddenly wary.

"You both love the meadow and you both have trouble with your father. At least, Lassiter says that Boss Mac has trouble. Apparently his father wants heirs to the McCall empire and Boss Mac is in no hurry to provide them."

"That's what I hear, too," Rye assured her, his voice dry.

"I wonder why? Most men are eager to have sons."

"Maybe he hasn't found a woman who wants him as much as she wants his money."

"Really? Is he that cruel?"

Rye looked startled. "What?"

"A woman might refuse to marry a man who is too poor or too lazy to provide for the children she would have," Lisa explained patiently, "but the only time I've ever seen a woman refuse to marry a rich man was when he was simply too cruel to be trusted with her life, much less that of any child she might have by him."

"That is not Boss Mac's problem," Rye said flatly. "He just wants a woman who would want him even if he didn't have two dimes to rub together in his pocket."

Lisa heard the tightness in Rye's voice and knew that he spoke for himself, as well. He was poor and very proud. She had seen enough of American life to know that dating cost quite a bit of money; it was rather like an informal "bride price" that men were required to pay before being granted the right to marry. Rye obviously didn't have any money to spend. It must have stung his pride not to be able to court a woman.

"Maybe," Lisa said carefully, "Boss Mac has been looking at the wrong kind of woman. My father never had money and never will. My mother never cared. They share so many things in common that money just isn't important to them."

"And I suppose you would be happy living the rest of your life in a skin tent and eating from a communal pot."

The sarcasm in Rye's voice made Lisa wince. He must be very raw on the subject of women and money.

"I could be happy, yes."

"Then why did you come here?" he demanded.

"I was . . . restless. I wanted to see my own country."

"And now that you've seen it, off you'll go again, following your husband from one outback outpost to the next."

Lisa blinked, wondering if she had missed something in the previous conversation. "My husband? The outback?"

Rye silently cursed the anger that had loosened his tongue. Boss Mac might know about the future love life of Dr. Thompson's charge, but a broke cowhand called Rye wouldn't.

"Since Boss Mac won't be showing up in the meadow this summer, you'll be going back to school in the fall, won't you?" demanded Rye.

Lisa wondered what Boss Mac's presence—or lack of it—had to do with her going back to school in the fall, but Rye looked so fierce that she simply said, "Yes, I guess so."

"Well, it doesn't take a genius to figure out that you'll meet some anthropology type at school and marry him and go skipping off around the world to count beads with the natives." Rye glared at the camera. "You finished yet?"

"Er, not quite."

Rye grunted. "When you're finished, come to the cabin. I'll teach you how to use an ax so that you and your over-educated husband won't freeze to death in the middle of some damned forest."

Speechless, Lisa watched as Rye strode angrily across the meadow without a glance back over his shoulder. A phrase she had heard Lassiter use came to her mind.

Who put a nickel in him?

Six

The sound of steel sinking into wood rang across the meadow in a steady rhythm that paused only when Rye bent to reposition the shrinking log. Usually the act of chopping wood soothed his temper, so long as he didn't think about what had made him angry in the first place. With each stroke of the ax Rye promised himself that he would watch his tongue more carefully when he was around Lisa. It was none of his business what she did or didn't do when she left his meadow. She could marry a Zulu warrior for all he cared. Hell, she could marry ten of them.

The ax sank so deeply into the wood that Rye had to stop and lever the steel loose. Cursing, he examined the cutting edge of both blades. It was a moment's work to touch up the edges to lethal sharpness with the whetstone. Then he peeled off his shirt, tossed it onto the woodpile and settled in for some serious exercise. He was careful to think of some-

thing besides Lisa while he chopped. Thinking about her
had a ruinous effect on his self-control.

Gradually Rye gave himself over to the age-old rhythms
of physical work. Swinging the heavy ax correctly required
both power and finesse. There was an elemental grace in the
repetitious movements that became almost an end in itself.
Like the beating of drums in an unvarying rhythm, the act
of chopping wood suspended time.

Lisa stood motionless beneath a trembling canopy of aspen leaves just beyond the stream, watching honey-colored
chips of wood leap from beneath gleaming steel. Rye
wielded the big ax with liquid ease, as though the long
hickory shaft and four-pound ax head were an extension of
himself. As he worked, sunlight and sweat ran in golden
rivulets down his back, making his naked skin glow. The
black, wedge-shaped mat of hair on his chest glittered with
random drops of sweat. His arm muscles flexed and then his
arms straightened and swept down. Steel whistled through
air into wood.

Rye twisted, lifted the ax, then brought it down again with
a sleek, powerful motion that fascinated Lisa no matter how
many times she saw it repeated. She didn't know how long
she had stood there watching Rye before he finally set aside
the ax, went to the stream and scooped up water in his big
hands. He drank deeply, then sluiced his head and shoulders with great handfuls of water, washing away sweat.
When he was finished he knelt for a few moments by the
stream, tracing ripples and currents with his fingertips.
There was a sensual delicacy to the gesture that contrasted
vividly with the blunt power of his body.

When Lisa looked from Rye's hand to his eyes, she saw
that he was watching her. For an instant it was as though he
had been tracing the outline of her body instead of the surface of the cool, rushing water. Warmth stirred within her.

It expanded slowly, sending soft tongues of fever licking through her.

With a single lithe motion Rye stood and walked toward her. When he stopped, his body was only inches away from her. The scent of cool water and warm male flesh curled around her, making her breath catch. He was so close that she could have licked drops of water from his skin. The thought of doing just that sent more heat sliding softly through her.

"What are you thinking?" Rye asked, his voice low, husky.

Very slowly Lisa lifted her glance from the diamond drops of water nestled in his thick, dark chest hair to the clarity of his eyes watching her. She tried to speak but could not. Unconsciously she licked her lips. She sensed as much as heard the sudden intake of Rye's breath as he watched her tongue.

"Thinking?" Lisa made a choked sound that could have been a laugh or a cry of despair. "What I do around you doesn't qualify as thinking." She swallowed and rushed on, saying the second thing that came to her mind, because the first thing would have been to ask if she could sip the water from his skin. "Do you think I'd chop wood better if I were stripped to the waist, too?"

She had meant it as a joke, but the way Rye's glance traveled slowly over the buttons of her blouse was no laughing matter.

"Hell of an idea," he said, his voice deep, his hands reaching for the top button. "Wonder why I didn't think of it."

"It was a joke," she said desperately, grabbing his hands. They were hard, warm and had a latent strength that shocked her.

"Take your blouse off and we'll see who laughs first."

Lisa tried to speak, couldn't and then saw the glint of amusement in his eyes. She groaned, caught between relief and something very close to disappointment.

"I've got to stop doing that!" she said.

"Offering to take off your blouse?"

"No! Falling for that deadpan humor of yours. You get me every time."

"Little one, I haven't even gotten you once."

Suddenly Lisa realized that she was holding both of Rye's hands within her own, hanging on to him as though she were drowning. And that was how she felt when she looked in his eyes. Falling and drowning and spinning slowly, held in the gentle storm of the fever stealing through her in shimmering waves.

"How about it?" he said.

"Getting me?" she asked in a high voice.

His slow, off-center smile made her heart turn over.

"Would you like that?"

"Help," she whispered.

"That's what I was offering to do."

"You were?"

"Don't you want to learn?"

"Learn . . . what?"

"How to chop wood. Why, did you have something else in mind?"

"I have no mind around you," she said. "How could I have anything in it?"

Rye threw back his head and laughed, a sound as rich and warm as sunlight itself. Lisa found herself laughing with him in turn, not minding that it was herself she was laughing at. There was no malice in Rye, simply a sensual teasing that she had never before encountered and could neither resist nor resent.

"I'll get better at this," she warned him.

"At what?"

"Teasing."

He gave her a startled look followed by a smile that made her toes curl. "You like teasing me, do you?"

She grinned. "Sure do."

"It's called flirting," he said. "Most people like it."

It was Lisa's turn to look startled. "Is this how cowboys flirt?"

"It's how men and women flirt, honey. How did they do it where you came from?"

Lisa thought of sidelong looks from sloe eyes, lush hips moving that extra inch, breasts swaying proudly. "With their bodies."

Rye made a strangled sound and burst out laughing again. "Tell you what. You teach me how to do it with my body and I'll teach you how to chop wood."

Lisa had the distinct feeling that the "it" he was referring to and the "it" she was referring to weren't the same thing. She opened her mouth to point that out, only to stop as she saw the laughter lurking just beneath Rye's carefully neutral surface. He was waiting for her to walk into the gently baited trap.

"No you don't," Lisa said quickly. "Uh-uh. Not this greenfoot or tenderhorn or whatever you cowboys call idiots like me. If I ask you what this 'it' is that I'm supposed to teach you to do with your body, you'll ask me what I think 'it' is and then I'll start telling you and you'll laugh and there I'll be with my tongue tied in knots and my face the color of dawn."

"Can you really tie your tongue in knots?"

"No, but I can fold it up at the edges just like Mother could. See?"

Lisa stuck her tongue out flat, then folded it neatly up so that the opposite sides almost touched each other. An instant later the delicate pink flesh vanished behind her teeth once more.

"Again," he demanded.

He watched in fascination as she repeated the process. "I'll be damned. Now I know how butterflies do it."

"Do what?"

"It, what else?"

"Hook, line and sinker," Lisa groaned.

"Sounds like a painful way to do it." Rye ducked and laughed at the same time. "If you push me into the stream, you're going to get wet."

Lisa measured Rye's size against her own and sighed. He was right.

"You're taking unfair advantage of someone who's smaller than you are," she pointed out.

"Clever of you to notice."

"Where's your sense of fair play?"

"I took it off with my shirt." Rye waited for a moment, watching Lisa struggle to control a rush of incautious words. "Let me do that for you."

"What?"

"Bite your tongue. I'd do it very gently. I wouldn't even leave a mark."

Suddenly Lisa couldn't breathe. She looked at Rye with a combination of curiosity and yearning in her amethyst eyes. Then she remembered that this was simply Rye's way of teasing a girl who wasn't accustomed to the deadpan, leg-pulling Western style of humor.

"I'll settle for having you teach me how to leave marks on a log," Lisa said. "Big marks."

For an instant she would have sworn that Rye looked disappointed, but the moment passed so swiftly that she wasn't sure.

"Big marks, huh?" he asked.

"Chunks. Like the ones you get."

Rye's mouth turned up at one corner. "Don't hold your breath, honey. To chop like me you'd have to be built like me." He looked at the pronounced rise of Lisa's breasts and the flare of her hips and wondered how he ever could have mistaken her for a boy, no matter what the distance. "You definitely aren't built like me."

"It's just as well," Lisa said solemnly. "I'd look terrible with a dark beard."

Amusement flared in his pale eyes. The curve of a smile showed briefly beneath the dense shadow of beard stubble. "Let's see what we can do about your chopping style."

Rye held out his hand. Lisa took it without hesitation. The hard warmth of his palm sent a shiver of sensation through her that made her breath catch.

"Ready?" he asked.

She started to ask what she was supposed to be ready for, then decided that so long as Rye was holding her hand she was ready for anything.

"I'm ready."

"Okay." He turned toward the small stream. "On three. One, two, *three.*"

Still holding Lisa's hand, Rye took two long running steps and then leaped the sparkling ribbon of water. Lisa was right beside him, launching herself into the air without hesitation. Laughing, holding on to each other, they landed on the far side just beyond the silver margin of the stream. They were still smiling as they walked to the chopping stump. Rye levered the ax free using only one hand, for the other was still held within Lisa's gentle grasp.

As Rye looked down at Lisa's unusual, vivid eyes and unself-conscious smile, it occurred to him that it had been a long time since he had felt so at peace with himself and the world. Being with Lisa put him in touch with a kind of laughter that he had rarely known since his mother had died so many years before. Lisa had the same ability that his mother had shown, a way of finding joy no matter what the circumstances in which she found herself, and sharing the joy with a smile or a glance or a word, making everything around her somehow brighter than it had been before.

For the first time Rye wondered if it hadn't been his father's search for just that rare quality of joy that had sent him on an endless round of dating and mating which had brought pleasure only to the women who had cashed his checks. It had been the same for Rye's younger brother, who had married and divorced twice before he turned twenty-five. At least their sister, Cindy, had learned very quickly to tell the difference between men who wanted her and those who wanted only an entrée into the McCall checking account.

That was one thing Rye didn't have to worry about with Lisa. She couldn't be smiling at him because of his money for the simple reason that she thought he was too poor to buy a new work shirt much less to pour diamonds into her hands. But she watched him with admiring eyes anyway. That made her smile all the more beautiful to Rye. Not having to question why Lisa enjoyed being with him was a luxury that money literally could not buy. It was a unique, addictive experience for Rye; for the first time in his life he was positive that he was being enjoyed simply as a man.

Belatedly Rye realized that he was standing with an ax in his right hand, Lisa's warm fingers in his left and an unaccustomed grin on his lips.

"You have a contagious smile," he said, squeezing Lisa's fingers once before he released them and handed her the ax. "You'll need both hands for this. When I chop, I hold the ax down at the bottom of the handle. You shouldn't do that. The length of your arm is a bad match for the length of the handle. Hold it farther up. When you swing the ax back, let your right hand slide up the handle. When you swing the ax forward, let your right hand slide down again. But whatever you do, always hold on hard with your left hand. Like this.''

Rye demonstrated the proper technique. Lisa tried to keep her eyes on the ax and his hands. It was impossible. The supple flex and play of his back muscles moving beneath his sun-darkened skin fascinated her.

"Want to try it?" he asked.

Lisa barely prevented herself from asking just which *it* he was offering to let her try. When she took the ax, her fingers brushed over his hands several times. The vitality of him radiated through her at each touch, a warmth that was more than simple body heat. Her hands were unsteady when they closed around the smooth, hard shaft of the ax. She mentally reviewed what he had just told her, took a deep breath, lifted the ax and brought it down on the chopping stump.

The ax head bounced once, barely scratching the scarred wood. She repeated the motion. The ax head bounced. She tried again. The same thing happened. Nothing.

"Did I forget to mention that you're supposed to put your back into it?" Rye asked after the third swing.

"'It' is quite busy enough already without having to deal with my back, as well," muttered Lisa.

For a moment Rye was nonplussed. Then he remembered just how many subjects had been covered—or uncovered—by the word *it* so far today.

"It has been very busy," Rye agreed.

"It certainly has. As a matter of fact, it just went on strike. No its allowed. Be specific or be quiet."

His lips twitched with his efforts not to smile. "Right. Here, let's try it—er, chopping—this way. This should give you an idea of the right rhythm and swing."

Rye stepped behind Lisa and reached around her until his hands were positioned above and below hers on the long handle. Every time she breathed in, a blend of evergreen resin and warmth and man filled her senses. His skin was smooth against hers, hot, and the hair on his arms burned beneath the sun in shades of sable and bronze. She could feel his breath stir the wisps of fine hair that had escaped her braids.

With each motion Rye made, his chest brushed against Lisa's back, telling her that barely a breath separated their bodies. The realization was dizzying, like feeling the earth turn beneath her feet. She hung on to the ax handle until her knuckles whitened, because the smooth wood was the only solid thing in a world that was slowly revolving around her.

"Lisa?"

Helplessly she looked over her shoulder at Rye. He was so close that she could have counted his dense black eyelashes and each splinter of color in his gray eyes. His mouth was only inches away. If she stood on her tiptoes and he bent down, she could know again the sweetness and resilience of his lips.

Rye took the ax from Lisa's unresisting hands and sank the blade into the stump with a casual flick of his wrist.

"Come closer," he whispered, bending down to her. "Closer. Yes, like that."

Rye's last words were breathed against Lisa's lips as his arms tightened around her, arching her into his body. She felt the warmth of his chest, the hard muscles of his arms and then the pressure of his mouth moving over hers. Blindly she put her hands on his biceps, bracing herself in a spinning world, holding on to his muscular strength as she savored the sweet resilience of his lips and the contrasting roughness of his beard stubble, and she wished for the moment never to end.

Suddenly Rye's arms loosened and Lisa found herself set away from him once more.

"What's with you?" Rye asked curtly. "You come on to me like there's no tomorrow, but when I kiss you, nothing happens. I might as well be kissing my horse. Is this your idea of a joke?"

Conflicting waves of heat washed over Lisa, desire and embarrassment by turns staining her face red. "I thought it was yours."

"It?" he said sardonically.

"Kissing me," she said. "It's a joke for you, isn't it? But the joke's on me." She took a deep, uncertain breath and rushed on. "I know that you're showing me just how much of a tenderfoot I am and I'm trying to be a good sport about that, because you're right, I'm a total tenderfoot when it comes to kissing. I've never kissed anyone but my parents and whenever you kiss me I get hot and cold and shivery and I can't breathe and I can't think and—and I don't know anything about kissing and—and the joke's on me, that's all. When you finish laughing you can go back to teaching me how to handle an ax, but please don't stand so close because then the only thing I can think about is you and my knees get weak and so do my hands and I'll drop the ax. Okay?"

The tumbling words stopped. Lisa looked anxiously at Rye, waiting for his laughter.

But he wasn't laughing. He was staring at her, hardly able to believe what he had just heard.

"How old are you?" he asked finally.

"What day is it?"

"July twenty-fifth."

"Already? I turned twenty yesterday."

For a long, electric moment Rye said nothing. Lisa stood without moving, afraid to breathe. He was looking at her from the shining platinum crown of her braids to her toes peeking out from her frayed sneakers. The look he was giving her was as intense as it was—possessive.

"Happy birthday," he murmured, as much to himself as to Lisa. After a last, lingering glance at her pink lips, he met her eyes. "There's a fine old American custom on birthdays," he continued, smiling gently at her. "A kiss for every year. And, little one, when I kiss you it will be a lot of things, but it sure as hell won't be a joke."

Lisa's lips parted, but no words came out. She was looking at his mouth with a curious, sensual hunger that was as innocent as it was inviting. Rye saw the innocence now, whereas before he had seen only the invitation.

"No one but your parents?" he asked huskily.

She shook her head without looking up from his lips.

He took her hand, gently smoothed it open with his fingertips and kissed the center of her palm.

"That's one." He kissed the ball of her thumb. "That's two." The tip of her index finger. "Three."

Lisa couldn't stifle a small, throaty sound when Rye's teeth closed slowly on the pad of flesh at the base of her thumb. She felt no pain, simply a sensuous pressure that sent pleasure flaring out from the pit of her stomach.

"F-four?" she asked.

He shook his head, rubbing his cheek against her palm. "There's no limit on bites. Or on this."

His head turned slowly. The tip of his tongue flicked out to touch the sensitive skin between her first and second finger. Before he moved on to the second and third finger he tested the resilience of her flesh with his teeth. He did the same all across her hand, the tender vise of his teeth followed by hot, humid touches of his tongue. When he caught her smallest finger between his lips and pulled it into his mouth, stroking her skin with tongue and teeth, she shivered wildly. Very slowly he released her, caressing her every bit of the way.

"Do you like that?" he asked.

"Yes," she sighed. "Oh, yes, I like that."

Rye heard the catch in Lisa's voice and wondered what it would be like to hear that again and then again, yes and yes and yes as he tasted every bit of her until she moaned the final *yes* and he eased into her untouched body. The thought of being inside her made him clench with urgent need. Feeling the slow, hidden tremors sweeping through her flesh from her toes to her fingertips did nothing to cool the heat and heaviness of his own desire.

"Did you like having my lips on yours?" he asked.

But before Rye finished asking the question he was bending down to Lisa, for he had seen the answer in the sudden darkening at the center of her eyes. Her amber eyelashes swept down, shielding the telltale expansion of her pupils as she turned her face up to him with the innocence and trust of a flower drinking in the morning sun. Her innocence pierced his desire with a sweetness that was also pain. He knew he should tell her not to trust him so much; he was a man and he wanted the untouched secrets of her body, he wanted to caress and possess every aspect of her, he wanted to feel her softness yielding to his hard flesh, clinging to him, sheathing him in ecstasy.

"Closer," he whispered. "Closer. I want to feel you going up on tiptoe against me again. Closer...*yes*."

Rye made a thick sound of pleasure when Lisa put her hands on his naked shoulders and arched into his arms. He caught her lips almost fiercely, kissing her hard, feeling her stiffening in surprise when his tongue prowled the edges of her closed lips. With an effort he forced himself to loosen his grip on her supple, responsive body. He leaned his forehead against the pale coils of her braids, fighting for control of his breath and his unruly passion.

"Rye?" Lisa asked, troubled, unsure.

"It's all right." His head lifted and then bent to her again as he nuzzled at her lips. "Just let me...just once...your mouth...oh, honey, let me in. I'll be gentle this time...so gentle."

Before Lisa could say a word, Rye's lips were brushing over hers once more. Again and again he savored the softness of her lips, skimming gently, barely touching, increasing the contact so slowly that her arms locked around his neck, pulling him closer in unconscious demand. When she felt the hard edge of his teeth close tenderly on her lower lip, her breath rushed out in a soundless moan.

"Yes," he murmured, licking the tiny marks he had left. "Open for me, little one, want me."

Lisa's lips parted and she shivered as Rye's tongue licked over her sensitive flesh as though it were his own. The shifting, elusive pressure of his caress teased her lips farther and farther apart until no barrier to his possession remained.

"Yes," he said thickly. "Like that. Like *this*."

The gliding, sensual presence of Rye's tongue within Lisa's mouth wrung a small cry of discovery from her. A wave of heat swept out from the pit of her stomach, a fever that turned her bones to honey. She clung to Rye's strength without knowing it, for all she could feel was the rhythmic penetration and retreat of his tongue caressing her. She abandoned herself to the rising heat of her own body and to him, returning the gliding pressure of his tongue with her own, enjoying the intimacy of his taste and textures, lured deeper and deeper into his hot mouth until she was giving back the kiss as deeply as she was receiving it.

After a long, long time Rye slowly straightened. He held
Lisa gently against his chest, trying and failing to control the
shudders of desire that swept through him. When he realized that the same wild trembling was sweeping through her
body, he couldn't stifle a thick masculine sound of triumph
and need. She was utterly innocent, yet a single kiss had
made her shiver with desire for him.

"Five," Lisa murmured finally, dreamily, rubbing her
cheek across Rye's bare chest. "I can hardly wait for six."

"Neither can I. But I'm going to if it kills me. And I think
it just might."

Rye saw the puzzlement in Lisa's eyes and smiled despite
the clenched need of his body. "You're like a curious little
kitten. Didn't your daddy ever tell you that curiosity killed
the cat?"

And satisfaction brought it back.

The childhood retort echoed in Rye's head, but it brought
him no comfort. He wasn't about to take advantage of
Lisa's innocence by seducing her before she ever had a
chance to object. His conscience wouldn't let him take a
woman who didn't even know his name. Nor would he tell
her who he was. He didn't want to see dollar signs replace
sensuality when she looked at him.

Yet he still wanted her. He wanted her until he shook with
it. But he wasn't going to take her. Sex he could have from
a thousand women. Lisa's innocent smile could come only
from her.

Seven

———

Lisa hummed softly as she worked on making Rye's new shirt. Gray, luminous, with subtle hints of blue and green, the color of the fine linen cloth she was cutting reminded her of nothing so much as his eyes when he watched her. And Rye always watched her. From the moment he rode his big black horse into the meadow until the last look over his shoulder before Devil plunged down the steep trail to the ranch, Rye watched her.

But that was all he did. He didn't kiss her. He didn't hold her. He didn't take her hand or offer to teach her how to use the ax. It was as though those incandescent moments near the chopping stump never had occurred. He still laughed with her, teased her until she blushed and looked at her with hunger in his eyes, but he never touched her. The one time Lisa had brought up the custom of birthday kissing—and missing kisses—he had smiled rather grimly and told her that it wasn't his birthday.

That was when Lisa had realized that not only wasn't Rye going to kiss her again, he was careful not to touch her even in the most casual ways. Yet he came up to the meadow nearly every day, if only for a few minutes. Despite his baffling sensual distance, Lisa instinctively knew that it was more than the meadow itself that was bringing Rye up the long trail from the ranch.

He's just poor and proud, that's all, Lisa told herself as she finished cutting out the final piece of the shirt. *He can't afford to date and he has too much pride to court a woman unless he has money in his pocket. But Boss Mac's party is free.*

Then why hasn't Rye asked me to go? said a mocking voice at the back of her mind.

Because nice shirts cost money, and everyone wears nice clothes to a party, that's why. But this shirt will be free, and he can't refuse to take it because it's just a replacement for the one he ruined chopping wood for me.

Pleased with her logic, Lisa hummed to herself as she set out the simple tools she would use to sew the shirt. Needle, thread, scissors and the skill of her own fingers were all that she would use, because that was all she had. It was also all she needed. She had been sewing clothes of one kind or another since she had been old enough to hold a needle without dropping it. The pattern for the shirt had been taken from Rye's old one, which she had carefully picked apart into its individual pieces. Using the old pieces, she had cut new ones. The only alteration she had made was to add nearly two more inches in the shoulders of the linen shirt, for the old shirt had been cut too small to stretch across the bunching of Rye's powerful back and shoulder muscles when he worked.

What to use for buttons had bothered Lisa. She had thought of asking Lassiter to buy buttons for her, but he came to the meadow only once a week. Besides, she didn't think it would be fair to ask him to spend his free time shopping for just the right buttons for another man's shirt. She had tried to carve buttons from wood, but the result had simply been too rough-looking against the fine linen. Then she had discovered the solution to the problem literally at her feet. Each year the deer shed their old antlers and grew new ones. The technique of shaping antlers into useful tools was very old, far older than civilization. Carving antler and bone was one of the arcane arts that Lisa had learned along with how to pressure-flake glass into a makeshift knife.

As with most primitive techniques, about all that was required for a finished product was time, patience and more time. That wasn't a problem for Lisa. In the meadow she had fallen back under the spell of the slow rhythms of tribal time, when patience wasn't difficult because there was nothing to hurry toward. She had enjoyed watching the buttons gradually take shape. She had enjoyed painstakingly polishing each one and thinking of the pleasure Rye's sensitive fingertips would get from the satin smoothness of the buttons. It was the same while she worked on the incredibly fine texture of the linen itself; much of her satisfaction came from the knowledge that the soft cloth would bring pleasure to Rye while he wore it.

Humming a work song whose rhythms were as old as the techniques she used, Lisa basted pieces of the shirt together for later sewing. When she finally stopped for lunch, she remembered that she had been warming water to wash herself. She tested the temperature of the water in the barrel that Rye had moved to a sunny spot for her. The liquid was silky and warm. She dipped out a pan of water, carried it into the cabin and bathed with the efficiency of someone to whom bucket baths were an accepted part of life. When she was clean, she put on a pale blue blouse that had come from an open-air market half a world away. One of her two pairs of patched and faded jeans had finally worn completely through at the knees, so she had followed local custom and cut the legs off to make a pair of shorts. In August, the high meadow was more than warm enough for her to enjoy having her legs bare.

When Lisa went back outside, she carefully refrained from looking in the direction of the steep trail. If Rye came to the meadow at all today, it would be late in the afternoon. Often he only stayed for a few minutes, asking her if she needed anything from "down the hill," or if she had been feeling well, or if she had any cuts or sprains that might need attention. She would answer no and yes and no, and then they would talk for a bit about the meadow and the grasses and the turning of the seasons.

And they would look at each other, their eyes full of all that hadn't been said or done.

Lisa's mouth made a bittersweet curve as she caught her reflection in the water remaining in the barrel. The time she had spent in the meadow had brought a golden sheen to her skin, a hint of sensual ripeness that had been absent before. It was the same for her mouth. Her lips were somehow fuller, more moist, a rosy invitation for Rye's caressing kiss—yet his touch never came. She would awake from forgotten dreams with her breasts full, aching, her body in the grip of the shimmering, elemental fever that Rye had called from her very core.

Lisa dipped another bucket of water from the barrel, unbraided her hair and submerged the pale blond mass in the bucket. She stayed outside to wash her hair, knowing from experience that the process was too sloppy for a cabin or even for a tent. She didn't mind the mess. She luxuriated in the fragrant mounds of lather and the clean, warm water that left her hair silvery with life and light. Unbound, her hair was hip-length, thick and very softly curling. She toweled the long strands thoroughly and combed out her hair with steady sweeps of her arm. Then, feeling lazy, she carried her bedroll through the fence and into the meadow itself. There she stretched out on her stomach, letting her hair fan across her back and hips to dry. The languid breeze, warm sunlight and drowsy humming of insects soon made her eyelids heavy. After a while she gave up fighting the peace of the meadow and slept.

When Rye slipped through the fence and into the meadow, for one heart-stopping moment he thought that Lisa was naked except for the hair curled caressingly around her hips. Shimmering with every shift of breeze, her hair was a silken cloak whose beauty had only been hinted at while coiled in braids atop her head. He stood transfixed, barely breathing, feeling as though he had trespassed on the privacy of a nymph who had been shielded until that moment from human eyes.

Then the breeze shifted again, smoothing platinum hair aside to reveal the earthbound color of worn cutoffs. Rye let out his breath in a soundless rush. He knew that he should turn around, run back to the cabin, untie Devil and ride like hell down to the ranch. He knew if he went and knelt next to Lisa, he wouldn't be able to stop himself from touching her.

And he knew that once he had touched her, he might not be able to stop at all. He wanted her too much to trust himself.

So tell her who you are.

No! I don't want it to end so soon. I've never enjoyed being with anyone so much in my life. If we become lovers I'll have to tell her who I am and then everything will be ruined.

So don't touch her.

But Rye was already kneeling next to Lisa, and the silken feel of her hair sliding through his fingers drove everything else from his mind. Gently he lifted the hairbrush from her relaxed fingers and began brushing the silvery cascade of hair. The long, soft strands seemed alive. They arched up to his touch, curled lovingly around his hands and clung to his fingers as though in a silent plea for more caresses. Smiling, he brushed with slow, gentle strokes, and when he could resist it no more he eased his fingers deep into the sunwarmed, shimmering depths of her hair. The exquisite softness made an involuntary shiver run through him. He lifted her hair to his lips and buried his face in the shining strands, inhaling deeply.

Lisa stirred and awakened languidly, caught in the dream of Rye that had haunted her every time she slept. When her eyes opened she saw the flexed power of his thighs pressing against his taut jeans and the pale delicacy of her unbound hair clinging to his body. She sensed as much as felt the weight of her long hair caught in his hands, a sensuous leash made of countless silky strands, and each strand bound her to him—and him to her. Slowly she turned her head until she could see his face buried in her hair. The contrast of dark and fair, of hard masculine planes and soft femininity, made her breath fill her throat.

Then Rye opened his eyes and Lisa couldn't breathe at all. Passion burned behind his black eyelashes, a turmoil of need and emotion that exploded softly inside her, bringing fever in its wake. She looked into his eyes and saw the truth that she had sensed the first time Rye had ridden into the high meadow and found her trying to chop wood. She had no defenses against that elemental truth or his passion, no defenses against him.

"I tried not to wake you up," he said huskily.

"I don't mind."

"You should. You're too innocent. You shouldn't let me near you. You trust me too much."

"I can't help it," Lisa said, her voice soft, unhesitating. "I was born to be your woman. I knew it the instant I turned around and saw you sitting like a warrior on a horse as black as night."

Rye couldn't bear the honesty and certainty in Lisa's beautiful amethyst eyes. His black lashes closed and a visible shudder ran through his body.

"No," he said harshly. "You don't know me."

"I know that you're hard and more than strong enough to hurt me, but you won't. You've always been very careful of me, more gentle and protective than most men are with their own wives and daughters. In every way that matters, I'm safe with you. I know that, just as I know that you're intelligent and hot tempered and funny and very proud."

"If a man isn't proud and hard and willing to fight, the world will roll right over him and leave him flatter than his shadow in the dust."

"Yes, I know that, too," Lisa said simply. "I've seen it happen in every culture, no matter how primitive or how civilized." She looked at Rye's head bent over her hair as he smoothed it against his cheek. "Did I mention that you're very handsome, too, and have all your own teeth?"

Helplessly Rye laughed. He had never known anyone like Lisa—wry, sensual, honest, with a capacity for joy that glittered through everything she said and did.

"You're one of a kind, Lisa."

She smiled sadly. She had been one of a kind wherever she had gone with her parents. Always watching, never being a part of the colorful, passionate pageant that was humanity. She had thought it would be different in America, but it hadn't been. Yet for a time, when Rye had been near, she hadn't felt separate. And when he had kissed her, she had felt the slow, sweet fever of life steal through her, joining her to him.

Tentatively Lisa traced the full curve of Rye's lower lip with the tip of her index finger. He flinched away from the innocent, incendiary touch, not trusting his self-control. She dropped her hand and looked away. She was too unsophisticated to conceal her bafflement and hurt at his withdrawal.

"I'm sorry," she said. "When I woke up and saw you, and you had your face buried in my hair..." Her voice died. She looked back over her shoulder, giving him an apologetic smile. "I guess I'm too much of a tenderfoot with men to read the signs right. I thought you wanted..."

Lisa's voice faded again. She swallowed, trying to read Rye's expression, but there was nothing to read. Only his eyes were alive, glittering with the fever that he was fighting to control. She didn't know that; she only knew that he had flinched when she had touched him. When he closed his eyes, she saw the rigid line of his clenched jaw, and she believed that he was forcing himself to be kind and say nothing.

She turned away from Rye, only to find herself still bound to him by the shining lengths of her hair caught between his fingers. She tugged very lightly once, then again, trying to free herself without drawing his attention. Gradually she realized that there was a gentle, inescapable force pulling her back toward him, reminding her that there were two ends to the silken leash of her hair. When she faced Rye again she was watching her with eyes that blazed.

"We have to talk, little one, but not now. Once, just once in my life, I'm going to know what it's like to be wanted as a man. Just a man called Rye."

"I don't understand," Lisa whispered as Rye bent down over her, filling her world.

"I know. But you understand this, don't you?"

A small sound escaped Lisa as she felt the sweet firmness of Rye's lips once more. The caressing pressure slowly increased, parting her lips, preparing her for the tender penetration of his tongue. Yet he withheld even that small consummation from her while he rocked his mouth languidly against hers, sensitizing lips that turned hungrily to follow his seductive motions. She said his name, and the sound was as much a sigh as a word. Hearing it sent fire licking over him.

"Yes?" Rye murmured, nuzzling Lisa's soft lips.

"Would you . . . ?"

Her words broke softly when his teeth captured her lower lip. She made a tiny, throaty sound of pleasure, but the caress lasted only an instant.

"More," she murmured. "Please."

Lisa felt as much as heard Rye's laughter. She opened her eyes to find him watching her with an intensity that was almost tangible.

"Shouldn't I have said that?" she asked.

"Say anything you like," he said, his voice almost rough with the hammering of his blood. "I love hearing it, feeling you turn to follow my lips, knowing that you want me. I love that most of all. Having you want me and knowing that it's me, just me, that makes you tremble."

"Is that part of it?"

"It?" he asked, smiling crookedly.

"This."

Lisa eased her fingers into his thick, warm hair and pulled his mouth down to hers. With the same sensual deliberation that he had shown to her weeks ago, she traced the outline of his lips with the tip of her tongue before she closed her teeth with exquisite care on his lower lip. When she felt the shudder that rippled through his powerful body, she smiled and slowly released him.

"Trembling is part of the velvet fever, isn't it?" she asked softly.

Rye closed his eyes and counted his own heartbeat in the violent race of his blood. The thought of making love with a woman as honestly sensual and sensually honest as Lisa nearly made him lose control.

But she was so innocent that he was afraid of shocking her long before he would be able to fully arouse her.

"Will you . . . ?" She touched his lips with her fingertip.

"Do you want me to kiss you?" he asked, opening his eyes, looking into the amethyst depths of hers.

"Yes," she sighed.

"How do you want me to kiss you? Like this?" Rye's lips skimmed over Lisa's. "Or like this?" He skimmed again, then returned to linger. "Or like this?" His tongue drew a warm, moist line around Lisa's lips, between them, inside them, until she whimpered softly and opened herself for a deeper kiss. "Is this what you want?" he whispered.

When Lisa finally felt the moist invasion of Rye's tongue, her whole body tightened. He began stroking her mouth in slow, sensual rhythms that made her melt against him, moving as he moved, slowly, deeply. What had begun as a simple kiss became the sensuous consummation she had longed for. She clung to him, forgetting his warning against trusting him, knowing only that she was in his arms and it was even better than her dreams. When he would have finally ended the embrace she made an inarticulate sound of protest and tightened her arms around his neck, wanting more of his heat and sweetness.

"Shh," Rye said, biting Lisa's tongue delicately. "I'm not going anywhere without you. You're going to be with me every inch of the way if it kills me . . . every last inch."

SILHOUETTE DELIVERS FIRST-CLASS ROMANCE—DIRECT TO YOUR DOOR

Mail the Heart sticker on the postpaid order card today and you'll receive:

— **4 new Silhouette Desire novels—FREE**
— **an elegant pen & watch set—FREE**
— **and a surprise mystery bonus—FREE**

But that's not all. You'll also get:

Money-Saving Home Delivery

When you subscribe to Silhouette Desire, the excitement, romance and faraway adventures of these novels can be yours for previewing in the convenience of your own home at less than retail prices. Every month we'll deliver 6 new books right to your door. If you decide to keep them, they'll be yours for only $2.24 each. That's 26¢ less per book than what you pay in stores. And there is no extra charge for shipping and handling!

Free Monthly Newsletter

It's the indispensable insider's look at our most popular writers and their upcoming novels. Now you can have a behind-the-scenes look at the fascinating world of Silhouette! It's an added bonus you'll look forward to every month!

Special Extras—FREE

Because our home subscribers are our most valued readers, we'll be sending you additional free gifts from time to time as a token of our appreciation.

OPEN YOUR MAILBOX TO A WORLD OF LOVE AND ROMANCE EACH MONTH. JUST COMPLETE, DETACH AND MAIL YOUR FREE OFFER CARD TODAY!

Remember! To receive your free books, pen and watch set and mystery gift, return the postpaid card below. But don't delay!

DETACH AND MAIL CARD TODAY.

If offer card has been removed, write to:
Silhouette Books, 901 Fuhrmann Blvd., P.O. Box 1867, Buffalo, NY 14269-1867

MAIL THE POSTPAID CARD TODAY!

BUSINESS REPLY CARD

First Class   Permit No. 717   Buffalo, NY

Postage will be paid by addressee

Silhouette Books®
901 Fuhrmann Blvd.
P.O. Box 1867
Buffalo, NY 14240-9952

NO POSTAGE
NECESSARY
IF MAILED
IN THE
UNITED STATES

He shifted slowly, lowering himself onto the blanket, kissing the silky radiance of her hair as he fanned it out above her head in a silver-gold cloud. Watching her eyes, he stretched out beside her and traced the line of her cheekbone first with his fingertip, then with the back of his fingers. She caught his hand and pressed a kiss into it before biting him not quite gently on his callused palm. His response was a low, very male laugh. His eyes turned the color of smoked crystal as he looked at her mouth and the curve of her breasts beneath her blouse.

"Do you want me to kiss you again?" he asked in a low voice.

"Yes," she said, meeting his eyes. "Oh, yes, Rye. I want that."

"Where? Here?"

Lisa smiled when his fingertips touched her lips.

"Or here?"

She shivered when he traced the delicate rim of her ear.

"Or here?"

His fingertip smoothed over the line of her throat, pausing at the pulse that beat quickly just beneath her skin.

"How about here?" he murmured.

The back of Rye's fingers caressed the hollow of Lisa's throat and then slowly slid beneath the collar of her blouse. There was no bra between his skin and hers, nothing to dull the sensation when he stroked the firm rise of her breast and caught her nipple between his fingers. She cried out in surprise and passion and put her hand over his as though to stop him from caressing her so intimately again.

"Are you saying that you don't want this?" Rye asked softly, tugging at her velvet nipple with gentle, skillful fingers.

Sensations speared through Lisa, making speech impossible. She moaned softly and arched against Rye's touch, holding his hand in place on her breast.

"That's it," he murmured, thumbing her nipple and listening to her sweet cries, feeling the echoes of her pleasure tighten his body, filling him with a heavy rush of blood. "Tell me what you want, little one. I'll give it to you. All of it, everything you can imagine."

"I want—" Lisa's voice broke as Rye rolled the nipple between his hard fingers, sending pleasure bursting through her. "I—" Her voice fractured again.

Lisa gave up trying to speak. She held Rye's hand against her breast and pressed herself into his palm, silently asking for more. Smiling, he slid his hand from beneath hers, ending the caresses that had flushed her skin with passion.

"Rye?"

"Yes?" he asked. His fingers flicked open first one button on her blouse, then a second, then a third. As he started to pull the cloth aside, Lisa made a startled sound. Her hands came up to hold the edges of the half-unfastened blouse together.

"Don't you want me to touch you?" Rye asked softly.

"I—I've never—I don't know."

"Your body does. Look."

Lisa looked down at her breasts. The nipples that ached so sweetly were erect, pushing against the soft cloth, begging to be touched again. While she watched, Rye's fingers circled the tip of one breast, then the other, making the nipples stand even higher and sending sensations spearing through Lisa all the way to the soles of her feet.

"It will feel even better without the cloth," Rye whispered, smiling as he listened to the soft whimpers he was drawing from Lisa. "Let me see you, baby. I won't touch you unless you want me to. All right?"

Slowly Lisa nodded her head, not trusting her voice to speak. She didn't care what Rye did, so long as it meant that the ache in her breasts would be answered by his caresses.

Looking only at Lisa's eyes, Rye slowly pulled aside one half of the partially undone blouse. With teasing, sensuous care, he tugged the cloth across the hard, high peak of her breast before tucking the loose folds beneath the firm flesh. He saw her eyes half close, felt her shivering sigh as her breast tightened at the first warm wash of sunlight across it. The nipple pouted in deepening shades of pink, revealing the heightened rush of blood through her body.

"Yes," Lisa whispered, moving languidly, arching slightly. "Yes. The sunlight feels so good it makes me ache, but it doesn't feel nearly as good as your hand."

He barely stifled a groan at the sudden hammer blows of need that made him painfully rigid. She was more beautiful than he had expected, more beautiful than seemed possible. Her breast was smooth and full, the skin flawless as a pearl, and her nipple was a raspberry waiting to be tasted by his tongue.

Lisa saw the fierce clenching of Rye's body and the sudden stillness of his face as he looked at her breast nestled among folds of blouse.

"Rye?"

Heat pulsed through Rye as he heard Lisa call his name in a voice made husky by the same passion that was driving him to the very edge of his control. His whole body tightened until he could barely speak.

"You're burning me alive," he said hoarsely, "and I've barely touched you. You're so innocent. But I'm not. I want you so badly that I feel like my guts are being torn out. I want to undress you, to hear you cry my name when I touch you where no one ever has. I want to kiss every bit of you, to lay my cheek against your waist, to trace the curve of your bare belly with my tongue, to taste the smooth skin inside your thighs, to touch you every way a man can touch a woman. But you're so damned innocent, I'd shock you even if I did no more than kiss the tip of your breast.''

Lisa tried to speak, but could not. Rye's words had been like caresses, stealing her breath.

"Do you understand what I'm saying?'' he asked roughly. "I'm not talking about a few more hot kisses and then I ride back down the hill. I'm talking about lying naked with you and touching you in ways you can't even imagine, and when you're hot and crying for me, I'll begin all over again until you're so wild you won't even know your own name.''

Lisa's eyes widened and her lips parted over a silent rush of air.

"That's when I'll take you and you'll take me and for a time there will be no you, no me, only us locked together in the kind of pleasure that people kill or die for,'' Rye finished roughly. "Do you understand that? If I touch you the way you're begging to be touched, you won't leave this meadow a virgin.''

Eight

Eyes wide, Lisa watched Rye. She opened her mouth to speak, licked her lips and tried to think. It was impossible. His words kept echoing inside her, making her tremble. She hadn't thought beyond the pleasure of his kisses. She should have, and she knew it. She was innocent but she wasn't stupid.

"I'm s-sorry," she said helplessly, hating to know that she had caused him pain. "I wasn't thinking how it would be for you. I never meant any hurt."

When Rye saw Lisa's taut expression he swore harshly and sat up in a single, savage movement. Then he closed his eyes, because if he kept on looking at her, he would reach for her, kiss her slowly, deeply, seducing her before she had a chance to say yes or no.

Suddenly he sensed the warmth of her breath against his hand in the instant before her lips touched his skin. When she held his hand against her cheek and whispered apologies, he felt the trembling of her body and knew that right now there was as much fear and unhappiness as passion in Lisa. The realization chastened him, cooling the fever that had been on the edge of burning out of control.

"It's not your fault," Rye whispered, pulling Lisa gently onto his lap, soothing her with a gentle hug. "It's mine. I knew where I was going. You didn't." He smiled wryly. "But I didn't know I could want a woman the way I want you. It took me by surprise." He brushed his lips over her cheek and tasted tears. "Don't cry, baby. It's all right. I know myself better now. I won't take either one of us by surprise again, and I won't do anything you don't want. You can have as few or as many of my kisses as you like, however you like them, wherever you like them. Just don't be afraid of me. I'd never force anything from you, Lisa. You know that, don't you?"

The words reassured Lisa, but not as much as the soothing, undemanding kisses that Rye gave to her forehead and cheeks, the tip of her nose and the corners of her mouth. After a few moments she let out her breath in a long sigh and relaxed against his chest. He swept up her hair and draped it over his shoulder so that silky strands cascaded down his back. He wished that he was naked so that he might feel the texture as well as the weight of her beautiful hair. He turned his face into the pale, fragrant strands and inhaled deeply, stroking her hair with his dark cheek.

Seeing the sensual pleasure that her hair gave to Rye sent curious tremors through the pit of Lisa's stomach. She remembered the moment when she had awakened to find him turning his face from side to side in her hair as though he were bathing in the warm, flaxen cascade. She remembered a few weeks before, when he had nuzzled his teasing, sensual mouth into her palm, his tongue licking intimately between her fingers, his teeth closing on her skin until she couldn't stifle a moan. The thought of having her whole body caressed like that made her skin flush with sudden heat and sensitivity. The breeze blew and she stifled a tiny gasp at the feather touch across her still-bare breast.

"Lisa," whispered Rye.

She turned and saw that he was looking at her breast rising between folds of pale blue cloth.

"Do you trust me enough to let me touch you again?"

"Yes. No. Oh, Rye, I trust you but I don't want to make it worse for you. It isn't fair that you should hurt when you make me feel so good."

"It's all right," he said, smoothing his hand from Lisa's knee to her hip to her waist. "It's all right, baby. This will feel good to both of us. Unless you don't want it?" His breath wedged as he controlled himself, keeping his hand just below her breast, waiting.

"It?" she said in a high voice, caught between a virgin's nervousness and the fever that was burning down through her bones to her very soul.

He smiled crookedly. "My hand, and then my mouth. Here. Sipping on you, tasting you, loving you."

He bent down and almost touched his lips to the ruby peak that was reaching toward him even as he moved. Instead of cupping or kissing the sensitive flesh, he blew on her as though she were a birthday candle. Lisa's broken laugh at the teasing caress become a choked cry as his warm palm took the weight of her breast. Yet still he ignored the tight, pink crown, as though he didn't know that it ached for his caress.

Without thinking, Lisa arched her back, trying to close the distance between Rye's mouth and her breast. The world spun as he lifted her, turned her, stretched her out on the blanket once more. He swept up the weight of her hair, letting it tumble wildly above her head, and then buried his left hand in the silky warmth, twisting it slowly around his fingers until her head tilted backward, arching her back.

"More," Rye said huskily.

Lisa didn't understand, but the feel of his fingers kneading her scalp was so unexpectedly sensual that she tilted her head back even farther and rubbed against his hand like a cat. Her back arched more with the motion, tightening her bare breast, making the nipple stand even higher.

"That's it, baby," Rye murmured, flexing his fingers against her scalp, urging her to draw herself even closer to his mouth. He moved in slow motion as he bent down to her, teasing both of them by not quite touching her despite the mute pleading of her arched back. "Yes, higher. You'll like it even better that way...and so will I."

With supple grace Lisa arched her back fully, brushing the tight crown of her breast against Rye's lips. Only it wasn't his lips that touched her, but the hot, moist tip of his tongue. The unexpected caress made her back curve like a drawn bow. His right arm slid beneath her, holding her while his mouth slowly closed over her breast, gently devouring first her hard pink crest and then the velvet areola and not stopping until he was filled with her and his tongue was shaping her and his teeth were a sensual vise that made her writhe with pleasure. Her nails dug into his powerful shoulders as she called his name with each breath she took, ragged breaths that echoed the rhythms of his mouth tugging at her breast, setting fire to her body.

With a swift motion of his head, Rye turned and claimed Lisa's other breast, raking lightly through the cloth with his teeth until the nipple stood forth proudly. His teeth closed through the cloth with exquisite care despite the hunger that was making shudders run through his body.

Lisa's voice splintered as waves of pleasure visibly swept through her. She didn't feel the rest of her blouse being unbuttoned or cloth being peeled away from her skin. She felt only his hot, wild caresses on her naked breasts as fever raced through her. When he laced his fingers through hers and stretched her arms above her head, she arched gracefully toward his mouth, her back a taut curve, her breasts full and flushed with the heat of his kisses.

"Don't stop," Lisa moaned, twisting beneath Rye, trying to ease the throbbing of her nipples against his hard chest. "Please, Rye, don't stop."

The hard thrust of his tongue between her teeth cut off her pleas. She returned the kiss fiercely, wanting to crush her body into his, shaking with her wanting. His lips pressed down into hers, controlling her wild motions, slowly transforming them into the rhythmic movements of the act of love. She didn't protest. She wanted it as much as he did. She had never wanted anything half so much. She felt his hips settle between her legs, opening them. Then he arched suddenly against the hidden center of her passion, and she cried out in fear at the sensations that speared through her.

"Rye!"

"Easy, baby, easy," he said, fighting the urgent hammering of his own blood. "It's all right." He turned onto his side, bringing Lisa with him. For long moments he gentled her with voice and touch and body, phrases and caresses that soothed rather than set fire to her. "That's it, honey. Hold on to me. There's no hurry. There's just the two of us enjoying each other. Just us and all the time in the world."

Lisa clung to Rye while he stroked her slowly, calmly, his voice soft despite the tremors of passion that ripped through him at every shift of her breasts against him. After a few minutes he slowly unbuttoned his shirt, and his breath came out in a ragged sigh when he felt her nipples nuzzle through the black thatch of his hair until they pressed against his sun-darkened skin. The contrast of satin breasts and work-hardened muscle made his erect flesh strain even more tightly against the confinement of his jeans. He ignored the harsh urgency of his sex, knowing that whether Lisa became his lover that day or took no more from him than his kisses, she deserved better in her innocence and honesty than a hurried, nearly out-of-control man.

"You're more beautiful every time I look at you," Rye said, his voice deep and his breath warm against Lisa's ear. He bit her ear delicately, then with more power, enjoying the way she moved toward rather than away from his caresses. His strong hand stroked against her back, rubbing her gently against his chest. "Do I feel nearly as good to you as you do to me?"

Lisa laughed shakily, no longer frightened by the intense, unexpected sensations that had taken her body without warning. She was curious now, restless, hungry to feel that transforming pleasure again. "You feel twice as good. Five times. Nothing could feel better than you do."

As she spoke, she responded to the gentle pressure of Rye's hand by twisting in slow motion against him, savoring the shivery feelings that went from her nipples to the pit of her stomach and then radiated out softly, hotly, turning her bones to honey.

"Do you like—" Lisa's voice broke suddenly as Rye's knee moved between her legs, opening them. The warm, hard weight of his thigh slid upward until it pressed against her softness, rocking, sending a slow, sweet lightning radiating throughout her body. She made a low, involuntary sound of surprise and looked at him with dazed amethyst eyes. The sensation wasn't as sharp as it had been the first time, when he had lain between her legs, yet still the pleasure could hardly be borne.

"Do I like...?" Rye asked, moving deliberately between Lisa's thighs, accustoming her to being caressed. His body tightened hungrily when he felt the sudden, humid heat of her as she was taken by waves of pleasure.

"D-do you like being touched?" she asked, her voice trembling.

"Yes." He bent and kissed her slowly. "Do you want to touch me?"

"Yes, but..."

"But?"

"I don't know how," Lisa admitted, biting her lip. "I want it to be good for you, as good as you make it for me."

Rye closed his eyes for an instant, fighting the urge to pull Lisa's hands down his body until they rubbed against the hard, urgent flesh between his legs.

"If it gets any better for me," he said almost roughly, "it could be all over." He smiled crookedly at her. "Put your hands on me. Anywhere. Everywhere. Whatever you like. I want to be touched by you. I need it, baby. You don't know how I need it."

Lisa's hand trembled as she lifted it to Rye's face. She traced the dark arch of each eyebrow, the line of his nose, the rim of his ear. When that caress made his breath catch audibly, she returned to the sensitive rim, but this time it was her mouth that caressed him. With catlike delicacy she sketched the curves of his ear using the tip of her tongue, spiraling down and in until she felt the sensual shudder that rippled through Rye's body.

"You like that," she murmured.

"Oh, I don't know," he said huskily. "Could have been a coincidence. Maybe you better try it again."

She looked startled, then smiled. "You're teasing me."

"No, baby. You're teasing me."

He gave a low growl when her teeth closed on his ear in a caress that she had learned from him.

"Should I stop teasing you?" she asked, laughing at his soft growl.

"Ask me again in an hour."

"An hour?" Lisa said. The words were a soft rush of air against Rye's sensitive ear. "Can people stand that much pleasure?"

"I don't know," he admitted, "but it would be worth dying to find out."

Lisa's answer was muffled because her lips had become intrigued by the difference in texture between Rye's jaw and his ear. He didn't complain about the lack of conversation; he simply turned his head slightly, offering easier access to the soft explorations of her mouth. Too soon she encountered his shirt. He drew away for a moment, shrugged out of his shirt and threw it aside without a glance. But when he turned back to Lisa, he was afraid that taking off his shirt had been a mistake. She was staring at him as though she had never seen a man bare to the waist.

"Should I put it back on?" he asked quietly.

She dragged her glance slowly up to his intent eyes. "What?"

"My shirt. Should I put it on again?"

"Are you cold?"

The low sound that came from Rye could hardly have been called laughter. "Not very damn likely. You just seemed . . . surprised . . . when I took off my shirt."

"I was remembering when you came to the stream after chopping wood. You rinsed off your chest and shoulders and when you stood up the drops were like liquid diamonds in the sunlight. I wanted to sip each one of them from your skin. Would you have liked that?"

"Oh, baby," he whispered.

Rye caught Lisa's mouth beneath his and kissed her, loving her with slow movements of his tongue, both shaken and fiercely aroused by what she had said. Finally, reluctantly, he released her, because he knew that he was right on the edge of his self-control. He lay back on the blanket, his fingers interlaced beneath his head so that he wouldn't reach out to the pink-tipped breasts that peeked out so temptingly from her unbuttoned blouse.

"How good a memory do you have?" he asked huskily.

"I'm told it's very good."

"Close your eyes and remember every drop of water you saw on me. Can you do that?"

Eyes closed, smiling dreamily, Lisa said, "Oh, yes."

"They're yours, every one of them. All you have to do is take them."

Her eyes snapped open. She looked at Rye stretched out before her, watching her with a mixture of humor and sensual intensity that made her breath stop. Slowly she bent down to him, shivering as he did when her lips first touched his skin.

"There was one here," she said, kissing the base of his neck. "And here...and here," she continued, nuzzling the length of his collarbone toward the center of his chest. "And there was a tiny silver trickle here."

Rye closed his eyes as Lisa's pink tongue licked down the centre line of his chest, burrowing through his thick hair to the hot skin beneath.

"The drops went all the way down to your buckle," she said, hesitating, a question in her voice.

"God, I hope so."

Smiling, Lisa continued down past Rye's ribs, smoothing her mouth along the center of his body, testing the resilience of his flesh with her teeth and her tongue. When she reached the buckle she stopped, and Rye was tempted to tell her that the water had run beneath his clothes all the way to the soles of his feet. His breath came out in a rush when she kissed the skin just above his belt, nibbling all along his flat stomach. He locked his fingers together above his head to keep from reaching for her as her soft lips caressed in a random pattern across his ribs, stopping just short of a nipple hidden beneath curling black hair. When she continued on up to his collarbone without a pause, he made an inarticulate sound of disappointment.

"You missed some drops," he said thickly.

"I did? Where? Here?" Lisa asked, touching Rye's collarbone with the tip of her tongue.

"Lower."

"Here?" Her lips caught and tugged playfully on the hair curling in the center of his chest.

"That's closer. Now go to the right."

"Your right or mine?"

"Either way, honey. You'll find it."

Suddenly Lisa understood. She laughed softly. "Of course. How could I have forgotten that water gathered there?"

Rye couldn't answer, for she had found a flat nipple and was teasing it delicately, hotly, using teeth and tongue as he had on her. He made a hoarse sound of pleasure. When her fingers began to knead through the thick mat of his chest hair, he twisted his torso slowly, increasing the pressure of her touch. Her nails sank into his skin as she flexed her hands, loving the feel of the crisp hair and hard muscles rubbing against her palms. Her hands roamed up and down his chest, stroking him, enjoying the sensual heat of his skin.

In time she discovered that the hair beneath Rye's arms was as soft as a sigh. The ultrafine texture fascinated her. Her fingers returned to it again and again, just as her mouth kept returning to the tiny, rigid points of his nipples until he could bear it no longer. His hands unclenched and pulled her across his body until she was straddling him. Before she could say a word her blouse was pushed off her shoulders and discarded, leaving her breasts completely bare. The tips hardened as he looked at them, telling him that she wanted his touch as much as he wanted to touch her.

"Rye...?"

"Come here, little love," he said huskily.

Slowly Lisa leaned forward, bringing her breasts into Rye's hands. When his warm fingers found her nipples, she shivered with the exquisite, piercing pleasure his touch gave to her. She couldn't control the cries that rippled from her any more than she could stop the fever that flushed her body, heightening her sensitivity. She twisted slowly in his hands while he drew her ever farther up his body. She saw his lips open, saw the hint of his teeth as his tongue circled her nipple and then she was inside his mouth, captive to his hot, moist caresses. With a moan she stretched out full-length on his body, giving herself to his loving.

Rye's hands closed around Lisa's narrow waist, kneading it even as his mouth tugged on her breast. He shaped the rich curve of her buttocks, sinking his fingers into her flesh in a caress that made her bones loosen. His long fingers rubbed down her thighs, then swept back up again and down and up in a rocking motion that made her tremble. He slid his thumbs beneath the bottom edge of her cutoff jeans, tracing the full curve of her bare flesh.

"Rye," Lisa said, then shuddered as his thumbs burrowed farther up beneath the faded cloth.

"What?" he murmured, turning his head so that he could caress her other breast.

"I feel...dizzy."

"So do I, baby."

"You do?"

"Bet on it. If I weren't lying down, I'd be lucky to crawl."

Lisa's laugh was shaky but reassured. "I thought it was just me."

"Oh, it's you, all right. There's enough heat in that lovely body of yours to melt this mountain all the way to its core."

"Is that . . . all right?"

"No," he said nuzzling her breast. "It's much better than all right. It's incredible and sexy as hell. I've been missing you all my life and didn't even know it."

Lisa's laughter turned into a gasp as sensations streaked through her from the sensuous tugging of Rye's mouth on her breast. His hand moved between her legs, cupping her intimately in his palm, and she stiffened at the unexpected caress.

"This is part of it," Rye said, watching Lisa's eyes as his palm rubbed against her.

"It?" she said breathlessly.

And then her thoughts shattered into a thousand brilliant shards of pleasure with each motion of his hand. She moved helplessly against his palm, sending a cascade of shining hair sliding over him. He shivered at its whispering caress.

"This is the home of the velvet fever," he whispered against her lips. "Can't you feel it, honey? Hot and sweet, hungry and beautiful . . . so beautiful."

Rye made a low sound as Lisa shuddered against his hand, for the spreading heat of her body answered him better than any words could have. His hands moved and the snap closing the waist of her cutoff jeans gave way, followed by the soft hiss of the zipper sliding down. Gently, inevitably, his fingers eased inside the waistband. She lay full-length on top of him, trembling, saying nothing as she felt the last of her clothes sliding down her legs, baring her to the sunlight and to the man whose eyes blazed brighter than any sun.

Rye held Lisa naked on top of him, soothing her with long, gentle strokes of his hands, trying to still the wild need in his own body.

"R-Rye?"

"Hush, baby. It's all right. I'm not going to do anything that you don't want me to do."

She let out a shaky breath and slowly relaxed against him.

"That's it," he murmured. "Just relax and enjoy the sun while I enjoy you."

After a few moments the sun and Rye's soothing, loving hands made Lisa's uneasiness at being nude vanish. She sighed and stretched sensuously. Soon her hands itched to stroke Rye as she was being stroked, but when she ran her hands from his shoulders to his waist, his jeans were there, a barrier that reminded her that she was naked and he was not.

"This isn't fair," she whispered.

"I'll survive," Rye said tightly, misunderstanding.

"No, I meant your jeans."

"What about them?"

"They're in my way."

There was an electric silence, then, "How shockproof are you?"

"Quite."

"You're sure?"

"Yes," Lisa said simply, meeting his glance. "Very sure."

Rye went utterly still when he realized what Lisa was saying.

"You don't have to," he said, his voice rough with the restraint he was imposing on himself.

"I know. I want to..."

"But?" he asked tautly, reading the question in the unfinished sentence.

"I don't know how. And I want to please you. I want that so much."

Rye held Lisa close as he turned onto his side and kissed her tenderly. "You please me," he said huskily.

He gave her tiny, biting kisses before thrusting his tongue into the sweet darkness of her mouth. She opened to him, drawing him in even more, wanting the mating of tongues as much as he did. Reluctantly he ended the kiss and stood up. He took off his boots and socks, unfastened his belt buckle and looked down at Lisa.

She was lying on her side, her hair flying around her in silken disarray, her pink nipples peeking out from the white-gold strands. The curtain of her hair parted on either side of her hip, revealing a pearly curve of flesh and a pale tangle of much shorter, curlier hair.

"It's not too late to change your mind," Rye said, wondering if he lied.

Lisa smiled.

Watching her, he unfastened the fly of his jeans and peeled them down his body, taking his underwear in the same motion. He kicked the clothes aside and stood with his breath held, praying that she was as shockproof as she had said, for he was more aroused than he had ever been in his life. He wanted her to take the same pleasure in that as he did, but she was innocent and he expected her to be afraid.

Lisa's eyes widened until they were amethyst pools within her shocked face. She saw the violent pulse leaping at his temple and throat and farther down, where he thrust rigidly forward.

And then he was turning away, reaching for the clothes he had just discarded.

"No!" Lisa said, coming to her knees in a cloud of flying hair. She flung her arms around Rye's legs and pressed her face against the top of his hard thigh. "I'm not afraid. Not

really. I've seen men wearing almost nothing, but not ...
not ... It just startled me.''

Rye stood and trembled when Lisa's hair settled over his
hard flesh like a loincloth of silk. "It?" he asked, his voice
like a rasp. "You do love that word, don't you?"

She looked up and saw the humor glittering through the
passion that made his eyes blaze and his skin burn hotly beneath her cheek. She knew at that instant that her instincts
had been right; Rye wouldn't hurt her, no matter how great
his strength or his need.

"This," Lisa said, brushing her cheek over the full length
of his erect flesh, "startled me."

"Baby," Rye whispered, sinking to his knees because he
could stand no longer, "you're going to be the death of me.
And I can hardly wait."

His fingers skimmed beneath the shimmering curtain of
Lisa's hair, then curved around the back of her thighs,
rocking her up against his body. Her breath caught and held
as his fingers stroked down her thighs and then returned to
the bottom of her buttocks again and again, each time sliding deeper between her legs, parting them just a bit more
with every caress.

"Do you know what it did to me when you rubbed your
cheek over me?" he asked, biting her ear and then thrusting in his tongue.

"N-no."

"This," he whispered.

Lisa bit back a moan as his palm smoothed down her
belly and his fingertips parted her tight curls, seeking and
finding skin that was moist, unbelievably soft. With each
gliding motion of his fingers she trembled more. Her eyes
closed and she swayed in front of him like a flower in the
wind.

"Put your arms around my neck," Rye whispered, sliding farther into her body, preparing her for the much deeper joining to come.

Blindly Lisa did as Rye asked, clinging to him because he was the only real thing in a world that was spinning faster and faster with each touch of his fingers inside her. She felt neither self-consciousness nor shyness at the increasing intimacy of his caresses, for the elemental fever he had discovered in her had burned through everything, leaving only heat and need.

"That's it, baby. Hold on tight and follow me. I know where we're going."

Rye found and teased the sensitive bud that was no longer hidden within Lisa's softness. With each circular caress she moaned, feeling waves of shimmering heat sweep through her until she could hold no more and her pleasure overflowed.

"Yes," he said, biting her neck with enough force to leave tiny marks, teasing her now with the flesh that was as hard as she was soft. "Again, baby. Again. Share it all with me. It will make it easier for you, for me, for both of us. That's it. *Yes.*"

Lisa barely heard the words that wrapped around her, joining her to Rye as surely as her arms holding on to him and his body probing gently against hers. She felt herself lifted and carefully lowered to the blanket once more. Though he lay between her legs, he did not touch the moist flesh that he had teased into life. Her eyes opened and her head moved restlessly, feverishly.

"Rye?"

"I'm right here. All of me. Is that what you want?"

"Yes," she whispered, reaching down to touch him as intimately as he had touched her.

Rye closed his eyes as a shudder ran through his whole body. The feel of Lisa's small hand closing around him was more exciting than he would have believed possible.

"Baby," he whispered, "let me . . ."

He took her soft mouth with every bit of the fever that was burning him alive. When her tongue rubbed hungrily over his, he eased himself into her body until he felt the fragile barrier of her innocence.

"Rye?" she said. *"Rye."*

Deliberately he slid his hand between their partially joined bodies, rocking his hips slowly, caressing the hard bud of her passion.

Lisa moaned suddenly as fever flared wildly through her, a fever spreading up from Rye's hand and his hard flesh. He filled her slowly, moving gently, caressing her with his hand and body until pleasure swept through her in rhythmic waves, pleasure so great that it utterly consumed her, melting her over him again and again, and each time she called his name. She wanted to tell him she could feel no greater pleasure without dying, and yet he caressed her still, rocking within her. Deep within her. And then he was motionless, savoring the agonizing pleasure of being fully sheathed within her.

"Lisa," Rye whispered. "Baby?"

Her eyes opened slowly, dazed by the shimmering heat of being joined with him. "I thought . . . I thought it would hurt," she admitted.

"It did," he said huskily. "But the pain was buried by so much pleasure that you didn't know. Does this hurt now?"

He moved slowly. She made a soft, broken sound that was his name.

"Again," she said brokenly. "Oh, Rye, *again.*" She looked into the gray blaze of his eyes. "Or doesn't it feel as good to you?"

"Good?" Rye shuddered as he buried himself fully within Lisa again and withdrew and penetrated her once more. "There are...no words. Come with me, baby. Take me where you've already been."

He moved in an agony of restraint, holding back with all his strength. He had never felt anything to equal the velvet fever of Lisa's body, had never known a physical sharing half so deep, had never believed himself capable of anything that approached the intense sensual involvement he was feeling. He moved slowly within her, deeply, his expression both tormented and sublime, wanting it never to end and knowing if he didn't let go soon he would die of the sweet agony.

Lisa's cries glittered through the fevered darkness that had claimed Rye, telling him that she was on the other side of ecstasy, calling to him. He wanted to go to her and he wanted to stay where he was, stroking the fever in both of them higher and higher while a darkness shot through with colors swirled around him, a thousand tiny pulses of ecstasy pricking his nerves into full life, shimmering, pressing, demanding.... With a hoarse, broken cry he arched into her until he could go no deeper, and then he surrendered to the sweet violence ripping through his control, demanding to be released.

Rye's last coherent thought was that he had lied; he hadn't known where they were going. Lisa had taken him to a place he had never been before, wrapping him in the velvet fever of her body, burning away his flesh, killing him softly, fiercely, burning with him soul to soul in a shared ecstasy that was death and rebirth combined.

Nine

Lisa sighed and carefully pulled out the tiny stitches she had spent the last hour sewing into the fine linen. She had been thinking about Rye rather than about keeping the proper tension on the thread. As a result, the seam was too tight, bunching the supple fabric. Patiently she smoothed out the cloth with her fingers before running long basting stitches down the length of the seam once more, holding the two pieces together until she could sew the finished seam with much smaller stitches. It had taken her many practice attempts on scraps before she had begun to master the trick of the flat fell seams that she had seen for the first time when she had picked apart Rye's old shirt. The neatness of the seams had fascinated Lisa; not a single raw edge could be seen anywhere on the shirt. She wanted it to be the same for his new shirt, nothing unfinished inside or out.

And that was the way it would be, despite the added work such seams made for Lisa. The additional time to be spent on the shirt didn't register as a problem with her. There was no time in McCall's Meadow, simply the brilliant clarity of summer flying like a banner from every mountain peak. Were it not for the growth of the grasses she photographed faithfully every seven days, she wouldn't have had any idea at all of the passage of time. Summer was a long, sweet interlude punctuated by the sight of Rye riding his powerful black horse into the meadow's radiance.

The thought of grass growing reminded Lisa to check her makeshift calendar. She looked up at the windowsill of the cabin's only window. Six pebbles were lined up. Today would be the seventh. Time to take pictures again. Not only that, but sunlight had begun to creep across the windowpane, which meant that it was after the noon hour. If she didn't get busy, Rye might come riding into the meadow and find her working on his shirt. She didn't want that to happen. She wanted the new shirt to be a complete surprise.

The thought of how much Rye would be pleased by the shirt made Lisa smile. He would be relieved and happy to be able to ask her to Boss McCall's dance at last. There had been many times during the past weeks when he had started to say something to her and then had stopped, as though he weren't certain how to say it. She suspected that he was trying to ask her to the dance, or to explain why he wouldn't be comfortable going there in his worn work clothes. The last time he had started to speak to her only to stop for lack of words, she had tried to tell him that it didn't matter to her whether his clothes were expensive or threadbare, it was enough for her just to be with him, but he hadn't let her finish. He had stopped her words with hungry movements of his tongue, and soon she had forgotten everything but the fever stealing through her body.

Remembering the intensity of Rye's lovemaking caused Lisa's hands to tremble. The slender needle slipped from her fingers. She retrieved it, took a deep breath and decided that it would be better if she didn't work any longer on Rye's shirt. She would probably prick herself and bleed all over the fine, pale fabric.

A horse's snort carried through the clear air, startling Lisa. She came to her feet in a lithe rush, only to see that it was two horses walking up the old wagon road from the valley below rather than one horse alone. Even though one of the horses was dark, she knew that its rider wasn't Rye. When he came to the meadow, he always came alone. While he was in the meadow, no matter how long he stayed, no one else came.

The thought made Lisa freeze for a moment, asking herself why Rye was always solitary. Lassiter usually came with Jim. Sometimes Blaine and Shorty or one of the other cowhands would show up with film or supplies or a hopeful look in the direction of the campfire. Always the cowhands stayed only long enough to eat and check on her before they tipped their hats to her and moved on as though they sensed that somewhere out beyond the rim of the meadow, Rye was waiting impatiently for them to leave.

And Lisa was waiting impatiently for him to arrive.

"Yo, Lisa! You in the cabin?"

"I'll be right out, Lassiter," she called, hurriedly putting the shirt pieces on top of the closet shelf.

"Want me to stoke up the fire?"

"I'd appreciate that. I haven't eaten lunch yet. How about you and Jim?"

"We're always hungry for your bread," Jim called.

Lisa walked quickly out onto the porch, only to stop uncertainly as both men stared at her.

"Is—is something wrong?" she asked.

Lassiter swept off his hat in a gesture curiously like a bow. "Sorry. We didn't mean to stare. You always wear braids on top of your head, and now your hair is all loose and shiny. Lordy, it's something. Eve must have looked like you at the dawn of creation."

Lisa flushed, surprised by Lassiter's open admiration. "Why, thank you." Automatically her hands went to her hair, twisting it into a thick rope that could be coiled on top of her head and held with pieces of polished wood that were rather like chopsticks.

"Don't hide all that glory on our account," Lassiter said.

"I don't have much choice if I'm going to get close to a cooking fire."

"You have a point," he said, replacing his hat, watching sadly as the shimmering, gold-white strands vanished into smooth coils.

"Amen," Jim said. "Long hair and a campfire could put you in a world of hurt. Boss Mac would never forgive us if anything happened to you."

Lisa paused in the act of securing her hair on top of her head. "Boss Mac?"

Lassiter threw Jim a hard look, then turned back to Lisa. "Boss Mac is real particular about the health of the people that work for him. He told us to take special care of you, what with you being up here alone and all, and being such a little bit of a thing."

"Oh." Lisa blinked. "That isn't necessary, but it's very thoughtful of him."

"Beg pardon," Jim said, "but it's real durn necessary. All us cowhands take Boss Mac's words to heart, 'specially that Rye. Why, he must be up here to check on you pretty near every day lately."

Lisa flushed and looked down, missing the glare that Lassiter gave to Jim.

"The boys and me, we figure he might be getting sweet on you," Jim continued, ignoring Lassiter's narrow-eyed look. "That would be a real wonder, him being such a loner and all. Why, I'll bet—"

"Thought you said you were hungry," Lassiter interrupted.

"—we can look forward to seeing you at the dance, can't we," finished Jim, smiling widely.

Lisa sensed that she was being teased again but couldn't guess where the joke lay, unless it was in Jim's delight at seeing a "loner" like Rye asking a woman to the dance.

"Don't count on Rye asking me," she said, forcing herself to smile as she stepped off the porch and walked between the two men. "As you said, he's a loner. Besides, not everyone has extra money for party clothes."

"What do you mean? Boss Mac has enough money to—ow, Lassiter! That's my foot you're tromping on!"

"Doubt it," Lassiter muttered. "You already got both of them in your big mouth."

"What the hell you jawing..." A look of comprehension settled onto Jim's earnest face. "Oh. Well, shoot. What's the point of a joke if'n there's no punch line?"

"The only punch you got to worry about is on the end of Big Mac's fist. Savvy?" Lassiter shot a quick look in Lisa's direction. She was bending over the fire, stirring up the ashes. He bent closer to Jim and said in a low voice, "Listen, hoss. You better stay down the hill until Boss Mac's through with his joke. You spoil his fun and you're going to be looking for some far-off piece of range to ride. What would Betsy think of that, with you two having another little one on the way an' all?"

"Well, *shoot*," Jim said, frustrated. "You hold on to a joke too long and it's no fun a'tall."

"That's Boss Mac's problem. Yours is to keep your trap shut unless it's to shovel in food."

Grumbling beneath his breath, Jim followed Lassiter to the campfire.

Papers were scattered all across Rye's desk. Each one had a small yellow square of sticky paper attached to the much larger white square. The yellow was covered with detailed instructions as to what needed to be done. He squinted down at one of the little sticky squares, discovered that he couldn't decipher his own hurried note and swore. He grabbed a tablet of tiny yellow squares and began to write.

The ballpoint pen had gone dry. Disgusted, he threw it into the metal wastebasket with enough force to leave a dent.

"First thing this fall, I'm going to hire an accountant," he muttered. "I should have done it years ago."

But he hadn't. He had been determined to handle every aspect of ranch business by himself. That way no one could say that Edward Ryan McCall III hadn't earned his own fortune. Unfortunately, bringing the ranch back from the state of near ruin in which he had found it took an enormous amount of time. Never before had it bothered him that running the ranch left him with no time for a private life. The women who had found their way to his door hadn't tempted him away from his work for any longer than it took to satisfy a simple physical urge. Being with his family had held no real allure for him, either; in fact, listening to his father's long-winded lectures on the necessity of continuing the McCall dynasty had been a real deterrent to frequent family visits on Rye's part.

He glared at the papers and wondered if he shouldn't just pick up the telephone and order a bookkeeper the way he would a half ton of oats. Why bother with interviews and checking references and all the other time-consuming things that had prevented him from getting an accountant in the first place? Just pick a name, grab the phone and walk out of the office a few minutes later with the job done. Devil would be looking over the fence right now, waiting impatiently for his rider to appear.

But Rye wouldn't be appearing. If he didn't input into the computer at least some of the paperwork laid out before him, the ranch accounts would be in such a snarl that he would never untangle them—not even this fall, when there would be day after day after day of nothing but ranch work to look forward to.

Frowning, Rye turned his mind away from the end of summer. He never thought of endings when he was in the meadow with Lisa. There, time didn't exist. She had always been there, she always would be there, no past, no future, just the elemental summer that knows no time. Like Lisa. There was a timeless, primal quality to her that was both fascinating and compelling. Perhaps it was her capacity for joy. Perhaps it was simply that she was able to live entirely in the instant, to give her undivided attention to each moment with him. Time as he understood it had no meaning to her. No yesterday, no tomorrow, nothing but the endless, shimmering present.

Yet summer would end. Rye knew it, although when he was with Lisa he didn't believe it. When he wasn't in the meadow, everything looked different. Outside of the meadow, his conscience goaded him for not telling her that he was the owner of McCall's Meadow, not simply a threadbare cowhand with no past and no future. But when Rye reached the meadow, whatever he was or wasn't when he was down the hill simply faded beneath the incandescent light that was Lisa. Whether he lay with his head in her lap while he talked about cattle and men and changing seasons, or whether he lay deep within her and felt her passionate cries piercing his deepest silences, with Lisa he had found a peace that transcended ordinary boundaries of time and place.

That was why his words stuck in his throat and refused to budge when he started to tell her his full name. Each time he was with her, what they shared became more and more valuable, until now it had become so precious that it didn't bear thinking about. If he told her who he was, he would lose something that was beyond price. She would look at him and see Edward Ryan McCall III instead of a cowhand called Rye. The instant she knew who he was, time would flow in its regular channels once more. That would happen soon enough, at the end of summer, when she would leave and the meadow would be empty once more.

And so would he.

That's why I won't tell her. Either way, I lose. Each day that I don't tell her is a day stolen out of time. Summer will end, but it won't end one second before it must.

The phone rang, disturbing Rye's thoughts. As he reached for the receiver he looked at the clock and realized that he had spent the past half hour staring through the papers on his desk and thinking of a meadow and a woman who knew no time. The yearning to be with Lisa twisted suddenly in him like a knife, a pain surprising in its intensity.

To hell with the ranch accounts. I need to be with her. There's so little time left.

The phone rang for the fourth time.

"Hello," Rye said.

"Goodness, what a bark. It's unnerving to know that your bite is even worse."

"Hello, Sis," he said, smiling. Cindy was the only member of his family whose call was always welcome. "How's the latest boyfriend?"

"Funny, Bro. Really funny."

"That fast, huh?"

"Faster. We hadn't even ordered dinner before he led the conversation around to my family. I was using Mother's maiden name at the time, too. There I was, Cinderella Ryan, being wined and—"

"Cinderella?" interrupted Rye, laughing.

"Sure. A name that outrageous has to be real, right?"

"You've got a point."

"I should have used it to stick him to a board with the other insects in my collection," she said glumly. "They're getting smarter, but no more honest."

Rye grunted. He knew that "they" were the fortune hunters of the world. He despised all such people, but he reserved special contempt for the male of the species.

"Come live with me, Cinderella. I'll vet them for you. I can smell a money hunter ten miles away."

"I wish Dad could."

"Is he at it again?"

"In spades."

"Don't tell me. Let me guess," Ryan said. "She's tall, brunette, 42-25-40, and her major talent consists of getting clothes that fit."

"When did you meet her?" Cindy demanded.

"I haven't."

There was silence, then rueful laughter. "Yeah, I guess he's pretty predictable, isn't he?"

"Not surprising. Mother was tall, dark and beautiful. He's still looking for her."

"Then he should add IQ to his list of numbers," Cindy retorted. "Just because you're built doesn't mean that you have the brains of a double cheeseburger with no mustard."

Rye smiled to himself. Cindy was the image of their dead mother—tall, brunette, curvy and very bright.

"Speaking of which," Cindy continued.

"Which what?"

"Good question. When you have an answer, you know my number."

Laughing, Rye kicked back in his office chair and put his cowboy boots on the papers. It occurred to him that Cindy and Lisa would enjoy each other. The thought took the smile off his face, because Cindy would never have the chance to know Lisa.

"...my college roommate. You remember her, don't you? Susan Parker?"

"Huh?" Rye said.

"Ryan, brother dear, monster of my childhood years, this is your wake-up call. *Wake up.* You're having a roundup or hoedown or whatever in a week. A dance. Correct?"

"Correct," he said, smiling.

"I am coming to your ranch in a week," Cindy continued, speaking slowly, clearly, as though her brother were incapable of comprehending English spoken normally. "I am bringing with me a woman called Susan Parker. She went through college with me. We shared a room. After college, she made an obscene amount of money smiling for photographers while wearing the most hideous clothes woman-hating male designers ever fashioned. Are you still with me?"

Rye's inner warning system went into full-alert status. "Beautiful and rich, right?"

"Right."

"Wrong. You're welcome anytime, Cinderella, but leave your matchmaking kit at home."

"Are you saying that my friends aren't welcome at your ranch?"

Rye opened his mouth for a fast retort and then stopped, defeated. "Cindy, you're my favorite sister and—"

"Your only one, too," she interjected.

"Will you zip up?"

"Well, since you asked so nicely, I'll be glad to—"

"Cynthia Edwinna Ryan McCall, if you don't—"

"Shut up," Cindy continued, interrupting, her timing perfect.

Rye sighed. "Cindy. Please. No matchmaking. Okay?"

There was a brief pause, followed by, "You really mean it, don't you?"

"Yes."

"Have you finally found someone?"

Pain turned in Rye again, drawing his mouth into a thin line.

"Ryan?"

"You're welcome to come to the dance. Bring what's her name with you if it makes you happy. I'll even be polite to her. I promise."

"What's she like?"

"Hell, Cindy, she's your friend, not mine. How would I know?"

"No. Not Susan. The one you've found."

Rye closed his eyes and remembered what Lisa had looked like asleep in the meadow, sunlight running through her hair in shimmering bands of pale gold.

"Her name is Woman...and she doesn't exist," Rye said softly. "Not really. She lives outside of time."

There was a long pause before Cindy said, "I don't understand. I don't know whether to be happy for you. You sound...sad."

"Be happy. For a time I've known what it is to be loved for myself alone. She thinks I'm just a cowhand with patched jeans and frayed cuffs and she doesn't give a damn. She treats me as though I've poured diamonds into her hands, and I haven't given her one single thing."

"Except yourself."

Rye closed his eyes. "That's never been enough for other women."

"Or men," Cindy said, her voice low as she remembered her own painful discovery that it was her money, rather than herself, that had attracted the man she had loved. "I'm happy for you, Ryan. However long it lasts, I'm happy for you. I can't wait to meet her."

"Sorry, Sis. It just isn't in the cards."

"Won't she be at the dance? Oh. Of course not. She doesn't know who you are. Damn."

He smiled despite the pain twisting through him. "She wouldn't be able to come even if I were able to ask her. She hasn't the money to buy a decent pocketknife, much less something as useless as a party dress. Patched jeans or silk, it wouldn't matter to me, but I'd cut off my hands rather than make her feel out of place."

"So buy her a dress. Tell her you won the money in a poker game."

"She'd tell me to get a new shirt for myself—and mean it."

"My God. Is she bucking for sainthood?"

Rye thought of the sensual pleasure Lisa took in his body, of the feel of her soft mouth and hot tongue exploring him.

"Sainthood? No way. She's just too practical to spend money on a onetime dress when her man is too poor to buy a new work shirt for himself."

"I want to meet her."

"Sorry. Summer will end soon enough as it is. I love you, Sis, but not enough to shorten my time with her by so much as an hour just to satisfy your curiosity."

Cindy muttered something Rye chose not to hear. Then she sighed. "What does she look like?"

"Lassiter told me a few hours ago that Eve must have looked like that at the dawn of creation."

What Rye didn't add was that he had nearly decked Lassiter for even looking at Lisa.

"Lassiter said that? Holy cow. She must be a real world-burner."

"He was more respectful than lustful."

"Uh-huh. Sure. If you believe that, you better have your IQ recounted, Brother. With Lassiter, lust is a state of being."

"I didn't say he was *only* respectful. It's just that there's a quality of innocence about her that defeats Lassiter's standard approaches."

Cindy laughed. "That I believe. Only a true innocent wouldn't know who you are. Where has she lived all her life—Timbuktu?"

"Among other places."

"Such as?"

"She's a world traveler."

"Jet-setter? Then how come she didn't recognize you?"

"Cindy, I'm not—"

"No fair," she said, interrupting. "You won't tell me what she looks like and you won't tell me her name and you won't tell me where she lives."

"But I did tell you. She lives in a place out of time."

"So where do you meet her?"

"There."

"'In a place out of time.'" Cindy hesitated, then asked wistfully, "What's it like in that place out of time?"

"There are no words...."

For several moments Cindy closed her eyes and simply hung on to the phone, fighting the turmoil of emotions called up by the bittersweet acceptance in her brother's voice.

"My God, Ryan. You should be happy, yet you sound so...bleak."

"Winter is coming, little sister. We're supposed to have a killing frost in the high country before the week is out. Summer will be much too short this year."

"And you'll miss being in your meadow, is that it?" Cindy asked, knowing how much peace Ryan found in the high meadow he had let go back to a wild state.

"Yes. I'll miss being in my meadow." Rye's gray eyes focused suddenly on the peak that rose above McCall's Meadow. "That reminds me. I've got to get a batch of film up there before dark."

"I can take a hint, especially when it's delivered with a sledgehammer. See you next weekend."

"I'll look forward to it," Rye said.

But it was the mountain he was looking toward when he spoke.

He hung up the phone, grabbed the bag of film from the top of a filing cabinet and headed toward the barn with long strides. He had a sense of time unraveling faster and faster, pulling apart the fabric of his unexpected summer happiness. The feeling was so strong that he had a sudden rush of fear.

Something has happened. She's hurt or she found out who I really am. Something is wrong. Something.

The sense of imminent danger goaded Rye all the way up the steep trail. He urged Devil on in a fever of impatience, testing the big horse's agility and endurance. When he burst through the aspen grove at the rear of the cabin, there was no one waiting for him by the campfire. He spurred Devil into the opening of the meadow where the split-rail fence zigzagged gracefully over the land.

From the corner of his eye Rye caught a flash of movement. Lisa was running toward him, an expression of joy on her face. He slid off Devil, took three running steps and caught Lisa up in his arms. His hand moved over her hair, releasing it from its bonds. He buried his face in the flying, silver-gold cloud and held her hard, drinking in her warmth, telling himself that summer would never end.

Ten

Lisa looked at the pebbles on the windowsill. Five. She glanced at the long-legged bay gelding patiently waiting in the aspen grove. The horse had been on loan to her ever since she had bruised her bare foot wading in the stream and had wistfully asked Jim if she could borrow his horse in order to check the meadow fence. After letting her ride for a few moments under their watchful eyes, Lassiter and Jim had been surprised at her skill on horseback. They had also been full of advice on how to treat a bruised foot.

It had been the same when Rye had made an unexpected return trip to the meadow just before sunset that same day, leading the gelding called Nosy. He had watched critically while she rode Nosy, approved her style and told her gruffly that Boss Mac should have thought of giving her a horse to ride sooner. If she needed something, she could ride to the ranch, and if she was hurt and couldn't ride, all she had to do was turn Nosy loose. He would go back to the ranch better than any homing pigeon.

Lisa's glance went from the pebbles to the angle of the sunlight slanting through the windowsill. It was at least two o'clock.

He's not coming back again today and you know it, she told herself silently. *He said that Boss McCall was keeping everyone hopping getting ready for the dance.*

Rye had ridden up to the meadow that morning, coming to her with the dawn, teasing her from sleep into sensual wakefulness with a tender persistence that had made her shiver with the fever stirring in her blood. He had made love to her as though she were a virgin once more, caressing her until she was flushed with passion, then beginning all over, stroking her body until she was wild—and then he had begun yet again, loving her with his mouth instead of his hands, teaching her of a honeyed intimacy that stripped the world away, leaving only the velvet fever of her body and his intertwined.

The memory of Rye's hot, unbearably knowing mouth loving her made Lisa's hands shake. He had made her feel like a goddess worshiped by a sensual god, and when she thought she could bear no more, he had come to her, teaching her that there was no end to ecstasy, simply beginnings.

With trembling hands, Lisa reached for the brown paper shopping bag that she had set out by the door. She had almost given Rye the shirt that morning, when dawn had turned his skin a rich gold and made his eyes incandescent with pleasure. But she had wanted the shirt to be perfect, and she hadn't had time yet to master completely the old flatiron she had found in the cabin's only closet—along with a rusted Spanish spade bit, a broken hammer and a handful of square nails that had to be older than the flatiron itself. Cleaning and using the ancient, heavy iron had tested her patience and ingenuity to their limits, but it had been worth it. The shirt was beautifully smooth now, and the cloth shimmered as though it were alive.

For the tenth time Lisa assured herself that Boss Mac wouldn't be angry if she used his horse for a nonemergency trip to the ranch. The meadow wouldn't be hurt by her absence. All her photos and logbooks were caught up. Surely Boss Mac would understand....

Quit stalling, she told herself firmly. *Rye said that he wouldn't be able to come to the meadow for a few days, and the dance is the day after tomorrow. If I don't give him the shirt today, he won't be able to ask me to the dance at all.*

Lisa took a deep breath, picked up the paper bag and went out to saddle Boss Mac's horse.

Rye cursed the walleyed cow in terms that would have made a rock blush. The cow, however, was not a rock. She was a cow, which was something entirely different. Compared to a cow, a rock was intelligent.

"Boss Mac? You in there?" Lassiter yelled.

"Where the hell else have I been for the last hour?" Rye snarled, unhappy at being interrupted yet again. He had put off so many things since he had become Lisa's lover that the men were after him every ten minutes to make a decision on something that should have been settled weeks ago.

"You still doctoring that fool cow?" Lassiter asked.

"Hell, no. I'm making a damn paper doily."

Lassiter looked over the stall just as the cow's long, ropy, far-from-clean tail swished across Rye's face with deadly accuracy. The cowhand listened with real respect while Rye described the cow's ancestry, personal habits, probable IQ and certain resting place after death in searing, scatological detail. Meanwhile Rye continued swabbing antibiotic on the many cuts that the old cow had received when she had stubbornly tried to walk through a barbwire fence. And tried, and tried and then tried again.

"She sure did take a notion to leave that pasture, didn't she?" Lassiter observed.

Rye grunted and made another pass with the dripping swab. "You want something from me or are you just exercising your jaw?"

"Your sister just called," Lassiter said quickly. "Your pa's coming with her to the party, unless there's a meeting and he misses the early plane. If that happens, you'll have to pick him up in the city. He's bringing a pack of his friends. 'Bout eight, near as I can tell. Miss Cindy tried to talk him out of it. Didn't work, I reckon. Like death an' taxes, he's coming."

Eyes closed, jaw clenched, Rye controlled the impulse to take a swing at the bearer of bad news.

"Wonderful," Rye said through his teeth. "Just wonderful." Then he had a thought that made his lips twitch into a reluctant smile. "I can just see his latest glitter baby's face when she realizes that the dance floor is the bottom of a barn and the band isn't plugged into anything but two hundred years of tradition."

Quietly Lassiter let out the breath that he had been holding and smiled. "Yeah, that should be worth seeing. How long has it been since your pa came up here?"

"Ten years."

"Been a few changes since then."

"Dirt is still dirt, and fresh cow pies still stick to your boots."

"Boss, those things ain't never gonna change."

Rye took a last pass at the cow's right side, then moved to her left.

"The way she's cut up, it'd be easier just to finish the job and barbecue the old she-devil," Lassiter offered.

"We'd wear out our teeth on her."

Lassiter grinned. He knew that Rye had a sentimental attachment to the walleyed cow. She had been the first cow to calve after he had bought the ranch. She had had twins nearly every year after that, healthy calves every one. Ugly as she was, Rye called her his good-luck charm.

"I've got a call into Doc Long," Rye continued. "When he's through stitching up the Nelsons' crazy quarter horse, he'll come here."

"Did that old stud go through the fence again?"

"Nope. Barn wall."

"Lordy. That's one determined stud."

"Some damn fool tied a mare in heat just outside."

Lassiter laughed softly.

Beyond the big, open doors of the barn, someone began hollering for Boss Mac.

"Go see what he wants," Rye said, ducking another swipe of the cow's tail.

Lassiter left and came back within minutes. "Shorty wants to know how deep to dig the barbecue pit."

"What? He's from Texas, for God's sake!"

"Oklahoma. Stockbroker's son. Shaping up into a real good hand, though. Better with horses than anyone except Jim."

Rye sighed. "Tell Shorty to make the hole big enough to bury a steer."

Shaking his head, Rye went back to working over the tattered old cow. He was interrupted six more times before he finished going over the cuts. Between getting normal ranch work done and getting everything lined up for the dance, it seemed that no one could do without Boss Mac's guidance for more than ten minutes at a stretch.

Finally Rye straightened, stretched the kinks out of his back and went to the huge porcelain sink he had installed when he had built the barn. He sluiced off the worst of the dirt and spilled medicine, stretched his aching back again and thought longingly of Lisa up in the high meadow. But no matter how many times he rearranged what had to be done in his mind, he couldn't find the hours to ride to the meadow and hold Lisa once more.

Suddenly, savagely, he cursed the work that prevented him from being with her. He was still scowling blackly when he stalked back down the line of stalls to take a last look at the old cow. He discovered that in his absence she had left a present for him. Muttering beneath his breath, he grabbed a manure fork, not wanting to risk any more infection in the old cow's cuts.

"Rye? Are you in here?"

At first Rye thought he was dreaming. He spun around and saw her standing on tiptoe in the broad center aisle, peering into various stalls.

"*Lisa*. What the hell are you doing here?"

She turned quickly at the sound of Rye's voice. The smile she had on her face faded into uncertainty when she saw his expression. As he shut the stall door behind him and walked toward her, Lisa's fingers tightened even harder on the paper bag she was carrying.

"I know how busy you are and I don't want to get you in trouble with Boss Mac," Lisa said hurriedly. "It's just that I had something for you and I wanted to give it to you and so I rode down the hill and—" she thrust the bag into Rye's hands "—here it is."

For an instant Rye was too stunned to do more than stare at Lisa. Into the spreading silence came Jim's clear voice shouting across the barnyard.

"Boss Mac? Yo, Boss Mac? You around?"

"In here!" Rye shouted, answering reflexively.

Lisa's eyes widened. No wonder Rye seemed so shocked to see her. Boss Mac was close by and she was interrupting Rye's work. She had heard enough about Boss Mac's temper not to want to make Rye the target of it. She looked around frantically, wondering where Boss Mac was.

"Shorty wants to know how deep the bed of coals should be laid an' Devil just threw a shoe an' Lassiter told me to tell you that Doc Long has to check on a mare with colic before he can sew up your durn fool walleyed cow," Jim said as he entered the barn. The change from bright sunlight to the muted interior illumination made him blink. "Where the blazes... Oh, there you are. Shorty swears he saw that bay gelding you gave to Lisa tied behind the barn. You want me to check?"

"No," Rye said curtly.

"You sure? If'n Nosy threw her or..." Jim's voice trailed off into silence as his vision cleared and he saw Lisa standing just beyond Rye. "Oh, Lordy, Lordy. Me and my big mouth. I sure am sorry, Boss Mac."

Lisa didn't hear Rye's response. She was still paralyzed in the first shock of discovery.

"You're..." Her voice dried up. She swallowed convulsively as she looked at Rye's tight, bleak expression. "Boss Mac."

"Yes," he said, and his voice was as hard as his face.

Lisa stared at Rye, trying to order her chaotic thoughts. "I..." She made a small, helpless gesture with her hand when her voice failed her again.

"I'm sorry, Boss Mac," Jim mumbled. "I sure didn't mean to spoil your joke."

Jim might as well not have spoken. Rye stood motionless, his attention focused solely on Lisa as he waited for calculation to replace passion in her eyes when she looked at him.

All trace of blood left Lisa's face as Jim's apology to Rye sank through her paralysis.

I sure didn't mean to spoil your joke.

She didn't notice the cowhand's rapid, silent retreat from the barn, for she had suddenly remembered the first words Rye had ever spoken to her: *You're something else, little girl. If you'll settle for a diamond bracelet instead of a diamond ring, we'll get along fine for a while.*

Now, too late, she knew what that "something else" was. A fool.

Rye had warned her in the clearest possible words that he wanted only one thing from her, but she hadn't listened. She had taken her loneliness and nameless yearning and she had created a beautiful dream: a poor cowhand called Rye.

I sure didn't mean to spoil your joke.

Jim's words echoed and reechoed in Lisa's mind, haunting her.

A joke, joke, just a joke...all of it, from the first instant, a joke. Rye was Boss Mac, the wealthy womanizer, the man who wouldn't settle down and provide his father with an heir. Boss Mac, who came from so much money that no one in his family bothered to count it anymore. Like his women. No one bothered to count them, either.

Lisa's amethyst eyes went to the brown paper bag that held the shirt she had made for Rye. She could imagine what he would think of clothing made under the most primitive circumstances, clothing that had all the myriad flaws of handwork. The shirt's stitches weren't perfectly even; there were no two buttonholes precisely the same size; the finished shirt had been pressed by an antique flatiron heated on a stone hearth. And the buttons themselves were appallingly unsophisticated.

Color returned in a flaming wave to Lisa's face when she thought of the buttons, no two alike, carved from antler and rudely polished by hand. She looked at Rye with stricken eyes, trying to find words to explain that she had meant well, she just hadn't known who he was or she never would have presumed...

Another realization came to Lisa in a wave of color that surged and faded as quickly as her heartbeat.

No wonder Rye didn't ask me to the dance. He isn't just one of the cowhands. He's the owner of the Rocking M. Whoever comes to the dance with him won't be a girl who has no money, no formal education, and social graces learned around primitive campfires.

What a joke. On me. Definitely on me.

Wild laughter clawed at Lisa's throat, but she had just enough self-control not to give in. She knew with certain humiliation that if she did, the laughter would soon turn into a raw sound of pain. That wouldn't do. She was in civilization now, where people masked their emotions. That was a social grace she simply had to learn. Immediately. Now. This instant.

And then Lisa realized that she couldn't smile and congratulate Rye on his droll Western foolery. She simply wasn't that sophisticated. She never would be. She was like the meadow—open to both sunlight and rain, lacking protection, a haven with no barriers.

That was what she needed right now. The meadow's generous, uncalculated warmth.

Lisa turned and ran until she found herself in the blinding sunlight outside the barn. She raced toward Nosy and mounted with the wild grace of someone who had been raised riding bareback. The horse spun on its hocks in answer to the urgency of its rider, but a powerful hand clamped onto the reins just below the bit, forcing the animal to stay in place.

"Whoa, boy! Easy, there. Easy," Rye said, bracing himself against the horse's attempts to free itself. When Nosy snorted and settled down, Rye looked up at Lisa but did not release the reins.

The first thing Rye saw was her unnaturally pale skin, her face drawn into taut lines. Her expression was that of someone who had been struck without warning and was searching for a way to avoid further blows. She was looking away from him, toward the peak that rose above McCall's Meadow, and her body fairly vibrated with her urgency to flee. He knew without asking that she was longing for the meadow's timeless summer, its silence and peace. He longed for the meadow, too. But it was gone now, yanked from his grasp by a cowhand who couldn't keep his mouth shut.

Rye hissed a single, vicious word. Lisa flinched and tried to rein the gelding away from him. It didn't work. Rye's fingers were immovable.

"I tried to tell you a hundred times," he said harshly.

Lisa tugged futilely on the reins. There was no give. She realized that she wasn't going to get to the meadow's gentle embrace without first confronting Rye. Grimly she clung to what remained of her self-control.

"But you didn't tell me," she said, watching the meadow rather than Rye. She tried to smile. It didn't work. "Telling me would have spoiled the joke. I understand that. Now."

"Not telling you didn't have a damn thing to do with a joke. Not after we became lovers."

Rye saw Lisa flinch at the word *lovers*, saw the hot flush of embarrassment rising up her skin. She looked vulnerable, defenseless. Innocent. But she wasn't. He had taken that innocence from her. No. She had given it to him, hadn't she?

She gave it to a cowhand called Rye. But I'm Boss Mac. Why didn't I tell her?

Swearing at himself and the world, his temper slipping away word by hot word, Rye ducked under the horse's neck without releasing the reins and forced Lisa to face him.

"I don't know why I'm feeling so damned guilty," he snarled. "I had a good reason for not telling you who I was!"

"Yes, of course," she said politely, her tone uninflected, her eyes fixed over Rye's head on the peak that rose above the meadow. She pulled discreetly on the reins. Nothing moved. "May I go now or do you want your horse back?"

Lisa's careful, polite words had the effect of adding a torch to the spilled gasoline of Rye's temper.

"You know why I didn't tell you, so don't play innocent!" he said angrily, clenching Nosy's reins in one hand and the forgotten paper bag in the other.

"Yes. Your joke."

"It wasn't a joke and you damn well know it! I didn't tell you who I was because I didn't want you to look at me with dollar signs rather than desire in your eyes! Why the hell should I feel guilty about that? And before you answer, you better know one more thing. I know that you came to America because you wanted to find a husband who could either live like your parents or had enough money so that you wouldn't have to adjust to clocks and a forty-hour work week."

Lisa's expression became more confused with each of Rye's words. Seeing that didn't improve his temper.

"You weren't raised to live in the real world and you know it," he said roughly. "Tribal time just doesn't fit in twentieth-century America. So you went head-hunting a rich man or an anthropologist and you ended up giving yourself to me despite the fact that I was poor and sure as hell wasn't bent on studying Stone Age natives. I took what you offered and never promised you one damn thing in the way of marriage or anything else. So you can just drop the wounded-innocent routine. You knew that summer would end and so did I, and then you would ride down the hill into the arms of that jackass anthropologist Ted Thompson has all picked out for you."

Rye didn't ask himself why even thinking about the unknown man waiting for Lisa made his own body tighten in a killing rage. He didn't ask himself about the meaning of anything that he was feeling—he was too angry at sensing summer slip through his clenched fists as irretrievably as sunlight sliding into night. He needed Lisa's sweet fire and shimmering warmth. He needed it as much as he needed air; and he was fighting for it in just the same way as he would fight for air, no holds barred, no quarter given, no questions asked or answered, nothing of softness in him.

And he was losing anyway. Losing her. He had known he would, but he hadn't known it would come this soon and hurt this much. The pain enraged him, and the loss.

He felt the reins being tugged slowly from his clenched hand.

"No!" he snarled, tightening his grip. "Talk to me, damn it! Don't just ride out of here like I don't exist!"

The demand penetrated Lisa's single-minded determination to escape. For the first time she looked directly at Rye.

He had expected to see calculation and money dreams in her eyes. He saw nothing but the same darkness that he felt expanding through his own soul. Pain and loss and grief, but not anger.

The lack of anger baffled Rye until Lisa began to speak. The very care with which she chose her words, the ruthless neutrality of her voice, the slow trembling of her body—each told him that she was stretched almost beyond endurance. She wasn't angry because she couldn't afford to be without losing all control over herself.

"I don't know anything about an anthropologist, jack-ass or otherwise," Lisa said. "My parents sent me here to find a husband, but that's not why I came. I wanted to find out who and what I am. I didn't fit into any of the cultures I grew up in. I was always the white, skinny outsider, too aware of other traditions, other gods, other ways to live. I thought I must belong here, in America, where people come in all colors and traditions are something families invent as they go along. I was wrong. I don't belong here. I'm too...poor."

"That doesn't say anything about us, about you and me," Rye countered coolly.

Lisa closed her eyes as pain twisted through her, leaving her shaken. "What do you mean?"

"You're hurt and upset because I fooled you, and right now I'm mad as hell at everyone involved, including myself. But underneath it all nothing has changed between us. I look at you and I want you so bad I can hardly stand up. You look at me and it's the same. We're a fever in each other's blood. That hasn't changed."

Lisa looked at Rye, at the hard line of his mouth and the blazing gray of his eyes, and knew that he was right. Even now, with anger and pain churning inside her, she could look at him and want him until she was dizzy with it.

Fever.

Rye saw the answering desire in Lisa's eyes and felt as though the claws that had been twisting in his guts were being slowly withdrawn. The end of summer would come...but not today. Not this instant. He could breathe again. He let out a long, harsh breath and released the reins, transferring his hand to the worn softness of the fabric stretched across Lisa's thigh.

"There's one good thing to come out of this mess," he said roughly. "Now that you know who I am, there's no reason you can't come to the dance."

As soon as Rye mentioned the dance, Lisa remembered the wretched shirt concealed within the bag he still held. Suddenly she knew that she could survive anything but him looking at that shirt and seeing all of her shortcomings so painfully revealed.

"Thank you, that's very kind of you," Lisa said quickly, "but I don't know how to dance."

She smiled at him, silently pleading that he understand that it wasn't anger or pride which made her refuse. She was out of place down here, and she knew it.

But Rye wasn't in an understanding mood.

From the front of the barn came Lassiter's voice calling for Boss Mac. Rye swore viciously under his breath.

"I'll teach you how to dance," he said flatly.

She shook her head slowly, unable to speak.

"Yes," he countered.

"Yo! Boss Mac! You in the barn?" yelled Lassiter, his voice fading as he went into the barn. "You got a call from Houston waiting on..."

"You'd better go," Lisa said, gently pulling on the reins again.

Rye lifted his hand from her thigh and held on to the reins. "Not until you agree to come to the dance."

"Boss Mac? Yo! Boss Mac! Where in hell are you!"

"I don't think that would be a good idea," Lisa said hurriedly. "I really don't know anything about American customs or—"

"Shove customs," Rye snarled. "I'm asking you to a dance, not to take notes about quaint native practices!"

"Boss Mac! Yo!"

"I'm coming, damn it!"

The horse shied nervously at Rye's bellow. He simply clamped down harder on the reins and glared up at Lisa.

"You're coming to the dance," he said flatly. "If you don't have a party dress, I'll get you one."

"No," she said quickly, remembering all too well his comment about giving her a diamond bracelet if she pleased him. "No dress. No diamond bracelet. Nothing. I have everything I need."

Rye started to argue, but a single look at Lisa's pale, set expression told him that it would be useless.

"Fine," he said in a taut voice. "Wear your damn jeans. It doesn't matter to me. If you don't want to dance we'll just listen to the music. That doesn't require anything but ears, and you damn well have two of them. I won't have time to come up to the cabin and get you. I've spent too many hours away from here in the past weeks. If I don't get to work, there won't *be* a dance—or a ranch, either, for that matter."

Lisa smiled sadly as she saw Lassiter approaching from one direction and Jim coming at a trot from another, men descending on Rye like flies on honey. The thought of how much time he had stolen from his work to be with her was both soothing and disturbing. Rye might have had that kind of time to spare; Boss Mac obviously did not.

"I'll send Lassiter for you tomorrow afternoon," Rye said. "Early."

Hesitantly, knowing that it was a mistake, Lisa nodded her head. She could no more resist seeing Rye again than water could resist running downhill.

Relief swept through Rye, an emotion so powerful that he nearly sagged beneath its weight. He looked up searchingly at Lisa, trying to see beyond the shadows in her eyes to the warmth and laughter that had always been beneath.

"Baby?" he said softly, tracing Lisa's thigh with his knuckles while he held on to the paper bag. "I'm sorry that I didn't tell you sooner. I just didn't want things to... change."

Lisa nodded again and touched Rye's hand lightly. When one of his fingers reached to curl around her own, she removed the paper bag from his grip, squeezed his hand and simultaneously tugged on the reins, freeing them from his grasp. By the time he realized that the bag was in her hands, Nosy had backed up beyond his reach.

"Lisa?"

She looked at him, her face pale, her eyes so dark that no color showed.

"Didn't you ride all the way down the hill to give me that bag?"

She shook her head and tried to make her voice light. "This was for a cowboy called Rye. He lives in the meadow. Boss Mac lives down here."

Rye felt the cold claws sliding into his guts once more. "Rye and Boss Mac are the same man."

Lisa reined the horse toward the mountains without answering.

"Lisa?" Rye called. "Lisa! What did you want to give me?"

The answer came back to him, carried on the wind sweeping down from the high peaks.

"Nothing you need...."

Rye stood for a long time, hearing the words echo in his mind. He sensed something sliding through his grasp, something retreating from him. He told himself that he was being foolish; Lisa had been shocked and hurt and she had taken back whatever present she had intended to give him, but she was coming to the dance with him. He would see her again. Summer hadn't ended yet.

Nothing you need....

Suddenly he sensed an abyss opening beneath the casual words, a feeling that he had lost something he could not name.

"Nothing has changed," he told himself fiercely. "She still wants me and there's no money attached to it. Nothing has changed!"

But he didn't believe that, either.

Eleven

The morning of the dance, Lisa awoke to an unearthly landscape of glittering diamond dust and a sky of radiant sapphire. Aspen leaves shivered in brilliant shades of citrine that made nearby evergreens appear almost black by contrast. Lisa's breath was a silver cloud and the air itself was so cold and pure that it shone as though polished. She stood in the cabin's open door and drank the meadow's beauty until her own shivering could no longer be ignored.

Only once did she think of Rye, who was Boss Mac, who was not Rye.

No. Don't think about it. There's nothing I can do to change what happened any more than I can run back through the night into yesterday's warmth. I have to be like the aspens. They would love to have the sweet fever of summer forever, yet they aren't angry at its end. They save their greatest beauty for the final, bittersweet moments of their summer affair.

And so will I. Somehow.

The jeans that Lisa pulled on were stiff with cold and patched in as many colors as the morning itself. She finished dressing quickly in a T-shirt, blouse, sweatshirt, windshell, socks and shoes, all but emptying out the closet.

Outside, the sunlight was so bright that the campfire's flames were invisible but for the subtle distortion of the heat waves rising into the intense blue of the sky. The coffee smelled like heaven and tasted even better as it spread through Lisa's chilled body. The contrast between cold and heat, frost and fire, heightened all her senses. Suspended like the aspens between the season of fire and the coming of ice, she watched in rapt silence while frost crystals sparkled and vanished as shade retreated across the meadow before the still-powerful sun.

When the final gleaming hints of frost had gone and all the plants were dry, Lisa slipped through the meadow fence with the camera in her hand. It would be the last time she recorded the height of plants against their numbered stakes, for the frost had been as hard as it had been beautiful; it had brought the end of growth in its glittering wake.

The meadow had not been taken by surprise. It had been preparing for that diamond-bright morning since the first tender shoots of new growth had unfurled beneath melting spring snow months before. The feverish rush of summer had already come to fruition. Grasses nodded and bowed to each passing breeze, their plumed, graceful heads heavy with the seeds of the next summer's growth. Beyond the grasses, aspens trembled and burned, their leaves such a pure, vivid yellow that Lisa could not bear to look at it without narrowing her eyes.

She moved through the meadow with the silence and ease of a wild thing. Her hands were light, quick and sure as she cut seed heads from grasses, taking only what Dr. Thompson needed from each plant and leaving the rest for the meadow and its creatures. Back at the cabin she sorted the numbered collection bags and set them aside. She pasted the pictures she had just taken into the log, entered the necessary comments and put the notebook aside, as well.

The angle of the sunlight and Lisa's growling stomach told her that it was past noon. The realization yanked her from the tribal time into which she had retreated, letting its slow, elemental rhythms soothe the turmoil inside her. She ate a cold lunch while she heated water for washing her hair. Long before the smoke-blackened bucket began to steam, she heard hoofbeats. Her heart beat wildly, but when she turned around it was only Lassiter.

What did I expect? Rye—Boss Mac—said he would send Lassiter, and that's just what he did.

"Hello," Lisa said, smiling through stiff lips. "Have you eaten lunch?"

"Afraid so," Lassiter said regretfully. "Boss Mac didn't want me to fool around up here before I brought you down the hill. Then just as I was leaving his pa called. The boss had to drive all the way into the city to pick him up. I'll tell you true, Miss Lisa, by the time Boss Mac gets back this evening, he'll be in a temper that would shame a broken-toothed grizzly."

"I see. Well, pour yourself a cup of coffee anyway while I get some things from the cabin. I won't tell Boss Mac we took a few extra minutes of his time if you won't."

Lassiter swung down from his horse and walked toward Lisa. His eyes searched her face. "You feeling okay?"

"I'm fine, thank you. And no, I didn't cut myself or sprain anything, and I don't need supplies or film from down the hill," she added, forcing herself to smile as she went through the familiar list.

Lassiter smiled in return, even though his question hadn't been meant as part of the quiz Boss Mac administered to any cowhand who had seen Lisa. Lassiter watched Lisa closely while she put out the small campfire with a thoroughness that spoke of long practice. He sensed something different about her, but he couldn't decide just what it was.

"I see you got a good frost last night," he said finally, looking from the blazing yellow aspens to the deceptively green meadow.

"Yes," Lisa said.

"It will stay hot for a few days more, though."

"Will it? How can you tell?"

"The wind shifted late this morning. It's from the south now. Guess we're going to have an Indian summer."

"What's that?" Lisa asked.

"Sort of a grace period between the first killing frost and the beginning of real cold. All the blessings of summer and no bugs."

Lisa looked toward the aspens. "False summer," she murmured, "and all the sweeter for it. The aspens know. They're wearing their brightest smiles."

She ran quickly to the cabin and emerged a few moments later carrying her backpack, her braided hair hidden beneath a bright scarf tied at the nape of her neck. Lassiter had saddled and bridled Nosy for her while she was in the cabin. As he handed over the reins, he looked at Lisa and realized what had been missing. There was no laughter in her today, but yesterday laughter had been as much a part of Lisa as her matchless violet eyes.

"He didn't mean no harm," Lassiter said quietly.

She turned toward him, confused, for her mind had been with the transformed aspen leaves burning like thousands of candle flames against the intense blue of the autumn sky.

"Boss Mac," Lassiter explained. "Oh, he's got a temper on him sure enough, and he won't back up for man nor beast, but he's not small-minded or vicious. He didn't mean for his joke to hurt you."

Lisa smiled very carefully, very brightly, her eyes reflecting the blazing meadow aspens. "I'm sure he didn't. If I haven't laughed in all the right places, don't worry. I just don't understand all the fine points of Western humor yet."

"You're sweet on him, aren't you?" Lassiter said quietly.

Her face became expressionless. "Boss Mac?"

Lassiter nodded.

"No," she said, reining the gelding toward the wagon trail. "I was 'sweet on' a cowhand called Rye."

For a moment Lassiter simply stood with his mouth open, staring at Lisa as she rode away. Then he mounted quickly and followed her out of the meadow. All the way down to the ranch he was careful to keep the conversation on Jim's teething baby, Shorty's barbecue pit and the walleyed cow that had more stitches in her hide than a pair of hand-tooled boots. Though Lisa still smiled far too little to suit Lassiter, she was more like herself by the end of the ride, and if sometimes her smile didn't match the shadows in her eyes, he saw no need to make an issue out of it.

When Lisa and Lassiter rode into the yard, there were expensive cars parked every which way, their paint gleaming like colored water beneath a coating of dust from the rough ranch road. There were battered pickups from nearby ranches, plus several strange horses in the corral. A big, candy-striped awning stretched down one side of the barn, protecting long tables from the afternoon thundershowers that often rumbled down from the mountain peaks. People shouted greetings and called to one another as they carried huge, covered dishes from their cars to the ranch kitchen. Everyone seemed to know everyone else.

A familiar feeling came back to Lisa, a combination of wistfulness and uneasiness that came from being the one who didn't belong at the gathering of clans. Welcome—yes. But a member of the tribe? No.

"Well, I see the Leighton kids came in over High Pass the way they used to 'fore the state highway come through," Lassiter said.

Lisa followed his glance to the corral, where three strange horses lipped hay from a small mound that had been dropped over the rails. "High Pass?"

"The trail you asked about just before we crossed the first stream and after Boss Mac's shortcut comes into the wagon road. The trail goes out over the mountain to the Leighton place. From there it's only a mile or two into town." Lassiter scanned the parked vehicles again and swore beneath his breath. "I don't see Boss Mac's pickup. That means his pa missed the early plane. Hellfire and damnation," Lassiter said, sighing and pulling his hat into place with a sharp motion of his hand. "The boss will be chewing nails and spitting tacks, no two ways about it. C'mon, let's get you settled so he won't have that to jaw at me about."

"Settled?"

"Boss Mac said for you to put your gear in his room." Lassiter spoke casually, looking anywhere but at the sudden rush of color on Lisa's face. "It's the big one just off the living room. His sister and her friend and his pa and his friends will take over the rest of the place," Lassiter continued hurriedly, "so there wasn't much choice."

"No problem," Lisa said tightly. "I won't be staying the night, so I'll need the room only long enough to wash up and change clothes."

"But Boss Mac said—"

"Shall I put Nosy in the corral or the pasture?" Lisa interrupted, her words crisp.

The thought that Rye—no, not Rye, *Boss Mac*—had assumed that she would calmly move into his bedroom infuriated Lisa. For the first time since she had discovered who Rye really was, she felt not only sad and foolish but insulted, as well. She could accept the end of summer without real anger, for living among various tribes had taught her that the passage of seasons was as inevitable as the progression from light to dark and back to light again.

But she could not accept becoming the latest of Boss Mac's women.

"I'll put Nosy in the barn," Lassiter said, watching Lisa warily, seeing the anger that had replaced the first flush of humiliation. "He could use some oats after being on grass for the last few weeks."

"Thank you," she said, dismounting. "Will you leave the tack on the stall door?"

"He told me to put it away. He told me you wouldn't be needing it anymore, or the horse, neither." Lassiter cleared his throat and added uncomfortably, "It's pretty plain that Boss Mac expects you to stay here."

"In his bedroom?" Lisa inquired, raising one platinum eyebrow in an elegant arc. "With him? That's not very likely, is it? I just met the man yesterday. He must have me confused with one of his other women."

Lassiter opened his mouth, closed it and smiled reluctantly. "He didn't say nothing about where *he* was planning to sleep. Just where he was planning for *you* to sleep. He's never had a woman here overnight. Not once."

"Good heavens. I certainly wouldn't want to spoil his spotless record. Especially on such short acquaintance."

Slowly Lassiter's smile dissolved into laughter. He leaned over the saddle horn and looked at Lisa admiringly. "Guess you're gonna get some of your own back, huh?"

"I'm going to what?"

"Get even," he said succinctly.

The idea hadn't occurred to Lisa in just those terms. Once it had, the temptation was very real. Then she thought of the aspens burning silently, each yellow leaf a proclamation both of the summer's bounty and the end of heat. She had no more chance to beat Rye at his own game than the aspens had of staying green through winter.

Lisa dismounted, resettled her backpack and went into the house as Lassiter led Nosy away. Even to her uncritical eye, the ranch house's furnishings were Spartan, with the exception of the office. There was nothing spare, worn or second-rate about the computer, just as there was nothing cheap about the cattle, the horses or the wages of the men who worked for Boss Mac.

I wonder what he pays his women?

The answer to that unhappy thought came as quickly as the question had.

Diamond bracelets, of course.

There was no doubt as to which bedroom was Rye's. It was the only one with a bed big enough for him. Attached to the bedroom was a bathroom with an oversized shower. Lisa shot the bolt of the bedroom door behind her. She removed the length of amethyst cloth from her backpack, shook out the long piece of linen and hung it over a hanger in the bathroom. She took a long, luxuriant shower, relishing every hot drop of water, feeling like a queen in a palace bath. When she finally emerged from the shower, the steam had removed most of the wrinkles in the linen. The rest succumbed to the small iron she found in Rye's closet.

After a few tries she got the knack of the bright pink blow-dryer that had been left out on the bathroom counter. She couldn't imagine Rye using the device any more than she could imagine him using the scented soap and shampoo that had been in the shower. She almost hadn't used them herself, because the bottles had been unopened.

Maybe Rye brought women here more often than Lassiter thought.

Unhappily Lisa brushed her hair until it was a fragrant, silver-gold cloud clinging to everything it touched. She outlined her eyes in the manner of Middle Eastern women since the dawn of time. Mascara made her long amber lashes as dark as the center of her eyes. She colored her lips from the glossy contents of a fragrant wooden pot no bigger than her thumb. The scent she used was a mixture of rose petals and musk that was as ancient in cosmetic lineage as the kohl lining her eyes.

She gathered the silky wildness of her hair and wove it into a gleaming, intricate mass, which she secured on top of her head with two long ebony picks. The picks were inlaid with iridescent bits of seashell, as were the six ebony bracelets she put on her left wrist. Slipper-shoes of glittery black went from the backpack to her feet. She picked up the rich amethyst strip of linen and began winding it around herself in the manner of an Indian sari. The last four feet of the radiant cloth formed a loose covering over her hair and made her eyes look like huge amethyst gems set in skin as fine grained and luminous as pearl.

"Lisa? Are you in there? Open up. I have to take a shower and Cindy's camped in the other bathroom."

Lisa jumped at the unexpected sound of Rye's voice. Her heart went wild.

That can't be Rye. It's too soon.

A quick glance out the bedroom window told Lisa that the afternoon had indeed slipped away. She started toward the bedroom door, only to stop as her hand touched the bolt. She wasn't ready to face Rye and smile as brightly as the meadow aspens. She wasn't sure that she would ever be that brave.

"Lisa? I know you're in there. Open the damned door!" Before she could speak, Lassiter's familiar cry rang through the house.

"Boss Mac? Yo, Boss Mac! You in the house? Blaine says that walleyed cow is chewing out her stitches. You want to call the doc again or you want to sew up the old she-devil yourself?"

What Rye said in response convinced Lisa that Lassiter had been correct; right now Rye was in a mood to give a sore-toothed bear lessons in how to be obnoxious. She heard his boot heels punctuate every one of his strides between the bedroom and the front door. When the sound of his swearing faded, she peeked out, saw no one and hurriedly left the bedroom. As she rounded the corner into the living room, she nearly ran into a tall, slender woman who had hair the color of freshly ground cinnamon, the carriage of a queen or a model—and a very expensive diamond bracelet on her elegant wrist.

"My God," the woman said, staring at Lisa. "Since when did Ryan start keeping a harem?"

"Ryan?"

"McCall. As in Edward Ryan McCall the third, owner of this ranch and a few million other odds and ends."

"Oh. Another name. Wonderful. Good question about the harem," Lisa said, giving the word its Middle Eastern pronunciation—har*eem*. "I'll bet he has the answer. Why don't you ask him the next time he buys you a diamond bracelet?"

"Excuse me?"

"There you are, Susan," said another woman. "I thought I'd lost you to that silver-haired, silver-tongued devil."

Lisa turned and saw a tall, young, beautifully curved woman walking in from the front porch. Her skin was flawless, her eyes were like clear black crystal, and she was wearing a red silk jumpsuit that had Paris sewn into every expensive seam.

"My God," Lisa said, unconsciously echoing Susan. "He does have a harem?"

"Lassiter?" asked the black-eyed beauty. "Why, yes, I'm afraid so. But we forgive him. After all, there's only one of him and so many, many needy women."

"Not Lassiter—Rye. Ryan. Boss Mac. Edward Ryan McCall the third," Lisa said.

"You left out Cindy's brother," said the brunette dryly.

"Who?"

"Cindy," Susan said, smiling, "introduce yourself to this little houri before she stabs you with one of those elegant ebony hair picks. Where did you get them, by the way?"

"In the Sudan, but they were trade items, not a local craft," Lisa said absently, not taking her eyes from the tall brunette. Next to her and Susan, Lisa felt like a short fence post wrapped in a secondhand rag.

I should have stayed in the meadow. I don't exist down here. Not really. Not the way these women do. My God, but they're beautiful. They belong. They're real. And I'm not. Not here, with all these people who know each other and Rye/Boss Mac/Ryan/Edward Ryan McCall III.

"And the eye makeup came straight from Egypt, too, about three thousand years ago. The dress is a variation of the sari," Susan said, ticking off each item on her fingers, "and the shoes are Turkish. The eyes are right out of this world. The coloring is Scandinavian with that perfect Welsh complexion thrown in, and the body is beautifully proportioned, if a bit short. Heels would solve that problem. Why don't you wear them?''

"Susan is a former model who is now running a fashion house. She doesn't mean to be rude," the other woman explained.

"*Moi?* Rude?" Susan said, lifting her perfectly shaped brows. "The ensemble is unusual but absolutely smashing. Is it rude to point out that the effect would be enhanced by heels? I'd offer mine, but you'd have to cut them in half. God, I'd kill for such delicate feet. And those eyes. Is your hair really platinum blonde, or did you cheat just the tiniest little bit?''

"Cheat?" Lisa asked, puzzled.

Susan groaned. "It's real. Quick, put her in a closet or none of the men will look at me."

Lisa blinked, too surprised at being envied by the tall, cinnamon-haired beauty to say anything.

"Let's start all over again," the brunette said, smiling. "I'm Cindy McCall, Ryan's sister." She laughed as Lisa's expressive face revealed her thoughts. "That look of relief is more flattering than a wolf whistle," Cindy said. "Not that I blame you. Competing for Ryan with Susan around would be more than enough trouble for anyone, without throwing an overbuilt brunette into the bargain. Unfortunately I'm afraid you're both out of the running for my brother. Ryan already has found someone and it's all very hush-hush. But there are other single men here, lots of good food, and I even saw some wine lurking at the bottom of the beer cooler. In short, there are more reasons to smile than to wail."

Lisa closed her eyes and stifled her cry of disbelief as Cindy's words echoed silently. *Ryan already has found someone.*

"She doesn't believe you," Susan said. "Do you think she has a name, or did Tinkerbelle drop her off on the way to chase an alligator?"

"I think it was a crocodile," Cindy said.

Susan shrugged. "Either one makes great shoes. Ah, she's back. If we're very quiet, maybe she'll tell us her name."

Lisa smiled wanly. "I'm Lisa Johansen."

"Ah, I was right about the Scandinavian genes," Susan said triumphantly.

Lassiter suddenly appeared behind Susan. He bent slightly, said something only she could hear and was rewarded by a heightened sparkle in her eyes and an outstretched hand slipped into his.

"Bring her back before dawn," Cindy said, watching Lassiter and Susan leave.

"You have any particular day in mind?" asked Lassiter.

Cindy laughed and shook her head. Lisa looked closely but saw no jealousy or pain in Cindy's face.

"You don't care?" Lisa asked.

"Lassiter and Susan?" Cindy shrugged. "They're of legal age. I'd hoped that she might catch Ryan's eye, but there's no chance of that now that he's otherwise involved."

"Where is she n-now?" Lisa asked, stumbling over the last word.

"Who?"

"Rye's—Ryan's woman."

Cindy smiled oddly. "Do you know any place around here where they don't keep time?"

"What?"

"He told me that 'her name is Woman' and she 'lives in a place out of time.' He goes to her there. That's why I can't meet her. Too many clocks at the ranch."

Bittersweet tears burned behind Lisa's eyes when she realized that she was the one whom Rye had described to his sister—and he knew, too, that Lisa didn't exist down here. She existed only in the meadow, which knew no time, where a poor cowhand called Rye came to see her whenever he could.

"But I want to see them together," Cindy continued wistfully. "Even if it's only at second hand, I want to see what it's like to be wanted for yourself, not for your bank account."

Lisa heard both the yearning in Cindy's voice and the echoes of Rye's determination. *Once, just once in my life, I'm going to know what it is to be wanted as a man. Just a man called Rye.*

Lisa hadn't understood what he meant at that time. She did now. She understood, and it hurt more than she would have believed possible. Not for herself, but for Rye. She loved him as he had always wanted to be loved, and he would never believe it, for he wasn't a cowhand called Rye. He was Edward Ryan McCall III, heir to too much money and too little love.

"Oh, look at that gorgeous baby," Cindy cried softly.

Lisa glanced over her shoulder and saw Jim holding a baby in his arms. The cowhand appeared both proud and a bit apprehensive at being left in sole charge of his son. Jim's expression changed to pure pride when he spotted Lisa and hurried over.

"There you are. Betsy told me to be sure to show off Buddy's new tooth."

The baby waved his fat fists and stared with huge blue eyes at Lisa. She smiled in delight. After an instant, Buddy smiled back. The new tooth gleamed in solitary splendor against the baby's healthy pink gums. One fist wobbled er-

ratically, then found its target. Buddy gummed his fingers
with juicy intensity.

"He's cuttin' another one, too," Jim said, his tone divided between pride and resignation. "Teething babies are
'bout as touchy as a rattler in the blind."

Cindy blinked. "Beg pardon?"

"A rattlesnake that just shed its skin can't see," Jim explained. "It'll strike at anything that moves. Rest of the time
rattlers are pretty good-natured."

"If you say so," Cindy answered dubiously.

Buddy whimpered. Jim shifted him uneasily, much more
at home with a rope or a saddle than his baby son. Buddy
sensed that very clearly. His whimper became a full-fledged
announcement of impending unhappiness. Jim looked
stricken.

"May I?" Lisa asked, smiling and holding out her arms.

With a look of pure relief, Jim passed over the baby.
"He's so durn little I'm always afraid I'll break him or
something."

Lisa's laugh was as soft as her smile. Automatically she
rocked Buddy slowly in her arms while she spoke to him in
a low, gentle voice. His eyes fastened on the bright amethyst cloth draped over her head. Little fingers reached,
connected and pulled. Cloth tumbled down and gathered
around her shoulders like a shawl. The baby's attention immediately went from the cloth to the pale crown of her hair
where the shell-inlaid ebony sticks glittered. With tiny hands
he reached for the tantalizing ornaments, only to discover
that his arms were much too short. His face reddened and
clouded with frustration.

Before he could cry, Lisa plucked out both sticks, knowing that if she left one in place, that would be the one Buddy
wanted. The baby gurgled and reached for the black sticks,
only to be sidetracked by the rapidly unraveling cloud of

Lisa's hair. Long strands slid downward slowly, then with greater speed, until everything was undone and her hair hung like a heavy silk curtain all the way to her hips.

"Oh, Miss Lisa, now he's gone and messed up your party hairdo. I'm sure sorry," Jim said, a stricken expression on his face.

"That's all right," she said softly. "Buddy's just like children everywhere. He loves things that are soft and shiny."

She tucked the ebony sticks into her bodice, picked up a handful of her own hair and began stroking the baby's cheeks with it until he laughed in delight, displaying both his new tooth and the reddened spot nearby where another tooth was attempting to break through.

"Sore gums, little man?" she murmured.

Gently Lisa rubbed her fingertip on the spot. Instantly Buddy grabbed her finger and began gumming and drooling in earnest, a blissful expression on his face. Laughing softly, rocking slowly, she hummed an intricate African lullaby to him, as lost to the outer world as the baby in her arms was.

Cindy stared, caught by the image of the baby sheltered within shimmering veils of Lisa's unbound hair. The slow movement of her body as she rocked sent light rippling the length of each silken strand, but as extraordinary as her hair was, it was not as astonishing as the wordless, elemental communication shared between herself and the child.

Her name is Woman and she lives in a place without time.

Cindy didn't know that she had whispered her thoughts aloud until she heard Rye's bleak voice beside her.

"Yes."

Lisa's head came up slowly. Rye looked into her eyes, afraid to see the very money hunger for which he was searching—and finding only darkness and violet mystery, the essential Lisa retreating from him, gliding away among the shadows of all that had not been said.

"Where'd Little Eddy run off to?" boomed a male voice from across the room.

"He's with me, Dad," Cindy said, turning to look over her shoulder.

"Well, drag him on over here! Betty Sue and Lynette didn't fly all the way out from Florida just to talk to an old man."

Rye set his jaw and turned to give his father the kind of bleak stare that would have stopped any other man in his tracks. The stare was met by Big Eddy's determined smile. Eddy put a hand on each woman's bell-shaped fanny and shooed them toward his son.

"There he is, girls, my oldest child and heir, the only person on the face of the earth who's more stubborn than yours truly. First gal that gives me a grandson will have more diamonds than she can hold in both little hands."

A wave of laughter rippled through the room.

"I begged him not to do this," Cindy whispered.

Rye grunted.

"Introduce him to Lisa," Cindy said quickly. "Maybe he'll get the picture."

"The only way he'll get the picture is when it's tattooed on his nose with a sledgehammer. You know something? I'm looking forward to it."

"Ryan, you can't!"

"The hell I can't."

"He's your father. Even worse, it won't do any good. He's so desperate for an Edward McCall the fourth that he's been trotting eager studs through *my* house lately."

"So that's why you dragged what's her name up here."

"Er...ah..."

Rye hissed a savage word as his father appeared two steps away, a well-developed brunette clasped in each hand.

Cindy closed her eyes, thought a fast prayer and said quickly, "Hi, Dad. I'd like you to meet someone very special. Her name is Lisa Johansen and she...she..." Cindy's voice died as she turned around to draw Lisa forward.

No one was behind Cindy but Jim and the baby son sleeping peacefully in his arms.

Twelve

Though a full moon shone brilliantly, drenching the land in silver light, Rye didn't dare take the steep, rugged short-cut to the meadow. Instead he took the wagon road, following the single set of hoofprints that had been incised into earth still damp from a late-afternoon thundershower. He concentrated only on those hoofprints and let the rest of the world fade into nothingness. He didn't want to think about the shouting match he had had with his father in the barn, or about the shadows in Lisa's eyes, or about the anger and cold fear he had felt when he had turned and found her gone as though she had never existed, leaving not even a word for him, not a touch, nothing.

Summer isn't over, he thought fiercely. *She can't leave.*

Thin, windswept clouds rippled in sheer veils across the face of the moon, softening its brilliance briefly before dissolving until only night and stars remained. Evergreen boughs sighed and moaned as their crowns were combed by transparent fingers of wind. It was the same everywhere he looked, bush or grass, tree or silver stream. The night itself was subtly restless, caught between heat and chill, breezes turning and twisting, returning and unraveling, never still, as though the air were seeking answers to unasked questions in the darkness that lay beneath the blind silver eye of the moon.

But the meadow was hushed, motionless except for the spectral stirring of aspen leaves whispering softly of summers come and gone. A horse's low nicker rippled through the night. Devil answered and trotted quickly toward the rope corral that had been strung among a grove of aspens.

The sound of hoofbeats brought Lisa upright in a tangle of sheets and blankets. She hadn't slept for more than a few moments since she had returned to the meadow. She had hoped that Rye would come to her after the dance, but she had been afraid that he wouldn't. Even now she didn't trust her own ears. She had wanted to hear hoofbeats coming into the meadow so much that she had heard them every time she drifted off to sleep, and then she had awakened with her heart hammering frantically and hoofbeats echoing only in her mind.

But this time the sounds were real.

She came to her feet in a rush and opened the cabin door. Aspen leaves shivered in slow motion, each languid rustle a whispered reminder of long hours spent sated beneath the sun. Her hair stirred in a vagrant breeze, shining as the aspen leaves shone, silver echoes of summer past.

"Lisa?"

She ran to him through the moonlight, unable to conceal her joy. He caught her in his arms, held her high and close, let her hair fall in moon-bright profusion around his shoulders. The heat of her tears on his skin shocked him.

"I was afraid you wouldn't come," she said again and again, smiling and crying and kissing him between words. "I was so afraid."

"Why did you leave?" he demanded, but her only answer came as tears and kisses and the fierce strength of her arms around his neck. "Baby," he whispered, shaken by emotions he couldn't name, feeling his eyes burn as hotly as her tears. "Baby, it's all right. Whatever it is, it's all right. I'm here... I'm here."

He carried her into the cabin and lay with her on the tangled blankets, never releasing her, his own anger and questions forgotten in his need to comfort her. After a long time the hot rain of tears slackened, as did the sobs that turned like knives in his heart.

"I'm s-sorry," Lisa said finally. "I was going to b-be like the aspens. They smile so brightly, always, no matter what, and suddenly I c-couldn't and I... I'm sorry."

Rye hushed her with gentle kisses brushed across her lips and tear-drenched eyelashes, and then he held her closer still, wrapping her hair around his shoulders, letting her presence sink into him like sunlight into the meadow. Slowly Lisa relaxed, absorbing him even as he was absorbing her. She became supple once more, her softness fitting perfectly against each muscular ridge of his body. He closed his eyes and held her, breathing in her fragrance, savoring her gentle weight and warmth until her breathing was even and deep once more. He felt the gentle kisses she pressed into his neck and he smiled, feeling as though a weight had been lifted from his heart.

"Ready to tell me what that was all about?" Rye murmured, rubbing his cheek against the cool silk of Lisa's hair.

She shook her head and looked at him through shining veils of hair, her eyes glowing with something close to desire and not far from tears.

"It's all right now," she said, nuzzling against his cheek, breathing in the scent of him. "You're here."

"But what . . . ?"

Rye felt the heat of Lisa's tongue gliding along the rim of his ear and forgot the question he had been trying to ask. His hands shifted subtly on her back, savoring rather than comforting her. The change was rewarded by a hot tongue thrusting into his ear.

"You're going to get into trouble doing that," he warned softly.

"I'd rather get into your shirt," she murmured, running her right hand delicately over his chest, lightly raking his nipple to attention.

His breath broke. "Let's compromise. How about my pants?"

She smiled and bit his ear with sensual precision. When she turned to capture his mouth he was waiting for her with a hungry smile. She teased him as he had once teased her, nuzzling lightly at his mouth, running her tongue along the sensitive inner surface of his lips until he could bear it no longer. He moved swiftly, trying to capture her mouth for the deep kiss he wanted so badly that he groaned when she eluded him.

"Come here," Rye said, his voice gritty, hungry.

Lisa's laughter was a soft rush of air against his lips as she obeyed. She sought him in the warmth and heat of his own mouth, shivering violently as his taste swept across her tongue. The kiss deepened and then deepened again until it was the slow, sensual mating of mouths that she had learned from him.

And that was just one of the things he had taught her.

A tremor of anticipation shook Lisa at the thought of the many ways in which Rye had teased and pleasured her. She wanted to arouse and to satisfy him in those same ways, if he would allow her the freedom of his body. Would he mind being loved by her hands, her mouth? Would he sense in her touch all the things that she couldn't say, the meadow being transformed silently by frost, the aspens blazing their most beautiful smiles in the face of the certain loss of summer?

"Rye . . . ?"

"Kiss me like that again," he said huskily, seeking Lisa's mouth even as he spoke. "No ending, no beginning, nothing but the two of us."

Lisa fitted her mouth to Rye's, seeking him as hungrily as he sought her, sinking into him while time hung suspended between the season of fire and the coming of ice. The kiss changed with each breath, now teasing, now consuming, always touching, sharing, growing until both of them could hold no more. But no sooner had the kiss ended than he pulled her mouth down to his once more with an urgency that could not be denied.

"Again," Rye whispered against Lisa's lips. "Don't stop, baby. I need you too much. When I looked for you at the ranch, you weren't there. *You weren't there.*"

Lisa heard all that Rye didn't say, his anger and his bafflement, his wordless rage that everything had changed before he had been ready for any change at all, frost-scattered light blinding his eyes, summer's end.

"I don't belong down there," Lisa whispered, kissing Rye between words, loving him, preventing him from saying any more. "I belong up here in a summer meadow with a man called Rye. Just a man called Rye . . . ?"

The slow, deep kiss Lisa gave Rye made him groan with the passion that had grown greater every time she had satisfied it. Beneath his clothes, his powerful body became hot, taut, gleaming with the same hunger that had his mouth seeking hers, finding, holding, drinking with a thirst that knew no end. Beneath her searching fingers, the buttons of his shirt opened and the cloth peeled away. He groaned with the first sweet touch of skin on skin, no clothes between, nothing but her warm hands caressing him, smoothing the way for her teeth and the hot tip of her tongue.

"Baby, come closer," Rye whispered, pulling Lisa across his body until her legs parted and she half sat, half lay on top of him. "I need your mouth. I need . . ."

Lisa felt the shudder that ran through him when she slid from his grasp, evading him until her teeth closed delicately on his tiny, erect nipples. Teasing him, hearing him groan, feeling his skin grow hotter with each of her caresses, excited her almost beyond bearing. She forgot everything except the man who was giving himself to her sensual explorations, watching her with eyes blazing hotter than a summer sun.

She smoothed her face from side to side on his hard chest while her hands kneaded from his shoulders to his waist. Her fingers slid beneath his waistband, searching blindly, stroking, caressing, nails raking lightly over hard bands of muscle until she could bear the restraints of cloth no longer. She reached for his belt buckle, her hands shaking, wanting him.

And then Lisa realized what she was doing. She looked up at Rye, silently asking him if he minded. The glittering passion in his eyes made fever burst in the pit of her stomach, drenching her with heat.

"What do you want?" he asked in a voice so deep, so caressing, it was like a kiss.

"To undress you."

"And then?" he asked, smiling.

"To . . . pleasure you," she whispered, biting her lower lip unconsciously, then licking the small marks. "If you don't mind?"

Lisa felt the lightning stroke of response that went through Rye, tightening his whole body.

"I always hoped that someday I'd die of your sweet, hungry mouth," he whispered.

She said his name, husky and low, a promise and a breathless cry of pleasure at the same time. He reached for her but she slid through his fingers again, down the length of his body, leaving his hands softly tangled in the silken ends of her long hair. Her hands closed around first one of his boots, then the other, then his socks, until there was only warm skin beneath her caressing fingers. Her fingers rubbed beneath the legs of his jeans, easing upward until his calves flexed against her palms. As hard as ebony, hotter than sunlight, the clenched power of his muscles both surprised and excited her.

Slowly she worked her fingers back down to his ankles once more, pricking his skin lightly with her nails, smiling when she felt his response. She rubbed her palms up the outside of his jeans, slowly savoring the power of his thighs, hesitating, then sweeping up past the hard evidence of his desire without touching it. He stifled a groan of protest and need and pleading, for he wanted only those caresses that were freely given to him, and she had been so very innocent when she first had come to his meadow.

This time there was no hesitation when Lisa touched Rye's belt buckle. She undid the clasp, reached for the row of steel buttons that fastened the fly, then paused, trying to control the shaking of her hands.

"You don't have to," Rye said softly. "You're still so innocent in many ways. I understand."

"Do you?" asked Lisa, shivering. "I want you, Rye. I want everything with you. I want it tonight. I want it ... now."

Rye's indrawn breath made a ragged sound as Lisa's fingers slid into the openings between the warm steel buttons. He twisted slowly beneath her and then shuddered heavily at the first touch of her fingertips on his hard, naked flesh. When she realized how intensely he enjoyed her caresses, her own body quivered within the grip of the same fever that made him hot to her touch. The last of her hesitation vanished as heat shimmered and burst within her, transforming her. She unfastened each steel button with growing anticipation, freeing him for her soft hands and even softer cries of discovery.

"You make me feel like a present on Christmas morning," Rye said thickly, wanting to laugh and to groan with pleasure at the same time.

"You are a present," Lisa murmured, stroking the length of him with her fingertips. "You're wonderful...but still much too well wrapped," she added, smiling and plucking at his jeans.

"Finish the job," Rye offered, his voice breaking between laughter and a need so great that it was tearing him apart.

Lisa had no hesitation about undressing Rye this time, but she was reluctant to give up what she had already unwrapped, even if only for a few moments. Rye was just as reluctant to lose the exciting heat of Lisa's fingers. Slowly, with many heated distractions, the rest of his wrappings slid down his legs. Without looking away from him, she threw his clothes into the darkness that lay beyond the shaft of moonlight pouring through the open cabin door.

Then Lisa stepped into the darkness, vanishing. When she reappeared moments later, drenched in moonlight, she was as naked as Rye. As he looked at the hardened tips of her breasts and the pale triangle at the apex of her thighs, his breath came in with a harsh sound and went out as a husky sigh. The sounds were like a cat's tongue stroking her, hot and raspy at once.

"Where were we?" Lisa teased, but her glance was already traveling down the length of Rye's lean, powerful body stretched out on the blankets. "Yes, I remember now," she said, her voice catching. She knelt, letting her hair sweep over his nakedness in a caressing veil. "It was summer and the meadow was a clear golden bell that trembled when we did, ringing with our cries. There was no yesterday, no tomorrow, no you, no me, just sunlight and...this." She caught up a handful of her hair and leaned down to him, brushing his hot flesh with the cool silken strands, following each slow stroke with the even greater softness of her tongue. "Do you remember?"

Rye started to answer, but could not. Delicious pleasure racked him, stripping him of all but a need so fierce that his breath unraveled into broken groans. Each sound sent another rush of heat through Lisa, shaking her. Her fingers flexed into his buttocks and stroked his thighs, glorying in the depth and power of his clenched muscles, the fiery heat of his skin and the intense intimacy of exploring him so completely, hearing his response, feeling it, tasting it.

"Baby," he said thickly, "I don't know how much of this I can take before..."

The last word splintered into a hoarse sound of pleasure. The dry, cool caress of Lisa's hair sliding across his loins was a violent contrast to the moist heat of her mouth savoring him. He tried to speak again and could not, for he had no voice, he remembered no words, nothing existed but the ecstasy she brought to him. He abandoned himself to her hot, generous loving until he knew he must be inside her soon or die. He reached for her, only to be shaken by a wild surge of pleasure when he looked down and saw her pale hair veiling his body and simultaneously felt the heat of her intimate caress.

"Come here," Rye whispered. "Come here, baby. Let me love you."

Lisa heard the words and felt Rye's need in every hard fiber of his body. With a reluctance that nearly undid the last measure of his control, she released him from the sensual prison of her mouth. When his hands captured her nipples, she moaned softly. She hadn't known until that instant how much she needed his touch.

"Closer," Rye coaxed, caressing Lisa's breasts, urging her to slide up his body. "Yes, that's it, closer. Come to me. Closer. Come closer, baby. I want you," he said, slowly biting her inner thigh, kissing away the mark, glorying in the violent sensual shudder that went through her when he caressed her soft, incredibly sensitive flesh. "Yes, that's what I want," he said thickly. "I love the heat of you...the velvet fever.... Closer, baby. Closer, come closer...*yes*."

Lisa swayed and bit her lip against the force of the sensations ravishing her body. A low moan was ripped from her, but she didn't hear it. She was deep within an ecstasy that devoured her so sweetly, so fiercely, that she could not say when it began or whether it would ever end. Suspended within the hot triangle of his hands and his mouth, she wept and called his name while he repaid her sensual generosity many times over, sharing her pleasure even as she had shared his, until she could bear no more and begged to feel him inside her again.

Slowly, with a sensuous anticipation that made his eyes blaze, Rye lifted Lisa, easing her down his body until she could feel the hard length of his arousal seeking her. At the first touch of him parting her soft flesh, fever radiated out from the pit of her stomach, drenching her with rhythmic pulses of heat and pleasure. When he slid into her, she made a hoarse sound and moved her hips over him very slowly, abandoning herself to him and to the waves of ecstasy sweeping through her. He tried to hold back, but the feel of her satin convulsions was too exciting. His hands tightened on her waist as he buried himself fully within her, sinking deeply into the velvet fever, giving of himself again and again until finally the last, lingering pulse of ecstasy had been spent. Even then he held on to her, staying deep inside her, savoring every shift and hidden warmth of her body stretched out on his chest.

After a long time Lisa lifted her head. He made an inarticulate sound of protest and snuggled her close once more. She kissed the swell of his biceps, then licked the mist of sweat from his skin with languid deliberation. When she turned her head and nuzzled through chest hair to the flat nipple beneath, she felt him tighten inside her. The sensation was indescribable, as though whole networks of nerves were being brushed with gentle electricity.

Rye smiled when he felt the telltale softening of her body, as though she were trying to sink into him as deeply as he was in her.

"Look at me, baby."

Lisa looked up. The movement tightened her body as Rye had known it would. He smiled even as he felt his own body tightening in anticipation. He kissed her lips, felt the racing of her heart against his chest and saw the sudden, heavy-lidded intensity of her eyes as she felt the growing tension of his body.

"This time we'll take it slow," Rye said, his voice husky with the renewed thickening of his blood, "so slow you'll think you're dying."

She started to say something, but he was moving within her and nothing else was real to her. She clung to him, following him, holding the end of summer at bay with every

touch, every soft cry, every dizzying race of ecstasy. Each
shift of body against body, each caress given and doubly
returned, each sensation shared and enjoyed, each one was
a brilliant aspen leaf shimmering against an autumn sky.
Moonlight and midnight blurred together until time was
suspended, all beginnings and endings swept aside and forgotten, leaving only man and woman intertwined, neither
knowing nor wanting to know where one ended and the
other began.

Lisa awoke at the first brush of dawn on the high peaks.
She memorized Rye's peaceful expression before she eased
from the tangle of blankets and dressed without waking
him. She put a few final items in the backpack, shrugged
into it and silently walked out into the white dawn. Frost lay
everywhere, glittering doubly through her tears, a chill so
deep that even the midday sun would not be able to deny the
changing of the seasons. Leaving shadow footprints in the
white, she saddled the patient gelding and urged him out
over the lip of the high meadow into the world beyond.

The raucous call of a whiskey jack pulled Rye from sleep.
Eyes closed, he reached for Lisa and found only empty
blankets. He went to the door, opened it and looked toward the campfire. The world was still white, frost scintil-
lating with each shift of the breeze. There was no sign of
Lisa, no smoke rising from the direction of the campfire, no
invisible twists of flame warming the chilly air. He stared for
a moment longer, feeling as though something about the
camp had changed, deciding finally that it was just the different perspective that came from the mantle of frost.

"Lisa?"

No answering voice came lilting back to him through the
meadow's silence.

"Lisa!"

Rye's call echoed and then silence returned, broken only by the empty rasping of a whiskey jack flying over the ice-rimmed meadow.

"Lisa!"

The meadow's chill penetrated, making Rye realize that he was naked and shivering. He turned back to the room and pulled on his clothes as hurriedly as they had been removed the night before, telling himself the whole time that nothing was wrong, Lisa was simply out in the meadow checking on the plants and she hadn't heard him, that was all.

"Damn," he muttered as he yanked on his boots, "I'm real tired of turning around and finding her gone. Once I get my hands on her again, she's going to find herself wearing a short leash. The meadow doesn't need her attention half as much as I do."

The memory of the previous night returned to Rye with a vividness that sent heat snaking through him, changing the fit of his jeans within the space of a few breaths. He cursed his unruly body even as he remembered the caressing heat of Lisa's mouth. He had never known a woman so sweet and yet so abandoned, wanting only him, taking nothing from him, asking nothing of him.

And he had given her just that. Nothing. Yet still she had run to him through the darkness, wanting him. Just him. A man called Rye.

Rye froze in the act of grabbing his jacket from the floor. The uneasiness that he had been trying to ignore since he had awakened without Lisa stabbed through him, and in its wake came questions he could no longer evade.

She wanted just a man called Rye. But I'm not just Rye. I'm Boss Mac, too, and Edward Ryan McCall III.

He wondered if that was why Lisa had cried last night—had she expected something from him? Yet she had asked for nothing. Not once. And when her tears had been spent, she had made love to him as though he had poured a river of diamonds into her hands.

Restlessly Rye went to the cabin door and looked out over the white expanse of meadow, seeking any sign that Lisa was out there. Only the aspens seemed alive, their yellow leaves more brilliant than a thousand smiles. Memory tantalized him, something that Lisa had said last night, something that he hadn't understood then and couldn't quite remember now, something about aspens and smiles. He raked the meadow with his narrow glance once more, then turned back to the cabin, trying to shake the apprehension that was seeping through him as surely as the cold.

"Might as well make coffee," he muttered to himself. "Whatever she's doing, she won't be long. It's cold out there and she doesn't have a decent jacket. Hell, she should have had the sense to take mine."

Even as Rye said it, he knew that Lisa would never have taken his jacket or even have thought of taking it. She was too accustomed to making do or doing without things that most people took for granted. Suddenly the idea of giving her a soft, warm jacket made him stop pacing and smile. The gift would be unexpected and all the more cherished for it. He would buy a jacket that matched her eyes, and laugh with her as he zipped her into it, making her snug and warm and protected against the worst cold that winter could deliver.

Still smiling, Rye went out to the campfire. Halfway there he stopped walking, feeling uneasiness crystallize like frost in his blood.

There was no fire ring beneath the frost, no grate, no soot-blackened pot, no tools laid out for quick use. It was as though Lisa had never built a campfire there, never warmed her hands there, never fed hungry men freshly made bread and strong coffee.

Rye spun and looked at the meadow, realizing too late what had been bothering him. There were no tracks in the pristine frost, no sign that Lisa had slipped through the fence to check on the plants without awakening him. He opened his mouth, trying to call Lisa's name, but nothing came out except a low sound of disbelief and denial.

She was gone.

Rye ran into the cabin, telling himself that he was wrong, she couldn't have left. He flung open the closet door—and saw not a single piece of clothing. Nothing remained of Lisa's. No backpack. No camera. No film. No log or seed packets. Nothing but a creased brown paper bag that had been put on the farthest corner of the highest shelf and forgotten.

He stared at the bag for a long moment, remembering the last time he had seen it, remembering the hurt in Lisa's eyes when she had discovered his identity; and then she had taken the bag from his hands, telling him that it had been for a man called Rye, not for Boss Mac, who had no need of her gift.

Slowly Rye brought the abandoned gift out of the closet. He opened the worn bag, reached in and touched a fabric so fine that at first he thought it must be silk. He upended the sack, letting its contents slide into his hands.

Luminous gray cloth spilled over his skin in a cool caress. Tiny glints of blue and secret hints of green gleamed from the fabric with each shift of his fingers. He walked slowly to the sunlight streaming through the open cabin door and shook the cloth out. It became a man's shirt, which shimmered in his hands as though alive, a gray that held elusive hints of all colors, all tints, all moods. The fabric itself was such a fine weave that he could barely accept what his sense of touch told him; he was holding linen of unbelievably high quality.

He stroked the fabric very gently, as though it were smoke that would vanish at the least disturbance. The surface of a button slid beneath his fingertip. The satin texture caught his attention, as did the subtle patterns within the button itself. Slowly he realized that he was looking at ivory or antler cut very carefully so as to use only the cream-colored parts. The same care was obvious in the collar, which had no puckering at the tips and whose stitches were almost invisibly small.

"Where on earth did she get this?" he whispered. "And how in hell did she afford it?"

Rye looked on the inner side of the neck where most shirts carried a label. There was none, but the workmanship was superior to anything he had ever seen. He opened the shirt and searched in the side seams, where the most exclusive designers often left their labels. Again, there was nothing to be seen but the incredible care with which the shirt had been made. Every seam was finished so that no cut edges were visible anywhere. The seams were smooth, flawless, ensuring that the fine cloth would hang perfectly.

Unbelieving, he went over each seam again, running his fingertips over the myriad stitches, telling himself that it couldn't be true, she couldn't have made this for him with nothing more than the few tools she carried in her backpack. She couldn't have cut buttons from antler and polished them with her own hands until each button felt like satin beneath his fingertip. She couldn't have spent hour after hour sitting cross-legged on the cabin floor, taking tiny stitches, smoothing the cloth, taking more stitches and then more until the light failed and she had to put the shirt away until the coming of tomorrow's sun. She simply couldn't have ... and yet she had. And then she had found out who he was, and ridden off without even mentioning the gift that had taken so much care to create.

What's in the bag?

Nothing you need.

Rye closed his eyes for a moment, unable to endure the pain of the truth that he held in his hands, all questions answered except one, and that one was tearing him apart.

I was going to be like the aspens. They smile so brightly no matter what.

But she had wept ... and then she had followed summer, leaving him alone.

Why did you leave?

I don't belong down there. I belong in a summer meadow with a man called Rye.

Last night he hadn't asked her what the words meant. This morning he was suddenly afraid that he knew. Summer was over, and she had discovered that the man called Rye had never existed outside of the timeless meadow.

The shirt slid caressingly over his hands, tangible proof of what he had been too blind to see. He had been protecting himself so fiercely that he had wounded her unbearably, and he hadn't known that, either. Until now.

What's in the bag?

Nothing you need.

Rye stared at the shirt until it was blurred by the wetness that ran down his cheeks in scalding silver streams. Slowly he removed his jacket and faded work shirt and put on the gift that Lisa had made for a penniless cowhand called Rye.

It fit him as she had. Perfectly.

* * *

Lisa reined the gelding onto the trail that led away from the wagon road. The trail led over High Pass and to the neighboring Leighton ranch. Nosy immediately decreased his pace to a kind of slow-motion walk. Lisa urged him with her voice and finally with her heels. Grudgingly the horse speeded up. The instant she relaxed, Nosy's feet slowly became glued to the ground again. He wanted to go back to the Rocking M's barn and he wasn't prepared to be gracious about going in any other direction. He shied at every shadow, dug in at every blind turn in the twisting trail and kept his ears back in a way that announced his bad temper to anyone with eyes.

"Look," Lisa said, glaring at the stubborn animal's flattened ears as Nosy balked again. "I know this isn't the way back to the ranch, but it's the trail I want to take."

"You sure about that?"

Her head snapped up. She stared in disbelief at the trail in front of her. Rye was sitting on Devil, watching her. The horse's black coat was gleaming with sweat and his nostrils were wide as he drank in great gulps of air. Bits of evergreen and aspen clung to unlikely parts of the bridle and saddle.

"How did you . . . ?" Lisa's voice faded.

"Shortcut," Rye said succinctly.

"You shouldn't have come," she said, fighting not to cry. "I wanted you to remember me smiling. . . ."

"I had to come. You left something important behind."

She watched helplessly as he unbuttoned his jacket. When she saw the luminous shirt she went pale.

"You d-don't understand," Lisa said painfully, giving up the uneven battle against tears. "I made th-that for a cowhand called Rye. B-but he doesn't exist outside the summer meadow. And neither do I.''

"You're wrong. I'm very, very real, and so are you. Come here, little love.''

The soft command made Lisa tremble. "I don't think…''

"Let me do the thinking," Rye said, his voice husky, coaxing. "Come closer, baby. Closer.''

With an anguished sound she shut her eyes, unable to bear looking at him without touching him. He was so close, but he was forever beyond her reach.

With no warning he spurred Devil forward, leaned over and lifted Lisa from the saddle into his arms. He buried his face in her hair, making no attempt to conceal the tremors of emotion that ripped through him when her arms slowly came around his neck to hold him as tightly as he was holding her.

"Meadow or ranch house, summer or winter," he said, "Rye or Boss Mac or Edward Ryan McCall the Third, it doesn't matter. They all love you. I love you. I love you so much that I can't begin to tell you.''

Rye kissed Lisa slowly, wanting to tell her how much he loved her, needed her, cherished her, but he had no words, only the warmth of his body and the tenderness of his kisses. He felt the sudden, hot glide of her tears over his lips and heard her love for him told in broken whispers. He held her close, knowing that he would never awaken alone in the meadow again.

They were married in the meadow, surrounded by the aspens' brilliant smiles. He wore the gift of her love that day, and on that same day of every year thereafter. Seasons came and went within the meadow, cycles of renewal and change, growth and harvest, the elemental rhythm of tribal time. The golden bell of the meadow rang with the laughter of their children and their children's children, and each of them discovered in the fullness of their lives what the aspens had always known.

The velvet fever known as love is bounded neither by seasons nor by place nor by time.

* * * * *

Silhouette Intimate Moments

Rx: One Dose of

DODD MEMORIAL HOSPITAL

In sickness and in health the employees of Dodd Memorial Hospital stick together, sharing triumphs and defeats, and sometimes their hearts as well. Revisit these special people next month in the newest book in Lucy Hamilton's Dodd Memorial Hospital Trilogy, *After Midnight*—IM #237, the time when romance begins.

Thea Stevens knew there was no room for a man in her life—she had a young daughter to care for and a demanding new job as the hospital's media coordinator. But then Luke Adams walked through the door, and everything changed. She had never met a man like him before—handsome enough to be the movie star he was, yet thoughtful, considerate and absolutely determined to get the one thing he wanted—Thea.

Finish the trilogy in July with *Heartbeats*—IM #245.

ATTRACTIVE, SPACE SAVING BOOK RACK

Display your most prized novels on this handsome and sturdy book rack. The hand-rubbed walnut finish will blend into your library decor with quiet elegance, providing a practical organizer for your favorite hard-or soft-covered books.

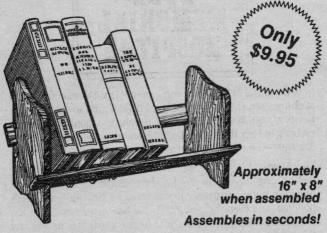

Only $9.95

**Approximately
16" x 8"
when assembled**

Assembles in seconds!

To order, rush your name, address and zip code, along with a check or money order for $10.70* ($9.95 plus 75¢ postage and handling) payable to *Silhouette Books*.

Silhouette Books
Book Rack Offer
901 Fuhrmann Blvd.
P.O. Box 1396
Buffalo, NY 14269-1396

Offer not available in Canada.

BKR-2A

*New York and Iowa residents add appropriate sales tax.

Silhouette Desire

COMING NEXT MONTH

#421 LOVE POTION—Jennifer Greene
Dr. Grey Treveran didn't believe in magic until he was rescued by the bewitching Jill Stanton. She taught him how to dream again, and he taught her how to love.

#422 ABOUT LAST NIGHT...—Nancy Gramm
Enterprising Kate Connors only had one obstacle in the way of her cleanup campaign—Mitch Blake. Then their heated battle gave way to passion....

#423 HONEYMOON HOTEL—Sally Goldenbaum
Sydney Hanover needed a million dollars in thirty days to save Candlewick Inn. She tried to tell herself that Brian Hennesy was foe, not friend, but her heart wouldn't listen.

#424 FIT TO BE TIED—Joan Johnston
Jennifer Smith and Matthew Benson were tied together to prove a point, but before their thirty days were up, Matthew found himself wishing their temporary ties were anything but!

#425 A PLACE IN YOUR HEART—Amanda Lee
Jordan Callahan was keeping a secret from Lisa Patterson. He wanted more than their past friendship now, but could the truth destroy his dreams?

#426 TOGETHER AGAIN—Ariel Berk
Six years before, past events had driven Keith LaMotte and Annie Jameson apart. They'd both made mistakes; now they had to forgive each other before they could be...together again.

AVAILABLE NOW:

#415 FEVER
Elizabeth Lowell

#416 FOR LOVE ALONE
Lucy Gordon

#417 UNDER COVER
Donna Carlisle

#418 NO TURNING BACK
Christine Rimmer

#419 THE SECOND MR. SULLIVAN
Elaine Camp

#420 ENAMORED
Diana Palmer

Silhouette Special Edition

NORA ROBERTS'S 50TH SILHOUETTE NOVEL

In May, SILHOUETTE SPECIAL EDITION celebrates Nora Roberts's "golden anniversary"— her 50th Silhouette novel!

The Last Honest Woman launches a three-book "family portrait" of entrancing triplet sisters. You'll fall in love with all THE O'HURLEYS!

The Last Honest Woman—May
Hardworking mother Abigail O'Hurley Rockwell finally meets a man she can trust...but she's forced to deceive him to protect her sons.

Dance to the Piper—July
Broadway hoofer Maddy O'Hurley easily lands a plum role, but it takes some fancy footwork to win the man of her dreams.

Skin Deep—September
Hollywood goddess Chantel O'Hurley remains deliberately icy...until she melts in the arms of the man she'd love to hate.

Look for THE O'HURLEYS! And join the excitement of Silhouette Special Edition!

SSE451-1